ALSO BY PIPER CJ

The Night and Its Moon

The Night and Its Moon
The Sun and Its Shade
The Gloom Between Stars
The Dawn and Its Light

No Other Gods

The Deer and the Dragon

a Chill in the Flame

PIPER CJ

Bloom *books*

Published by Bloom Books, an imprint of Sourcebooks
P.O. Box 4410, Naperville, Illinois 60567-4410
(630) 961-3900
sourcebooks.com

Cataloging-in-Publication data is on file with the Library of Congress.

Printed and bound in the United States of America.
LSC 10 9 8 7 6 5 4 3 2 1

To spaghetti—
You and time have a lot in common.

Continent of Gyrradin

Pact Encampment

the unclaimed wilds

Sulgrave Mountains

western Red outpost

the Frozen Straits

Raascot

Gwydir

the Etal Isles

the university

Uaimh Reev

Stone

Raasay Forest

Farleigh

Velagin

Farehold

Priory

Aubade

the Temple of the All Mother

Henares

Amurah

Tarkhany Desert

the Zatra Oasis

Kafarem

Valor Mast

the Dying Sunset

Midnah

LISTEN ALONG WITH OUR
villains

PART I

Martyr – Megan Dixon Hood
Monster – Chandler Leighton
Become the Beast – Karliene

PART II

How Villains Are Made – Madalen Duke
Fool – Margo
Fighter – Christian Reindl, Power-Haus

PART III

Six Feet Under – Oshins, Leslie Powell
I Don't Take Insults Lightly – Madds Buckley
Don't Save Me – Chxrlotte

PART IV

Nobody Wants to Be Alone – Christian Reindl, Atrel
The Devil – Banks
Product of My Own Design – Artio

PRONUNCIATION GUIDE

CHARACTERS

Anwir—AN-weer
Berinth—BEAR-inth
Caris—CARE-iss
Ceneth—SEEN-eth
Eero—Arrow
Guryon—GER-yon
Ophir—oh-FEAR
Firi—FEAR-ee
Sedit—seh-DETT
Tyr—TEER

PLACES

Aubade—obeyed
Gyrradin—GEER-a-din
Gwydir—gwih-DEER
Henares—hen-AIR-ess
Midnah—MID-nuh
Raasay—ra-SAY
Raascot—RA-scott
Tarkhany—TAR-kah-nee
Yelagin—YELL-a-ghin

CONTENT WARNING

One instance of non-graphic attempted suicide.
Find the complete list of content and trigger warnings at
pipercj.com.

PROLOGUE

I N THE BEGINNING, THERE WAS PAIN.
These had been forests once. Desolate lands that now
stretched into the horizon had boasted trees and lakes and seas.
The snaking sand blowing across cracked ground had been
rich, healthy soil. The mountains that had long ago sheltered
sheep and birds and towns had long since abandoned their
snow, erupting into lands that swept the world with heat, fire,
and suffering. In the cruelty of neglect, little thrived. Sulfur
choked out natural-born life, with scarcely a rodent left to
gnaw at the straw and weeds that clung to the hot fissures
between rocks. Vegetation wilted and died.

People, whether human or fae, remained in their pockets
of the dried spaces between things.

The monsters that roamed the land were born of violence,
fear, and anger. Little remained of the herbivores or carni-
vores of lore—natural-born beasts said to have once flour-
ished. Gentle creatures had wandered the forests and grazed
on the grasses, thriving beneath the lovely warmth of the sun.
Now, humans struggled to cling to life, remaining as scarcely
more than slaves to the cruelest of fae who had been powerful
enough to withstand the changes of the world. Perhaps the

race of humans had been fortunate to be kept alive in a world that offered no reprieve, no grace, no kindness. Maybe they had not been fortunate at all.

Perchance it was surviving that was the curse.

She'd had a name once.

She'd been born of parents, as one often was. Her birth was one of fear, hunger, terror, and dread. She'd been raised as a child with the slender ears and too-large irises of the fae—eyes that squinted against the baking sands and whipping winds, eyes that saw no kindness, eyes that hadn't known love or joy or peace. Her mother had been gaunt. Her father had been thin. Her childhood had been one of caves, hunger, hiding, terror, and suffering. She'd been born in the end of times.

She was the beginning of times.

Her first miracle was water.

The dried lips of her mother and dusty husk of a dehydrated father created a need, and her desire to see them live birthed a simple cup filled with cool, liquid life.

Their words were few.

She was their secret as much as their salvation.

Her second miracle was the shelter that protected them from the red sparks and brutalities and terrors of the world beyond. The creatures that prowled did so with cruelty and agony. The sky was a mixture of scarlet and brown. Green was a concept, not a color. Life was a stolen escape between carcasses, petrifactions, and stone. If it hadn't been for the fairy tales from the mouths of her wilted mother or the gentle heart of her sickly father and the vibrant fantasies of a wishful child, she would have had no imagination for anything good.

In the papery breaths of tales and bedtime stories that were carried off in the winds, people whispered lore of a time before.

Whether or not they understood the circle of time, they

had reached the end of their eon. It was the age of the ouroboros to bite its tale and begin its draconian circle once more.

She'd walked beyond the sheltered walls of their created sanctuary with the confidence of someone with nothing to lose. Where her feet were meant to land on death, she summoned life. She dreamed of the broadleaf plants and their shade, of fruit-bearing trees, and of grass underfoot that she'd only heard of in her parents' stories. They said that long ago, life had grown upward, reaching toward the sun, and she made it so once more. Her journey found her with rivers to cool her feet, lakes in which she could swim, waterfalls and seas. Her walk resulted in the companionship of the once-fictional beasts like the gentle deer, the clever fox, and the noble falcon.

Her parents had clung to the barest edges of life long enough to see her walk among the gift of creation. Their wonder. Their salvation. She was not the first of her kind, but she was among the rarest. The mother and father who had brought her into this world could not walk with her on her journey. She was meant to traverse this path alone.

When she grew lonely, she did not return to the ramshackle prison of a shelter she'd built for herself, nor did she clutch the memories of her parents. She built for herself a manor, then a city, then an empire.

When she grew lonely, she dreamed of the long-forgotten race of mortals and brought forth a human. The man walked with her as her partner and companion as she spread greenery and life across the earth, lifting her hands and smiling as she spoke into existence a new and beautiful world.

In her time with the man who loved her, held her, and stood beside her, she'd forgotten why the fae and humans struggled to join one another. She clutched the hands and held the face of the man she'd created, and her heart was full. She felt comfort. She felt happiness. She felt selflessness and motivation and comfort until the day his face began to etch with the treacherous lines of age, his hair began to gray, and

3

his body began to fail. She felt herself crack as the one she'd loved and had made from the very air withered to become one with the dust.

He was not the first death she'd experienced, but he would be the last.

When he grew old, she created for herself a companion who would not break her heart with time. A fae woman was made from thought and light, breathed into existence. This new fae was her equal in many ways. She shared the physical characteristics of the woman herself, though the woman on her journey had not wanted to create a copy, so she'd invented a beautiful, different breed of fae—one with wings she needed to set herself free. She had called to the magic of the world and asked it to manifest as it saw fit. This woman could come and go as a dove to the sky. The fae was the bird, and she was the tree.

In the beginning, there was pain.

In the middle, there was life.

In the end, there was forgetfulness.

The circle could not be broken. It was a serpent destined to swallow itself once more. This was the curse of time and the world upon it. They would forget the pain, the snake, the tail. Those who walked the earth would forget how time and fate were destined to ebb and flow like the tides of the seas. They would lie in the sun and eat nice things and sleep with lovers and bear children and convince themselves that the world had always been this way and would be this way forever.

She'd had a name once.

Now, some called her the All Mother. Some felt her a deity; others weren't convinced she'd existed at all. She had been fae, though many had called her a goddess. What was a goddess, after all, if not one who could create and destroy. Her immortality allowed her eternity, and her manifestation had allotted her a life not limited to the physicality of her flesh and granted her the ability to spread throughout the forest—a network of trees as prolific and beautiful as the charged sparks in the brain.

Manifestation was the rarest gift. It was the power of the old gods.

Those who manifested possessed creation itself in their very fingertips, and with that ability came an immortality beyond the simplistic understanding of an undying life.

Manifestation could be beautiful, incredible, powerful, and good.

Manifestation could be destructive, wicked, and terrible.

Manifesters were the end of the world.

Manifesters were its beginning.

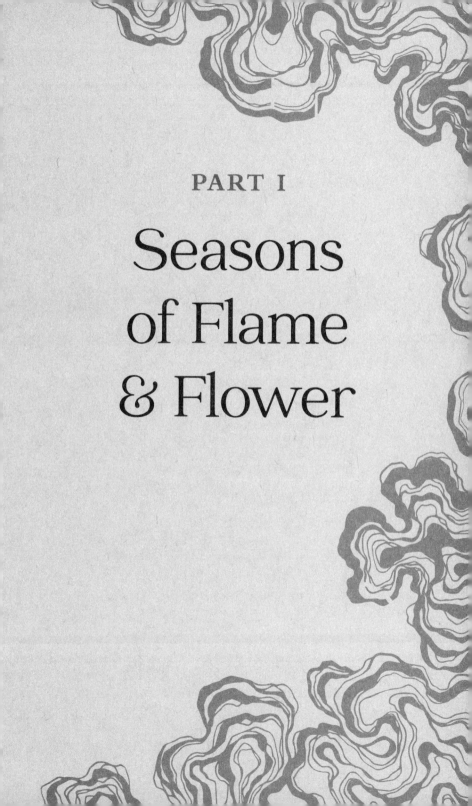

PART I

Seasons of Flame & Flower

ONE

✦　　✦　　✦　　✦

NOW

S HE'D NEVER ENJOYED BEING COLD AND WOULD PREFER NOT to die shivering.

Sea spray had flecked Ophir's face for so many years. She gazed across the salty water, paying special attention to the silver moon rippling on its surface, as she wondered if there was someone on the shores of the Etal Isles staring back at her. She'd always wanted to visit the Isles. It was one of the many things she'd hoped to do. There were so many foods and drinks she'd wanted to taste. Mouths she'd wanted to kiss. Lives she'd wanted to live. They didn't matter now.

She abandoned the shore and stepped into the blood-dark waters. The warm, night-black liquid sent her spiraling into visions of gore once more. She flinched against the onslaught of clanging metal, of lifeless eyes, of pushing and screams and the horrors that led her to this moment. Her hands were clean now, but she looked upon her thin, pale fingers in the moonlight and was only able to see the crimson-stained memories of her failure.

She wouldn't have to withstand it much longer.

The goddess must have approved of Ophir's plan, for no one stopped her that night. She eyed the diamond-bright stars and guessed the time at just past the four o'clock bell, which explained why Aubade was so quiet. It was too late for drunkards and too early for bakers. This was the only hour when even a princess could wander barefoot in a flimsy, cotton shift through the castle.

It was time.

Ophir waded into the waves and frowned as water saturated the dress's thin material. The clinging fabric was unpleasant. She balled the shift in her fists and pulled it over her head to stand bare beneath the crescent moon. Her nakedness felt appropriate, as if it were the last thing to declare that she had nothing to live for, and nothing to lose.

Another step and the waves licked her calves. One more and they were at her knees. Ophir wondered how far the sand would stretch before it fell off into the ocean below. Perhaps it was an answer she should have known, but the king and queen had never allowed her to wander more than a few arms' lengths into the sea. Fae could live splendidly long lives if they weren't cut short by a riptide, or something as stupid as trusting a man.

Men. Ophir's lip twitched in a thinly controlled sneer as the poisonous word touched her.

Her sister, Caris, had known how to swim but knew little of men. Ophir, on the other hand, considered herself an expert in the rougher sex, but when it came to the water, she'd managed a few basic lessons before deciding the sea was best left for merfolk and sailors. If the sisters wanted to see the ocean, they could sit on a pleasure boat with other members of high society and sip mulled wine while an aged captain told tales of the high seas. It was the safest way to dabble with either danger.

Such caution was useless to either of them now.

Caris, delicate and fair, was a flower snipped before it could fully blossom. Where Caris was soft, Ophir was rough. Where Caris was the selfless humanitarian, Ophir took life for a ride. Caris's eyes sparkled blue like springtime rain, her cheeks bloomed rosy, her voice was a sweet song, her hair glimmered like sunlight. Ophir had inherited the hardness of her father's crown-gilded eyes, the subdued plainness of her mother's gold-brown hair, and a face that felt common in comparison with her sister's angelic features.

Caris was the people's princess. Their beacon. The hope of a kingdom.

She was Ophir's better in every way, though she would have rebuked Ophir for thinking such.

Sorrow and rage turned sour in the pit of her belly as she pushed aside her final view of Caris—the sister who should have lived.

A piece of sea kelp brushed against Ophir's leg, though she paid it no mind. Whether it be weeds or eels or fabled water wraiths, it didn't matter. Warm, rhythmic saltwater swallowed her thighs, then her hips, then her navel, then her breasts. She kicked off the sandy bottom and relaxed onto her back. The steady pounding of waves against the cliffs became a dull thrum as she submerged her ears and looked up at the stars. The moon was traveling across the sky faster than she liked. In an hour or so, the castle would stir. By the time the attendants found her empty bed, it would be too late.

Ophir closed her eyes and let the current carry her. The waves' nostalgic rocking returned her to infancy, as if in her final moments she might find comfort in her life ending just as it had begun. This was the last bassinet.

A blast of cold water enveloped her, and she knew she'd finally left the safety of the sandy bottom and drifted into open ocean. She frowned against the unpleasant chill. The waves became less like a cradle and more like an assault as they broke over her. Ophir sputtered out the water, gagging on the brine as she tried to remain on her back. Her eyes stung from the salt, but any attempt to rub them offset her balance. Another wave shoved her to the side, pushing her under the water.

"Fuck." Ophir emerged from the black water and choked

on the curse. Instinct took over as she struggled to tread the dark water, if only to keep her head above the waves.

Her panic tied itself to the cold. She didn't want to die in discomfort. She was supposed to float off in peace.

Another briny wave attacked her eyes, ears, nose, and throat. It was a struggle to find her way to the surface as her hands and legs fought to call upon the muscle memory required of treading water, creating tired circles with her arms and legs.

"Goddess damn it," she coughed as she struggled to orient herself.

There.

The castle was still almost completely dark, save for the distant twinkles of a few orange flames that marked its perimeters. She was so much farther from shore than she'd thought.

Something brushed her leg, and this time she wasn't so sure it was kelp. An involuntary yelp tore from her belly, and the jolt required to bring her leg away from the unseen danger sent her beneath the waves once more.

No, no, no. Not like this. This wasn't how it was supposed to go.

The desire to die clashed against her most primal urge: the need to survive. Instinct overpowered her as she attempted a breaststroke, but her weak arms were powerless. She whirled through her options in the blink of an eye as she put herself on her back once more and kicked toward shore but was quickly overturned by the rolling waves.

"Help," came the weak, involuntary plea. Her nose and throat stung of salt and fish. She choked on her exhaustion as she remained pointed toward the shore, perhaps praying, perhaps calling to whatever flicker of fight rested dormant within her. "Please help me."

She reached out, grasping for anything, but there was nothing to grab. There were no ropes, there were no rocks, there was no boat. She had chosen the time and the place specifically so that there would be no one around to witness her final moments.

Another wave took her under, and she knew with some certainty that she would not be resurfacing. She'd gotten what she wanted the moment she'd stopped wanting it. This was it. She was a fish in a net being dragged to the bottom as she thrashed and struggled. Ophir clawed for the surface but couldn't tell up from down. The sky was as dark as the sea below. Her lungs burned as they begged her for air that would not come. Down, down, down she went. There was no white shift dress to create an angel of her sunken form. She was no princess. She was merely a pale girl in the murky depths—another victim of the sea.

Something bit into her skin, and she knew the sharks of the deep had arrived to pull her limb from limb. Teeth and claws dragged her deeper and she cried against the final insult, which gave the sea its opening to fill her lungs.

To her utter shock, it was not the ocean floor that she hit but the water's surface as she breached, choking and gagging all the while. She tried to call for help, to banish the shark, to do *something,* but was shocked by a woman's voice. She struggled to see what held her in its teeth, what had dragged her by its claws, but nothing made sense.

The voice spoke through grunts as it struggled to keep them afloat. "There you go, cough it up. I need you to hang on for a little while longer, okay?"

Ophir was quite certain she was hearing things. Surely, she had died and an angel was now escorting her to the All Mother. She was disappointed to learn the afterlife stank of seaweed and shellfish. Her body spasmed with each cough and began to thrash, rejecting the water that scalded her throat.

"Oh, no you don't," scolded the voice. Her voice was strained as she said, "Drowners always try to take someone down with them. Either you hold still, or I bind your damn arms."

The goddess wasn't as friendly as Ophir had imagined she'd be.

She tried to turn her head to see the shore but instead saw the pale flesh of a woman dragging her against the riptide. The woman's hair was as black as the sea around it, plastered to her neck, shoulders, and any other bit that Ophir couldn't see.

"Goddess damn you, hold still. Don't make this harder."

She wasn't quite sure why she obeyed, but she did. Ophir succumbed to her back as she was dragged through the sea. The temperature changed again as they drew near to shore.

"Am I alive?" came Ophir's hoarse question.

"Afraid so," said the voice.

The stranger dragged her fully up the beach and onto the sand. Ophir coughed up the remnants of seawater swashing in her lungs, then blinked against the sting of salt in her eyes as she looked at the woman. Tiny rocks and broken shells bit into her cheek as she lay heavy against the sand. A wave licked around the parts of her that still dangled in the ocean, salt burning the tiny cuts that covered her naked body. It was fortunate that she had no use for emotions like shame, as she didn't possess the energy to cover her nakedness even if she'd wanted to.

Her thoughts were as heavy as a lodestone. Perhaps she was delirious, for the only thing she could think to ask was, "Are you a mermaid?"

The woman stopped wringing out her hair and laughed. "Do you see a tail?"

Ophir tried to push herself up onto her elbows but was too weak. She had been treading water for too long. It took every drop of strength before she was finally able to sit up. The stranger patted her on the back while she coughed. She struggled through the fog of exhaustion, mind sharpening just enough to attempt to demand answers.

"Mermaids are a cute fiction, aren't they?" the woman said. "Mermaids, dragons, centaurs...such delightful nonsense."

"Dragons *did* exist," Ophir muttered. "They'd make a hell

of a lot more sense than a strange woman swimming against the ocean's current before the dawn's bell."

"Well." The stranger clapped her hands. "I'll be sure to speak to the All Mother about mermaids and dragons next time I speak with her. Any other complaints while you're busy whining to the person who saved your life?"

"Who are you?" Ophir meant it to come out with authority, but no conviction remained. Her spirit was as tired as her body.

The stranger offered a smile. Even in the final moments before twilight, she could distinguish the glint of moonlight on the woman's sharpened canines, then shot a glance to her arched ears. The stranger, like Ophir, was fae. Fae was the only similarity they shared, as the woman didn't look like anyone Ophir had met. She didn't possess the pale features of Farehold, nor the bronze skin and wings of the northern fae. The stranger's foxlike eyes matched the dark ink of her hair. The woman's attire was also unlike anything the princess had seen. Her rescuer wore something skin-slick and shimmery, almost as if she were in a dress made of water and moonlight.

"I'm Dwyn." The woman leaned backward onto her hands as she eyed Ophir.

"What kind of name is that?" The princess coughed again, spitting sand and salt onto the beach.

"The kind that belongs to someone who just rescued you. What are you doing swimming naked in the middle of the night? I've borne witness to some terribly executed plans, but that has to be the stupidest idea I've ever seen. Unless, of course, you're on some sort of suicide mission."

Ophir looked at the waves. Her eyes unfocused as the same monstrous visions that had driven her to the sea returned. She saw her sister, the shapes of men, and the sticky pools of Caris's spilled life. She hated herself for living in a world without her sister. She hated herself even more for being grateful her reckless attempt had failed. Seabirds' cries signaled the first grays of dawn, jolting her back to the present.

Dwyn stiffened. "Oh, I'm sorry. I had no idea. I still wouldn't have let you do it, but…"

Ophir narrowed her eyes, "I'm sorry—what were you doing in the ocean in the middle of the night?" She found some strength as she leveled her gaze. "There were no boats nearby. You're asking a lot of questions for someone who doesn't have a leg to stand on."

Dwyn smiled. "I have two legs to stand on. Not a mermaid, remember? But unlike you, stranger, I have gifts for water."

Ophir wanted to scowl but couldn't quite bring herself to the expression.

"And you? Do you have a name, or should I just refer to you as the Naked Woman?"

"I'm Ophir," she replied, throat still raw. She curled up a leg and lowered an arm to help cover her nudity. Other than the brown-gold hair that remained sea-slick against her shoulders and parts of her breasts, she remained utterly exposed.

Dwyn's lips turned down in a frown, though her eyebrows quirked as if half of her face was amused. "That's the name of the youngest princess."

Ophir gave a staccato, humorless laugh.

Dwyn blinked. "You're the youngest princess?"

Ophir's stomach roiled. She was going to be sick. She spewed salt and bile onto the sand beside her, then wiped away the acidic spit with the back of her hand. "The only princess, now."

Visions of the king and queen flashed before her. She heard her mother's keening and her father's tears. The loss of one child had shattered them. The loss of two might have finished the job. Her selfishness for robbing the kingdom of an heir was another in a long list of reasons fueling her self-loathing.

Ophir made her first weak attempt at standing. Sand clung painfully to every part of her. She fell forward on her knees and palms. Broken shells and tiny rocks bit into her flesh, each scrape and cut screaming from the salty burn of seawater. She couldn't stay here, naked and vulnerable with some stranger. She tried again to move and failed once more.

"Say," Dwyn chided softly. Her lower lip was in something of a pout as she eyed the princess. "Let me help you. I'll get you back to the castle, Princess Ophir."

She responded before thinking. "My friends call me Firi. At least, my sister did."

Her stomach twisted again, this time with regret. What a stupid thing to say. She wasn't sure why she'd responded at all. This stranger—Dwyn—wasn't her friend, and she had no intentions of making any new ones. She certainly didn't want to think of her sister.

Perhaps Dwyn understood why the statement gagged her. It didn't take much sleuthing to piece together that Ophir had sought a watery grave over reality's horrors.

But she'd lived, for better or for worse. As much as she hated to admit it to herself, she didn't want to die. She didn't want to be alive, either, but the terror she'd experienced in the final moments before Dwyn had rescued her sealed her fate. She was a survivor.

If she was going to continue to walk this cursed earth, then she didn't want to do so under the lock and key of suspicion. She'd failed at dying—as she had with everything—and being caught would only make things infinitely worse.

"They'll find me. I can't explain this. No one can know. I don't..." Ophir's thoughts drifted hopelessly.

Dwyn's eyes twinkled. "Then we'll have to be sneaky, won't we."

TWO ⊙

✦   ✦   ✦   ✦

THIS WAS EITHER A NIGHTMARE OR DREAM, OPHIR WAS certain. She felt disconnected from her body as she allowed the beautiful stranger to guide her forward. Dwyn wrapped a supporting arm around her as Ophir led them to a crevice in the cliff until they came to a halt in front of a sand-colored door.

"This leads to the castle?" Dwyn asked. She looked from side to side as if checking for prying eyes. "Any riff-raff could come in from the sea. That doesn't seem very safe."

"And what riff-raff we are," Ophir responded with a sigh. "There are a few secret passageways left over from the royal family who reigned before my grandfather took the throne. I'm not sure that many know about this door."

A hush pressed over them once they crossed the threshold into the passages. Ophir knew the maze-like halls well from a rebellious youth spent avoiding courtly responsibilities. They were forced to pause whenever they heard the early-morning sounds of waking servants and shuffling attendants to avoid detection. She had no idea how she'd explain herself, should they be spotted. She looked down at the gooseflesh covering her shivering form and scowled. She remained fully nude, dripping wet, and covered in sand. That would be hard enough to explain without the presence of the unfamiliar, soaked, dark-haired fae woman clad in slippery starlight.

Fortunately, years of delinquency lent themselves to successful sneaking. Relief washed over her the moment she slid her chamber's iron lock into place. She frowned between Dwyn and the door, then put a chair in front of it for good measure.

Dwyn left soggy, sandy footprints on the stones and rugs of Ophir's suite while exploring the princess's room. She was still leaving wet fingerprints on an oil painting when Ophir abandoned the stranger to draw a bath. The scents of kelp and fish scales and rotten crabs were replaced with the gentle honeyed smell of her soaps. Eager to have the itchy salt washed from her body, she stepped into the still-too-hot tub and sank into the bubbles. She sucked in a lungful of air before disappearing beneath the surface.

"Are you going to drown yourself in there too?"

Ophir popped her head up from beneath the safety of her warm, wet cocoon. She'd survived the night, yes, but she did not feel safe. Her heart was a violent, angry place just as her soul was an empty, silent void. In her conflict, she grasped for the barest semblance of normality.

"Come here, stranger." She began as a princess commanding a subject, but her tone softened as she looked after the woman. "I just mean… Will you sit with me? You pulled me from the middle of the ocean. You came out of nowhere. I think I deserve to know my rescuer."

Dwyn arched a brow. "Fortunately for you, I'm rather bored."

The dark-haired fae leaned against the edge of the bathtub and dangled a hand in the soapy water just to test its temperature. The scent of freshly crushed mint wafted over the honey bubbles as the fae's unique perfume filled the room. Perhaps Ophir would have noticed it earlier if she hadn't been on the brink of death. The comfort of her bedchambers just before dawn offered the perfect opportunity to see what else she'd missed about her savior.

She opened her mouth to ask a question, but her breath was stolen. Dwyn gathered handfuls of glossy fabric and slowly pulled the starlit dress over her shape. Legs, hips, stomach, breasts, shoulders, neck, chin. Goddess, she was beautiful.

"What are you…" Ophir stammered. The dress dangled from Dwyn's arm as she waited for Ophir to finish the sentence. When the princess did not stop her, she let the fabric puddle at her feet. "I…I don't know if this is common behavior where you're from, but—"

"Are you asking if my entire kingdom is as comfortable with their bodies as I am based off one interaction? Tell me, Princess, does everyone in Farehold swim into the ocean to die under the moonlight?"

Ophir stared blankly.

Dwyn winked. "Precisely. There are just as many sticks up the asses of my people as there are wills to survive with yours. I am wholly myself, irrespective of kingdom or culture. I suspect the same is true of you."

Perhaps it would have been polite to look away, but Ophir wasn't one to turn away from a challenge. Her eyes lingered on an elaborate tattoo that crawled from Dwyn's left knee up her hip like a vine, ending just beneath her ribs.

"Are you staring at this?" Dwyn gestured to her ink. "Such a waste. My tits are up here."

Ophir choked on her retort.

Dwyn swung her legs over the edge of the tub opposite the princess and lowered herself into the waters. Her legs intertwined with Ophir's beneath the suds, which sent a jolt through the princess. Ophir blinked through her confusion as she fought to make sense of the scenario. Perhaps she had, in fact, died under the waves. Maybe these were the final nonsensical thoughts and visions as the mind winked out and relinquished the soul to be with the All Mother. That was easier to believe than accept that a stranger had truly just stripped and invited herself into the bath.

In another life the princess would have savored the

wonderful opportunity to share her tub with a beautiful woman. Ophir had known lust, even if love had never fully shown her its face. On another night, she would have leaned into the legs that interlaced with hers. She would have run her hands along their soft curves, feeling her way along the hips and waist and breasts beneath the bubbles. On another night, another life, their lips would part, their eyes would flutter closed, their gentle tongues would meet with exploratory slowness as they became acquainted. If tonight were any other night, Dwyn's presence would have been a gasp of pleasure. Their sounds would have been nothing but a harmony to the melody of the sloshing waters.

But this was not another night.

"I'm sorry, but who are you?" Ophir forced authority into her tone. She was rigid against the farthest edge of the tub. "Wait, no. I'm not sorry." Ophir gripped the ledge as stress spiked through her. She fought to make sense of things as she demanded, "Who the *fuck* are you?"

"I'm Dwyn," she said while playing with the foam, carving shapes into it and making it stand atop itself. "I've already introduced myself. Listening is a valuable skill." She blew a handful of bubbles into the air, watching as they popped. Dwyn sucked one into her mouth and gagged against the bitterness of its unpleasant, chemical flavor.

Ophir's flash of anger faltered. This person was impossible.

Changing the subject entirely, Dwyn asked, "Do you have anything to drink?"

Ophir looked on incredulously.

The fae stood unceremoniously from the conciliatory bubbles. She splashed all about as she exited the tub, drenching the rugs and floor. Ophir watched her disappear around the door until she returned with a pitcher of drinking water that had been resting on the writing desk. Dwyn drank deeply of it before offering it to Ophir. She wanted to say she'd lost control of the night, but she hadn't had a drop of control to begin with.

Dwyn rejoined her beneath the suds with a shrug. "I told you, I spend my time on the water."

"You're being intentionally vague."

Dwyn splashed some bathwater onto the princess in an ongoing show of irreverence.

Ophir stared. "Do you even care that you're in a castle or in the presence of a monarch?"

"Not in the least," Dwyn replied. From the carefree way she blew the bubbles, Ophir believed it. "But since you insist on bringing up your crown: the royal family is said to have an assortment of gifts. Let me guess…you make flowers grow, or something sweet and soft like that?"

Ophir rolled her eyes. She raised a hand from the water and created a cup with her fingers. A ball of fire sprang to life, hovering in the empty space above her hand, despite how it still dripped water from the bathtub.

Dwyn looked impressed. "Conjuring flame is far cooler than flowers, I'll give you that. I've seen fae speak to an already-burning flame, but I've never met someone who can create a fire while dripping."

"Your turn."

Dwyn complied. "I have a few gifts, but they're best served in the sea. Both my abilities, and my needs."

The last word stuck in the back of Ophir's head like a thorn. Needs were often a harbinger of one of the darker gifts. Light gifts fueled a user. Dark gifts drained their fae until they found a way to replenish. What could she have been doing in the sea to replenish, unless…?

"Are you a siren?"

Dwyn shrugged and began to scrub at her scalp among the bubbles. "Sure." She smiled at the term. "You could call me that. What people say of me doesn't matter. I've never found any title particularly useful."

Ophir pressed, "But you can breathe underwater, right? That's what sirens do? Is that why you were out in the ocean? Sailors don't realize they can't breathe until it's too late…"

Dwyn offered an exaggerated roll of her eyes at the fateful tale told to the seafaring. "Sailors are just as likely to be violent criminals as they are to be good, kind men. The world doesn't need all of them."

"So you've killed," Ophir replied. She kept her tone level as she watched the fae for a reaction.

"I've survived," Dwyn countered. "Does it matter how that happens? Though I suppose not everyone has my desire to stay alive."

Ophir deflated. It was true. Her will to live was thin at best.

Two days ago, she'd loved her life. Forty-eight hours prior, she would have agreed with Dwyn that life was for living. Of course, she'd defined living a little differently. Life was for drinking and sex and experiences. Life was for breaking the rules, for sneaking out of the castle, for going to late-night parties in the homes of strangers. Life was for dragging your sister to debaucherous masquerades even when she pleaded with Ophir to turn around and bring them back home.

Gentle, virtuous Caris was always the responsible one.

Life was for Caris, the selfless humanitarian destined to bring peace to the kingdoms, the sister who deserved to live. Ophir's heart cracked, hot tears lining her lids as she sat with the knowledge that her sister should have been the one who made it out alive. Instead, Ophir was left with a shattered heart and hands that would never feel clean enough to wash away the spilled blood.

No, life was not for surviving.

"Do you want to talk about it?"

Ophir leaned two wet arms on the edge of the tub, resting her chin where they folded. "No," she said. "Not in the slightest."

Dwyn began to wring the water from her hair, twisting it as she stood. She left destructive puddles in her wake as she rifled for a towel. "Can I tell you what I think?"

"I assume you will anyway." Ophir closed her eyes. Visions of gore and men and bodies filled the black space behind her lids. Ophir forced her eyes open and watched Dwyn twist the towel around her hair. "You can take a second towel. There's no need to stay naked."

"With a body like this?" She leaned against the edge of the bath, allowing the lip of the tub to cut into the curve of her thigh as she looked at the princess. She unwrapped her hair as if to emphasize that she required no towel at all. "But here's what I think: tragedy happens to everyone, and we have three paths offered to us in the midst of horror."

"You know what *I* think? You're nude and I don't know you."

"You're focusing on the wrong thing here, Princess." She put her hands on the edge of the tub and leaned forward, breasts pressed together by her inner arms as she leaned in conspiratorially with her secret. Inky tendrils of hair dangled about her shoulders, stray pieces sticking to her neck, her chin, her chest.

Ophir spoke on instinct rather than curiosity. "And what are those paths?"

"The first one is the most obvious, and the most boring. The first is to heal, to forgive, to move on." She shrugged.

Ophir would have laughed if only to keep from crying. This was what Caris—the princess of goodness and quiet resilience and light—would have wanted. Her older sister would have prayed to the goddess for comfort. She would have turned her grief into triumph through the beauty of a life well lived. She would show her fortification through her unwavering spirit.

But Ophir was not Caris. She would not be healing. There would be no forgiveness.

"The second is what you very nearly accomplished tonight, Firi." The princess winced at the use of the nickname. She may have told the stranger to use it, but it was just another wound in her already raw heart. "There are many escapes. People escape through drink, drug, sex, travel, addiction, gambling, harm, and…well…the escape that travels in only one direction. Though choosing the ocean—"

She didn't want to talk about the second option any further. "And the third?"

Dwyn smiled, softening her voice. She touched the princess lightly on the nose. "The third, dear heart, is vengeance."

THREE

✦ ✦ ✦ ✦

THAT NIGHT

"ONE DRINK, THEN WE LEAVE." CARIS PULLED HER HOOD over her head, which was perhaps the single most conspicuous thing she could have done. It was already a masquerade. The princess's additional secrecy was overkill.

Ophir laughed. "I'm not going anywhere until we've had ten."

It was a beautiful night, mixed between late spring's fresh air and early summer's warmth. Every woman's arms were bare, their dresses scooping daringly to expose their backs or plunging to reveal the curves of breasts. Caris was the only one on the estate wearing a hooded cloak, and it was drawing more than a few stares. They hadn't even entered the estate and they were already making a spectacle of themselves from the moonlit grass of the lawn.

"It's too hot for that cloak. You're already sweating." Tiny beads of moisture dotted the older sister's forehead. Ophir clucked her tongue disapprovingly.

"I'm sweating because I'm nervous. And it's still spring."

"It feels like summer. That hood of yours is like announcing to the entire party that you're a poorly disguised princess. Relax."

Caris dropped her voice to a hiss. "How am I supposed to relax?"

Ophir unclasped her sister's cloak and draped it over her arm. "Can you at least try to have fun? It'll be great once we get a few drinks in you. I promise."

The night hummed with festive energy. It was the nerves of prospective socialites, the perfumes of women and the burn of the bright stars overhead. Ophir grinned as she buzzed with the night's animation. "I'll return this to you after you've had your first five."

"*One*." Caris extended her hand uselessly to grab her cloak.

"Three, and that's my final offer. Besides, are you really so selfish that you'd deprive the people of seeing how lovely you look in this dress?"

Caris frowned down at her blush-rose gown.

Caris looked like springtime personified. She'd braided tiny peach flowers into her hair. Half of her golden locks created a crown of elaborate plaits while the other half cascaded down her back. Her mask began in the braided crown of her hair, covering half of her face with a pearly veil of gauzy material. It didn't hinder her sight but hid her features just enough to keep others from recognizing her. She was golds and pearls and pinks stitched into the loveliness of a blossom that had come to life. While Caris was the picture of virginal elegance, Ophir had opted for drama.

Ophir couldn't go anywhere without making an entrance, and this party would be no exception. While most of the women filtering into the estate had opted for the colors of spring, she had selected a plunging black gown. The elaborate black lace of her mask matched her black-painted lips and the lace gloves that wound their way up to her elbow. Ophir had admired herself in the mirror for an hour before the party, loving that she looked far more like a dark enchantress than a princess.

She left her toffee hair completely down, though she had

swept it dramatically to one side. The sisters did not look like they had dressed to attend the same party. They didn't even look like the sort of women who would affiliate with one another, let alone be from the same family.

"Are you ready?" Ophir asked.

"Not at all," Caris grumbled miserably.

With the socialites who entered the manor seemed to be in elaborate assortments of masks, a dark-haired man with a simple, single black band around his eyes was leaning against the door, scanning the crowd. Ophir eyed the marvelous tailoring of the black tunic that clung to his chest and shoulders, the tick of his jaw, the golden tan beneath the mask, contrasted against the sallow pinks peeking through so many others. She wondered if it was too early in the night to start thinking of conquests, because if he was willing, she was game. His attire was refreshingly tasteful compared to the gaudy suits and attires of the others in attendance, and she wasn't the only one who'd noticed. A woman in violet brushed her hand against his chest and attempted to lure him into conversation, but he made a polite, dismissive gesture before shaking her off. The youngest princess had been watching the exchange with amusement when he caught her looking. She blushed and averted her gaze, but when she looked back, the man was gone.

Ophir grabbed Caris's hand and shuffled them in with an entering bevy of young women, all with elaborate updos, masks, and gorgeous gowns for the occasion.

The occasion, of course, was that the weather was nice and they were wealthy. It was occasion enough if you were bored and had money to burn. Ophir had been blessed that, as the younger sibling, she'd had very little responsibility fall on her shoulders. While Caris had dutifully studied the politics and sat through her lessons and done all of the right and proper things a monarch must do, Ophir had dabbled in a variety of very un-princess-like behaviors. She'd taken more than a few lovers, escaped the castle walls to watch a necromancer summon the dead in the middle of the night, and had once disappeared for three days as she'd joined a troupe under a false identity so that she might run off to experience the life of a circus before her guard had found her and dragged her home.

King Eero and Queen Darya of Farehold were good, gentle, intelligent people, and Ophir knew that, though they tried to understand their youngest child, they weren't quite sure where they'd gone wrong. It wasn't unusual for fae to have experimental years. As the years wore on, one might have a few dalliances or dabble in paths, but the sisters were still within their first century of life. Caris was just shy of her seventy-fifth birthday, and Ophir—an infant by fae standards—had just blown out the candles on her fifty-first cake.

She loved the flavor of chaos far too much to step into the calm, duty-filled path expected of a princess. This party would be another in a long line of things that she wanted to do, perhaps solely because she wasn't supposed to.

August and Harland were going to kill her for this, of course.

August had been Caris's personal bodyguard for the past sixty years. August was in his seventh century of life, and though fae were supposed to be ageless, the stress Ophir put him under etched the years on his face. It was fitting, as he both looked and acted the part of a father figure. While Caris did have a spectacular talent for patience, empathy, and wisdom, her fae power was the gift of memory. She could recount anything she heard, read, learned, or saw with perfect replication, making her an excellent student and a brilliant scholar. While this impressed her tutors and reaffirmed to everyone that she would be the best suited for the throne— armed with all of the laws, consequences, politics, genealogies, and information a monarch might need—her gifts were not particularly useful when it came to defense. She was agile, sharp of hearing, and long of life as were all fae, but her physical safety had been August's responsibility for a long time.

This meant in no uncertain terms that August had spent sixty years detesting Ophir.

The tender, compassionate Caris would never willingly go anywhere without his protection. She was courteous and mindful of both the laws of the kingdoms and the well-being of those around her. Caris's empathy had always extended to August and his duties. As her tawdry younger sister, on the other hand, Ophir had made a reputation for herself by abducting Caris and slipping past the guards whenever she got the chance. She made his life so much harder than it needed to be.

She almost felt bad about it.

Almost.

Harland—a chestnut-haired fae with a face meant for smiling—was one in a long line of guards who had come and gone into Ophir's life, as most of them had quit, been fired, or vanished under mysterious circumstances. Harland had only lasted as long as he had because he absorbed Ophir's chaos with good humor. She'd made it her mission to seduce him the moment she laid eyes on him, if only for the challenge.

If he could outlast her resistance of convention and appreciate her subversions of tradition, perhaps he was the best suited to guard her.

When she endangered Caris's life, however, the guards were not so understanding.

The guards called Ophir a wildfire—every bit as destructive as she was powerful. Her elder sister was as vulnerable as she was important to the future of the continent of Gyrradin. If Ophir was the flame, Caris was the flower.

She thought of the exasperated expression Harland would offer coupled with the furious reprimand that would undoubtedly follow from August and decided if they were going to get in trouble anyway, she might as well make the most of their night.

All Ophir had to do was to say that she was going with or without her, and Caris felt the protective impulse to accompany her little sister.

Ophir fancied herself a strong, capable woman. She feared nothing and answered to no one. She could save herself and her sister through sheer cockiness and confident smiles if she put her mind to it. At least, that was what she'd believed.

But they were not wolves.

They were lambs amidst lions at the lord's estate.

FOUR

+   +   +   +

R AUCOUS MUSIC CANNIBALIZED ALL OTHER SENSES. CARIS made another attempt to bolt before they crossed the threshold, but temptation overpowered Ophir's caution as she dragged her sister into Lord Berinth's estate. Ophir had never met a party she didn't like, but if his reputation was to be believed, Lord Berinth might put other wild nights to shame. She'd heard whispers of the hedonistic Lord of Indecency for nearly a decade, but the stars had never aligned for her to attend. According to the sort of gossip and rumors that snaked through the city, there was a reason he required the concealment of one's identities. Even the madams at brothels would clutch their pearls if they heard what went on behind his walls. Ophir felt quite certain that she'd die of curiosity if she didn't find out what went on in his estate.

"Oh no. Absolutely not. No, no, no." Caris tried again to turn on her feet.

Excitement crackled through Ophir's body. "Oh hell *yes.*"

This party was the single most shocking, bawdy, scandalous if not outright blasphemous thing she'd ever seen. She couldn't decide if she hated it or loved it.

The high-vaulted rooms were packed from wall to wall

with food, wine, music, glittering jewels, tawdry laughter, and, above all, the melding bodies of men and women performing the most carnal acts on one another on three stages. One man laced his fingers through the hair of a male submissive on his knees as the man bobbed up and down on the swollen cock. Across the room, two women writhed against one another with their legs interlocked. A human woman—one of only a few mortals in attendance—stood atop the center stage while three fae men serviced her.

Caris's voice trembled as she said, "This is insanity."

"This is glorious," Ophir countered. "They're putting on a show, Caris. If you want to go, you can. But I'm staying."

Dark music joined the laughter and devilry to drown out Caris's remaining protests. The air was thick with roses and sex. Ruby velvets, opulent paintings, and obsidian leathers decorated the estate from wall to wall. Ophir's gaze followed a stately black pillar from its anchor in the marble floor to where it disappeared against the black, palatial ceilings.

A woman jostled them as she forced her way past the princesses toward a group of waiting friends. The moment she arrived, a companion handed her a drink and began undoing her corset.

"She's not going to—" Caris wasn't able to finish her sentence before the woman dropped her corset to her feet. The companion pulled on a silken belt before her dress fell open like a robe, baring her before the world.

Ophir was too enraptured to worry about her sister's modesty.

This was the reason Berinth had earned such a reputation: half of the partygoers in attendance were in various states of undress. Lovely women serving drinks wore only their masks and elaborate shoes, completely naked to the elements for all the world to see, the pinks, purples, and browns of their painted lips carefully matched to the shades of the most sensitive parts of their peaked breasts. A well-muscled man walked by with a tray of drinks, wearing nothing but his mask.

"Firi, let's *go*." It was clear from Caris's tone that she would never, ever forgive her younger sister for involving her in anything so scandalizing. It was improper. It was absurd. It was a new level of abhorrence. From her voice alone, Caris sounded like she might molt her precious, gentle wrappings to whip the younger princess out of sheer horror and disgust.

Caris's unwillingness to let go and have fun only made the challenge more exciting.

Ophir's blood sparkled with a cocktail of nerves and wickedness as she eyed the spectacle, afraid and excited in equal portion. Perhaps this would be something she hated. If so, she'd apologize profusely to her sister and spend all of the necessary weeks in restitution begging for forgiveness. On the other hand, they might have the time of their lives and unlock new levels of pleasure and desire if they allowed themselves to be open.

"Wait." Ophir's eyes widened. "Is this your first time seeing a naked man? You are such a virgin."

Guilt pecked at her as the words left her mouth. As shocking and fun as it was to witness events meant to jolt and incite, it was admittedly more than what Caris had consented to seeing.

She frowned at the pieces of Caris she could see from behind her sister's opalescent mask. From the fresh, round pink of her cheeks, the crystalline blue of her eyes, and the golden curl of her hair, she'd always managed to glide through life as the honorable, innocent virgin. The duty-bound firstborn had been promised to King Ceneth of Raascot—a man she was supposed to have met only once prior to the wedding but who had captured her heart so completely upon their first introduction that the pair concocted a bottomless array of excuses to see each other as often as they could—and had every intention of saving her maidenhood for their union. Much to Ophir's dismay, this promise wasn't just one of law that she could circumvent or pressure her sister into forgoing but one of love and hope. The firstborn princess glowed every time she spoke of Ceneth and her marriage.

Though she empathized with Caris's position and understood why her sister was acting so miserable, she hoped Caris would be selfless enough to let her have a memorable experience.

"I've seen a naked male body," Caris mumbled.

"I don't believe you," Ophir replied definitively. "You would have told me. Unless…you aren't counting when we were children playing in the fountain with the heirs of the Duke and Duchess of Yelagin? We were toddlers!"

Caris folded her arms over her chest defensively.

"Fine, I'm sorry," Ophir admitted, and she was. At least, a little. "Maybe this isn't the best exposure to sexuality outside the marital bed. I didn't mean to traumatize you. But it's a little late, right? The trauma has come and gone. You can't unsee the beautiful people fucking. We might as well make the most of it."

"There have been so many signs to leave, Firi. This place is practically covered in omens telling us not to be here." She might have gone on speaking had the couple in front of them not stopped just shy of the dance floor. The masked woman hiked up her skirt and bent at the waist to reveal that she was wearing nothing beneath. The woman's hair was an unnatural shade of red, with lips to match. Her silver mask covered a bit more of her face than several of the other partygoers, perhaps to protect the anonymity of someone who liked a particular brand of wanton exhibitionism in her sex life. The man untied his britches and spit into his palm before lubricating his exposed manhood and sliding into her. The woman's groan of shock and pleasure joined the chorus of moans, of the wet suctions and dribbles of intercourse, of the thrusts and slaps of flesh.

"I'll grant you that this is not meant to be a party attended by family members." Ophir grimaced.

"Because this would be a romantic date night for a couple?" Caris's question was rife with incredulity.

Ophir lifted one shoulder. "If the couple was interesting…"

"It's hard to believe we were raised by the same parents," Caris said as she lifted a hand to shield her eyes. "Hurry up and find me a drink so I can meet your stupid quota and leave."

"That's the spirit." Ophir grinned. "Forbidden things always taste better with alcohol."

"Wait! Are you going to leave me?" Caris demanded.

"Just to get drinks. Plus, I won't leave you alone. Someone wants to talk to you! Be friendly." She gestured to a tall, fae gentleman in a reflective black mask of polished metal that obscured the top half of his face as well as his hair, ending in the pointed ears of an onyx wolf. He brushed past the attendants and the sweaty bodies of partygoers as his sights remained fixed on the sisters.

"Firi!" Caris said her sister's name with the angry squeak of a frightened mouse. "You are not going to leave me alone with a stranger. I don't want a drink anymore. Stay here."

"Play it cool. He doesn't know who we are," she assured her sister. "We're just two pretty girls at a party. Ask him to fetch us a few flutes of sparkling white wine."

The man crossed the remaining space between them. His teeth glinted in the light with a sinful delight as he reached for Caris. He swept up her hand and planted a kiss on her fingers. Even through his mask, it was clear he was fae. His large irises glistened in shades of a brown so rich it was nearly crimson. "My, what a lovely flower you are. It's rare I see such innocence in a home like this." Rather than dropping her hand entirely, he replaced the space of his palm with a glass of champagne. "Come, won't you have a drink with me?"

Caris took an uncomfortable step backward before bumping into the bare chest of a bystander. She gestured her apology, and Ophir could practically see the years of conditioned politeness not to scream and run churning through her sister. The bodies of masked guests pushed into her, preventing any clean escape as they shuffled in the space beyond.

"I'm afraid we must be going," Caris said.

The man tsked and used a swooping gesture to plant his hand on her lower back, guiding Caris deeper into the party, leaving Ophir to stand on the edge of the dance floor alone. Something changed in her the moment she saw the strange man touching her sister. She'd wanted him to fetch them drinks, no more. She moved to follow them, but the spaces between bodies closed, creating a wall between Ophir and the disappearing shape of her sister's pink dress.

She struggled to find a gap between partygoers to lock eyes with her sister. Though obscured through the pearly veil, Caris's energy reverberated one word: *no*.

Ophir fought to keep up with them, but the strange man only had eyes for Caris. With a hop and a light shove, she wound between partygoers and wrapped her fingers around the man's forearm. Ophir cleared her throat. "I'm sorry, but she isn't interested—"

He cut her off with curt, firm authority. "It's rude to refuse a drink with the host, my lady. Has no one told you that?"

This was his party.

"You're Lord Berinth," Ophir said through the lump in her throat.

"Guilty as charged, my lady, though I do suggest you keep that gem to yourself." He tapped his mask. "The point of a masquerade is for us to enjoy life's pleasures without the consequences of identity." He lifted his champagne glass to his lips in a toast, and Caris politely sipped at the flute he had pressed into her hand, making a bitter face as she drank the liquid. Perhaps this wasn't a high-quality champagne. Bernith motioned to a lithe man in a black jaguar mask as he approached. "Aemon, there you are. Please meet the two most beautiful guests of the evening. Get this charming young lady a drink while I chat with the lovely damsel, would you?"

Aemon took Ophir by the arm before she could protest. He guided her between the bodies of the partygoers, weaving through the crowd toward the polished bar where the drinks were being served. She attempted to shoot an apologetic look Caris's way but couldn't see her sister amidst the throng.

"Excuse me," Ophir said to the man, "but I really don't want to be apart from my sister."

"Have a drink," he replied dismissively.

The stranger called Aemon quickly snatched a flute from a tray and pressed it into her hand with spectacular grace. Between his posture and his thin, hard muscles, the point of his canines and feline ears of his mask, she couldn't help but feel as though the man might shape-shift into a predatory jungle cat at any moment. Ophir accepted a glass of the bubbly champagne and began sipping at it just to give herself something to do with her hands as she scanned the packed room for signs of pink. Unfortunately, the nervous energy meant she was consuming the liquor rather quickly. He was telling her all about his hunting hounds and the exciting blood sport of foxing when she realized she could no longer see Caris.

"Thanks for the drink, but—"

"Sisters, you say?" He flashed a too-white smile. "How daring your proclivities must be to attend this soirée with a sibling."

She nearly gagged. "That's a horrifying thing to say. She's family. We had no idea what we were getting ourselves into."

"Suit yourself," he said with a shrug. Aemon snatched another flute from atop a tray as a servant passed by and switched it out for the empty one in her hands. "Beautiful people shouldn't be restrained by such conventions."

Ophir drank from the flute before replying, "Beauty has no correlation to morality."

The host gestured as if to indicate that he didn't believe her, but that, as he seemed to count himself among the beautiful, he would not be taking her input to heart.

Aemon was pretty. He was not handsome, but he had a loveliness often worn by someone who intended themselves to look innocent. Yes, pretty was the correct word. She was sure it was an effective trap for many women, but she didn't find herself particularly invested in anything this fae had to say. Any hope of a fun night soured. The smell of roses was too strong. The music was too loud. Anxiety intermingled with a sense of responsibility at having abandoned Caris, a woman who'd been radiating the terrified energy of a startled deer from the moment she'd entered.

Ophir would need to cut this man off if she had any hope of reuniting with her sister.

She made a gesture to excuse herself from the conversation, stopping him in the middle of his sentence. "I'm sorry—I've lost my sister. I need to go find her." She moved to push past the bodies, both clothed and unclothed, when he grabbed her elbow with more force than seemed necessary.

"I'm quite certain she's fine," he purred. "Why don't you relax and let her enjoy the party? Here, have another drink."

She hadn't remembered finishing the second glass. Wasn't it full just a moment ago? Ophir shook her head in an attempt to argue. He procured a brand-new glass of champagne seemingly from thin air, snatching the empty one from her hand. Her head swam with the pulsing song as it overtook her. Was the music louder? Why was the smell of roses so strong? She needed fresh air. She needed a window. She needed to sit down. The dull throb of a migraine began to bloom behind her eyes.

"No, I'm sorry. Thank you for your company, but I need to find her." She'd intended for the words to come out with firm assuredness, but they slurred as if she spoke with a mouth full of molasses. She stumbled toward the nearest table and reached out a hand to steady herself.

He tightened the grip on her elbow before she could reach the ledge. His words came out as anything but friendly. "I said she's fine. Leave her be."

In a moment of lucidity, she snapped into her sense of authority.

Ophir clamped down on his hand and summoned fire

through her palm, singing a hole cleanly through the lace of her glove.

He screeched as he winced away in a whimper but then returned with an icy fist of his own. Icy powers battled against her flame in a war so quiet, so covert, that no one around them seemed to have noticed.

Aemon's ice bore into her hand, quelching her fire as their powers remained trapped by the press of their flesh. He attempted to maintain his smile as he snarled, "How dare you use magic on me, witch. This is a party. No need to get violent."

Her vision swam. Sweat spiked across her forehead as she struggled to keep her eyes open. His cold was winning. Ophir released the champagne flute and heard the high-pitched sound of glass and bells as it shattered to the marble floor.

She knew in that moment she had been drugged.

A male arm slung itself around Aemon's shoulders, smiling broadly as he clapped the pretty, icy man on the arm. She recognized the handsome newcomer from when she'd first entered the party, identifying the simple black, silk band around his eyes with holes cut for his vision. A muscle in his jaw flexed with an unreadable emotion. She blinked through an ever-growing blur as she traced the line from his chin, down a tendon in his neck, and landed where the dark corners of a tattoo seemed to be peeking up from his shoulder on one side, stopping as if they were vines prepared to reach up his throat. She'd never seen a courtier or nobleman with a tattoo, but then again, there was plenty at this party she'd never seen before.

He said, "Thank you for finding my lady. She's always wandering off. Are you okay, love? You're looking a little pale. Let's get some fresh air."

Ophir's knees buckled as the stranger braced her for her fall. "My sister—"

He had his arm around her in a second, pushing past the people who'd pressed in on them as he guided her away from

Aemon. He dropped his voice so no one around them would hear.

"You have to get out of here."

The world rippled like the surface of a pond. "I don't feel well."

A wave of nausea overtook her the moment she spit out the words. She threw out a hand to stop them from walking, holding her hair while she emptied the contents of her stomach onto the floor. The partygoers shrieked in both amusement and disgust.

"Sorry, but we don't have time for this," the man said. She'd barely finished throwing up before the stranger scooped her from the floor and began to shove people to the side in his haste for the door.

"Stop," she protested weakly as another wave of nausea rolled through her.

No. She would not be taken again. She would not be taken anywhere.

A resurgence of fight and fear pulsed through her. She didn't know this man. She didn't know where he was taking her. The small relief that had come from the vomit dispelling some of the drug from her system rushed her wits back into her as she threw a handful of flame onto the stranger who gripped her. He cried out in surprise and loosened his grip, but the small distraction was all she needed in order to push away. She began running the moment her feet hit the floor, stumbling through the crowd as up and down tipped and tilted. She pushed her way through finery and naked bodies, shoving off the hardened abs of a male attendant as she fled. Ophir turned just long enough to see the stranger pursuing her.

She burst from the enormous hall and rounded the corner into the corridor. She grabbed the first handle she saw and yanked it open, then another, then another. Each had some manner of sex, lust, drugs, or violence contained within its walls. Screams, whips, blood, and blades joined the slamming

41

of flesh, the sounds of sucking and fucking, the moans of climax.

"Caris?" she shouted into one room after another. She didn't care if she was giving away their names; she needed to find her sister. The wooziness of the drug in her body tripped her against the smooth floor. Her ankle twisted as she slipped and bruised her knees on the marble. With a slap, stumble, and crawl, she was on her feet again, throwing open another door. Her voice escalated in pitch and terror with each new unsuccessful thrust of a handle.

"Caris? Caris!" She struggled to say her sister's name through the dizzying lure of unconsciousness.

The stranger caught up with her as she stumbled through the opulent hall, still attempting to pull her from the manor. "Get outside," he urged. "I can find your friend. You *need* to get out of here."

Hysterics won. She choked on her panic as she screamed, "I'm not leaving without her. She needs help! I know she's in trouble."

She reached the final room at the end of the corridor. Either she'd suddenly lost her strength or something was blocking her efforts. She grunted as she threw her body into the door and forced it open. It cracked open just enough for her to see a large, dimly lit bedroom. The black rectangle of the bed was nearly concealed by the terrible crowd of men.

At its center, she found her sister.

FIVE

✦　✦　✦　✦

NOW

"YOU'RE DREAMING." STRONG HANDS SHOOK HER AS SHE screamed. Her throat was raw, ravaged from her nightmare. She continued to wail, barbed wire tearing from her stomach through her mouth as she cried.

Her body tipped as someone pulled her into a sitting position and crushed her into what was meant to be a comforting hug.

"Don't touch me!" Ophir pushed backward. She struggled to open her eyes through the sting of tears only to see Harland. She gagged, choking on the lingering scent of roses, only to realize she was smelling smoke. It had been a memory. A nightmare.

The horror of reality crashed into the present moment. Harland's hands were red and swollen with blisters and pain. Her nightdress had singed, falling to ashes as fire had claimed her in her sleep, swallowing her whole in its angry, orange flame. She commanded the fire and it vanished, but that did nothing for the destruction it caused in her sleep. He'd reached through the fires night after night to shake her from her horrors, freeing her from the unspeakable memories that broiled her from the inside out.

"Your mother is here to see you, Princess," Harland said, teeth clenched against the pain.

Ophir winced at the sight of his blisters. "Harland, I…"

She wanted to apologize. Not just for his hands, or for yet another pile of ashes in a long line of ruined royal furniture, but for everything. For Caris. For being the reason Aubade wept. For the fundamental brokenness within her. The one thing she didn't want was to be left alone with her mother.

"You have nothing to apologize for." She didn't notice the attendants cowering at the doorway until he beckoned them in. One woman threw a robe around her shoulders while others began to sweep the sooty evidence of her night terrors. The attendants were a flurry of hairbrushes, perfumes, healing tonics, dressing gowns, and every such power necessary to make the room acceptable for the queen.

Ophir rarely met with the king and queen. Their titles as mother and father were secondary to their roles as monarchs to the land. Farehold was their firstborn child.

As children, the girls had taken at least one meal per day with their parents in the formal dining hall. Her mother had loved to play with them in the garden, and her father had enjoyed attempting—and failing—to teach his daughters archery and horseback riding. As the years had gone on, their visits had become more infrequent. The king and queen had a kingdom to attend to, and duties on which to focus. They'd join their daughters for meals several times per week as the years stretched on, but Ophir had rarely darkened the doorway of the war room. She'd made herself intentionally scarce in all matters of politics and diplomacy, and they'd allowed her to distance herself from the responsibilities of monarchy.

She'd stood dutifully beside her parents at Caris's funeral, but there had been no bittersweet embraces, no comfort, no kindness. They'd have to be fools not to know that Ophir was responsible for Caris's death. She couldn't bring herself to ask.

"Can you stay?" Ophir whispered to Harland.

His shoulders slumped. "I'll be right outside."

Harland ushered the attendants out the moment Queen Darya entered, closing the door behind her.

Ophir looked around uncertainly for somewhere for her mother to sit. The woman's expression was strained but not unkind as she perched on the edge of the ruined mattress. She patted the unburned patch of cloth beside her. She took Ophir's hands in her own as soon as her daughter took a seat.

"I like what you've done with the place," the queen said quietly. Her eyes were glassy with the threat of tears. The corner of her lips twitched in the barest of smiles.

"I'm redecorating," Ophir replied, matching the weak attempt at humor.

"Ophir..." The queen closed her eyes. A single tear spilled over her cheek as she did so. The queen tightened her grasp on her daughter's hands. "Your father and I fear we're losing you, too."

Ophir's throat constricted as she watched her mother's face. They knew of Caris, yes, and of Ophir's nightmares, but she wouldn't have chosen these words if Harland had informed his king and queen about her night at sea or the long-gone wet stranger in her room.

Good. They had enough on their plates without adding that burden.

"I don't know how to stop picturing it," Ophir replied at last. "She's there, even when I sleep."

"It's breaking me to know I've lost one child while the other was returned to me broken. We need you to be strong, Ophir. Your title comes with privileges, and with responsibilities. Your sorrow is not yours alone. You carry all of Farehold with you, and the people need to see your chin held high. If it helps, there are tonics for your suffering," said the queen. Her eyes fluttered open. Her tears found their stride as she looked into her daughter's eyes. "I'll send for a healer who can help you with a dreamless sleep."

Ophir wanted to say that a healer might treat a symptom but would do nothing for the problem. She didn't want a healer. She wanted to be held. To be heard. To share tears, rather than hear from the servants' whispers that the queen had been crying herself to sleep night after night. She opened her mouth to explain herself, but nothing came out. Instead, she stared at the woman who was more queen than mother and who would visit, as was proper, but who so rarely gave Ophir the maternal love she craved.

"Give your burdens to the All Mother," the queen said. "I'll pray with you. Close your eyes."

So, Queen Darya led them in an empty prayer. It was a petition to protect the kingdom, to heal Ophir, and to guard Caris's soul in the afterlife. When the queen left, Ophir felt emptier and more alone than if her mother hadn't visited at all.

Three weeks had passed since the kingdom mourned the loss of their beloved princess. Three weeks had crawled on its hands and knees over glass. Four times throughout that bitter month, Queen Darya had made Ophir think that perhaps the woman knew how to be a mother, after all. Four miserable, aching nights, she had let herself into Ophir's room at night when her sobs were too loud for the castle to bear and touched her hair until she fell asleep. Three weeks were marked by ruined bedsheets, by burning furniture, and by a sleep-deprived Harland bursting through the room and battling the fire to get to her. The night guard who typically relieved him during sleeping hours had been chased away by Harland's unwillingness to leave her to face her demons alone.

Ophir found no peace in sleep. Visions of the tragedy raged behind her closed lids when she was awake, and she relived their savagery in her dreams.

The servants murmured about the loss of their kind, gentle royal. The advisors needed the world to remember that not only had Farehold lost its saintliest monarch, but Raascot had been robbed of its future queen. Ophir clutched her pain, knowing it was her final tie to her sister. Anguish was not an emotion she wanted to share. She resented King

Ceneth and his suffering as the world looked only at his loss, rather than hers. The King of Raascot and his people had attended the burial ceremony with his armed guard, grieving the loss of his betrothed. They'd planned for peace and unity for the continent's humans and fae. Together, he and Caris were going to usher in a new era of prosperity. When she died, all hope had perished with her.

Ophir took a small solace in the vengeance enacted by the royal family.

Berinth's manor had been brought to rubble. Nothing remained of his estate, and his grounds had been salted and cursed. The lord had not been recovered, but any man affiliated with their fateful soirée had been burned without ceremony and left in the unmarked graves of the manor's ruins. Investigations into the nature of his profane and terrible gatherings had met a number of dead ends, as no one seemed to know much about the mysterious lord, nor the other men Ophir had found in the room that night. From the little they'd learned of the man, he'd arrived in the lands beyond Aubade only one decade prior, after inheriting the lands and title from his wealthy, established uncle.

If Ophir had to be awake, she'd spend the time in prayer. Dwyn had suggested vengeance, and goddess almighty, how Ophir longed for a world with justice. She'd never been religious, but if there was an All Mother, perhaps the goddess would do what she could not and smite Lord Berinth where he stood.

And so the days had gone on, with Ophir praying to a goddess she didn't believe in, drowning her sorrows in red wine, shriveling and pruning in the bath, and dozing in and out of sleep for weeks.

Night after night, Ophir woke to Harland's frantic attempts to help, just like he had the night of the party. Somehow, Ophir's ever-vigilant guard had awoken that morning knowing some horror had befallen. He hadn't knocked in those first lights of dawn.

Harland had burst into Ophir's room with the ferocity of someone who knew something was terribly, terribly wrong. He'd startled the night guard who had fallen asleep on watch and tumbled from his chair. After yelling at the negligence of the overnight guard and flinging open the door, he'd found her bed empty. A servant had discovered a despondent Ophir hours later.

They hadn't anticipated that a grieving member of the royal family would need increased security detail to ensure she stayed in her room while Aubade planned a funeral, but a mere forty-eight hours after Caris's death, Harland had been shocked to find a naked stranger with a towel in her hair and a soapy princess surrounded by the sandy evidence of her trip to the beach. Dwyn had been all too happy to tell Harland that his charge had attempted to kill herself. She patted him on the shoulder and told him to do a better job before slipping into the shimmery, salty starlit gown that she had worn when she'd carried Ophir in from the sea. Dwyn had disappeared from the castle without another word.

The weeks had stretched into more than a month, and the young princess had not seen the siren again. Memories of Dwyn and wishful thoughts of vengeance were fleeting. Ophir supposed she'd never know if the All Mother answered her prayers for justice, which was just another helpless thing worth mourning.

She hadn't answered questions about Dwyn. She hadn't answered questions about Caris. She hadn't answered questions about anything. Ophir had disappeared into herself, growing quieter and smaller with every day that passed. She was slipping away while the fire ate her.

"It won't hurt me." Ophir frowned at Harland's blistered, bandaged hands.

"It's already hurting you," he replied.

Once she was fully awake and knew she was safe, he would leave her room once more, and she would go back to being completely and utterly alone.

Ophir had been strong once. She had been wild and charming and powerful. She hadn't needed protection from anyone or anything.

Until she did.

One month became three. Early summer had grown unbearably hot, its sweltering air boiling the residents of Castle Aubade no matter how many charmed fans or spelled objects they used to keep themselves cool. The sweltering weather was the only thing that pushed Ophir from her room, chasing her beyond the cliffs to sit on the edge of the waters, allowing her to dissociate into the horizon where sky met sea and the waters could lap against her feet. The hottest summer on record slowly faded into the early, cooling days of autumn. No matter how many suns set or moons passed, her heart would not heal.

Others seemed to be moving on with their lives. Caris's bedroom had been sealed shut, never to be used again. Portraits and statues were commissioned to honor her. Commemorative charities were started in her name. A holiday of cherry blossoms was named for the late princess, to be honored every year on the anniversary of her death. The days went on and clocks continued to tick away their time as if nothing had changed; people resumed their duties and their laughter and their visions for the future. Yet Ophir grew smaller, and smaller, and smaller.

She'd wasted into such a gaunt, sallow state that healers had been called and servants were ordered to sit with her and monitor her nutrition, reporting back on her daily intake of food. Spiritual advisors from the All Mother and even from the temples of the lesser-known deities were called to her bedside to beseech anyone who would listen on behalf of their youngest daughter. Holy priestesses from temples across the continent were summoned, though they had no answer for how to heal that which had broken within her.

The king and queen had already lost one daughter, Ophir supposed. They couldn't risk another.

Ophir had abandoned her life of parties, preferring to drink herself to sleep most nights and wake up with a pounding headache and a sick stomach with every passing morning. As she had done in the summer's blistering heat, she continued to wander down to the beach and allow the shells to cut into her bare feet. She'd walk into the ocean up to her calves while Harland, her ever-present shadow, stayed at a careful distance. She wandered the shores and cliffs a few times per week whenever the weather allowed, but never again did she see the strange woman who'd brought sand and salt into her bedroom and crawled into the tub's soapy waters with her. The fae hadn't only saved her from the ocean that day. Dwyn's bizarre levity in the moments following the incident had kept Ophir from breaking. The treacherous way in which Dwyn had informed Harland of her attempt had been an act of kindness, even if it hadn't felt that way.

She knew it wouldn't bring her sister back, but Ophir would search for the siren's shape along the dots of the horizon as a final, strange tether to the most awful night of her life.

Once again, she had left her room half-drunk and begun to wander toward the sea. Her guard followed several paces behind, unwilling to let her leave his sight. Through the corridors and toward the back wall of the castle, she exited where Castle Aubade's vertical, cream walls met the sheer cliffs that dropped into the sea below.

Fourteen weeks had come and gone, forcing her to live with a reality worse than death. Fourteen weeks with the familiar empty space stretched out before her. In the nearly four months that had spread from early summer to the chill of late autumn, there had been no sign of life beyond the fish and crabs that washed up on the shore. She would continue her cycle of waking, drinking, vomiting, burning, screaming, walking into the water, and wishing she had been taken instead of her sister. No relief was coming for her. Ophir was all alone.

Until one day, she wasn't.

A slim silhouette was relaxing on the cliff, dangling her feet over the edge without a care in the world in the hour before sunset. Ophir stilled at the exit to the castle, clutching at the door when she saw the shape. Her guard doubtlessly recognized the woman from the naked figure that had greeted him all those mornings ago. His hand flew instinctively to the hilt of his sword, but Ophir placed a hand on his wrist, pausing him.

"I'd like to talk to her" was all she said.

Harland promised he'd be nearby if she needed anything. He leaned against the door to the castle's outer walls and eyed them warily as the shapes of the two women stood out against the horizon.

Ophir had the strange déjà vu that she might be dreaming once again as she felt the sea spray hit her face. The calming sound of waves breaking on the rocks below intermingled with seagulls that bobbed and dove through the pinks and reds of the evening sunset. Dwyn was lounging on the cliff as if it were the most natural thing in the goddess's lighted kingdom.

"Dwyn?" Ophir closed the space halfway between the custard-colored wall and the spot where the strange, dark fae sat. She meant to speak the name with a sense of authority or recognition, but her rasp had almost no volume at all. The name was stolen on the breeze, lost to the caws of the seagulls that dove and flapped overhead.

Over the gentle, distant sound of the waves, a lilting voice called, "It's been a while, Firi. How's the vengeance coming along?"

The princess walked toward her as if approaching a mirage. One wrong move, and surely the dark-haired fae would ripple away and leave her all alone once more. Ophir was a step away from waking up to a fresh sense of abandonment. Any moment now, she'd jolt awake and find herself entirely empty.

Each step she took filled her with increasing confusion

as the silhouette grew and Dwyn's features sharpened into reality against the oranges and pinks of late evening. Was Dwyn truly here? Ophir took a seat beside the fae on the reddish dust. Her hands pressed into the grime and sand of the cliff to support her weight.

"It's not," she said, finally answering the question that had been asked of her. Her voice was quiet. She rarely spoke. Her throat was only exercised through the night terrors that shook her from her sleep, dragged and shredded by the thorny stems of roses that ran up and down her vocal passages each and every night.

The siren nodded. "So I hear. The walls have ears, as do the cliffs, and the waves, and the birds." The wind coming off the sea moved her dark hair around her face and neck as if it were kelp under the waves. Her hair did not tangle or knot against the salt in the air as the hair of so many others did. Instead, she seemed to have a dark halo of cloud-like hair. Dwyn had so many deeply unusual features that one did not typically find on the continent. Ophir hadn't noticed the shape of her eyes or the gild of her skin the last time they'd been together. She'd been too numb to absorb details. The events following the massacre at Berinth's home had been a bizarre, dreamlike sequence that she hadn't been sure if she'd imagined.

"It seems like you haven't taken my advice very seriously." The woman's voice had a musical, foreign quality to it. She spoke the common tongue with a peculiar spice and flavor that Ophir hadn't remembered from their time together.

"I've prayed for vengeance," Ophir replied.

"I didn't think you were religious."

"I'm not." The princess deflected. "Are you from the Etal Isles?"

Dwyn smiled. "Sulgrave, born and bred. I did come south for the fabled isles, and yet here I am on the cliffs of Aubade. Have you ever met anyone from the Etal Isles?"

Ophir hadn't. She'd never met anyone from Sulgrave,

either. While the people of Farehold tended to possess pink undertones and colorless hair, the only other races of humans and fae she'd known on the continent were the bronzed fae from Raascot, and her time in the throne room as a child when ambassadors from the Tarkhany desert had visited. She'd played with a young Tarkhany boy who claimed he was Prince of the Sands. Dwyn wasn't from Raascot, nor was she from Tarkhany. Her skin was not the deep northern tan, nor was it the rich, dark browns of the Tarkhany people. There was a faint gild to the undercurrent of Dwyn's skin, and a tilt to her eyes that Ophir had never seen before. Truth be told, she didn't give a fuck where Dwyn was from. Any citizen from any kingdom willing to dive into the deepest waters to save her might as well have traveled from the moon.

Dwyn pressed on. "Do you know anyone who's gone there? The Isles, that is. Does your kingdom conduct any trades with them?"

They didn't.

"It's odd, yes. But do you know the strangest part of the Etal Isles?" Dwyn arched a manicured brow as she looked at the princess, studying her face. "The most peculiar thing about the Isles is that no one else finds them unusual. Everyone seems to act like it's perfectly reasonable for there to be a kingdom and its people a short sea vessel trek away, and yet they've never visited. No one from the islands comes to the mainland, just as no one from the continent goes to the Isles. We all pretend it's not suspicious." This was clearly something that had been on Dwyn's mind for a long time.

Ophir didn't have the energy to argue. She offered, "We don't trade with Sulgrave, either."

Dwyn's laugh was like tinkling bells. "Of course, you don't. Sulgrave is nearly impossible to reach. Crossing the Frozen Straits is a suicide mission for mortals and fae alike. No one expects trade between our kingdoms. The Etal Isles lack an excuse. They should be only a few days of seafaring from Aubade."

"Is that why you were in the water that night? The Etal Isles?"

She shrugged. The wind whipped Dwyn's hair in sharp, dark lines across her face as she gazed at the horizon. "Perhaps it is, perhaps it isn't. Maybe it's why I'm in the water every night. For all the world knows, I might be the leading scholar on the Isles. First, I have to figure out how to get there."

Ophir looked off into the horizon as if she might see the distant shape of a mountain that she hadn't noticed in her decades of life by the sea. "Is that what you need me for? You want me to get you a ship?"

Dwyn giggled at that as if it were the most ridiculous thing she'd heard. Her gaze flitted away from the princess as she watched another seabird bank against the cliffs, plunging for the water. "No, Firi. There's nothing you can do for me. This is about what I can do for you."

"Don't call me that," Ophir muttered. The scabbing wound on her soul was reopened and salted by the nickname.

Dwyn's brows pinched ever so slightly in the center. Her voice softened. "Isn't that what your friends call you?"

Ophir was quiet for a moment. "I don't have friends anymore."

Dwyn clapped her hands together, attention fully present. "Yes, *this* is what brings me here. There are three paths forward after a tragedy, and you have already attempted the path you're on. You tried giving up. You swam into the waters with the intent to die, and I saw you in the moment you realized you wanted to live. I witnessed your struggle to keep your head above water. I know there's a fighting spirit in there somewhere. Though"—Dwyn scanned her body slowly—"it may be buried rather deep."

Ophir looked over her shoulder to where Harland continued to rest against the wall. He hadn't let them out of his sight. Perhaps she should take a lesson from his caution.

Her eyes narrowed. "Why are you here, Dwyn? It's been months. I haven't seen you, or heard from you, or so much as—"

"Tell me, Firi: what do you want?" She swung her bare feet over the cliff with a fairy-like levity. She was perfectly unbothered by their interaction. Ophir found it refreshing to be around someone whose heart wasn't broken and who didn't see her for the husk that she was.

"I want Caris back."

"Well, that's not helpful. Try again."

Ophir felt hot tears threaten to spill over her lids and was glad of the salt spray, as it gave her an excuse for watery eyes. "I want to have been a better daughter and a better sister. I wish I hadn't been such a bastard. I want to go back in time and—"

"You're not even trying."

The fire within Ophir flashed with anger. Her question became a demand as she repeated, "Why are you here, Dwyn?"

"Didn't you hear me? I came south for the Isles."

"No," she said firmly, "why are you here on this cliff? Why bother to return after all of this time? You came into my life and then you left me. I felt like I was crazy—like it had never happened. Why did you leave? Furthermore, why did you bother coming back?"

The Sulgrave fae hummed while she considered. Her breath was a thoughtful, low note scarcely discernible above the sound of the birds and waves. She cocked her chin to the side, allowing the yellow-orange bars of sunset to light her profile.

"Maybe after all of these failed attempts to get to the Etal Isles, I've run out of things to do in the south and needed a new project."

"I don't believe you."

"Maybe our bath together was just so ravishing that I can't get your body out of my mind."

Ophir's eyes became slits. "I don't believe that, either."

Dwyn feigned offense. "Why? You don't think you have a nice body? Your self-esteem should be higher than that, Princess."

Ophir motioned as if to get up and leave the cliff when Dwyn waved her down.

"Fine," she sighed. "I saw you last week standing in the water. You just stood there for nearly an hour, seeing nothing, not moving, just standing knee-deep in the sea. I kept waiting for you to so much as blink, but you didn't." Dwyn repositioned her posture so that she turned to fully face the princess. "Of course, I've thought about you from time to time—this drowned royal rat of a hopeless princess I'd fished out of the ocean—but I'd assumed things had gotten better. When I saw you... I've known suffering, Firi. I'm back because I know what it is to suffer."

"I asked you not to call me that."

"Well, too bad. When we first met, you told me it's what your friends call you. Like it or not, I'm your friend."

"I don't like it."

"Now it's my turn not to believe *you*." Dwyn cocked her head to the side.

Ophir raised her chin and met the woman's gaze. She didn't wear the pitying look of the citizens of Farehold, nor the concealed blame that her parents tried to keep from casting on her. It wasn't the look of helplessness she saw in Harland's eyes, nor the heartbreak in the faces of the servants. The Sulgrave fae did not pity her.

Dwyn wrapped her fingers around Ophir's and squeezed them. Her eyes went dark as she whispered, "Tell me what you want."

"I want the goddess to be real. I want her to be someone who answers prayers. I want to believe she's doing something about injustice."

"Liar."

Anger flashed through Ophir. "How dare you."

Dwyn met her glare with a challenge. "No one wants prayer. Cut out the middleman, Ophir. Tell me what you truly want."

She held the challenging stare, but Dwyn did not back

down. Thoughts of the night that would not leave her, even now. She still heard the screams. She saw Caris's blank, unseeing sapphire eyes. She felt the slick sensation of gore between her fingers and the ashes that covered her night after night as the flame consumed her. "I want everyone who hurt my sister to experience ten times over every bit of pain that they caused her. Death is too good for them. I want them afraid. I want them to suffer."

"Perfect."

SIX

✦   ✦   ✦   ✦

THAT NIGHT

AUGUST'S EYES BULGED LIKE THOSE OF A FISH. OPHIR'S HOPE for rescue had been struck down the moment it arrived. His hands relinquished his weapon and it clanged to the polished floor with a sinking, metallic sound. His large, calloused hands went to meet the shape that protruded from his chest. Ophir stared in horror at the blood-soaked steel that pierced his armor and severed lungs, vital meats, and bones in one sickening puncture. The blood hadn't blotted on his front as it might have if he had been wearing a tunic, but instead a small, horrible waterfall of sticky crimson began to pour from the base of his breastplate as his life dripped out to his feet.

Ophir cried his name in anguish. She reached for him through the deep well of shock and horror. The man who'd stuck him yanked his sword out with a swift jerk, sending August to his knees. The wet, garbled sound of death muted his words as he looked at Ophir.

"Save her," he said before he collapsed to the ground.

She winced as she braced herself for the assailant to attack, but the gruff cries of new bodies stole his attention. Ophir whipped her head to see if anyone was advancing on her, but the tangle of limbs and swords and masks paid her no mind.

August must have been right on her heels, as he'd burst into the room moments after Ophir's arrival. She hadn't seen him at the party. She scarcely saw him now, even as he stood before her. She struggled to understand wave after wave of horror as they crested and broke, drowning her in one impossible horror after the next.

His rallying warrior's shouts had still contained hope. Perhaps he'd hoped Caris's bright, blue eyes still retained a spark of life, a speck of recognition, a moment of hope as he'd come to save her.

His last choked plea had been a command to help her sister, and Ophir would die trying.

Ophir begged the fire to answer her cries, but the drug in her system pressed down on her. She held her hands out before her and willed her power toward the men, watching her weakened flame sizzle and spark as she crumpled to her knees.

"Please," she pleaded with her flame. "Please."

When it did not answer, she began to drag herself across the room toward her sister's exposed body. Shreds of rosy fabric still clung to the place around her waist where her dress had been indecently ripped down the middle. Her veil was nowhere to be seen, revealing her blank, unseeing face to the room. Caris's fair skin was marred with signs of restraint and struggle. Ropes had bound her wrists and ankles to the bed. There was something strange on Caris. Something foreign and terrible and unknowable.

"Caris?" Ophir blinked at the slick, odd twists of reds and purples and browns and blues that piled atop her sister. Caris stared back soundlessly, unmoving as the odd, wet shapes remained.

Ophir wanted to scream, but the involuntary sounds gagged her, suffocating her.

There were far too many men in the room. The space was littered with so many bodies. August had taken several down—the carnage of his fight staining the floor with liquid pools of crimson before he'd fallen. Ophir hadn't been looking for movement behind or around her; she could only see her bound, mutilated sister and the fallen guard who'd been her only hope of their escape. Wait, how many had fallen? How long had Ophir been on her knees? Time swam, intermingling with the blood and guts of infinite nothingness.

Hands yanked her suddenly.

With no warning, Aemon latched on to Ophir by the ankles, dragging her backward. She yelped as rough hands yanked her further from the bed onto the floor, smearing her through the lakes of blood. She hadn't heard or seen him enter the room in the commotion. Her eyes had been fixed on her sister, her eyes and ears deadened by the gore around her. She cried out again in protest, kicking and twisting as she tried to crawl. Ophir's hands slipped on the floor as she grasped toward Caris, desperate to reach her sister. Ophir's black dress slid against the marble floor as the angry man grabbed at her gown. His pretty face was twisted in horrible delight as he flipped her onto her back to look at him.

"You're not going anywhere, princess" came his blood-thirsty growl.

Ophir called to her fire again, but no flame would answer. She tried to scream, but no sound emerged. Aemon's hands were at her bodice, gripping at a knife and tearing her breasts free with the aid of his dagger, when all of a sudden, he stilled. He'd gone from cutting to frozen in the span of a second as an odd, high ringing sound filled the room. A dark line began to spread across Aemon's throat, and with glacial slowness, his head slipped from where it had perched atop his neck. His body collapsed down onto Ophir, crushing her under his weight.

Now the screams found her, ripping from her throat in a sick, feral sound.

The stranger who had tried to get her out of the manor was holding a strange, curved sword drenched in Aemon's blood. The hilt appeared to be made from bone itself. He didn't have time to stop and help her as his blade was swinging once more at another attacker in the room, allowing Ophir the time she needed to push Aemon off of her and close the space to where Caris was tied to the bed. She grabbed her sister, and she could hear the stranger shouting above the noise to stop.

Why would she stop? She needed to free Caris. She needed to save her.

She reached for the ropes that bound Caris, still not understanding the bizarre shapes and textures and colors atop her sister's bare torso. Her fingers were too thick and heavy and stupid from the drug to work the knots that bound the eldest princess. She abandoned the restraints and grabbed her sister's body.

She began to pull Caris against her as the stranger's commands grew louder. He was yelling for her to let go—commanding her to step away.

She clutched her sister to her tightly as she felt something terrifying, horrible, and liquid.

A cloud seemed to descend upon her, filling her mind with a thick, blinding agent and her lungs with smoky rage. She couldn't understand what she was feeling. She refused to believe the evidence before her. She pulled away from her embrace to touch the strange substance on her sister's body. Her hands were not meeting solid flesh. There was a smooth, terrible squish against rope-like shapes and soft, circular meats that had been exposed from within the elder princess. Ophir pulled up her crimson-colored hand as she finally understood the blank glaze of Caris's sapphire eyes.

She froze, staring at the blood on her hands.

The stranger had her over his shoulder in a swift, sweeping motion. The world bobbed as he turned and ran. She was numb. She stared after the carnage in the room as they sprinted from it, leaving her sister's disemboweled, lifeless corpse behind, along with August, Aemon, and the demons who had worn masks of flesh and blood.

Organs. Caris's organs had not been inside of her body as they should. Ophir had seen the smooth tissues and vermillion cells and slippery evidence of something so evil, so foul and unholy, that her brain had been unwilling to comprehend the sight.

The party had scattered, guests screaming and sprinting from the premises once the battle had spilled from the bedroom into the hall. Tables were overturned, drinks shattered as pitchers and glasses and lights and mirrors and every manner of thing toppled to the ground in the desperate need to escape. Naked bodies sprinted across the yard of the estate toward the city, breasts and buttocks and skin exposed against the elements of the night as they were consumed with the sole purpose of survival.

"My sister," Ophir mumbled into the stranger's shoulder as they ran from the building to where the horses were tethered.

The masked man had a small cloak in his saddle bag and wrapped it around her, both for the shock and for the havoc Aemon had wreaked on her bodice. Between the dissociative state and the sedatives in her system, Ophir wouldn't be able to sit on a saddle. The stranger mounted his midnight-colored horse and tucked her against him, urging the steed into a trot, then a canter as they rushed from the estate.

The man remained silent as he held her tightly against him. He asked nothing yet seemed to know precisely where to go. She wasn't sure how much time passed on horseback before they arrived at the castle, but the man was dismounting and making his horse promise to stay put before she realized they'd arrived. He scooped Ophir off the saddle and continued to hold her as he carried her in through a side door.

She should ask questions. She should demand to know how she knew he was a princess, or even more alarming, how he'd learned the castle's hidden entrances and exits. She should be worried. She should feel something, anything. But she didn't.

The stranger ducked into the first alcove he could find. He laid Ophir on a chaise before he spoke. "Are you hurt?"

She looked down at the blood on her hands and then back at him vacantly.

"Were you cut? Do you need a healer?"

Ophir tried to shake her head but had no idea whether or not she'd been hurt. She didn't know anything. She stared with unseeing eyes as he quickly and roughly assessed her to ensure she hadn't been punctured. He didn't touch her—simply ensured that the blood that soaked her did not belong to her.

She did not speak, and he did not say goodbye. The man disappeared like a dark phantom in the night.

Ophir didn't lie there for long.

She stood to go look for her sister. She needed to find Caris. She needed to help her. She needed to find a healer. She needed the royal guard, the constabulary, the knights. She needed...

Ophir stumbled to a halt as she realized the full weight of what she had seen. Understanding hit her as brutally as though she'd been struck in the back of the head with a brick.

Her feet did not need to find the healer's hall. She didn't need to return to Bernith's manor. She didn't need anything, because Caris no longer lived. She'd taken her sister to a party, and it had gotten her killed. She was the reason her sister was dead.

A sickening curl—that of a poisonous weed growing roots and vines and branches—began to grow from her belly. The wicked plant twisted within her for two days until it had reached her mind. While the castle planned the firstborn sister's funeral, Ophir clung to one thought, and one thought alone: she wanted to join Caris. The noxious plant with its twigs and thorns and barns told her that the only thing she could do was to leave. While others slept, she spent two nights awake, picturing the noxious weed and its shadows upon the ceiling until that wicked curl within her brought her to the beach. Its roots urged her onto the beach, aching within her as she stared at the water. It knotted more deeply inside of her, urging her to make the pain go away. It told her that everything could be washed away if she stepped into the waves. The memory of Caris, the sight of her lifeless eyes, the pain and guilt and shame of what she'd done could drown with her among the waves.

She removed her shift and let the wind carry the thin fabric to the black waters before she knew what she was doing. She marveled instead at how warm the waters were. Almost as warm as if she'd waded into Caris's blood.

SEVEN

✦   ✦   ✦   ✦

NOW

W AKE UP! GODDESS, YOU HAVE TO WAKE UP!" HARLAND'S cries were louder than the screams that had shaken her from her night terror, her sister's body the last image behind her eyes.

"For fuck's sake!" A second, angry female voice cut through the darkness.

Ophir came fully conscious in a room filled with steam, not smoke. Water sizzled and misted against the red-hot stones of her room. She gasped and sputtered as a second wave assaulted her, cooling the remaining embers.

Ophir couldn't see the speakers through the thick cloud of mist, but she understood who'd come to her rescue. Harland's muttered gratitude sounded conflicted at best. The woman's mocking *"You're welcome"* solidified what she knew to be true.

"Wake up, Firi," Dwyn called through the steam. "It's time for breakfast."

The sentence was absurd, but then again, her life had been upended months ago. Why should things start making sense now?

Under different circumstances, she would have been surprised at how quickly her parents had welcomed Dwyn.

Instead, the castle was so desperate for a solution that they'd rejoiced when Dwyn was introduced. Harland had given King Eero and Queen Darya a brief report of the situation, but they hadn't needed more than a few words. Not only was it an incredible relief to learn that Ophir had a friend, but the fact that this friend was a fae with the powers of water was a miracle from the All Mother, according to the queen.

Ophir supposed the Sulgrave fae hadn't fully understood what she was signing up for as the royal family had her fully moved into new, unburned rooms along with their daughter. She was promised she would be compensated handsomely for the miracle she brought to their family, and the king refused to look a gift horse in the mouth. King Eero neither knew nor cared why she'd traveled south from Sulgrave, or how she knew his daughter. He would have been thrilled if she'd found a wet log in the forest that had quelled her destructive fears. The only thing that mattered to him in the world was that he kept his only remaining child alive.

"Hurry up, Firi," Dwyn sang, tone mocking as she said, "It's impolite to keep your goddess-given miracle waiting."

If the All Mother had begun answering prayers, Ophir preferred that the deity focus on justice and leave her to her sooty demise. She answered through the sweltering mist. "I haven't decided if you're a blessing or a curse."

"That's what happens when you pray for someone else to do your bidding," Dwyn said. Her dark shape emerged through the cloud, water droplets hissing as they evaporated the moment they hit the floor. "If you want things done right, you're going to have to take them into your own hands."

Ophir's face fell. She looked at the destruction she'd wrought, heart sagging. "I can't."

"Oh, Firi," Dwyn said softly, snatching her hands. "If anyone can, it's you."

EIGHT

+   +   +   +

THAT NIGHT

Goddess dammit!" Tyr cried out in anger, punching the castle's exterior. "Fuck!"

The impact drew blood and sent a shock of pain from his knuckles to his shoulder. It hurt his bones, his joints, his shoulder. He winced against the shallow pain of scraped skin as the sea breeze brushed against it. This night was built on the backs of misery and disappointment. The dark waves breaking against the cliff muffled his outburst, mingling his frustration with the endless noises of the sea.

He'd been so close. He'd followed the wretched siren south to find her circling Aubade's royal heirs like a vulture. He'd beaten Dwyn to the party. He'd had the princess in his arms. He'd been so certain he'd robbed Berinth of his victory, that he'd bested the witch, that he'd saved the royal heir to live another day. But his unyielding focus on Ophir had blinded him to Berinth's prize.

Tyr never let himself get angry like this, but this was no normal night.

Wisdom dictates that one not speak ill of the dead, but if it weren't for goddess-damned Caris, everything would be fine. Instead of saving lives and preserving his ongoing place in the race for knowledge, he'd fucked up with such spectacular thoroughness that he didn't even know where to start.

A distant sound told him that if he didn't get moving, someone would find him near the castle. He'd have no trouble staying hidden, but his horse had not been blessed with such a gift. They'd see his black mount and it would only be a matter of moments before they began searching. They'd find the princess where he'd left her on the chaise. She'd tell them about Lord Berinth and his party. The whole kingdom would know about Caris's death within the hour, he was sure of it. He had to be on the road before all of Aubade was looking for him.

"Come on, Knight. We have to get out of here."

Knight snorted in low agreement.

This was Berinth's fault.

Tyr had had his eyes on the lord for months. The man and his retinue kept their secrets safeguarded, but there was nothing on the continent Tyr couldn't uncover. It was his gift, after all. He dealt in secrets.

Berinth wasn't his real name, but that was as far as he'd gotten down that line of inquiry. The man had appeared around the same time that Dwyn had slithered out of the ocean. If he hadn't been following the wretched water demon, he wouldn't have found himself in the right place at the wrong time.

Four parties locked in a race, but Tyr was the only one who knew all the players. Dwyn was a close second. She knew of the band in the mountains. She knew about him, of course, and would very much like to see his head on a spike. The feeling was mutual. Murder, unfortunately, wasn't something he could act on, no matter how desperately he wanted to see her dead. He wasn't even certain the goddess would consider Dwyn's death murder. A favor, more likely. The continent would be a better place without her.

Still, if he hadn't been tracking Dwyn, he wouldn't have been there to snatch the youngest princess from death's door. Poor Princess Ophir. She had no idea what she'd been swept up in. If she was lucky, it might stay that way. Perhaps he could find a way to resolve the largest disaster the kingdom had ever known while the world—Ophir included—went on believing Caris's death was little more than a senseless murder.

How, then, had Lord Berinth beaten every other player in the race?

Dwyn didn't know about Berinth, he was almost positive. Perhaps she never would have known there was a third player if his sloppy attempt at slaughter hadn't taken Caris off the table. Compared to the two of them, he was certain Berinth was in the dark as to just how many of them he'd been competing with—nary an inkling as to Sulgrave and its activities. The lord knew nothing aside from his own objective.

Knowledge was power, yes, and Tyr knew things.

But all the research in the world didn't matter if Berinth had beaten them to the princess.

He'd known with certainty that if he waited long enough, Ophir would show up. She had a reputation for her inability to resist a good party, and the lord had spent months, if not the better part of a year, setting trap after trap. Tyr had loitered in the spaces between things, keeping his eyes open for Ophir party after party. No one had expected the prim, quiet Caris to leave the castle—she was too well mannered to be seduced by the call of a good time.

It had been Ophir's game to lose.

All he had to do was keep her out of Berinth's clutches. He was only there to prevent Berinth from winning the race. He'd spotted the youngest princess in her black dress the moment she stepped foot onto the property and had been rather sure she'd seen him as well. Ophir had entered with a friend, and he'd been too focused to realize she was accompanied by her sister. Her perfect, pure, virginal sister had been the one in the pink.

"Fuck, fuck, fuck." His curses were practically snarls. How could he have been so ignorant? Tyr prided himself in knowing things, yet Berinth had seen what he hadn't.

He kept Ophir from Berinth's knife, but what had it cost him?

Knight whinnied softly as they approached an inn.

"Shh, hush boy." He stroked the horse's neck as he dismounted, shifting into the place between things. He continued to lead the horse forward, but he was no longer visible to the eyes of men or fae, unseen as long as his ability concealed him. He led the horse into the stable behind an inn and promised it he'd return. The honest, homey smells of fresh straw and farm animals filled the rugged structure. It was a welcome relief from the relentless scent of the ocean.

Knight whinnied his displeasure as he entered a vacant stall.

Tyr snagged a bag of alfalfa from the wall for the creature. "I always come back for you, don't I?" He took the saddle off and stashed his bags in the corner of the stall. "Maybe if we're lucky, they'll brush you down for me. You belong to some other patron, if anyone asks."

The horse chuffed in response.

Tyr had preferred animals to people since birth. Animals were loyal, and pure, and possessed a freedom he could only dream about. He'd never met a creature he hadn't liked and had spent his childhood hand-raising any bird that had fallen from its nest, nursing any rabbit that had been attacked by a cat, and freeing foxes that had stepped into snares.

His compassion for animals had not been met with kindness.

Perhaps his need to prove himself masculine and powerful had been a result of the taunting of his peers. Maybe he wouldn't have spent years training, fighting, and learning if it hadn't been for their names, their cruelties, their punches and exclusion. Maybe he wouldn't have needed to use those skills if it hadn't been for the fire, the shadow, the ice, the abilities the boys had wielded on the day they'd killed Svea. Six years. Six wonderful, perfect years had not been enough. They could have spent eternity together and it wouldn't have been enough. Maybe he wouldn't need the most powerful blood magic on the continent if she were alive.

Maybe, maybe, maybe.

He supposed it didn't matter. Revenge was the only thing he cared about.

His lip curled as he thought of the three vile reasons he'd ventured south. Flame, ice, and shadow. He wouldn't return to Sulgrave until he'd mastered them.

Every ember, every frozen shard, every dark power that had been used to cut, and slice, and hurt Svea, he'd inflict on them. They'd experience everything she'd felt. Every moment she suffered, they'd suffer. He repeated their names like a prayer, using the violence of their actions to fuel him. He never let himself forget her fear, her cries, her pain. It burned within him. It drove him across the very earth. It had entered him into the race.

The three would pay. When they met their comeuppance, it would be at his hand.

NINE

✦ ✦ ✦ ✦

NOW

I'VE NEVER HAD A SLEEPOVER," DWYN SAID AS SHE CRAWLED onto the bed.

"I wouldn't call this a sleepover" came Ophir's exhausted response. The invitation she'd extended to Dwyn would serve a few purposes. For one, having someone else present to monitor her would give Harland a chance to sleep through the night. Dwyn's gift for water was a perfect complement to Ophir's destructive flame. She'd been rushed to Ophir's room on more than one occasion in the middle of the night since taking up residence in the castle, but the time it took for her to be shaken awake and sprint down the corridor wasted valuable, destructive seconds. Dwyn had suggested many times that she stay with the princess in her room, and after executing her fourth middle-of-the-night rescue mission, Ophir conceded.

"Why? Sleepovers don't have dozens of bowls of water scattered about the room and a bathtub filled to the brim?" Dwyn's question was wry, but not in bad humor. She'd argued that she'd handled Ophir's fire without issue every other time, but Harland insisted it would be easier to manipulate that which was already present. If they were awoken in the night by an inferno, they didn't need to waste precious moments scrambling for a source for her power.

The contained fire within the hearth head already begun to die, and there was no effort to relight it for the night. The summer was too pleasant for the need of fire, and the burgundy glow of the dim, remaining light was too soothing to invite flames back into the room.

"Caris and I would share our beds all the time. We were inseparable," Ophir said quietly. She pulled the sheets over her lap to distract herself from the familiar spike of heat beginning to creep up her neck as another onslaught of tears threatened her.

Dwyn pouted. She plopped her head on the pillow and stared up at the canopy bed.

When she didn't respond, Ophir looked at the siren and tried again. "You smell like mint. Has anyone told you that?"

Dwyn nodded. "They have. All fae have a unique scent, though I'm sure you know that. I'm told it's quite intoxicating for humans, the poor creatures. They don't have much of a shot at life, do they. I suppose you probably don't get to see a lot of humans, right? Little princess locked up in her tower." She pouted for the plight of mortals and isolated fae princesses alike, then waved it away, returning the conversation to herself. "I wish I could bottle my own and experience what others do."

"It's a common ingredient. You could just visit the kitchen."

"And cook? Please" came Dwyn's sleepy scoff.

Ophir sighed. "Caris said I didn't smell like anything."

Her dark brows gathered in the middle as she rolled toward Ophir, gently taking a handful of hair and bringing it to her nose. Her frown deepened as she released the hair, bringing her face terribly close to Ophir's neck, lips and nose nearly grazing her skin as she inhaled. Gooseflesh rippled down Ophir's neck, arms, and spine at the proximity.

"Caris was wrong."

Ophir twitched ever so slightly. "What do I smell like?"

After a pause, she said, "Like the sun itself."

Ophir shook her head. "The sun doesn't smell like anything. And Caris—"

Dwyn twisted her mouth to one side. "Firi, can I stop you? Thinking about Caris is good, but I need you to practice something with me."

Ophir used the back of her hand to wipe at her tear. "What's that?"

"Tell me how angry you are."

Ophir had already begun rolling into a ball against the painful memory of her sister, hugging her knees to her chest. "What?"

Dwyn folded her feet beneath her, sitting on her knees atop the bed. She clasped Ophir's hands in her own. "Right now, your emotion is an animal. It's a hurt deer limping through the forest. It's a dolphin watching a shark approach. It's a kicked puppy. These are the spirits I see and feel when I look at you."

"Thanks." She wiped at a second tear.

"No, listen. I need you to tell me: what's the most terrifying creature you can think of?"

"I don't want to do this."

Dwyn's lips became a hard line. "There are lots of things we don't want, and just as many things that we do. Unfortunately, wishes and wants are useless unless we do something about them. I'm trying to help you. Now, what is the scariest beast in the lands?"

Ophir thought about the beasts that roamed the forests. Bears, wolves, bats, and enormous cats with fangs and teeth would wait for you in the trees and hills with glowing, yellow eyes. Spiders could crawl beneath your sheets and approach you while you slept, attacking you in the night.

"I hate snakes."

"Good." Dwyn nodded encouragingly. "Close your eyes, Firi. See a forest. See its trees, its dirt, its roots and shadows and darkness. Are you there?" Dwyn waited for a sign of acknowledgment before continuing. "Good. Keep those eyes closed.

Picture the limping deer in your heart as it walks through the forest. Envision the helpless, wounded deer of your sorrow, and watch as his fur begins to fall away. See his coat fall to the ground around his hooves until he has no hair. Look at the deer's antlers as they shed, and see his eyes move from atop his snout to the sides of his head. See your deer lie down on the ground. Watch as his legs disappear into his body and his scales begin to grow. Watch him lengthen. Look at his fangs. Look at his size. Can you see him? Can you see the enormous snake that was hiding where the deer once was?"

Ophir scrunched her face behind her shut lids. She forced herself to see the deer as it twisted and transformed into a large, horrible serpent.

"Describe it to me. What color is it? What's it doing?"

She swallowed as she envisioned the slithering beast in the forest. She still wasn't comfortable with the exercise, but she exhaled slowly as she focused on the picture in her mind. "It's black. Everything about the snake is black, from its belly and its scales to its eyes and teeth and tongue. Its mouth is open. Venom is dripping from its extended fangs. It's coiling like it's going to strike."

"Firi, you *are* the snake. You are no wounded deer. You are a terrifying, dangerous creature. What can you do as a snake?"

Ophir opened her eyes. "Nothing. I'm not—"

Dwyn's eyes flashed with a sharp, scolding agitation. "What can a snake do? You're a snake—what can you do?"

Ophir gnawed on her lip. This couldn't be any more useless than her unanswered prayers. Reluctantly, she offered, "I can...strike?"

"That's exactly right." Dwyn's voice was grave. She burned with intensity as she squeezed the princess's hand more tightly. "Next time you feel sad about your sister, I want you to take that sorrow and channel it into rage. Your grief must become fury. See your emotion as a physical beast. You are not wounded, princess—you are provoked. You are the serpent."

For the barest of moments, Ophir felt empowered. Then Dwyn was stripping naked from her nightdress and the princess was shaking her head in shock. "What the hell!"

"Oh, I don't sleep with things on. I try to avoid clothes whenever I can. Hope that's not a problem." She blew out the candle on her side of the bed and waved a hand to indicate she was done speaking for the night.

Of all of the people Ophir could have met in this world, she'd been brought together with the most peculiar alien fae in all of the land. She'd never met anyone from Sulgrave before this and speculated as to whether or not it was problematic to wonder if they were all so strange. She was still blinking with bewildered eyes as she blew out her candle and rested her head against the pillow, acutely aware that the stripped body of a siren was mere inches away.

+   +   +   +

Cold. Panic. Terror. Water. Confusion.

The arctic, soaking blast of water flung her from her sleep. Ophir sputtered as she looked up into wide, dark eyes. Pale skin. Dripping water. A familiar, vine-like tattoo wrapping elaborately from one knee up over her hip. It was Dwyn who stood over her, feet planted on the mattress as she panted.

"Goddess damn you, Princess. I knew it was bad, but surely the night terrors should be less frequent by now?"

Ophir's throat ached from her screams. She tried to make sense of her surroundings but discovered from the gray dust covering her skin that yet another sleep dress had been reduced to ash. Dwyn had cut the terror short, sparing the mattress and leaving only the barest hint of steam as evidence that her water had washed away the princess's nightmares.

Harland threw open the door only to instantly avert his gaze with an embarrassed flush. The women looked to him with a mix of bewilderment and indignation as Dwyn was still completely nude on top of the bed and now Ophir was covered in soot in a similar state of undress.

76

He shook his head against the confusing surge of visuals and emotions. "Is...does...um..."

"Spit it out," Dwyn said impatiently.

He pinched the bridge of his nose as if to focus. "Was your friend burned, Princess Ophir? Do you need extra healing tonics?"

"We're fine," Ophir answered for them both. Perhaps she should have checked to see that Dwyn wasn't covered in blisters before she'd made such a definitive statement, but she was ready for Harland to leave. He closed the door behind him, saying something about ensuring fresh blankets would be fetched, but it had come out rushed and muffled against the quick turn of his back as he'd disappeared.

"I'm sorry," Ophir mumbled, closing her eyes against the naked woman standing over her.

"Okay, maybe I was wrong." Dwyn lowered herself to the mattress. She sat on the part of the bed that hadn't been singed in the flame, slowly folding her feet beneath her. "You don't just feel sorrow. You're also terrified."

Ophir sniffed against the scent of smoke and singed fabric. She stood from the bed to grab towels so she didn't have to sleep in a puddle of water and the embers that remained from her burned clothes. The silken sheets had begun to melt beneath her. She spread out the towel and curled up on it.

Ophir closed her eyes, doubting that sleep would come a second time. She rolled away, ignoring the Sulgrave fae. She bunched a handful of remaining sheets between her fingers, doing her best not to cry into them as she clutched the fabric. The night terrors, vulnerability, and utter lack of control were a source of humiliation. She hated the nakedness that her flame had forced upon her. She felt raw and sick and empty. Her back was to the dark-haired fae, so she was surprised by the contact when Dwyn wrapped an arm around her, pressing her body into the curves and grooves of the princess's back and legs as she cuddled her. Ophir could feel the press of her breasts, the curve of her hips, the warmth of her skin, and the sharp, minty scent of her hair.

Her entire body blushed in response. Her reaction wasn't just because Dwyn was a beautiful naked stranger, or because they were in bed together. Pain reddened her cheeks and constricted her throat as she struggled to remember the last time someone had wrapped their arms around her with tenderness. "What are you doing?"

"I'm holding you, and you're going to let me, because I think deep down you know it will help. You're not alone, Firi. Once you feel it, maybe you'll be able to turn that sorrow and fear into the weapon it needs to be."

TEN

+   +   +   +

THEN

H ARLAND WAS JUST SHY OF ONE HUNDRED AND FIFTY YEARS of age when he'd been assigned the honorific title of Princess Ophir's personal bodyguard. While many expressed their congratulations over the prestigious rank he'd achieved at such a young age, far more had wished him luck.

He'd never met the princess, save for the occasions where the royal guard had been summoned in its entirety to appear before the royal family. She'd seemed informal compared to the firstborn heir, but surely, her reputation couldn't be nearly as bad as the gossip that rippled through the ranks.

"Harland, I take it?" A fae man in his seventh century of life offered a casual salute as a greeting. "I'm August."

"Caris's personal bodyguard," Harland noted. August smiled apologetically in response. Perhaps the regrets stemmed from the permanence of August's position; meanwhile, the turnover rate in watching Ophir had provided unprecedented advancement for Harland. He knew that no one expected him to last, but he didn't let their doubt deter him. Her previous guards had been quite old, after all. Perhaps his youth would allow him more flexibility in adapting to her mercurial nature than their traditional ways.

"I hope to serve alongside you for many years to come," Harland replied.

"I do too," August said on an exhale. "For everyone's sake."

His first few days were uneventful. Promising, even. Ophir seemed content to remain confined to her rooms, leaving Harland to occupy himself in the hall with thoughts of lasting success in the castle. He spent two days, then five, then seven, wondering if Ophir was in fact a very well behaved heiress who'd been sorely misrepresented in public opinion.

Her looks certainly didn't win her any favors when it came to demure conformity, and perhaps, he thought, an unfair culture had punished her for it.

Caris may have been conventionally lovely, but Ophir had the terrible, fierce beauty of a white-capped stormy sea, and she knew it. Her movements demanded respect and awe, even if the wise knew enough to fear her. Every expression she made was worthy of its own museum, he thought. Her bravery, her wit, her bold, clever disregard for convention were a natural disaster in a perfect, fae body.

He tried not to think such thoughts about her, but, if he wasn't mistaken, she returned several too-long glances in the hall, a smirk as the door closed, a wink, once, unless he imagined it. The love between a princess and her guard was a fairytale in the making, he thought. He reminded himself for a week, then a month, then four months, that these thoughts would not serve him, but he had little to do aside from think. So he allowed himself the reprieve of his imagination.

Her gold-brown hair was a marvelous shade of caramel, with the sort of ochre, gilded eyes that demanded that anyone who looked upon them tumble, utterly lost, into their carefully interwoven depths. Her mouth was quick to reveal her impishness, both in speech and in the crooked way her lips would twitch with delight. She relied on her wit and charm, and they did not fail her.

Four months into his new position, he fell victim to her guiles.

"Harland?" She said his name with such innocence.

He was quick to respond. The man opened her door to see what she needed, abandoning his post in the hall.

"Would you help me with this?" She fidgeted with the buttons at the back of her bodice near her armoire.

Heat crept from his neck onto his cheeks. "I'll fetch one of your maidservants, Your Highness."

"That's unnecessary. Please don't bother them. Just shut the door behind you and give me a hand?" She made her voice so innocent, like cream and milk and sunlight. She twisted to look at him over a bare shoulder.

"I don't know if I..."

"Just here," she insisted, jiggling the top of her clasp. "Please."

He obliged. His thumb grazed along the skin along the side of her throat as he summoned the sort of gentleness required for tiny clasps and fine bodices. He blushed at the unintentional intimacy, muttering his apologies at the touch, praying she couldn't see how his manhood pressed against his pants.

"Oh, wait," Ophir said quietly.

Harland froze, terrified he'd done something wrong.

"Lock the door, would you?"

She feigned fumbling with the bits that were meant to interlace as she beckoned him further into the room. Having locked the door, he returned to the space beside her with all of the gallant helpfulness of a knight and the discomfort of a saint.

"I really shouldn't." Harland's voice was low as she grabbed his hand, guiding it to the buttons.

He'd barely begun to connect one side to the other when her hand met his again, this time to still him. She looked into his eyes until he felt his resolve melt. She twisted until she was facing him.

She lifted to her toes, parted her lips, and leaned toward him. It was an invitation, but he'd have to accept her bid.

Harland feigned resistance, though he did so in a way that begged her to see through his words, to read his body language, the want in his eyes.

It was a dance he needed to do. He made murmured excuses about his station that he longed for her to refute. He held the back of her neck while he breathed into her shoulder about how he couldn't be with her, though his expression begged her to continue. He prayed her sensitive ears hadn't heard the thundering change in his heartbeat when she pulled at the threads of his tunic. She dragged her fingers over his chest, then her mouth over his neck. He knew he was lost the moment her fingers ran along the seam of his britches. Her mouth moved to his neck, dragging the flames of hot kisses along his bare throat. He attempted one last utterance about duty, honor, and respect, all the while digging his fingers more deeply into her flesh and needing her to know that she could—and probably should—stop at any moment.

Harland wanted her. He knew it. She knew it. He hoped she knew he never would have so much as looked at her with disrespect, let alone live out his darkest, most passionate fantasies if she hadn't initiated. But here he was.

Harland would be the first to admit that he'd been primed to fall.

He said she tasted like water in the desert and like prayers on the desperate lips of the wicked. It was the sort of thing you only said to someone when you'd given yourself over, body and soul. And so, she took. Ophir savored his mouth, his hands, his manhood until she was satisfied through every kiss, touch, and stroke she desired. Their night commanded the movement of hips, hair, and hands that eliminated all doubt, erasing any memory of anyone who had come before. She claimed what he'd known for a long time: he belonged to her. At first, she led their dance, taking charge when she rode atop him. He flipped her onto her belly, lifting her hips while she stretched her chest against the bed. He pounded into her, desperate to fill her with every quaking movement, from the clap of his hips against her to the way his rough hands gripped her delicate body.

He swore their time together was a religious experience.

He whispered sweet nothings, told her of his past, talked about the only other woman he'd been with and how she'd broken his heart into enough pieces that he'd retreated into the life of the guards with no hope of gaining a wife or building a family. He held nothing back.

He awoke cum-drunk and blissfully rested after their tumble.

He reached for her but knew before his hand hit the empty space behind him that she was gone. The wild, lovely Ophir had bested him in the throes of passion, then slipped out of the castle, unnoticed. She visited a poppy den that night, falling asleep among the opium clouds of its patrons. Her smile was the hazy, half-present quirk of tilted lips when he found her to bring her back to the castle.

He wanted to be angry, but he only admired her all the more.

It would be dishonest to be angry with her for using him. He'd wanted to be used. He'd read everything into their shared tumble that he'd wanted to read, and left with a lesson. She was beautiful, clever, and free.

She expressed interest in continuing their dalliances, followed by grumbled protests over boundaries he set after their night together.

He existed to ensure her safety, he said, and he couldn't guard her properly if he was beholden to her whims.

She insisted that her gift for flame enabled her to protect herself just fine.

Following their exchange of power, his gentle rebukes were met with frustration. He stopped her, blocked her exits, and prevented her movements in ways that she met with nearly wry flirtation. While Harland had very little control over where Ophir went, he always did his best to follow, even if just in the shadows. He'd been rash and naïve, but he maintained every intention to live up to his sovereign title as the princess's protector, no matter how difficult and perilous she made the job.

Her halfhearted attempts to dodge her responsibilities took her to the far tower with a bottle of wine, as they had so many times before.

His job was not for the faint of heart.

But he wouldn't trade it for anything.

✦ ✦ ✦ ✦

Ophir mustered a smile. "You look beautiful. Are you nervous?"

The ladies in waiting had left the sisters alone in Caris's chambers so that she could have a few moments of peace before the northern king arrived. Today the eldest princess was in a lovely shade of light green, looking very much like young leaflets in the early days of spring. Her long golden hair was left down in relatively informal curls given the seriousness of the occasion. Caris's beauty had been a thing of murmurs of admiration across the continent. Her soft voice and gentle spirit were just as charming as the rose of her cheeks and the bright blue of her eyes. Ophir was in awe of her.

Caris shook her head, smiling with a deep, genuine joy. Her loveliness was as much a part of her good soul as it was her delicate features. "No, I'm always excited to meet with him. He's going to change the world, Firi."

Ophir smiled. Caris was wrong, of course. Ceneth was not going to change the world. If the continent had any hope for evolution, it would be because of what the two of them might achieve together. Their vision for a sanctuary for fae and solace for humans was one that might end centuries of fear, mistrust, and bloodshed. The two shared their passion with the unity of a single heartbeat. While advantageous diplomatic marriages were traditions as old as time, Princess Caris and King Ceneth had truly been blessed by the All Mother to not only share their vision for how the world might be, but also to have the ability to achieve it together.

What they shared was so much more than their vision

for the continent. They'd been blessed with twin hearts that desired a life together.

The winged king of Raascot had a much easier time traveling with his gift of flight and was more than happy to make the journey as often as he could. It was customary to wait until after the fae bride's seventy-fifth birthday before a royal wedding. While Caris had insisted for the better part of a decade that she was eager and ready to become Raascot's queen, her parents had insisted she adhere to tradition, and Caris had obliged, albeit impatiently.

The sounds of hooves and carriages joined the great thunder of wings that sounded the Raascot party's arrival. Caris sparkled with giddiness as she rushed to greet them.

Ceneth and his procession were greeted at the castle with fanfare and open arms. While it was splendid, it was nothing compared to the warmth of Caris's face as their eyes locked and she ran to him. Ceneth had swept her up in front of family and friends, holding her aloft as he squeezed her with tenderness and excitement. His exclamations of how she smelled of the fresh rain in spring, the shower of kisses on her cheeks and forehead, the pet names were all a bit too much for the public. It may not have been the most appropriate show of affection for two unwed monarchs, but as they were promised to one another, the demonstration was received with appreciation rather than admonishment. How lucky were they to have found not only shared dreams but to have fallen in love? If the joy had belonged to anyone other than her sister, Ophir would have been sickened.

While the kingdom's monarchs made their way to the dining room, Ophir used the distraction to slip free from supervising eyes and duck into the kitchen for a bottle of wine. She had been expected to join them in the room, but everyone knew she wouldn't come. She'd smelled the roast ham and apple glaze, the braided rolls, the tarts and sweets and greens mixed with fig to balance the vegetables' flavor with natural sugars, and she'd felt nothing but irritation. A special dinner for their special guest. A lovely meal for the lovely Ceneth. She'd spotted the only thing she wanted in the kitchen and left the food for the perfect family. After roughly twenty minutes, Harland found her on the castle wall overlooking the sea with a fine bottle of merlot.

She hadn't bothered to bring a glass.

Harland slid into the space near the wall across from her and extended his hand for a drink. Their relationship was too familiar for a guard and his lady according to any and all outside opinions, but the world had no way of knowing this informality was the strained, barely salvaged friendship of a man who'd survived her seduction and rejection with a bruised ego and a chuckle.

Harland took a swig of the dark wine.

Ophir pouted, looking between the bottle and her guard. "I didn't bring enough for two."

"You're in luck," he said. He fished in his breast pocket for a small flask. "Keep your wine. I'll stick to whiskey."

If he was trying to make her smile, he'd succeeded. She'd felt on more than one occasion that, apart from her sister, he was the only friend she had. On the matter of courtiers and lords and ladies, Ophir knew her likability had nothing to do with who she was and everything to do with her title. Everyone wanted to be close to the crown. Harland, however, had nothing to gain from her—not anymore, at least. She was glad he'd stuck it out and remained on the job after surviving her preferred form of humbling men. She was even more relieved that he'd remained steadfast, patient, quick to smile, and ready to leave the past behind them.

"Shouldn't you be sober on the job?"

He made an exaggerated smacking sound as he drank his whiskey. "Shouldn't you be in the dining room right now with your parents, sister, and future brother-in-law? The food smelled great." He returned the alcohol, and she proceeded to take three deep swallows before wiping the purple droplets from the corner of her mouth with the back of her hand.

"The hero and heroine will do just fine without me. Their mission to save the world doesn't need a distraction." She continued to gaze at the horizon, refusing to fully engage in his attempts to chastise her. "Are you asking because if I'm there eating, you'd get to eat, too?"

"You caught me."

She smiled humorlessly. "Go, Harland. Fix yourself a plate. Snag me a roll. For now, I find it's quicker to get drunk on an empty stomach, and they certainly don't need my help with that task."

Harland's brows met in the middle. "It's important—what they're doing. That doesn't make your life any less valuable."

Her attempt to smile fell flat.

"You know," Harland mused as if to himself, "your eyes are usually so golden it looks like you wear your crown around your pupils. Not today though."

"Because the glitter fades when I'm hungry?" she asked, taking another drink.

"They give you away," he said. "They're ochre when you're sad. The light doesn't reach them."

She shifted uncomfortably and Harland took the hint, dropping the topic. She wished she'd brought a cloak or blanket with her onto the wall, as the late hour was beginning to blow a chilling wind off the sea. A large, wooden ship was docking in the ports after returning from what had presumably been a trip to one of their distant trade partners. She focused on the little dots of men who worked like a colony of ants to unload their cargo from the vessel onto the pier.

Besides, Harland was wrong. Her life was not important. Every dotted sailor she watched served a purpose in his chain of command, helping keep the ship together. One would tie the masts, the other would steer, one would keep lookout, and all would participate. They had more purpose than she did. Caris had taken enough purpose for the both of them. Ophir didn't resent her sister in the slightest. She admired

Caris not only for her wit and wisdom but for the unwavering confidence she had in an optimistic future.

The firstborn heir to the Farehold throne cast a very long shadow behind the brightness of her success. Ophir had no interest in competing with her elder sister's shine.

"My family is alive because of them, you know." Harland extended a hand for another drink of the wine.

She raised a brow curiously, encouraging him to go on as she passed him the merlot.

"Do you know what I do?"

"Yes. You harass my sense of privacy by following me all over the castle."

He chuckled with a friendly, throaty sound. If he was going to stare too deeply into her eyes, she might as well return the favor. It was easy to do with Harland. She inhaled his honest, freshly cut grass fae scent, savoring the inborn perfume. His eyes were a pretty, complex shade of hazel as they twinkled in the afternoon sun. The greens, browns, and golds etched through his irises were a map of the world. He took another drink and then gave it a swirl, realizing they were making it through the alcohol more quickly than the princess may have intended.

"Watch." He flexed his fist and punched into the wall of the outlook, directly into the stone. It crumbled and shuddered against the impact, leaving his hand intact.

"Show-off," she muttered, but the demonstration succeeded in eliciting a smile. "That's quite the neat trick. Is that how you got the job? You're terribly strong?"

"It is," he admitted, brandishing his knuckles to show that his skin had not broken from the impact. "But my mother and brother weren't so lucky with their abilities. My mother can commune with the dead, and my brother can speak mind to mind."

Harland didn't need to go on. She understood what he meant. People did what they did best: hated what they did not understand. The powers had long since been informally separated into abilities of light and dark. While those born with light gifts were often celebrated as blessings from the goddess, it wasn't uncommon for families, men, children, women, and strangers to turn up dead after their darker gifts had been revealed.

In the right setting, his mother may have been honored for her ability to commune with the afterlife. Those who could enter your very mind and thoughts, however, were never known for anything other than nightmares made flesh.

Changing the continent's dangerous misconceptions was the dream that Caris and Ceneth shared. While Caris had expressed a longing to be married from the moment she met Raascot's noble ruler, she adhered to the long-standing tradition of waiting until the age of seventy-five, building decades of goodwill with her people so they would trust her vision when they unified their kingdoms and ruled as one.

Through their combined efforts and relations across the continent, Caris and Ceneth had crafted a pipeline from Farehold to Raascot so that fae with darker powers might escape persecution and seek refuge. Raascot was an asylum for anyone who'd been branded "dark fae."

Humans or those called the "light fae" who were disquieted by the influx of dark fae in the north were invited to relocate to the southern kingdom. Farehold took on the population growth steadily, overseeing their movements and resettlements as people migrated across the borders.

Removing fae from immediate threat of death and danger was only step one of their plan. While vital in protecting against the urgent realities of violence, dividing the groups had the potential to breed further distrust and make matters worse unless the second stage of their vision was carefully implemented.

Separating the problems from their prejudices had already begun to show its fruitfulness in the years since the underground pipeline had been instated. After the immigrants had settled from one kingdom into the next and roots had been planted, Caris's marriage would unite two kingdoms into one. As long as they could remove the vulnerable populations from immediate fear of harm or persecution, they'd continue down their path before education and unity could be disseminated through the joined continent. Once unification had been achieved, they'd work to cultivate healthy relationships between fae and humans of all gifts and abilities.

The plan would not be achieved overnight, but it was a beautiful vision for how a future without violence and misunderstanding of power might look.

"Your brother is okay?" Ophir asked. They never spoke of Harland's family. In fact, aside from his age, his name, his title, and the amount of frustration she engendered in him, he generally avoided talking about himself at all.

Harland confirmed with a tilt of his head. "They're in Raascot, living just outside of Gwydir. He's going through formal training to learn how his abilities can be used for good, as much a part of their military as I am this one. If he had stayed in Farehold..."

They both knew exactly what would have happened if he had remained in Farehold.

Ophir took the final drink of wine and set it down beside her. Three-quarters of a bottle had been almost enough to give her a small, pleasant buzz, but it hadn't quite done the trick. She leaned against the wall as she continued to gaze out at the horizon.

"Once Caris leaves for Gwydir, do you know what you'll do?"

She shrugged. "I suppose I'll do what I've always done: whatever the hell I want."

Ceneth remained at the castle for a full week, and it was both too much, and never enough time. Caris had been as doting and lovelorn as any bride-to-be, but he'd matched her energy with equal ferocity. Ophir had never seen anyone look at a woman the way the winged northern king gazed at her sister. There was no doubt in Ophir's mind that he'd drain the seas for her, lasso the moon, and level kingdoms if she asked. He was a man whose soul had been fully given to his betrothed. They deserved each other, in every sense of the word.

Ophir absently wondered if their offspring would be born with or without wings. She tried to picture Caris's blond hair and blue eyes on bronze skin and set against the black feathers of a Raascot fae.

Ophir politely interacted with Ceneth at the dinner tables and whenever their paths crossed in the hall. She held no animosity toward the dark king, but she also didn't feel particularly inclined to get to know him. He'd always been abundantly civil with Ophir, but never more than that. The king gave her a proper, courteous kiss on the cheek as he parted. He held Caris for a long, beautiful stretch before he and his men returned to the north.

Ophir touched Caris's back as she stood at the gate, waving at the figures who disappeared into the distance. "You won't always have to say goodbye."

"I know." Caris wiped at a single, silvery tear.

"Fuck tradition," Ophir said. "Move up the wedding. Unless, of course, you think you'll have a change of heart before your seventy-fifth birthday?"

"Don't even joke about that. He's so wonderful. He's everything, Firi."

Ophir hated the pain on her sister's face. "But you're in love."

Caris shook her head, curls swishing around her shoulders as she did so. "You shouldn't rush something that's meant to last forever. Besides, there's more work to be done for us both. The people trust us as leaders of the separate kingdoms. We'd undermine our progress if we rushed the unification of the continent. It'll be worth the wait."

And that was only one of the millions of reasons that

Caris was the better person in every sense of the word. She was decent, selfless, and trusting to a fault. Ophir didn't know it then, but she understood now.

Caris's goodness would be her downfall.

ELEVEN

+ ／ + + +

T YR HAD BEEN GIVEN A GIFT. IT WAS ONLY RIGHT THAT HE use it.

He'd always been good at sneaking, but it shouldn't have been this easy. Not in a castle. If his priorities hadn't rested elsewhere, he might have brought the egregious security flaw to someone's attention. How old was this castle, that it contained a passageway that no one else knew about? Honestly, it wasn't even the princess's fault that she was coming and going at all hours of the night. Who wouldn't use points of access when they were as easy as stepping through a mirror? It had certainly been intended as a safety measure—a method for escape if the royal family needed to steal away undetected. In a sense, she was using it for its intended purpose.

Tyr had slipped into the princess's room as Ophir had returned from the kitchen with another bottle of wine. He'd thought she was going to take it in her bed, which had been both worrisome and understandable. He'd spent his own shares of nights in bottles of various spirits as he'd drowned his sorrow.

Her personal guard had followed her to take up post outside of her room. She'd locked the door behind her and then promptly pressed her way into the floor-length mirror. It released and gave way to a set of stairs that wound to the wine cellars beneath the castle. He never knew exactly what he was looking for when he stepped into the space between things, but that was the blessing and curse of voyeurism. Sometimes you had to be present for a long time before you learned something worth knowing.

Within a matter of minutes, she was sitting on the cliffs outside of the castle, completely unaccompanied. He was nearly impressed. The last royal hope of Farehold, and yet she could find absolute quiet and unguarded solitude whenever she wanted, even when they thought they had her under lock and key.

Surely, this was how she'd gotten Caris out of the castle.

Now it was how she got shit-faced on vintage red wines while watching the sunset in silence. He'd spent so many years in the invisible places between things that he'd long since lost the ability to feel shame for spying, but this did feel private. He got no sick pleasure out of watching the unwitting. When he courted partners or seduced lovers, it was with the full, enthusiastic desire of two or more passionate parties. Watching was for information. He'd followed Dwyn to Farehold with a purpose, and his tracking had led him to the princess.

He sat and leaned his back against the cream stones of the outer castle wall while Ophir drank straight from the bottle, watching seagulls dart beyond the cliffs. Seabirds reminded him of his post on the frozen coast, except these birds were louder and far bolder with their movements. All their screeches were so shrill, so piercing against the gentle consistency of the incoming tide. The day was extraordinarily humid, and everything tasted of fish and salt. He was envious of the green glass bottle pressed to her lips. He'd take woman or wine over the flavor of seaweed any day.

He felt...something.

He watched her take drink after drink while the orange

sun flooded the horizon, filling the seascape with pastels. It lit her features, setting her profile and the locks of her hair to the same flame for which she was famous. The humidity had turned to sweat, her hair clinging to her neck and bare arms in a sticky, curled mess. He didn't feel pity. It certainly wasn't disapproval.

Empathy. That was the emotion.

The secondborn daughter to the Aubade throne, reckless and wild and lost, was in pain, and somehow, despite barely clinging to her will to survive, she kept putting one foot in front of the other. Some days it was by drinking berry-flavored liqueurs, and others it was by spending the day in bed. Progress was not linear. She was surviving. He understood.

Maybe that was why he didn't feel angry when Dwyn strolled onto the cliff, despite how much he loved to hate her. Dwyn's curtain of black hair caught in the wind, whipping around her face as the breeze swept off the ocean and rushed onto the rocks. He hadn't heard her footsteps over the rhythmic sounds of the waves, but he wasn't particularly surprised at her presence. She was why he was at the castle in the first place. She was playing some game with the princess that he had yet to fully understand. Both he and Dwyn stared at a lock, so to speak, and Dwyn appeared certain that Ophir held the key.

He took as many silent steps as he dared until he was within earshot. He told himself it was because it would be a useful opportunity to hear Dwyn interact. The witch didn't know he was here, and goddess only knew what she may or may not share when she thought she and Ophir were alone. Hate Dwyn though he might, he saw how Ophir's shoulders relaxed ever so slightly at the witch's presence. Maybe he was angry that anyone liked Dwyn. Maybe he was jealous that it was Dwyn who spoke to the princess, Dwyn who comforted her, Dwyn who shared her bed.

He'd met the princess first in the flesh, after all, even if Dwyn had unwittingly led him to the royal siblings in the first place. He'd rescued Ophir at that party. He could be the one comforting her right now. The cliff could be silhouetted with the princess's small frame next to his strong, broad shoulders.

But alas, this was another in a long line of ways Dwyn had bested him.

He observed the pair as Dwyn slid easily behind her, planting one hand behind Ophir's back on the cliff so her arm supported the princess's back. She extended her slender fingers for the bottle and they took turns swigging from the wine. Ophir rested her brown-gold locks on Dwyn's shoulders, allowing her loose waves to cascade down the girl's back, their strands a mix of caramel and chocolate. He listened, but they didn't talk about spells or magic or power. They didn't talk about kingdoms or politics or loss. They didn't talk about anything.

They were just two people, sitting on a cliff at sunset, sharing a bottle of wine.

TWELVE

✦   ✦   ✦   ✦

OPHIR SET HER JAW. SHE CLENCHED HER FISTS. SHE BRACED herself to be yelled at, yet again.

"What are you?" Dwyn struck her across the face, the harsh, red welts already rising against her pale skin. Her sea-freshened face was pink against the wind that chafed it, but it was nothing compared to the harsh, clear evidence of Dwyn's act of intentional violence.

"Ow!" Ophir's hand flew to her face where the imprint of a hand was already hot against her skin, eyes wide with shock. She'd expected a scolding, not a slap.

The day was as terrible as her energy. The winds, the impending storm, the chill, the ferocity in every one of her lashes matched her as if one was a harmony and the other its melody. Ophir's eyes were as wide as saucers, the melted honey of her irises staring at Dwyn in a state of bewildered horror. It wasn't the first time Dwyn had attempted a rather violent form of therapy, but this was the first time the fae had hit her.

"Hey!" Harland shouted from where he stood off to the back.

"I know what I'm doing," Dwyn yelled dismissively at the

guard, returning her aggressive posture to the princess. There was no gentle energy in her tonight. She focused her dark brown eyes on the princess where she shrank.

Ophir blinked rapidly in shock, flinching preemptively. She'd been hit twice in her life, and both culprits had been dealt with swiftly and without mercy. This was the third time someone had laid a hand on her, and she had no idea what to make of it. She stumbled backward, a thin hand raising to touch the heat of the welt. She knew what Dwyn wanted to hear and swallowed through the thought.

"I'm a snake?"

"Say it again." Dwyn raised her hand, and Ophir winced in anticipation of the pain. Distant lightning over the sea made her look like one of the old gods from the time before the All Mother had brought order and love to the world. There was a dark ferocity in the typically aloof siren's face she'd never seen before.

"Goddess, fuck, stop!" Ophir flinched and lifted a hand to protect herself. Harland's stare intensified from where he'd been idling in the expanse above the cliffs. He was clearly uncomfortable but didn't know what to do or how to help. He hadn't let Ophir out of his sight in nearly seven months, save for the moments she slept or the times she excused herself to the bathing room. He'd become a permanent shadow, and following the tragedy that had befallen the castle, the princess no longer tried to evade him. No one was sure when he found the time to sleep, particularly as he no longer trusted any of the other castle guards to watch her.

Ophir's unusual relationship with Dwyn had resulted in the liveliest anyone had seen the young princess in months. No one questioned the Sulgrave fae's presence—she may as well have been from a village in Farehold, a border town in Tarkhany, or the Raascot capital of Gwydir for all it mattered—as long as it seemed to be doing what no one else in the kingdom had accomplished. Whoever she was, and whatever she was doing, it seemed to be working.

"Don't tempt me, Firi. I've been looking for excuses to smack you ever since I moved into the castle. You and your goddess-damned flame-soaked night terrors haven't let me get a decent sleep in weeks. Go on. Give me a reason."

"I'm a snake."

Harland relaxed at the exchange. Out of the corner of her eye, Ophir caught him chuckling to himself and begin to pick at tiny pieces of lint on his cloak. He seemed to be doing his best to give the women their privacy. It was impossible to miss the bizarre brand of psychology Dwyn seemed to wield. While healers and spiritualists had tried prayer, tonics, and drugs, and while her parents had gone to great lengths to offer their youngest child space and understanding, it was the Sulgrave fae's violence that appeared to be making true, noteworthy progress.

The cliffs were not quiet today. The clouds were dark with impending storm. The sea matched its ominous intensity, white caps breaking the otherwise steel shades of its waves. The wind whipped around them, making Ophir wish she had tied her hair into a braid. Her hair was a mix of muddy brown and dark blond, tangling in a cloud against her face as the wind moved it. She choked on a strand of her hair and spit it out, attempting to look fierce, and failing.

"Again! Say it until I believe you."

Ophir scrunched her face angrily. "You want to know what I believe? I believe that you're certifiably insane."

"Try again, princess."

"I'm a black snake! I'm a big, terrifying black snake!" She cried her assertions into the wind at Dwyn, fists balled in anger. Ophir doubted she looked threatening, but she pulled her lips back in a snarl to show the sharpened ends of her canines. It wasn't the desired expression of fury Dwyn was trying to elicit, but rather, a face of contempt and irritation at her so-called friend who wouldn't stop hitting her across the fucking face.

The siren lifted her hand to strike again and Ophir winced, raising her forearm up defensively to block the blow.

Dwyn's voice was growing higher and louder to combat the sound of the approaching storm. "Fight back, Ophir! Stop being so pathetic. You're acting powerless. Where is your rage?! Don't let me hit you. Don't let yourself be a victim. What are you?"

"If you don't want me to get hit, then stop hitting me!"

"Do you think the world will stop, princess? It will punish you as long as you allow it! Don't *let* it!"

Dwyn pushed her to the ground and the princess went flying, skidding through the dust, grime, and sand at the cliff's edge. Her hands scraped and chafed as they burned against the impact, a jolt of pain shooting up her arms. Her palms stung with the shallow scrapes, droplets of blood already beginning to form on her hands. She shot a panicked look to Harland just in time to see him straighten where he stood. His full attention was on the girls as her feral friend descended upon her.

"Where's your will to live!"

"You're insane," Ophir said, bewildered.

Through gritted teeth, Dwyn said, "I haven't shown you a drop of insanity yet. You have no idea how much I have to give."

Dwyn wound her foot up and kicked Ophir in the ribs. She reeled against the pain, stars populating her vision. That was the signal to intervene. Harland moved quickly toward them, his hand on his hilt, but Dwyn thrust a powerful stream of water directly from the ocean below at the guard that threw him against solid stone. His body made impact with a loud thud as her power crashed around him, cracking his body against the cream-colored outer walls of the castle. Water and chaos and pain erupted in a way that filled the very air, as if the impending storm was only a player in their terrible game. Dwyn pulled her foot back again and kicked Ophir in the stomach this time. The princess gagged and choked on her pain, feeling loss, betrayal, and terror consume her.

"What are you!" Her foot drew backward, ready to come

down in another terrible blow. Her next kick would surely draw blood.

With anger, Ophir spun on the siren. She pushed herself up with one hand and began to call her flame with the other, but Dwyn was too fast. The wind was the wail of a legion of banshees as it whipped off of the ocean's choppy surface, whistling and crying around them. Ophir's toffee hair had become painful whips of rope as they slashed and bit into the skin of her face and cheeks. Thunder cracked just beyond the bay, announcing its arrival to any who dared to remain on the seaside. Dwyn doused the emerging fire with her water and crunched the princess's hand beneath her foot.

"What are you!"

With a shriek so loud and unholy that it washed out the ocean around them, Ophir unleashed an explosion of anger. Her hands flew out in front of her as if to send another wall of flame at Dwyn in their death match. Her banshee cry opened a bottle of fury and the madness of long-held violence as she released a raw, untethered scream. "I'm a snake!"

And there it was.

Dwyn began to back away quickly, lips parted, eyes wide with surprise.

Harland had just begun to stand from where he'd been knocked nearly unconscious against the wall of the castle. He was gasping for air after having nearly drowned on dry land from the siren's blast of power and perhaps thought he might be hallucinating from the swallow of seawater.

Ophir stared in horror at the vile evil that had emerged from her explosion of rage.

A large, black serpent was poised to strike, its vitriol focused fully on Dwyn.

Manifestation was said to be the power of the All Mother. In her infinite wisdom and selflessness, she had breathed the earth and all its creatures into existence through the power of thought, energy, and air. The goddess had desired lush, green lands, and so she'd manifested vegetation. She'd wanted to quench her thirst, and so she'd filled the world with water. Animals filled her world, from the gentle herbivores to the terrible predators that kept the balance of life in check. The All Mother had desired companions and had crafted humans to live alongside her. They'd grown jealous and afraid of her power, so she'd made the fae to bridge the gap between the mortal and the holy.

Throughout recorded history, manifestation had been reported only three times. The first was said to have been possessed by a religious Speaker for the All Mother who used her words to bring harmony in war times, conjuring walls to end battles, chains to shackle enemies, and dividing the kingdoms to prevent their lust for blood. The second was said to have belonged to the original fae king of Farehold, as he'd created for himself the wealth and armies he'd needed to take hold of a kingdom, leveling the lands. The third had been killed at the gentle age of eleven when she'd shown the first inclinations of manifestation. Her parents had attempted to hide her gift, but the moment word spread, it had been decided by the church and crown alike that the gift was too powerful to be wielded on these lands.

Dwyn's shock and surprise had given way to a slow, private smile. She didn't seem to fear the monster before her, not even as the thunder cracked and the lightning of the approaching storm reflected against its scales. The edges of her lips twinged upward as the fallen princess, who still clung to the cliff's edge, and the shocked bodyguard examined the large, black serpent.

The siren motioned to Harland. "Can you take care of this for us?"

The serpent was the size of a large dog. Ophir wasn't sure how Harland was supposed to "take care of it" and keep his life and limbs intact, but Dwyn didn't seem concerned.

Ophir had manifested.

What was more, the siren had seemed to know she

could. This was why she'd spent weeks forcing the princess to envision the beast. She'd created a nightly meditation of how the creature looked, how it made her feel, the powers it possessed. She'd gone so far as to beat Ophir within an inch of her life to activate whatever remnants of survival remained in her weak, pathetic body.

The snake was enormous. It was the living embodiment of rage, venom, and fear. Still, it did not seem emboldened to move of its own accord. The creature remained coiled, as if waiting for a command. Seeing his opportunity, Harland brought his sword down in a sharp, clean arc. The unnatural viscosity of the black, thick blood that sprayed from its beheading was as horrifying as the appearance of the creature itself. Dwyn immediately began the process of shoving the serpent's body over the cliff's edge, as if her first priority was concealing the evidence. The wind fought against her efforts as the storm around them began to thunder over the sea, but Harland joined the siren in shoving the serpent's body over the edge of the cliff into the waters below.

They were joined in a mission to hide the evidence of what the princess had just done. No one could know about this, and they knew it intrinsically.

The rain began to pour down over them with the flurry of rocks and fists. Any evidence of the snake's blackened blood was washing away under the pounding of water as lightning cracked over the ocean. The waves were crashing with such intensity that their sea spray began to join the rain soaking the three who remained on the cliff.

Shock glued Ophir to the ground.

Harland scooped up the princess as Dwyn opened the castle door, guiding them through the corridors. She'd become familiar enough with Castle Aubade over the past few weeks to know how to navigate from the cliffs to the princess's chambers. Her rooms had changed a number of times, as the severity of her flame would often leave the bedchamber in such a state of charred disrepair that they'd need to relocate to a new wing until something could be done about Ophir, Flame Heart.

✦   ✦   ✦   ✦

"What do I do?" Ophir's voice sounded so small to her ears. She had been strong, once. Those parts of her had been laid to rest with Caris. She hadn't thought she was capable of signs of life until she'd created one of her own.

In the seconds that followed, she had gone directly from the storm-swept cliffs to her room where thoughts could flood through her mind just as the waters beyond the fortress. Her guard disappeared, presumably to clean up after her as he'd done so many times before. She was rife with anxiety, twisting her fingers against the wet fabric of her skirt as she flipped through the events of the evening like a tattered, paperbound novel, reading it forward and backward and again and again until the spine cracked. She'd waited in agonizing silence for Dwyn, Harland, or anyone to burst in through her door and demand to know how she'd created a snake.

She had summoned a serpent. No—she hadn't summoned it, for it had not existed.

Summoners called to that which occurred naturally. Some could speak to only present elements, like those who crafted metal, fire, or stone by wielding the elements before them. Ophir had been gifted with the ability to summon an element even when she found herself lacking its presence. She could summon fire, rather than simply move that which existed in hearths, candles, lanterns, and torches.

What Ophir had done was not summoning.

She had manifested.

She'd been foolish to think Dwyn's methods had been an exercise intended for healing.

Harland entered her room without announcing himself. He knelt before her as he had done so long ago, but everything was different now. Her clothes and hair were wet, as she'd been the morning he'd burst into her room following

104

the party. She sat atop her bed fretting over her creation, but this time she was not a distant husk. Fear had replaced her numbness, seeping into the world around her just like the damp, soaked spot on the duvet from where her sopping clothes and tendrils of hair rested firmly on the mattress.

His saturated armor mirrored her dress as it dripped onto her carpet. She knew from the twitch of his hands that he wanted to comfort her. Of course he wanted to be a good guard, a good subject to the royal family, a good friend and a good steward of magic and peace. Surely, he wanted to do the right thing, but how could one do the right thing when there was no clear path forward?

But she knew his pained expression went far beyond that of a man of duty. His face was that of a man who wanted to take her in his arms and hold her.

Ophir chewed on her words. "If people find out—"

"They won't," he said quickly. He abandoned his comforting post and stood, crossing his arms to force his hands to be kept to himself. He rubbed at his chin with a free hand while he stated the facts. "Your gift is flame, Ophir. It is well known throughout the kingdom. Everyone knows what power you possess, and they would never expect or believe that you'd come into anything further. It's unlikely that you would show an aptitude for such a radically different skill this late in life. No one will suspect you of possessing a new gift."

"Why would you hide this for me?"

His eyes were tight and serious. "You know why."

Her damp, brown-gold locks shook, water dripping from their tendrils. "Several fae have multiple powers. Dwyn can—"

His eyes strained as he turned to hear her finish her sentence. His words were taut with a low severity as he asked, "What can Dwyn do?"

She didn't want to incriminate the fae who had quickly become her only friend. No man would feel safe in the presence of a siren if they knew what she could do. Regardless,

Ophir wasn't sure she'd survive if Dwyn left. She'd made more healing progress, begun to gain healthy weight, and even stretched her nights of sleep further and further thanks to the Sulgrave fae's presence. "She has multiple water-related abilities. Not only does she manipulate it, but I believe she can also breathe in water." He didn't need to know what she used her powers to accomplish. Harland was no sailor. He was at no risk of falling prey to whatever dark whims a siren might possess.

"No one has to know about this," he repeated, as much to himself as to her. He pressed a hand to his heart as he looked at her, a silent vow in his action. Manifestation came with the kind of consequences that raised the ground, toppled dynasties, and created worlds. It was a power too great to be allowed to live on this earth. He said it as much with his eyes as he did with his gesture: he would not allow her to meet a manifester's fate. "But Dwyn knew."

"She learned when we did," Ophir replied.

"She knew," he said, expression grave.

"How could she have known?" Even as she asked the question, she held the same puzzle pieces that Harland gripped with uneasy hands. Dwyn had planted the image in her mind for weeks. She'd goaded her, pushed her, and beat her until the princess snapped with the power. This had been no healing exercise in freeing oneself from trauma. She'd been engaging with intent. The Sulgrave fae had known.

Harland shook his head.

"What do we do now?" Ophir asked.

He looked at her with pained, hazel eyes. "She's in a guest room now. She wasn't happy about being separated from you."

"Is she in trouble?"

Harland chewed his lip. "That's not the right word."

"We haven't been apart in weeks," Ophir replied. She wasn't sure what the inky snake had taught her about Dwyn, but a few facts remained. Dwyn had saved her. Dwyn had kept her alive the night of Caris's murder and continued to save her night after night, fitful sleep after restless slumber. Aubade was spared an ashen end because of Dwyn.

The line between suspicion and salvation grew thinner with every night that passed.

✦   ✦   ✦   ✦

For three days, Ophir did not see or hear from Dwyn. Harland had refused to answer any questions about the Sulgrave girl. In the moments following her manifestation of the serpent, everything else had blurred. Ophir was escorted out of her rooms only for meals.

For fifty years, Ophir had been adrift. She'd dodged responsibilities, deflected obligations that came with the crown, and indulged in the pleasures and victories of a princess who'd learned how to navigate as the secondborn. For the gut-wrenching, hopeless months following Caris's loss, she'd grieved, she'd prayed, and she'd suffered. For three days and three nights, she pictured herself on the cliff and the enormous, terrifying beast that had sprung from her fingertips.

She pushed the word out of her mind every time she was confronted by the implication that came with creation. The thought was too big, too important, too powerful for Ophir to speak aloud. She settled into a protective shock as the sun rose and set. Though she didn't name the power, one distinct change occurred.

For three consecutive nights, Ophir did not dream.

THIRTEEN

+   +   +   +

T HERE WERE ONLY THREE PEOPLE IN THE WORLD TYR HATED more than Dwyn. He'd see them all dead the moment he had the power he needed. He'd like to see her dead, too, even if he couldn't be the one to kill her.

"Get off me, dog!" Dwyn hissed. She wriggled against him, and he tightened his hold to keep the serpent in a woman's body against the wall. Her teeth flashed with anger, dark eyes smoldering like blackened coal. She held his gaze with a challenge in her eyes, as if refusing to give him the satisfaction of looking away.

He towered over her from where he had her pinned against the stones of the castle's outer wall. The wind and waves splashed against the cliffs behind them. His flexed muscular forearm crushed her windpipe as her feet struggled to find purchase on the soil.

"Did you think I wouldn't find you here? Did you think you were alone?" Water dripped from his hair, running down his jaw and neck, washing the tattoo that wrapped its way just past the collar of his shirt.

"I'm not in Sulgrave any longer, Tyr. The clan has no power in Aubade. If Anwir wanted me, he should have come for me himself." She released a frustrated grunt as she struggled, but her sounds were washed away by the cries of gulls and the waves.

"You're a small fish right now, and I think you know that."

Her eyes burned with hate as they bore into his dark eyes, his hair, his fucking tattoo. Goddess above, how he despised the matching ink that marred their skin. He'd pluck the knife from his hip and peel the tattoo from his skin right now if he thought it would free him, but their curse was far cleverer than mortal tools.

He returned the burning glare. His reflection in the mirror had once looked back at him with kind eyes. They'd been the rich colors of coffee and earth and the forest. As he pinned the siren to the wall, he hoped they were glazed like the dirt used to cover graves, not unlike the one he wanted so badly to put her in.

Motherfucking Dwyn.

He'd followed her across the Frozen Straits, though his hunt for the witch had begun far, far before that. He knew what she was. He knew who she wanted. He didn't know how, when, or where she'd infiltrated Farehold's royal family, but she'd beat him to it in spectacular fashion.

"What are you doing with the princess?" His question was a thinly veiled threat. It came out in a low, angry growl.

"You know why I'm here," she said through clenched teeth. "The same reason you are."

"Berinth won the blood race. It's over. Go home."

"After you," came her taunting reply. He searched her face for further explanation. When he didn't budge, she laughed. "Noble, stoic, stupid Tyr. Do you really think it's over? And, what, I've stayed in Farehold because I love their backwater culture? Why did the goddess curse me with such an idiot for a shadow."

His nostrils flared as he struggled to control his emotions. She wasn't wrong. At least, not completely. He'd followed

Dwyn across the Straits because she held the secrets he so desperately needed. He hadn't understood what had driven her to Farehold until he'd caught her skulking about Castle Aubade. International politics had never been of interest to him, but he struggled to understand how the southern kingdoms could be so ignorant and barbaric as to still utilize monarchies, unless they didn't understand the implications.

But, surely, they knew. Everyone knew. Didn't they?

"Ask me," Dwyn said, biting down on the words. "Ask me how I'm going to do it without you."

"You can't," he snarled.

"Oh, but I can."

A sound behind him told him she was summoning water, but he was as quick as shadow. He opened the door that led to the castle's back entrance before the salted waves crashed down onto them, dragging the siren into the corridor with him. Water rushed in at the seams and hinges, splashing under the doorframe and wetting their feet just as he slammed it behind them.

"I'm no threat to her." Dwyn slammed her foot down into Tyr's instep and he grunted, but it did not have the desired effect. He did not release her.

"You're no friend to her, either, witch."

She laughed. It was a dark, humorless sound. She was unfazed as she stared him in the eye and said, "There's more than one way to obtain a royal heart, dog."

He bared his teeth in an ongoing growl, and she mirrored the expression, sharpened canines reflected against the dim, flickering lights of the corridor.

He pressed harder on her windpipe. She gripped his forearm uselessly as she began to bargain. "You plan to focus your efforts on me while Berinth lives? You're a fool. You saw what he did with Caris. You know what he may yet accomplish. He'll have the southern kingdoms long before you and your precious band get what they want. If he succeeds, it won't matter what I'm doing with the princess." She spat and the froth of her spit clung to his face.

The sound of footsteps scraped from the distance before he had time to respond. Tyr slammed his hand down over her mouth just as she sucked in a breath to cry for help. She brought a knee upward in an attempt to harm his manhood, but he rotated in time so that she struck only leg. He had only moments before whoever approached caught him in the castle.

As the individual neared, Tyr vanished.

Dwyn kicked slightly until the tips of her toes met the earth. He could no longer be seen, but he wasn't going anywhere.

"Dwyn?" called a man's voice. Tyr recognized it as belonging to Ophir's bodyguard before the man rounded the corner. "Are you there? I need to talk to you about..." Harland's voice trailed off as his gaze raked over the awkwardness of her stance. Tyr flexed in frustration as he understood what the guard must see. She was not relaxing against the wall. She was not breathing easily.

Fuck.

Harland put his hand on the pommel of his sword just as he freed her. She sucked in a lungful of air as she tumbled from the hold onto her feet. Tyr's hands balled into fists as a string of curses took over his every waking thought.

"Harland. How nice for the princess's personal bodyguard to escort me."

She said the guard's title with too much vitriol as she shot a cold glare into the empty air, presumably at Tyr. He looked on with a curled lip. He hated Dwyn but didn't think she was stupid enough to give him away. If she revealed his presence, he'd spill her secrets before she could blink.

Harland examined her.

"Something is wrong," he said as he freed his sword from its sheath.

Dwyn's expression changed in an instant. She was relaxed and confident as she soothed him. "No, no. It's okay. I came back out here to practice a new technique with the water and just stepped inside. It's rather wet out there. I'm sorry to have alarmed you. I assume you want to discuss our sweet Firi?"

He stared at her without moving for a long while.

"What? You've never happened upon a girl on a stroll before? You look like you've seen a ghost."

Tyr didn't breathe as he watched the exchange. If Dwyn couldn't convince the man there was nothing wrong, they'd have to kill him. He was certain she knew as well as he that Harland's death would close more doors than it opened. *Come on, witch. Do what you do best. Lie.*

He exhaled as Harland nodded with unconvincing slowness. The guard said, "What happened on the cliff earlier—"

"Let's not talk about it here," she said hurriedly. She closed the space between them as she took his bicep in her hands. "Back to the room, shall we?" She urged him down the corridor, away from the threat that loomed just beyond the glimmer of sight.

Tyr remained at their heels, as silent as a house cat. He knew from the angered glare she cast over her shoulder that she knew he'd followed. She probably wished there was some way she could drown him while he trailed behind, but she could not fight what she could not see.

+   +   +   +

In just under a century and a half of life, Harland had learned that his gut was rarely mistaken. It had told him to put his name up for consideration when a position opened as Ophir's guard, and he had. It had urged him from his bed in the middle of the night to tell him something was wrong, only to discover Ophir missing from her bed while across the castle, a servant rang the alarm bell that the numb, silent princess had been found in an alcove, hands stained with blood and dressed for a masquerade. Days later, he'd entered Ophir's room to find his charge with a stranger—one who informed him that she had attempted to take her own life. And that same gut had looked at Dwyn with a distrust that refused to subside.

He led Dwyn to a rather plain guest room two halls over from Ophir's room while he wrestled with his thoughts.

She leaned into the writing desk, wooden lip biting into her hip as she relaxed into its edge. She pouted. "Why so serious?"

He gave her an unhappy look, which only made her laugh.

"Such a frown, Harland. You look too much like those happy, golden hounds to get away with such an expression." She smiled. Dwyn turned her back on him while pouring herself a glass of water from the pitcher on the desk, which gave him a moment to gather what he wanted to say.

Trapped between impossible choices, he neither wanted to confide in Dwyn nor tell anyone else what he had witnessed on the cliffs. Ophir had created something from nothing, and the siren was the only other witness.

Manifesting was the power of gods. It was something that could not be taken lightly. Once the king and queen were informed of the princess's gift, her life would never be the same. Given that she'd scarcely begun the healing process from a long and scarring trauma, he didn't know if he could subject her to the changes that would ensue the moment the world knew what she was capable of.

Ophir was not the only worry on his mind.

They'd grown negligent toward possible threats within their own walls in their desperation to see the youngest princess heal. The monarchs, the guards, and all their security checks had been entirely too lax. They'd allowed a Sulgrave woman into their walls without truly understanding who she was or what she was capable of. Harland had known enough when she'd been the one who'd saved Ophir from her attempt to take her own life on the night of the party. When the fae had reemerged with her gifts of water and offered peace in a time of turmoil, it had seemed like Ophir had grabbed on to a lifeline.

His princess may very well be alive because of this siren.

The castle had accepted Dwyn's presence readily. Some

had even suggested that Dwyn had been sent by the All Mother to help save the princess from herself in the wake of the tragedy. Harland forced down his thoughts time and time again, fighting against the urge to suggest that the so-called blessing had been a little too convenient.

He continued to examine her as she plucked a leather tome from the writing desk and wandered toward an overstuffed settee. She draped herself over the piece of furniture with the contentedness and ease of someone who belonged.

In many ways, she looked like any fae woman with ink-black hair. She possessed the arched ears, the irises larger than any human's, and the lithe grace that mortals failed to achieve. There were other things about her that gave him pause. Her irreverence, for example. Was it a trait of Sulgrave fae at large, and thus one he should adjust to, or was it a Dwyn-specific curiosity? Were her boldness, her flirtatiousness, her malice traits of a kingdom or the same flaws in personality that would have set him on edge, had anyone in Aubade possessed them?

He supposed it was his own fault for knowing little of Sulgrave. But, to be fair, no one knew much of the mountain kingdom beyond the Frozen Straits, save for the reassurance that they were neither immediate threat nor enemy to Farehold or Raascot.

The inhospitable stretch of ice and snow that separated the northernmost and southern kingdoms made travel between their distant, mountain kingdom nearly impossible. Trade was a doomed endeavor, as were diplomatic missions. Anyone who managed to make the pilgrimage in one direction didn't dare risk their fate twice by returning. Dwyn's foreign Sulgrave lineage had been curious, but not immediately problematic, nor cause for alarm. She had been odd in the way that all foreign customs and mannerisms were peculiar to someone who found them unfamiliar. Aside from her improper insistence of nearly constant nudity, the girl had been a rather lovely addition to the castle.

The Sulgrave fae was an asset in some ways, of course. For instance, Ophir slept more soundly as the nights wore on as long as Dwyn was present. The threat of burning the castle and those inside of it in their sleep seemed to be waning as long as a water guardian remained vigilantly beside her. Healing seemed as if it might be possible.

But then came the things that troubled him.

Everything had changed when the tar-like serpent sprung from Ophir's anger and pain.

Dwyn had to have known precisely what it would mean to be discovered a manifester, which explained why she'd moved so quickly to dispose of the evidence. Her hands had been on the snake's body shoving it off of the cliffs before she'd even turned to address the shell-shocked princess.

"You knew," he said, breaking the long silence.

Dwyn didn't bother closing her book. She blinked back innocently. "Knew what?"

He stayed near the door. "You're clever in many ways, Dwyn." He kept his voice level, large hazel eyes trained on her with militant intensity. "You've gained access to the castle. You're in the walls. You have her trust. Congratulations. But your acting needs work."

He didn't miss the way she refused to breathe as he shut the door behind him.

FOURTEEN

* * * *

THAT NIGHT

OPHIR REMAINED NUMB AS SHE STARED AT HER BODYGUARD. Harland watched the dark-haired stranger depart from her chambers. The princess snuck lovers into her bed more times than he or any of her former guards could count. This was different. Dwyn had told him what she'd done.

"Firi…" His voice was thick and low as he struggled to choke out her name.

"Don't" was her quiet reply. Bathwater dripped from her still-soaked hair onto her shoulders. She stared at the sandy footprints on the rug as she waited for him to speak.

He looked at her unflinchingly, though she did not return his gaze. "She said you tried to drown."

The man looked as though his heart had cracked. Under normal circumstances, Harland would have taken off after an intruder and interrogated them as to why they'd been present in the princess's room. Nothing had been normal about that morning.

"Caris is dead," she said, her voice somewhere between numb and asleep as she spoke from beneath the oceans of disbelief. He shook his head as he rejected the statement. These were just words. They had no meaning.

"I know."

"…It took me until now to understand what I saw. And once I let it sink in—once I truly felt it—I didn't want to be here anymore." Perhaps he felt like she had. This was a strange, awful joke. A mistake.

"Murder is unthinkable," he said. "I can't imagine what you're going through. But this isn't your fault."

"It is." She stared at the bathwater pooling on the rug near her feet. "I took her to a party, and it was like…it was as if they planned it. They separated us. They drugged us. The way it happened…" Her voice drifted. "You didn't see the way they cut her open."

He went rigid. "What do you mean, *cut her open*? Healers? The people who prepared her for the funeral?"

"Her killers," Ophir said, not feeling the words. "They cut her down the middle. They took out the very things that made her alive like they were pulling weeds from a garden."

She saw the mechanisms of his mind whirring behind his eyes as he pieced her words together. She understood the delay. It had taken her days to process the horrors.

"Ophir, are you telling me they killed her to take things from her?" When she said nothing, he emphasized, "Are you saying they killed Caris for her organs?"

Ophir went silent as Harland moved for the door and closed it behind him. His voice dropped a register. He spoke low and urgently as he pressed his back into it, barricading her from the world beyond.

"Are you safe?"

She nearly pitied him. The poor, good guard had no way of knowing that the threat was there in the room with them. She had taken herself into the sea. She had dragged Caris, against her will, into a party and convinced her to have a drink. Ophir had told Caris to relax and have fun. She'd encouraged her sister to drink the poison. She'd murdered her sister. She was the danger.

Ophir closed her eyes in a long, slow blink. She hadn't

slept. She had scarcely breathed, save for the odd moments she'd relaxed enough in Dwyn's presence to allow herself to think she might be dreaming.

Harland made her tell him everything, and in those numb, early hours, she obliged. She hid nothing. She recounted everything from the way her sister's hands had been tied to keep her on her back, and the colors of the men's masks, to the location of the party and the sickening feel of entrails against her fingers when she'd pulled Caris to her. She knew in no uncertain terms that August had come looking for her. The warrior had died trying to save his charge, and within the next few hours Harland would doubtlessly be hearing as much from the other staff. She was vaguely aware that someone had been there to help her, though she could not describe him. His voice had been musical, she said, though Harland more or less chalked more than one bit of information up to shock.

Ophir had killed Caris. She had killed August. She had killed so many by insisting they go to that party—a den of sin that her sweet sister would have never willingly entered. It had been her selfishness, her wanderlust, her need for excitement and thrill of disobedience that had urged her out of the castle that night with their dresses and masks. They'd slipped past the guards, evaded detection, and overlooked every possible opportunity to abort their foolish mission and turn back.

"Ophir, look at me." He was kneeling before her where she sat on the bed staring despondently into the distance. "I know this is hard, but this is very important. Explain what you meant when you said they cut her open."

She felt herself disappearing with every passing second. She blinked at him again, struggling to understand the relevance in any of it. She didn't want to be here. She didn't want to be anywhere.

"I've told you everything."

"You haven't," he insisted. There was a stress and comfort coupled in his two words. Though she didn't like what he was saying, he was right. She hadn't. Some scabs were too painful to reopen. His expression softened as he said, "Please, Ophir."

"Why?" She croaked the word.

"Because: it could be nothing. Or, it could be everything."

Seconds ticked into a minute, but his gaze did not falter.

"She was nearly naked when I found her. Her dress was still on, but it had been shredded down the middle. The stranger kept shouting for me to stop and not to touch her before he carried me out. Maybe he didn't want me to feel what it was like to truly feel horror. They'd cut open her belly."

"Just her belly?"

Ophir came sharply into her body, veins flooding with something cold and angry all at once. "What do you mean, '*Just her belly*'? Is that not enough?"

He reached out a comforting hand and she slapped it away. He struggled to look patient. "Please, I know it's hard, but try to remember. What else did you see in the room? Was it just men and a bed and your sister?"

He had used that word again—*just*. As if those three things weren't the single most horrifying combination in the goddess's lighted kingdom. She used to find him so comforting. He'd been a friend to her. A source of companionship. A safety net. What was he now?

"Just?"

"Firi—"

"Stop." Anger surged through her, and it comforted her. Fury was a beautiful emotion compared to the shock and horror that had consumed her. "What do you want from me? I don't have the energy to play whatever game this is."

He tightened his grip on her hand. "Think, Ophir. Was there anything else? Bowls? Books? Daggers? Metals? Was she missing any of her organs? Was she still wearing her... underthings?"

A high ringing sound filled her ears. She'd heard the

sound before in the moments before she'd been sick. It filled her now as a new and terrible nausea gripped her, raking through her body. She ran to the bathing room to grip the edges of the chamber pot, releasing whatever remnants of acid and liquid had remained in her stomach. She would not be answering any more questions. Not now, or ever again.

"Go fuck yourself," she snarled.

Harland would have his answers eventually. While the casket had been closed, it had been passed along from the medical examiner that she'd been missing her liver. There was no relief, no victory, no goodness in the world when a parent learned their child had died. The only small kindness was the knowledge that she had not been deflowered, though there was far more to sexual assault than the overly simplistic terms that they were disgustingly distilling the word into. Everyone had believed that Caris had been dragged into the room to be violated by the men in attendance who had been all too thrilled to get their evil, perverse hands on a princess.

Only a few people did not seem comforted by this information. For some sick, unknowable reason, Harland had seemed further disquieted at the knowledge that she'd died with her maidenhood intact. Perhaps crimes of a deviant sexual nature were easier to accept and understand than whatever unholy horrors had been attempted in the room that night.

The knowledge that they'd taken only her liver had bothered him deeply—he'd said as much. He didn't understand why they'd chosen that piece of the princess, except that perhaps their process had been interrupted before they could access more. When Ophir had screamed at him and told him that she'd shove a fireball down his throat if he ever spoke of her sister like that again, he'd gone fully silent on the topic.

Harland would mention nothing more of his suspicions.

Ophir dropped into a living comatose state. Whatever pieces of her that were still capable of feeling were surprised every day that the sun continued to rise and birds continued to sing. Beautiful blue skies mocked her. The happy faces of laughing children were an affront too grotesque to face, so she refrained from leaving the castle. She would spend autumn, winter, and spring in her room, draining the winery of its reds and whites regardless of their year or finery. She didn't want music. She didn't want companionship. She didn't want anything except for Caris to be alive. She wanted to be gone in her sister's place.

FIFTEEN

✦　✦　✦　✦

Y OUR PLAN IS SHIT, DWYN. YOU'LL JUST, WHAT, BE SILENT until the end of time so I can learn nothing more from you?"

Tyr had haunted her room for days. He knew that she wanted to salvage whatever remained of Harland's good graces, but the guard needed her to be forthcoming, and that was a risk she was unwilling to take while Tyr haunted her doorstep. So, Harland would interrogate her, she'd remain silent, save for her unhelpful shrugs and apologetic expressions, and the dance would go on.

Alone once more, she said to Tyr, "My plan is to let you starve to death. You'll need to leave eventually for food. You know what I had for dinner? The princess and I ate the loveliest hot breads with roasted garlic, fresh butter, and melted cheese—"

He relaxed against the wall. "I know what you're doing, and it won't work. I can wait."

She arched a brow. "So can I. I've lived a very long life, dog. Ophir isn't going anywhere, and neither am I. But you certainly can. You could leave for Sulgrave today and be back in your bed with your precious clan by the end of the month."

"It's an awfully long trip to have ventured to the southern kingdoms for nothing."

"And why did you come? Loyalty? Maybe you're more of a dog than I realized. Anwir really knows how to recruit his men."

He bristled at the mention of the clan leader. "You know nothing of why I'm here."

"Don't I?" She jerked up the hem of her nightdress, revealing far too much thigh and hip. His gaze flitted to her goddess-awful tattoo.

"Tell me why you've truly come, and I'll leave."

"I've told you." She glowered.

A muscle ticked in his jaw as he glared back.

"What will it matter? You know you're wasting your efforts. Berinth will beat us both to it. Then you'll have starved to death for nothing. Or again, you could run away. Go home. Ophir and I will be nothing but a memory. Think of it like a long, miserable weekend—a speck of dust in your life."

He hadn't bothered to conceal himself but had positioned himself so that if someone opened the door, he could shift back into the spaces between things, rendering himself invisible until he was safe once more. He rested the back of his head against the wall and closed his eyes. Tyr hadn't slept or eaten in several days. He hoped someone was taking good care of Knight, or there'd be hell to pay as soon as he left the castle. "You know I can't do that."

"Mmm, it would appear so. Because this isn't about me at all, is it? How flattering." Dwyn continued about her night as if she spoke to a ghost in the room. He glared as she washed her face, brushed her hair, stripped from her clothes, and crawled beneath the sheets, ignoring his presence entirely.

He'd been silent as she'd hummed obnoxiously to herself for nearly an hour. Finally, he said, "I've been patient, Dwyn. You know you're safe with me. Not because I want you alive—goddess knows I want you dead just as badly as you wish you could kill me. But I can't kill you for the same reason you haven't acted on anything with Ophir, right? We have no idea what Berinth accomplished. As long as another child of royal blood is alive..."

"Excellent thought. Why don't you focus on Berinth and leave Ophir to me? I promise you, she's in great hands."

He regretted his attempt at reasoning with her. "You have a better chance of killing me than getting me to leave."

"Die, then."

Dwyn closed her eyes and tucked an arm beneath her pillow, snuggling beneath the sheets. The move was rife with both disregard and disrespect.

"You haven't asked why I don't make a move with the princess."

She smacked her lips against her sleep, unbothered. "I assume it's because we both know you couldn't compete with me in matters of the heart even if you tried."

"You can't do anything," he said. "Your unwillingness to share has tied your hands. You're as stuck as I am."

"You're talking while I'm trying to sleep."

"I don't need the princess," he said. She cracked an eye open at this. "Ophir doesn't deserve what's happening to her."

Dwyn sat up. "You're right. She doesn't. So stop stalking her."

"I'm here because you're here, witch. If what you want is anything like what Berinth wanted with Caris, then she's not safe with you. I'm not here to hurt her."

Dwyn considered the information. "You'd leave me alone—me *and* Ophir, that is—if you learn to do what I can already do?"

Tyr waited expectantly. Perhaps, just once, Dwyn could be reasonable.

She lifted her index and middle fingers to her lips. "It's the little jewel at the apex of her sex. I find the most success with a combination of suction and gentle licks. When she starts to—"

There went his last thread of hope. "I know how to make a woman come."

Dwyn shrugged. "Such a tragedy you had the chance to take advice from an expert and you shot it down. As for the other thing? This isn't a race where winners can tie for victory," she said, head resting comfortably on her pillow. "You know that as much as I do. Only one of us will come out on top of this. And you're only following me because you *know* I'm leagues ahead of the rest of you. Berinth is your only real competition, and you're letting him get away. It's sweet to have such a fan, Tyr. Truly charming that you're so fixated on me." She finished their conversation in no uncertain terms, yawning to underline her boredom. She would not be answering any more of Tyr's questions.

"Why don't *you* go after Berinth?"

"Because I don't need him, or what he has. And, just so you know," Dwyn muttered from where she'd rolled away, her voice muffled from her pillow, "you're a bastard."

Tyr allowed himself to drift into a brief and fitful sleep from where he'd sat with his back rigid against the stone wall. It was not restful, but it was certainly better than nothing. He shifted into his gift as dawn broke, unseeable to the eyes of all within the castle. He eased the door to the Sulgrave girl's room open slowly and slid out, shutting it softly behind him without making a sound. His ability to elude sight didn't prevent others from hearing him, but if one was careful and light on one's feet, they could go undetected for ages. Tyr had long since suspected that ghost stories and hauntings could be rightly attributed to fae with his gifts. The voyeurism allowed with invisibility didn't outright prevent perception from the other senses. His gift was considered dark and wicked in more ways than one.

SIXTEEN

· · · ·

THEN

S ENSITIVE.
That's what they'd called him.

It was harder to criticize a man for caring for strays and mending broken wings if he could slit your throat in the night or bring you down before you could blink.

Tyr had been raised in the church but had left his parents behind in their blind worship after his second decade of life. He had never been interested in the trades. He hadn't wanted to be a tailor or guard or butcher. His fists needed more. The scales demanded balance if he were to possess a bleeding heart. He craved the symmetry that only battle would bring to his life.

The All Mother seemed like a creature of love and benevolence, but she also provided opportunities for expressions of righteous violence. Though his parents had encouraged him to use his strength and skills in service of the cloth and become a Red, he'd scarcely finished initiation as the sword arm of the church before he'd realized his abilities would be just as villainous in the hands of a religious leader who led without checks and balances as he might from any dictator. The All Mother may or may not have been real—at least, magic, good, and evil certainly seemed real—but the church's teachings had been so filtered through the agendas of man and fae that the cold had been the lens he needed to examine his skepticism.

He'd considered it. His parents had wanted him to devote himself to the church.

Consideration had been a luxury afforded him before Svea.

He'd walked straight to the church with mud on his hands, knees, and under his fingernails from her burial. He'd banged on the door until someone had answered. They'd taken him in and set him to training. Soon, he'd have access to the groundwater of magic that allowed the faithful to call on borrowed abilities. The strongest Reds were godlike with their manipulation of the elements and forces. He'd never let himself be weak again. He'd never let any pain come to someone or something he loved, because he could do little more than slip into the unseen space between things.

Tyr had taken the oath for the Reds, but he'd made little effort to conceal his beliefs, or lack thereof. No one would speak to him about his blasphemous theories, though he knew he couldn't be alone in his theological questioning. What if the All Mother had been a deified fae? What if she'd possessed an omnipotence they were failing to understand, worshipping rather than truly studying? If the strongest among them could call to any ability they wanted, what made them think that godhood wasn't something that could be achieved?

They didn't like the nature of his questions.

He was meant to be dedicated for service, not for gain.

Tyr's void of faith had taken root as something different—rather than an absence, he felt a craving. There was knowledge. There was potential. There was…something. They'd trained him, but his overseers had made no attempt to conceal their concerns. Perhaps not all fae were meant to access the groundwater. At least, not in the name of the All Mother.

He'd still been a Red when he'd met Dwyn, though he hadn't known her name or how the wicked witch of the sea would change the course of his life. Presently, they were both under the roof of Castle Aubade. Part of him would love to just kill her and get it over with, even if he couldn't. It would solve so many problems if he snapped her neck and sent her to whatever twisted afterlife she would surely belong in. Instead, he was resigned to observe. He was forced to watch, hoping she'd slip up, hoping she'd reveal an inkling or glimpse into her abilities. She'd already achieved far more than he and the others hoped possible for themselves. It was challenging to fathom how much more someone like her might achieve with her sights set on the southern princess. If she made a move on Ophir, he'd have to intervene, even if it meant losing his shot at the sort of power only the Reds and one blasted siren possessed.

Now that this witch he'd hunted for nearly fifty years was with the princess...maybe she was right. Maybe there was more than one way to secure a royal heart.

+   +   +   +

The first time he'd locked eyes with the witch was seared into his brain.

Sulgrave was situated in the northernmost mountains of the continent. Its seven territories, ruled by Comtes, sprawled among the mountains, ending at the Frozen Straits. The Reds hadn't liked him, and he understood why. His demand for knowledge had become a thirst. They didn't need him anywhere near the important stations of the church. It was perhaps the politest way the organization could more or less excommunicate him without dishonoring his family.

His parents were pious people, after all. They didn't deserve the shame a heretic would bring to their good standing in the church.

Scarcely in his twenties and low ranking among the Reds, he'd been given the least desirable outpost along the western shores where the mountains fell into the frozen sea. An arctic village of fewer than three hundred of Sulgrave's heartiest civilians lived near the sea as the last frontier for the kingdom. The shores weren't protected by the same seasonal enchantments that guarded their kingdom. While mild weather graced Sulgrave's residents in the seven territories, a never-ending winter swept the western shores and outlying regions of the northernmost mountain lands. There was a small building that served as the village's church and as well as the rationale for his presence, but the villagers more or less ignored Tyr, and he kept to himself as much as he could.

He hated every goddess-damned minute.

Tyr had served the sword arm of the All Mother for fewer than five years when he'd come across a damsel in distress, or so he'd thought. He wasn't sure what had possessed him to ever see himself as altruistic, save for the lens society has cast on a man of the cloth. As he looked back on the event now, it would be the first and last time he assumed the victim and the aggressor based on gender alone.

Screams had come from beyond the icy shores.

He'd been certain he'd heard wind playing tricks on him. A sound came again across the ice, and he began to fear that perhaps a villager had fallen into the ice. He'd never been so cold, nor had his faith ever been more fragile. Every moment since his arrival at his post had weakened his resolve. The sun rose and fell for months. In the summer, it stayed with him from morning throughout the night, glowing red even in the midnight hours. He was now in the perpetual twilight before the village plummeted into months-long winter. The sky was a cold gradient of lavenders and indigos, speckled with stars and the silver crescent of the moon. He wrapped the furs of the aboriou hide around him more tightly and ran into the whipping winds in search of the voice's owner.

The wind chafed his skin and froze his joints as he scanned. He could see nothing from the outpost that had barely been enough for one man and his cot, and he began to climb a snowbank to look down onto the sea.

The sound came again, cutting across the glasslike shards of ice of Sulgrave's frozen shores. A woman was calling for help. He knew he wasn't imagining it. Tyr scrambled out of the cumbersome bundles of fur and ran for the shores in his leathers.

He stopped as soon as he saw her.

Her arms were bare. He could see the skin of her neck, of her upper chest, of her fingers without the warmth of cloak or gloves. Her bare feet walked along black sand, moving between broken chunks of glacial melt. She was in a strange, glossy dress that seemed to be made of oil and starlight.

He should have run to her, but everything within him screamed of danger.

He wasn't the only one to respond to her screams. A man was running to her from the village. His arms appeared to be thick with warmed bundles of cloaks and blankets for the near-naked shipwrecked woman.

Tyr knew he needed to stop the man. He called to him and began running. He angled his body for the villager, putting one foot in front of the other as the icy wind froze his fingers and reddened his nose. He'd run with a tenacity that hadn't compelled his muscles for months. Tyr's hand gripped his weapon, his teeth gritting against the frozen winds as he barreled toward them. The villager paid him no mind, eyes fixed solely on the woman. Her cries for help had stopped as the villager reached her.

Tyr skidded to a halt as the two touched.

The woman was close enough that he could see the shape of her eyes, the rouge of her cheeks, the cloud of her hair, and count the fingers that gripped the villager.

She'd been holding the man in an embrace until he fell limply before her. The man who'd come for her had withered, now mummified against the shards of ice and chilled seawater that lapped against her bare feet.

She looked up over the villager's body as it floated weightlessly against the lapping waves. Her gaze touched Tyr's.

By the time his wide eyes had absorbed the vision before him, her black hair had whipped around her in a cloud so beautiful and horrific that she may have been one of the terrible old gods made flesh.

He hadn't advanced. He hadn't raised his sword.

They did not look away from one another. His lips were still parted in a gasp. Her dark, glossy dress whipped around her in the winds, though her skin seemed unaffected by the sub-zero temperatures. She moved her head curiously. She wasn't looking at him with predatory hunger, nor with fear. She was merely interested in the man who'd sprinted for the black sand beaches only to skid to a halt so far from where she stood. The woman held such a casual interest, he could see the glimmer from where he stood.

It was the sort of moment that one might excuse as a dream.

With an uncaring coolness, the young woman turned and walked into the frigid sea waters. Her head disappeared beneath the waves as if she'd never existed. If it weren't for the floating body of the hollow man who bobbed and lapped against each cresting wave, he could have convinced himself that it had been a hallucination. Instead, Tyr knelt next to the wilted man and knew he'd come across a truly dark terror. This was the day Tyr became singularly possessed with the sort of dark magic that would scream for a man's help only to suck her rescuer of its life force.

He'd heard of the succubae who could kill men, though even women cursed with such a power couldn't do so with simply a kiss or touch as the witch on the shores had done. He knew of fae who could call to water. A common, helpful gift was the ability to warm oneself. He hadn't actually met anyone who could breathe water, though the stories of merfolk had filtered through the centuries. What powers was this fae collecting that had allowed her to accumulate more than what came naturally?

He and his fellow Sulgrave fae had grown up around whispers of blood magic, though talk of such things had been forbidden. Access to unnatural powers was a mission in suicide, as it drew on one's own life force to call to abilities that did not belong to you. The Reds who had served for decades were trained in the ability to access the groundwater of magic that flowed through life, but each time they did, their own blood cooled and struggled within them.

Many Reds died attempting to learn to call new powers.

But this… what if someone else could die in your stead? What if you could use the blood of another for your borrowed ability?

✦ ✦ ✦ ✦

Finding her the first time had been an accident.

Locating her a second time would be an exercise in obsessive intention.

Tyr left the seaside Sulgrave outpost that day and had never returned. He would never again affiliate with the Reds or the missions of the All Mother, whether or not such a goddess existed. Abandonment wasn't only immoral by religious standards and shameful within the community, it was illegal by the church and the laws of the Comtes alike. One did not simply abandon the Reds and live to tell the tale. If he was caught, he'd end up locked in an elaborately enchanted jail cell with no hope of redemption, if they chose to keep him alive at all.

Prayers had won him nothing.

Devotion was little more than a candle, and the All Mother would have needed the true power of a bonfire to convince him to stay.

Tyr was alone, but not without resources. He'd been trained as an assassin. He had been given the honor of serving as the All Mother's sword and then taken his skills, knowledge, and power and spit in the face of their organization.

None of it mattered until they paid. None of it meant

anything until he saw them burn with the cuts, the flame, the shadow, the torture that they'd shown Svea. If he couldn't so much as conjure three moments of a secondary power without falling to his deathbed, what was the point? Why had he learned? Why had he joined? He'd find no justice with them, and he knew it.

The church and its frivolous dispatches. The laws and its meaningless words. The outposts, the structure, the blind devotion were all useless in a world where ruthless fae could grow their powers in the villainous shadows without the chains of supervision.

But where was one to start?

He used his gift to step into the space between things, disappearing in plain sight as he shifted into libraries, learned the lores of peasants, and studied the ancient tomes buried in pagan sites. Locating the beautiful, demonic creature a second time had been the result of years of skill, education, planning, entrapment, and cultivation. The stranger he'd seen on the waves was as slick as oil and as evasive as shadow, but he knew what he'd seen. He knew she'd taken more than what the goddess had given.

Knowledge was supposed to be a blessing.

The thirst for knowledge that didn't belong to you was an all-consuming curse.

SEVENTEEN

✦   ✦   ✦   ✦

Tyr didn't discover the Blood Pact. They had found him.

As it turned out, he was not the first outcast to abandon the church. Exiled from society, they were the men and women who lived in the shadows. They were the Reds, the assassins, the guards who'd deserted their posts and forsaken their titles, banded together with a new solemnity more serious than death.

Tyr had waited in the ruins of a temple to the old gods until after nightfall before he'd shifted into his resting state of visibility. He'd been squinting over the muddled words of an old text that had said the same three things he'd already come to learn in his research. What he knew was this: most powers had the ability to give. The world was given light, energy, water, air, wind, luck, love, joy, and all manner of skills through the lighted expressions of magic. Feared powers like consorting with the dead, speaking mind to mind, infiltrating one's willpower threatened the world. Rarely, someone was born with an ability to take. Succubi, incubi, and any cursed with death's touch had to be exceedingly careful in learning how to control their inherent skills.

Then there was the third kind of power.

It was the acquisition of powers that didn't belong to you. Certain practitioners operated beyond the church and its boundaries. These fae, so the rumors went, had found ways to tap into magics that were not theirs to possess. They, like the church and its Reds, believed magic to be a singular unit—often called "groundwater" by magical zealots for the way it flowed and filled the earth—and fae manifestations of magic were merely the freshwater springs for that water. They believed that if all magic was sourced from the same place, then everyone should be able to access all abilities. The death toll grew as those who sought to expand their powers quickly learned a difficult truth: powers that did not belong to you drained you of your life. One could not access strange or unnatural magics without sacrificing themselves. In some ways, the consequence of stolen power was its own method of policing crimes against magic. Attempting magical theft was an errand in assured suicide. Anyone pursuing perversions of magic would perish at the hand of their own greed.

"It'd be a lot easier to read that particular piece of literature if you used a light, boy."

Tyr jolted, dropping the book. He reached for his sword only to realize how many had crept into the rubble around him while he'd stared at the words.

"Who are you?" He flexed, prepared for battle. He may no longer be a Red, but he was well trained.

The man smiled. "We're more interested in who *you* are. Perhaps if you let us know why you've spent the last several months researching blood magic, we might see if we can help one another."

"I'm a..." Tyr eyed the group and knew he would not fight his way out of here. They weren't dressed like thugs—this wasn't the thieves who mugged or the robbers who loitered along the roads for those weak in guard or spirit. They were lithe, armed, and would have been rather intimidating to a man with any normal sense for fear. They didn't seem like they had ill intentions. They watched him curiously as he assessed the group. "I was a Red."

A woman spoke up. "So were half of us."

He breathed out slowly. "I was a Red because I need access to something. For...personal reasons."

The leader made an understanding face. "Revenge drives more of us than you'd think, kid."

As an orange flame illuminated the broken, fallen stones and the people around him, Tyr identified the face that held the torch. He'd seen the face before in the sketches and drawings of wanted men. Anwir had been excommunicated from the church more than six hundred years prior. Tyr recognized him from the bounty on his head and the blasphemies he was said to have spread. He hadn't known the man still lived, let alone that he'd remained in Sulgrave. This man had spent centuries in the darkest corners building his empire of shadow and ruin.

"Blood magic?" Tyr asked. His voice sounded so hollow as it bounced off of the crumbling rocks. He did his best to count the party before him, but knew he was terribly outnumbered. How many had left the church and fled the law only to have found one another?

Anwir strode toward him. His voice remained cool as he plucked the book from Tyr's hands. "There's no use playing coy. We've been following you for some time. Besides, this book won't teach you anything that we can't tell you firsthand."

"*Mysteries of the Heart?*" the woman asked, guessing the title.

Anwir grunted his confirmation. "Reds borrow against their blood," he said to Tyr. "Half of them die in the process. Legend has it that some fae can use stolen powers without risking their lives for new abilities."

"They use someone else's heart," Tyr finished for him. "That's about as far as I made it in the book."

"Then you've made it far enough," Anwir replied. "We've spilled enough blood to learn what *not* to do."

"You've done what?" Tyr worked to control his expression.

"He's saying: a few corpses are missing an organ or two," the woman said. "We've taken them from the dead. We've cut them out of the guilty and innocent alike. We've even stuck our hands into still-beating chests. None of it works."

"Well, someone's figured it out," Tyr muttered.

Anwir's fingers tightened against the book. "What makes you say that?"

Tyr opted for the truth. He couldn't explain why, except that some secrets felt better when they weren't clutched to one's chest. He offered honesty, or a version of it. He didn't speak of Svea or her death. Instead, he told them he'd been posted on the western banks when he'd witnessed a fae take a life and then walk into the arctic waters. He'd been pursuing understanding of the incident ever since.

Mutters rippled through the group. Anwir asked, "What did she look like?"

The others muttered among one another briefly, knowing precisely of whom he spoke. That was the night Tyr learned her name.

Dwyn had traveled with the Blood Pact for a time but had quickly set out on her own. She was uncovering terrible truths and unlocking coveted powers more quickly than any of them had ever hoped to achieve. She'd left in the night, evading the Comtes, the church, the law, and the Blood Pact at once. She'd learned how to convert life into power, using the conduits of other souls so that her own blood remained unharmed.

It turned out they did want the same thing, though perhaps not for the same reasons.

Anwir wanted to wield blood magic without hurting himself, unlike the Reds, who sacrificed their lives for the sake of borrowed powers. Dwyn was the answer.

Joining the band of heretics had been more solemn and painful than his dedications to the church.

Tyr was branded with dark, elaborate ink—marked to set himself apart from society. His tattoo bound him to the Blood

Pact as he renounced the church and the laws of Sulgrave. He belonged to the shadows. He belonged to strength. He belonged to power. They were not the Reds who found themselves guided by the will of the All Mother. They were not the morally pure who had candles lit in their honor or were met with the smiles and gentle blessings of the goddess. They were nothing like the white knights or proud guards.

They were the dark things seeking answers to questions that one shouldn't ask.

Tyr belonged to the space between things.

The Blood Pact stayed the course. Their hunt to circumvent the consequences of stolen powers consumed them as it had for hundreds of years prior. Tyr's contribution remained his singular obsession: finding Dwyn, and learning how she'd not only found that which evaded the rest but had already put it to use. She was to be brought to Anwir and reunited with the clan she'd abandoned. The woman on the run was educated, slick, and clever. She had long ago learned to operate in the oily gray waters of the unimpeachable. Her advancements in power were about to meet their natural end in Sulgrave.

"You think you'll get her to talk?" Anwir asked before Tyr set forth.

"I think I've spent enough time in old libraries and ruins. And while I appreciate the Pact's dedication, I don't have the stomach for gouging beating hearts from innocents."

Anwir chuckled. "Show me one truly innocent man and I'll show you the All Mother's tits."

Tyr's lips twitched in response. "Is that what you're hiding under that tunic?"

The leader's smile faded. "I wonder..." He shook his head, brushing off the thought.

"Are we still thinking of tits?"

The smile returned, but his eyes did not match. "In a way. It's about Dwyn. She's not just running. She's...hunting. She's on a mission of sorts, and I can't help but wonder what she knows if she learned all we set out to learn, yet did not stop."

Tyr rolled the idea around in his head. "What more is there? If she can draw from the groundwater without harming herself, she's already the most powerful fae alive."

"Perhaps…" Anwir's thoughts trailed. "There may be one stronger, still."

Tyr lifted a brow. Suddenly, he understood the connection. "You don't think…"

"If you find her, you won't just be learning how to master blood magic. You may be on a mission to capture the next would-be goddess."

The words echoed through the hollowness of his chest. They rang clear and cold as he traversed the mountains, searched the valleys, met with scryers, interrogated outlaws, and hunted in the space between things.

Learn from a fae. Stop a god.

By the time he'd realized why she'd left the mountains, it had been too late.

The continent's royal blood lived in Farehold. Aubade was where he needed to go.

+ + + +

Perhaps he'd defected, just as Dwyn had. What else prevented him from dragging Dwyn by her hair to confront the Blood Pact once he'd found her skulking about Castle Aubade? The answer didn't elude him. He'd been after her long before he'd met the others. She knew things he didn't. If Dwyn wanted a princess, then he'd been focused on a minnow while neglecting a shark in the water.

The truth was, he had no allegiance to Anwir.

Tyr didn't care about the Blood Pact, their cause, or their leader.

His mission for vengeance belonged to Svea, and her alone.

Arriving in Farehold had quickly alerted to him as to

how many were closing in on the princesses and the keys they held in unlocking magical advancement. His dry mouth hadn't been the only one in need of quenching. Thirst for knowledge had leached throughout the continent. Dwyn may have led him to the lower continent, but she wasn't alone in her hunt. The princesses were a dark beacon for the ill will of dark magics. They set off a chilling light without ever knowing or understanding the critical role they might hold for everyone in Gyrradin.

The stakes heightened as time marched on.

Berinth hadn't resurfaced since Caris's death, but he may very well pose a greater threat to the future of man and fae than any other witch or crime syndicate or church combined.

No one who knew Tyr would consider him good. He inspired neither confidence nor fear. He was that which disappeared between the shadows. He was his own.

The race to godhood would have only one winner.

EIGHTEEN

✦ ✦ ✦ ✦

NOW

S OME THINGS HAPPEN SLOWLY.
Dwyn had once heard that one could boil a frog if
the water began at a comfortable temperature. The creature
wouldn't understand its fatal flaw until it was too late. The
successful erosion of kingdoms happened gradually, void of
fanfare, without detection.

Patience is a virtue, yes. Patience is also a ploy.

Dwyn was not in a hurry.

She'd carried a quill and stack of parchment with her to
bed and doodled Sulgrave's distant mountains as she waited.
It took three days, but at long last, she heard a knock at her
door.

"Who is it?" Dwyn called in a light, airy voice.

She smiled when Harland identified himself. This was
patience's reward.

A decade of vigilance had taught her what everyone
knew: Raascot was ruled by King Ceneth. He bore no heirs,
nor had his parents survived. Farehold's king and queen had
given birth to two daughters, Caris and Ophir. More careful
reconnaissance had helped her to understand the heirs for
who they were, and what she needed to do.

By the time she'd made her way to Aubade, Farehold's princesses were already fully formed fae well into their adulthood. Caris was the princess of goodness and spring. She was the continent's purest hope for love and unity, particularly after centuries of persecution of her people within the confines of her kingdom. Fae born with fearsome powers had been hunted nearly to extinction. Had Ceneth not opened his borders to Farehold's refugees, the southern barbarians would have continued slaughtering anyone deemed unsafe.

Ophir was the continent's afterthought. While the blood of centuries of monarchs coursed through her veins, little was expected of her. The eldest princess would marry King Ceneth and unite their sovereign kingdoms through a long-anticipated marriage. The youngest princess, on the other hand...

Caris and Ceneth would surely reproduce, multiplying Dwyn's opportunities, should she wait. Whether she appeared as a kind, benevolent aunt to royal children, or waited until a male heir was procured who could be beholden by her guiles, time was her ally. There were other strategies, of course. There was always something she could do, a friend she could make, a path she could take, should she want.

The Blood Pact had nipped at her heels for decades, though they knew little of how she did what she did, let alone how to achieve their ultimate goals. When new players were revealed on the continent, her timeline was shoved forward with harsh, indelicate hands.

Further boldness came in the form of Berinth. She'd adapted before, and she could do it again. He'd arrived to snatch the noble title of Lord from someone he claimed to be his uncle, though any discerning party would have more than a few questions as to how such a peculiar stranger had tumbled upon this prominent role. He'd tried his hand at shows of opulence. It was a brazen, indelicate strategy.

Dwyn had watched from a distance as the other player in her blood sport attempted to summon an audience with the royal family. He'd thrown lavish parties, hosted dinners, sent invitations, and made countless attempts to draw the women to him. While Dwyn's strategy had been one intending to curry gradual favor, Berinth had attempted to lure. While she'd planned to ingratiate herself through trust and self-control, he had laid shameless, sparkling traps.

They were perfect opposites.

His impudence had revealed all of his cards to anyone who knew how to read the game.

The game was power, and the players were ones who knew how to advance.

The knock came again and she sat up with a light, kind smile on her lips for the royal guard as she called for him to enter. He didn't need to see anything alluring or predatory from her. She withheld the vibrancy she utilized for sailors on the waves. She settled into a patient, somewhat indifferent smile as he entered her rooms. She arched a curious brow.

"Harland, is our princess okay?"

Her use of the possessive pronoun was intentional. She wanted him to know that she considered Ophir her monarch as well, even if it sounded unnatural coming from the foreign lilt of her words.

He was unmoved. "It's time for honesty. I need to talk to you about what happened on the cliffs."

Dwyn didn't need to lie. She wasn't interested in any too-hasty placating that might bite her further along the line. She hadn't been left with only the past few days to think about her response but with decades far prior to the events that had brought him to her door.

"I'm ready," she said, prompting the guard to speak first. She sat with a respectable rigidity to her spine, inclining her attentive, delicate features toward the man. She'd taken to borrowing a few of Ophir's more modest pieces, covering up during the day to help herself appear somewhat less preda-tory. It seemed to be having the desired effect on all but the clever guard.

His expression was more than a little disconcerted. He closed the door behind him but did not move any closer to her.

"Dwyn, in your own words: tell me what happened on the cliffs."

"Yes," she said with cool certainty. "Princess Ophir conjured a snake."

His brows lifted. He tripped over his inquiry as he pressed, "And you—you knew she had such abilities."

This was where a lie was required, though all of the world's best lies were born from truths. She answered his question with one of her own. "How do you manifest your abilities in Farehold?"

Parallel lines pinched between the guard's ever-expressive brows. "Excuse me?"

"Your power, Harland. How was it discovered?"

"What does this have to do with what I can or can't do?"

"Answer the question."

He reached as if to rub the back of his neck, but stopped himself before giving into the informal gesture. "I've been able to do this since I was young, though I supposed I discovered it when I had been shut into a pantry and needed to escape. I punched a hole through the door with the strength of a battering ram. I was ten."

She made a show of considering his information. "Is it safe to say that you uncovered your power in a moment of distress?"

She saw his expression change the moment Harland knew where she was taking her argument, and he didn't care for it. "If you intend to imply that you put Ophir in distress to help her uncover her ability, then your logic is flawed. Not only has she possessed flame since she was a child, but I've seen you react to her fire. You've helped her in her night terrors, and you intentionally drenched her flame on the cliff when she was distressed so that she'd be forced to find another way to survive. You know she calls to fire."

"Fire, yes—"

"You knew, Dwyn. Somehow, you knew there was more."

Dwyn made no attempt to deny him. "I knew that her fire was not enough to keep her alive! Our abilities are meant to aid us in distress! I had no reason to believe summoning willpower or psychological stamina would be any different from manifesting power. It's no secret that Firi has shown very little will to live. My hope was that she'd have as much power and strength in basic survival as she might in magic. What use is fire if she possesses no reason to stay on this earth? She didn't lack supernatural ability. Your princess had no fight left in her."

They were performing the careful steps of an eerie dance. The music was strange, but the movements were ones she'd made before. Her words were right. Her logic was firm. She knew enough of men to spy that he saw through her impishness, and more, still, to know that he had no counterargument.

Yes, she was aware she'd entered the castle under more than mysterious circumstances. She'd greeted the guard with the sort of iconoclastic irreverence of either a dream or a nightmare, fully nude in the princess's bedroom with a towel wrapped around her wet hair just before daybreak. She hadn't wasted her breath on a hope that the guard would ever trust her. If he was an intelligent man, however—and she didn't take him for a fool—she counted on Harland seeing the value she brought to Ophir's life. The man didn't have to like her to appreciate that Ophir was finally eating, sleeping, and healing.

Yes, she'd appeared out of nowhere and, within months, was sleeping in Ophir's bed, whispering in her ears, and glued to her side. Yes, suspicion was natural. But Dwyn was willing to bet that Harland valued Ophir's happiness over Dwyn's removal.

Her gamble paid off a thousand fold

"You knew," he repeated. It was the only point he had.

She arched a carefully manicured brow.

"I have no idea what you're talking about."

The guard shook his head. "Either cut your act or join a

troupe to hone your skill, Dwyn. Violence has been used to manifest abilities, not to psychologically overcome trauma. If you were searching for a new ability, nothing would have been curated as it was. You made her picture a snake for weeks. I've heard her mutter that beast's description until you made her believe she'd become it. This was no mistake."

Dwyn puckered her lip in her best gentle, disarming pout. She'd sent many men to their knees with her doe eyes and gentle smile. She was clever enough to know that beauty and charm could be used to convince one's opponent of the inverse. If she possessed the necessary cunning, Harland might walk away from their exchange believing she truly was an innocent, pretty, simple thing.

They stared at one another for a long moment, her brows knit, his eyes calculating. She hoped it would be enough, then saw the instant her attempts fell short. It seemed Harland would not be crumpling to her wiles, but she refused to incriminate herself.

"We both want what's best for the princess," she said seriously. It wasn't an answer, but she would give up nothing more today.

As he left her room and closed the door behind him, she wondered if he could feel her satisfied smile.

NINETEEN

✦   ✦   ✦   ✦

S HE'D DONE IT ONCE. SHE COULD DO IT AGAIN.
    One week prior, Ophir had created a snake. She
hadn't created just any snake—she had manifested the very
serpent she'd envisioned from its size and the color of its scales
to the twinkle of its eye and the coil of its poise. The very
venom she'd pictured dripping from its fangs had dripped
from the points of its horrible teeth onto the lip of the cliff
below.

Harland had moved with such swiftness to behead it. It
had been with equal speed that he'd begun to shove its body
over the edge of the bluff. Dwyn had joined him without
needing to be told. They knew without words that the events
of their stormy evening must remain concealed. Its enormous
body plummeted to the rocks below to be smashed and
battered by the waves as they broke against the shore. By the
time its bloated carcass was discovered, it would be indiscernible from any of the great, mysterious beasts of the ocean's
unknowable depths.

She should be scared.

She should be shocked.

There was a host of emotions that a rational person was

meant to feel. Maybe she would experience the logical gamut of feeling if her year had not been one from hell. Perhaps if she hadn't suffered the brutalized, excruciating loss of her sister as a consequence of her own selfish desire for fun and experience, she'd have a heart primed for discernment and fear. If the past fourteen weeks hadn't been spent in various gaunt states of numb, emotional paralysis, Ophir may have encountered the familiar, knowable sensations of fear or worry.

She'd been numb for so long that instead she felt the dark, blackened coal in her stomach reignite. It had been so cold, so heavy for months and months and months. Just the barest edges of it glowed with a reddened flame as it began to glow. She felt... something.

Dwyn was right, even if the woman's methods of instruction had been somewhat barbaric. Ophir rubbed her cheek at the distant memory of Dwyn's slap. She didn't have to be the weak, limping deer. She was a snake, and snakes could strike.

Ophir knew that Harland would be waiting in the hall. She crept on the quiet tips of her toes to move a chair to the space beneath the door, wedging the handle into place. It wouldn't stop the worried entrance of an angry guard, but it would at least sound an alarm if he had to smash through wood to break down her door.

She was almost disappointed that he hadn't learned her other methods of escape. It didn't show a lot of initiative if he hadn't been able to assess her possible points of exit.

The window was too obvious. A castle guard was always pacing the space beneath the glass of her iron-latticed window. There had once been an adjoining door between her room and the room that had belonged to Caris, though they'd blocked off its entrance decades before Caris's death. Ophir couldn't be trusted with unrestricted access even to her sister's room. The one thing they'd never discovered was the movement of her floor-length mirror.

One had to push it slightly inward, carefully easing the

mirror's pressure into the wall more deeply before it released and revealed a stairwell to the catacombs beneath the castle. Aubade had been built by a rather mistrustful king, and the palace had been littered with false walls, moving bookcases, and ladders that dropped down from the ceiling. The mirror had been a secret that she'd managed to keep to herself. She hadn't even shared it with her sister. If she was careful, this beautiful escape hatch could last for fifty generations more without ever being found.

Autumn on the sea was chilly, but not too cold for a cloak and the fur-lined pants and tunic that helped her conceal her identity. She summoned the barest ember of fire into the space above her palm, allowing the little flame to illuminate the pressing dark of the stone passage. She could squelch or reignite her flame at any time and was grateful for its glow whenever she found herself picking through the dark of the night.

She'd come in and out of the castle this way on many occasions. The only footprints in the dust appeared to be her own. She knew exactly where to turn and how to navigate the corridors that would eventually release into a wine cellar. A latch allowed her to ease open the solid back of a wooden rack in the depths of the castle's belly, letting her into the secret space beneath the kitchen. She could easily conceal the rack once more and reenter the castle through more normal means with the argument that she'd simply gone to the kitchen in search of alcohol.

The custard stones wove in a complicated labyrinth beneath the castle. If she followed the smell of fish and salt, she could find where it released onto the cliffs. She extinguished the ember that had hovered in the space above her hand and allowed herself to be guided forward by the moonlight. A small dock of rowboats had been pitched and was replaced every year or so in case escape was ever necessary. Instead, she navigated beyond the boats and picked her way along the slick stones that dotted the shore. There was no sand on this part of the beach, only the slime and barnacle-marred protrusions that met the air during low tide alone.

The reddish cliffs had a particular alcove that revealed itself only at such times of the day or night when the sea was at its lowest. A crab scuttled over her feet, and she kicked aside a piece of kelp as she wandered into the shallow cave just as she'd done so many times in her childhood. This hiding place had been the perfect way to escape without ever going too far. They'd never search for her in this dip of the cliff. If she was lucky, they wouldn't even know she'd been missing before she was safely back in her room.

Ophir called a ball of light and allowed it to hum in the center of the hollowed limestone. Any wayward sailor would see the warm, ethereal glow of her flame from his ship, but she and her light were invisible to anyone in the castle, as she and her cave were perfectly beneath the structure, embedded in the very cliff on which it sat. Her orange flame hung like a low chandelier, unbound by constraints as it lit the water-slick curves and grooves of the cave.

Now it was time for the reason she'd come. She had manifested once. She was ready to do it again.

She wiggled her hands in front of her and pictured a snake.

Nothing happened.

She narrowed her eyes and focused. Dwyn had forced her to see everything about the serpent for weeks. She knew its size, its weight, even its foul scent. She had believed in the beast and turned the pain of her trauma into a physical, reptilian monster in her mind long before she'd conjured it. It had been anger, pain, and survival that had made her imagination a reality.

She thrust a hand out before her and envisioned the serpent leaping from the tips of her fingers.

Again, she was met with silence. Only the gentle lapping of the waves at the lip of the cave mingled with her frustrated kick and grunt against her failure. She tried again and again, doing her best to recapture the scenario that had led to the monster and its manifestation. She kicked against the wall of the cave with too much force, crying out in pain as the shock of impact lanced up her leg.

An idea pricked her.

Dwyn had ignited her survival instinct. She'd heard of such methods used in some training camps among soldiers. Pain and panic were powerful tools in triggering one's will to live.

On that stormy cliff in front of Dwyn and Harland, she had manifested the snake from the primal place within her that fought for life. She'd created a warrior to battle on her behalf when she'd been kicked within an inch of consciousness. The princess began to wander around the slippery floor of the cave in search of a loose stone. Unfortunately, the carving nature of the ocean had made every surface exceptionally smooth. A tidal pool had been created toward the back of the cave where the grooves had naturally collected water, allowing a tiny ecosystem of shrimps, colorful corals, and the white-sand bottom of a little beach to live in the sea cave regardless of the tide and its height. She splashed around in the pool, hoping to find a loose rock, but only succeeded in wetting her hand and startling a baby octopus who'd been hiding under an old oyster shell.

Ophir scanned the space around her, searching for anything that might effectively trigger her survival instincts.

Perhaps her half-formed plan to smash herself over the head with a stone was best left thwarted. Besides, she wasn't sure if she could provoke survival instincts while knowing that she would doubtlessly hold back on the true danger she needed as a catalyst. She wouldn't have hit herself hard enough to genuinely believe she was about to die. She supposed she could jump into the ocean, but she wasn't sure if conjuring a serpent would serve her well if she was in the midst of drowning. Ophir needed to feel like she was dying—not actually die.

She sat on the cave floor and allowed the damp seawater to

leach into her clothes, soaking through to her legs. The warm glow of the flame she'd conjured cast interesting shadows on the far wall. It made her think of bonfires on the beach with her sister, or how they'd curled up against the hearth on late winter nights to drink melted chocolate and discuss their hopes and loves and dreams. Ophir would tell her all about her latest conquest, and Caris would gasp and hit her playfully as she lived vicariously through Firi's immoral ways, soaking in every detail.

Tears licked at her lower lids.

Her first reaction was to slam down the cover on her emotion and to sink back into the numbness that had protected her for months. The feeling stirred something in her greater than memory. She realized that there were more excruciating pains than the physical. There were horrible, terrible ways to feel like you were dying without ever letting anyone touch you. So, she did what she'd spent months and months preventing herself from doing. She did the very thing that caused her to jolt awake screaming, burning her clothes and her bed.

Ophir opened herself up, and she let herself feel.

She went to the place in her mind that she'd never let herself go while awake.

She opened the darkened door once again to see the men who'd crowded around her sister. She allowed herself to see every single detail. She looked into their faces, soaking in the lines around their eyes, the shades of their hair, the presence of stubble, their builds, their heights, the shapes of their jaws. She looked into her memory and stared unflinchingly at Caris and how they'd kept her alive. Harland had suggested they'd wanted her to stay a virgin. While the idea that she had not been forced had comforted her parents, he'd stiffened with a darker horror. It was as though Ophir's heart ripped in two.

The pain lanced through her with excruciating slowness as she lived her waking nightmare. Tears spilled over her lids before she knew what was happening. She heard the sound echo and reverberate off the walls as if listening to someone else's suffering. Her disembodied, uncontrollable sobs turned into the angry, howling screams of the unhinged. She was not sad. She was not hurt. She was not afraid. She was furious. Her mouth grew wider as she bared her teeth against the sound. Her lips pulled back. She allowed her anger to burn hotter and brighter than the fire in the room. She let it eat her, filling every membrane and curve and cell. Her muscles sizzled with her fury. Her tendons ached against the blistering heat of her pain. Her face had contorted into the supernatural, open-mouthed, full-bodied scream of a banshee. There was no sound in her ears but that of her own searing, thrashing rage. She didn't care if they heard her in the castle. She hoped all of Aubade stirred in their beds and jolted awake at the feral, otherworldly sound of her hot, scorching misery.

She forced her pain into anger.

She envisioned the savory, satisfying ways she would peel Berinth's skin away from the muscle and bone, burn his eyeballs until they melted in the sockets, and make him beg for forgiveness before leaving him to die like a dog in a ditch. She'd cut his compatriots from neck to navel and punch her fist into the cavities of their stomach while they lived, watching the torment in their eyes as she cooked them from the inside out. She'd be the serpent, sinking her fangs into them time after time until every last one of them twitched and gasped and begged for mercy at her feet.

Her trauma went from a murky, bloody thing to a strong, firm shape.

Still screaming with the raw and unbridled rage of the woman on the brink of living hell, she brought her hands in front of her and brought her pain to life.

Her anger gave birth to an enormous, black serpent.

She was stunned. She hadn't known if this would work. She was bewildered at her own power.

Her screaming stopped. Its final echoes crawled from the cave, hollow as the sound escaped over the waves. Her throat ached from the exertion. Her eyes burned from the tears that had stung her. Now that she'd created her monster, she didn't know what to do with it. Harland had been so quick to behead her snake when they'd been on the cliff. Dwyn hadn't looked even the least bit afraid. Now that she was alone with the animal, she started to remember why she'd chosen the image of a snake in the first place. She found them utterly terrifying. They were the most horrible thing she could imagine, and now she was sharing a suffocatingly small sea cave with the coiled tendril of an enormous reptile.

It swerved as it observed its surroundings, slowly unraveling itself like rope on a dock. It had been interested in the flame in the center of the room until Ophir made the mistake of taking a sideways step and catching its attention. It whipped its head around with unnatural speed.

She raised her hands to placate it, but her heart began to pick up its pace. Fear crept through her as she attempted to speak. "I created you, snake. Stand down."

What was she saying? It didn't speak the common tongue. It was a scaly brute.

It flicked out its tongue to taste the air around it and unhinged its jaw, revealing the horrible venom she'd spent weeks envisioning as it dripped from the creature's fangs.

"It's okay, snake," she tried to say, but she didn't believe her own words. Sensing her uncertainty, it began to rear its head.

Though the princess's heart was in an arrhythmia of panicked humming, she locked in on an idea. She raised a hand and began to manipulate her ball of light, drawing the creature's attention to the movement of the orb while she slowly backed out of the cave. The serpent moved with unnatural ease as it cocked its head, continuing to flick its tongue as it tested the air around it. Ophir continued to move the ball of light toward the back of the cave, drawing the serpent to the shallow pool. Her back was to the sea as she took step after step, putting more and more distance between herself and the snake. The tide was beginning to come in. The waves were louder as they broke on the cliffs and had begun to conceal the slippery rocks that had allowed her access to the cave.

She didn't want to put her back toward the serpent, but once she reached the mouth of the cave, she needed to turn and run if she wanted to get to shore before the waves made it any higher. In her foolish haste, she'd scarcely made it onto the second, sea-slick rock before a wave cracked against her legs, knocking her feet out from beneath her. The wave shoved her with rough hands from the boulder and rammed her body into the vertical cliffs of Castle Aubade.

Ophir thrashed for the surface, finding air as the wave withdrew. She knew it was preparing to crash again as she reached for the boulder. Her fingers scraped against the sharp, glasslike shards of the mussels and mollusks that clung to the protrusion, desperate to find a way to grip the perilous rock. She held on tight as another wave crashed down on her, filling her mouth with seawater and bits of sand. Her body was not thrown into the cliff this time, giving her just enough time to pull her knee up onto the stone and attempt to stand. A deep, gory slash carved across her leg as a broken barnacle bit into her flesh, but she made it to her feet.

She had mere seconds to jump to the next rock when she realized her flame had gone out. The dark silhouette of a reptile was slowly slithering its way out of the cave. It was following her.

Adrenaline and fear drowned out the sounds of the rising tide and crashing waves. She leapt onto the next rock. Pain shot through her wounded leg and found her on unsteady feet, crunching down onto her knees with a horrible, squelching impact. The snake's attentions whipped to her movements as its huge, rope-like body finished slithering from the sea cave completely and onto the rock, fixated on her.

She turned for the snake and called upon fire once more, flinging the ball into the sky to tempt the beast's attentions.

Her flame needed to be high enough so that the punishing water would not extinguish it, but as the sea around her rose, the waves came down with increasing intensity. She couldn't watch to see if her attempt was successful, making yet another jump for one in a line of five more slippery boulders before she was safely on shore. She yelped unwillingly as the gash in her leg and pain in her knees caused her stomach to churn.

She jumped again, slipping on the disgusting, slick surface that came from years of seaweed, muck, and grime, making traction impossible with the rising tide. She slipped again and this time, the ocean succeeded in shoving her into the tight space between the boulder and the cliff. The moment she hit the water, she felt the terrible impact of her skull as it bounced off of the sheer, unforgiving wall of the cliff. She couldn't so much as gasp in surprise as seawater pushed itself down her throat. The wave pulled away, but she didn't have time to grab for a rock before she was being shoved against the cliff once more.

A rough, horrible feeling lanced through her as her neck jerked backward and upward. A man had a handful of her hair and was yanking her from the water like one might grab the scruff of a kitten. His other hand gripped her shirt, yanking her indelicately from the only two places he'd been able to take hold. He had her up and out of the water just as another rising wave smothered them. Fortunately, the man was anchored by enough weight and traction from his heavy boots that he was not knocked from where he knelt. It was not Harland.

"Can you walk?" The stranger yelled the question over the sounds of the sea.

She wasn't sure if she could, but as her eyes caught the dark movement of the snake, she knew her fire had gone out once more. She tried to raise her hands, but he seemed to know what she intended.

"Forget it," the rough, masculine voice insisted. "We have to get out of here."

He grabbed her by the elbow both to urge her forward and to steady her as they covered the remaining distance to reach shore, escaping the violence of the rising tide. She wanted to collapse upon the sand, but the snake was closing in. It seemed to have a problem with the water as it slithered over the slippery stones and swam when the waves pressed in.

"The snake," she gasped.

"Command it!" he yelled at her.

She coughed up bile and seawater.

"I—"

"Command it, Ophir."

"I told it to stand down and—"

"Snakes can't stand!" the man barked in response.

She blinked up at the dark stranger and then at the snake as it closed in on them. The princess didn't have time to argue. They didn't have time. She raised her hand and shouted at the beast, "Stop."

It obeyed. It tilted its head with what may have looked like curiosity. Though its large face stayed still, its body continued its slithering journey to join the rest of its vertebrae and coil beneath it on the rock nearest the shore. It tasted the air as it had done in the cave.

She coughed again and he slapped her roughly on the back to help her dispel whatever remained of the salt in her belly.

"Get rid of it," he said.

Conflicting emotions jolted her. "You want me to kill it?"

"I don't care what you do with your monster. But if you don't get rid of it, it's going to hurt someone."

She looked at the snake. It opened its mouth again with the same venom-drenched fangs. She realized somewhere deep in her gut that it had not been trying to hurt her. It had merely shown her what she had manifested, down to the very last drop. The creature had been following its maker, not attacking.

"Go back to the cave," she said uncertainly.

It tasted the air once more before turning and slithering away. With the snake gone, she could focus. It had barely begun its retreat before the princess turned her attention to the stranger.

"What the hell!" She gagged on the taste of salt as she stared up at the man. A wave splashed against them as its white foam raced up the sandy beach, and she winced as the salt filled the open gash on her leg. They were off the danger of the rocks and cliffs, but there was still a stretch of sandy beach before they could make the climb toward the castle.

He grabbed for her shirt, and she started to fight him.

"Don't move," he grumbled, procuring a small knife, stilling her with the pressure of one hand.

"Stop!" She panicked, trying to twist away from his knife.

"I'm trying to help you. Hold the fuck still." The man held her prone as he cut a strip of cloth from the base of her shirt, ripping the white fabric cleanly so it scarcely hung from her breasts to the top of her belly. He tied the fabric tightly above her wound to create a tourniquet. "You're losing a lot of blood. We have to get you back to the castle."

"Who are you?"

"Can we talk about that after we've stitched you together?"

The adrenaline had not yet leached from her body. Her teeth began to chatter as she shivered. "No. I want to talk about it now! I want to know why strangers are always pulling me out of the water outside of my castle."

He was not smiling, though his tone held an undercurrent of distant amusement. "Probably because you keep throwing yourself in the ocean. Are you going to get up or am I going to have to carry you?"

She glared through the salt and pain. "You wouldn't dare."

"Watch me."

TWENTY

✦　✦　✦　✦

T HE STRANGER DID NOT PICK HER UP AS ONE MIGHT A
damsel in a fairytale but threw her over his shoulder as
if she were a root vegetable sack at the whims of a working
hand. Ophir shrieked with every drop of obstinance she
possessed. She kicked with her good leg, but he tightened his
grip, immobilizing her efforts for defiance. She attempted to
beat at his back, but he only chuckled at her while walking
up the beach and toward the narrow, hidden walkway that
might return them to the tunnels.

She called a ball of flame and thrust it into his back. He
growled, lowering her to the ground rather indelicately so
that she bounced on her bottom. He grabbed her roughly by
the arms. His dark eyes, the swimming, interwoven colors of
coffee and earth and coal, burned into hers as he growled,
"Fine. Die out here."

She stared back at him with wide surprise, her eyes grazing
over her unnamed savior. There was something familiar about
him. He was on one knee, wiping salt water from his face
while she examined him. His eyes, his dark hair, his tattoo…

"You're him."

He stood, seemingly understanding what she'd meant.

"Yes. I'm the one who saved your ungrateful ass from the tide. I'm sorry to be the one to let you bleed to death on the beach."

"You were the one at the party. You were there. You tried to get me out of Berinth's house."

His voice stayed level. "I don't know what you're talking about."

Ophir attempted to get to her feet, wincing as every part of her ached. Terrible pain lanced through her. She was pretty sure she'd broken her kneecaps, though they were probably just bruised to oblivion. Her head throbbed from where it had been bashed against the cliff. Her vision dimmed from the blood loss. "You might want to do a better job hiding your tattoo if you're going to lie about your identity."

She tried to take a step but swayed, tumbling downward.

A strong hand shot out and caught her before she bit the sand with her full body weight. Her cheek pressed into the fine grit of the beach. From where she tasted shells and rocks, she heard the male voice above her ask, "Are you ready to stop being difficult?"

She didn't have the energy to fight him. "Take the entrance by the rowboats. There's a tunnel system—"

"I know."

She shook her head. "No, the wine cellar—"

"Has a passage to your room. I know."

"How do you know?" Ophir squirmed as fear wriggled its way into her senses. He shouldn't know about her passage. He shouldn't know about her bedroom. No one knew.

"Fight me later, princess. I'll sit still for you to throw a punch if you can do me the favor of staying conscious for the next ten minutes. Can you do that?"

She attempted to glare but wasn't sure that her eyelids were responding to her summons. The night's stars were blinking out slowly as if the black sky was gobbling them whole. This time when he carried her, it was with a gentleness that allowed her eyes to remained fixed on the stars.

They made it to the edge of the castle when he eyed her.

"Ah, shit. We can't have a trail of blood from the beach to your room. Hang on."

He set her down once more and let her back rest against the custard stones of the castle's outermost wall just before the entrance to the tunnels. He reached directly over his head and grabbed his shirt from the center of his back, pulling it off in one swift motion. His black tunic was grimy with salt and sand, but they were more worried about concealing the evidence of their entrance than risking infection. He revealed his broad chest and the demarcations of his stomach with the swift tug of cloth. If they could get safely inside, they could access whatever medicines and tonics they needed. While her makeshift tourniquet had helped to slow the blood flow, his dark shirt absorbed the pooling, telltale signs of her injury on the stone floors that might give them away.

With his shirt off, she could see how his tattoo spread from the base of his neck down one pectoral and wound its way elaborately down his arm. She opened her mouth to comment on it, but her vision swam, which weakened her resolve. Her loose grip on consciousness must have been painted clearly on in her eyes.

"Hey, none of that." He gave her three quick taps on the face with his hand. "We had a deal, remember? You have to stay conscious."

"I'm conscious," she said with unconvincing slowness. She dared a glance at her hand to see its grayish pallor. It had been a particularly chilly night, and she had not been dressed for the weather even before she'd been half-drowned in the ocean. The slightest breeze set her to shivering once again.

When he picked her up this time, it was with increasing delicacy and gentleness. "Keep talking, Princess. Tell me what you were doing in the cave."

"It's…not…your business."

A low growl rumbled through his throat as he navigated his way through the underground tunnels. "Tell me about your favorite food."

"I…"

"Hey." He jolted her against him so that her eyes blinked open rapidly. "Food. Tell me."

She attempted to shrug, but her limbs were too heavy to move. "I like all foods."

"Goddess damn you are unhelpful. Tell me about your first kiss."

She smiled, though her lips were cold against her teeth. "Now that's a good story."

He continued moving swiftly as he maneuvered the tunnels beneath the castle. He seemed to be covering ground quickly. They were nearly to the wine cellar. "I want to hear it. What was his name?"

With the slowness of the absent, she said, "What makes you assume it was a male?"

"Well, aren't we full of surprises. We're almost there, Princess. Keep talking."

The bounce and jostle told her they'd begun mounting the stairs. They should be no more than three flights away from her chambers. Somewhere in the distant reaches of her mind, she knew she had a healing tonic in her bathing room, just above her washing basin. She'd need to demand answers about how he knew about the secret entrance to her room. No one was supposed to know about that entrance. Maybe after she slept for a bit, her headache would go away and she could think more clearly. She was terribly chilly. Sleep would answer all of her questions; she was certain of it. She just needed to let her eyes close.

"Princess? How about that kiss?"

"I'm not…" Her eyes stayed closed.

"What was her name?"

"It was a boy," she mumbled.

"What?"

"My first kiss was with a boy," she responded, her words slurred with chill and sleep. "I just thought it was presumptuous for you to have assumed."

He chuckled darkly at that as he reached her mirror, finding the pressure release so that it slowly opened into the room. Her chambers were just as she'd left them. He set her wet, brine-covered body on her bed. She hated how filthy she felt and wished she hadn't been forced to dirty her duvet, but she didn't have the energy to argue.

"Where do you keep your tonics?"

She didn't answer. He'd figure it out. She just needed to sleep for a little while.

"Hey." This slap was rough, reminding her of how Dwyn had hit her on the cliffs. "I need you to be an active participant in your survival. Where are your tonics?"

She lifted a hand to gesture to the bathing room, and before she'd had a chance to fall asleep on the bed, he was hauling her into the empty bathtub with all of her clothes on. He tugged the dark, filthy shirt off the wound with less gentleness than she might have liked. The gash was so much more horrible-looking in the clean light of the castle. It was no surface scratch. It appeared she had slashed cleanly into muscle.

The stranger spoke with the emotionless assuredness of a physician. "I just need to wash it and then I'll put half of the tonic on the wound itself and have you drink the rest. Are you with me? Princess?"

Ophir didn't bother nodding. She figured he would probably do whatever he wanted regarding her injury no matter what she said. He hadn't been particularly accommodating to her delicate sensibilities so far, and Ophir didn't imagine he was about to start. He dumped her into the bathtub fully clothed and began to run the water. She let out a painful gasp as the water washed over her gash. He began rummaging through the things above her washing basin and grabbed a clear bottle of medicinal astringent.

"This is going to hurt. I'm just going to kill the worst of it before we knit the wound together. Are you ready?"

"No." She gritted her teeth, wincing preemptively. He

began to pour the clear, burning liquid over her cut and she grunted with the low, sustained moan of excruciating misery. Her ears popped from the searing agony. Once it was done, he poured the healing tonic on the gash. He tried to hand the rest to Ophir to drink, but she seemed to be losing consciousness once more, as much from the pain as from the blood loss.

"Open your mouth, Princess." The man grabbed her chin and tilted her head back. The pressure of his fingers against her jaw forced her mouth open as he began to bottle-feed her the remaining tonic. She choked at first, coughing and rejecting the liquid until she managed to swallow. Once the brown glass bottle was empty, the stranger seemed satisfied. He'd done what he needed to do.

She blinked rapidly at him after the tonic began to work its way through her belly. "Are you going to tell me who the fuck you are?"

He offered something of a crooked smile. "You're not very ladylike. Did you know that?"

"It's been implied."

He was in heavy, sand-covered boots and sea-dampened black pants, but he remained shirtless. She didn't want her eyes to linger too long on the divots of his muscles or the way his body rippled. He spoke with low, calm seriousness. "I'm Tyr, so that's the name you can use when you overcome your attitude and are ready to thank me."

She scowled at him from where she sat like a grimy, wet doll gripping the edges of the bathtub. She was sitting in roughly three inches of standing water and appeared to have brought half of the beach back home with her. She wanted to take a real bath. She was sure that once she rinsed her hair and scrubbed herself clean, she'd have more sand in the bathtub than she knew what to do with.

"What are you, my guardian angel? Aren't angels supposed to be friendly?" She attempted to push herself up from where she sat in the bath.

"I wouldn't move yet if I were you."

"Turn around." She ignored him and began to peel her shirt off. Saltwater itched as it began to dry, and she didn't need another little misery added to her ever-growing list of pain and discomfort.

"Just so you know, I can see you in the mirror."

She looked up and narrowed her eyes as she caught his reflection looking back at her. He arched a brow that was far too playful for the severity of the situation, and she made a shooing motion with her hand. Still grinning, he rotated his body so he was facing neither her nor the mirror. Ophir continued the process, attempting to slide her pants down but wincing and gasping as they stuck to her legs. He rolled his eyes at her impropriety but kept his bare back to her.

She ran the water but didn't plug the tub, allowing the sand to run down and empty with the water that filled it. Ophir began to gingerly rinse various parts of her body. She grabbed a honey-and-almond-scented bar of soap and scrubbed it against her arms and legs, dipping one appendage beneath the water at a time.

"Get talking, Tyr."

His posture shifted as he found a more comfortable position. "What would you like to know?"

She grumbled. "My throat hurts. I'm tired. I've had a rough night. Don't be coy. Who are you, why are you here, why were you on the cliffs, what were you doing at Berinth's party, and how the fuck do you know how to get into my bedroom? Honestly, what *don't* you have to answer for?"

She watched his muscled back shrug as she ran her hair under the water, allowing as much sand as possible to escape where it had clung to her damp, toffee tendrils. Now that she'd stopped the water's drainage, she allowed the tub to fill around her.

"I'd love to be cagey, but seeing as how you seem to have successfully unlocked manifesting, I think maybe it's time you and I get on the same page. Though you could try to curse a little less. Obscenities won't help you."

She raised her head from beneath the water, stilling as she watched his neck and back while he spoke.

"What do you know about blood magic?" he asked, still facing the wallpaper.

She winced at an emotional pain more poignant than the gash in her leg. "Is that why you were at Berinth's the night of Caris's murder?"

He made a face as if contemplating whether to deny it. "You and your sister have attracted a few unsavory characters to Aubade—Berinth being one of them. Royal blood is a rather valuable commodity."

Harland had danced around this thought precisely. The blood magic of a royal. Her throat knotted as she drowned in the flood of ten thousand thoughts as violent and relentless as those crashing against the cliffs of Castle Aubade.

"The things that could be achieved with Caris's heart, particularly if she was a virgin..."

"Don't talk about her like that." Ophir choked out the command.

She could feel his apologetic frown even from the back of his head. He lowered his voice when he answered. "I'm truly sorry, Ophir. I'm not much of a guardian angel. I'm less interested in protecting you than I am in keeping their hands from what you can offer them."

"He didn't get her heart."

Tyr turned to her with fully widened eyes. Ophir's hands flew to cover herself as he gaped at her. His lips parted. "What? What do you know?"

"Excuse me." She clutched herself for comfort.

"Why would you say that?" Tyr demanded, moving toward the bath's edge. His coffee-colored eyes fixed on hers.

"The coroner." Ophir blinked back, horrified. "Her liver was missing—oh my goddess. Fuck off. I did *not* invite you in here. You are owed *nothing*. Get out."

His shoulders heaved, nostrils flaring as he pulled in air, but he forced himself to relax. The thoughts behind his eyes seemed to be clicking like the mechanics of a pocket watch. He closed his eyes slowly as he turned, obeying her wishes for privacy. "I'm sorry," he said. "I wish I could have left you alone."

"Then why didn't you let me die? Wouldn't that have solved your problems?"

Tyr gestured uncomfortably. "Can you get dressed so we can speak properly?"

"You're in my room. In my chambers."

"Fine," he squared, staring at her fully. "Then we'll talk with you naked. Trust me, I am more than fine with the arrangement."

It took Ophir a moment to relax after he'd spun on her. She swallowed at his request and focused on cleaning herself of the sand and evidence of the sea. She ran her hair under the water as she scrubbed a mint bar along her scalp, freeing the bits of broken shell and pieces of sand that had clung to her hair. She paused as she turned the bar of soap over in her hand, sniffing it again, wondering where it had come from. The scent was so overpowering, so familiar. It didn't smell like anything she remembered purchasing or being gifted. She frowned at the curious soap before running it over her body once more. Now was not the time to worry about peculiar soaps. She gave one final pass of her back and chest under the running water before deciding she was finished. It would have to suffice for as long as she remained unwilling to submerge the gaping wound on her leg once more.

"Close your eyes."

He exhaled, nostrils flaring. "They're closed."

She eyed him suspiciously for a second before lifting herself above the lip of the bath. Ophir reached for a robe that had been hung on a hook beside the bath and tied it tightly around herself. Its cloth absorbed the water droplets that clung to her body and collected the clean pools that continued to drip from her hair.

"Okay," she said carefully.

He swept his arm toward her room as if it were his to offer. "After you."

Ophir abandoned her tub, escaping from the lip of the basin. She crossed the room and sat on her bed but indicated that Tyr should sit on the chair as far from her as possible. He obliged but didn't hurry to talk. The strange man seemed to be enjoying the sight of the princess in her robe a bit too much, even if she was looking rather battered. Finally, he said, "You staying alive might be my best chance at drawing Berinth out to finish what he's started."

Ophir may as well have turned to stone. She soaked in the features she knew were not from the southern kingdoms, breath and heart hushed by her horror. He didn't look like anyone she'd met before. Her previous encounters with this stranger had been shrouded in the secrecy of his mask. "Splendid. I'm bait for a sadistic, blood-magic princess murderer. And that explains why you know how to get into my bedroom because...?"

"I'm pretty good at sneaking around. It's my gift. I've needed to keep an eye on the place. If I know all the entrances and exits, I can intercept more effectively. Which brings me to my next point. How well do you truly know Dwyn?"

She stiffened, though something about the gild of his skin and distinct angle of his face suggested that he hailed from the same remote mountain kingdom as the siren. Tyr was not the first man to question the siren's presence in her life. "What? How do you know Dwyn?"

His face tightened in a controlled expression as he leveled his gaze. "I followed her here from Sulgrave," he said.

She didn't mean to sneer with quite so much vitriol as she asked, "Unrequited love?"

His chuckle was black and humorless. "That bitch is the reason I know the things I do about blood magic, Princess. You should be a little more careful about who you let into your bed."

His words alone would have sent her into a state of

disagreeable shock. The handle to her bedroom door began to turn and her eyes widened, realizing her chair was still against it to prevent unwanted entry. She turned to Tyr to command him to hide, but he was gone.

The door sounded in quick succession.

She shot a look to where Tyr had been only a second before, then back to the door.

"Tyr?"

"Answer the door."

Ophir swallowed audibly. She gathered her senses with several swift blinks, wondering how much saltwater she'd swallowed, and limped over to the door. She moved the chair just as Harland was winding up to break down the entrance.

"Why did you block the door?" The whites of his eyes were as prominent as the rims of teacups. It was clear he'd been on the verge of panic. Ophir gave her guard no shortage of reasons to worry. She was the reason he didn't sleep at night, and she knew it.

She made a face. "Because you like to let yourself in whenever you like. Did you even knock? No? Then you have your answer." It was cruel of her to brush him off like this. He was a good guard with excellent intuition. He had been right to follow whatever sense had led him to her room, but she wasn't ready for that conversation.

He seemed moderately if unsatisfactorily pacified, until he soaked in her appearance. "You look like hell, Firi. What happened?"

Healing tonics worked well, but they weren't an instantaneous magical solution. She was glad the long robe covered the wound on her thigh. He was probably only seeing the bruising where she'd smacked her face against the cliff.

"I was getting out of the bath and tripped."

He looked entirely unconvinced. His hazel eyes were shades of deeper green as they softened, mingled with the browns and golds of his skepticism. "Are you okay?"

"The injury to my ego is worse than the bump to my

head. I've already taken a tonic. I should probably have a few more sent up the next time you see the healer. Now, what do you want? Why are you here?"

He looked a little wounded that she was being so dismissive. "Can I come in?"

The corners of her mouth turned downward. "I'm tired."

"It's about Dwyn."

Her mouth was still tightly closed, but her nostrils flared as she exhaled. She pushed the door open widely enough for Harland to enter.

He made a horrified sound, and she knew her mistake immediately. "Goddess, Firi, what did you do in here?"

She didn't have to fully turn to know what he'd found. Harland was holding up strip of fabric soaked with blood and crusted with salt and sand.

"You first. Tell me about Dwyn and I'll explain"—she waved her hand elaborately—"all of that."

"You didn't slip in the tub." It wasn't a question.

"What can I say—I'm crafty. What's wrong with Dwyn?"

He wasn't ready to deflect. He was still holding the bloodied strip a of cloth as he addressed her. "I can't protect you if you're still pulling this shit, Firi. How could you sneak out of the castle after all that's happened? How could you—"

"I'm sorry," she said quietly. For once, her tone wasn't jaded or defensive. She truly was sorry. She knew that Harland didn't just speak for her station, or for the kingdom. He cared deeply for her. He'd sworn fealty to her, he'd been her only friend, he'd been her lover, he'd been the closest thing she'd had to family in months. She knew precisely what it would do to her parents if they lost their only remaining child. Caris's death had torn the kingdom to ribbons. If she passed, there would be nothing left to comfort them. The guard's expression said all this and more as he searched her apology for sincerity.

Harland sank onto the bed and raked his hands through his hair. "Why must you insist on posing the greatest threat to your own safety?"

It was as if he'd hit her. She spoke with the quiet injury of the reproach when she whispered, "You loved that about me once."

He looked up to her with emotion lining his hazel eyes. "No, I'm really asking, Firi. What happened to make you so careless? Is being a princess so terrible? Is being here with your friends and people who care about you so boring that you always need to sneak out and deceive us? Why are you always trying to get yourself killed? Why..." He looked away, running his fingers through his chestnut hair again. He was rife with complex emotions neither of them could unpack right now. He repeated his question more carefully. "Why do you need to cut me out?"

Her eyes tightened as he spoke. His final question betrayed him.

"This is about you, then. You liked that I was an individual. You loved my recklessness. You're angry because I don't include you in what I choose to do with my life and my time." A hand went to her heart as if to soothe the physical wound of his words, gripping it against herself as she spoke her own.

He saw how bruised and scraped her hands were and got up from the bed to fetch the tonic from the bathing room. He was met with more sandy, bloodied clothes and an open bottle of astringent. He returned with a black male tunic. "Was someone in here?"

She bristled against her lie. "No. I used that to wrap my wound."

Disbelief weighed heavily on his shoulders. He was as tired of her lies as she was of telling them. Their dance was exhausting, yet neither of them would relinquish.

"Seriously." She parted her robe slightly to reveal her upper leg and watched as his mouth dropped in horror. "I used it to help stop the bleeding. I've cleaned it and used the healing tonic."

"The goddess has a sick sense of humor."

"Harland—"

Harland disappeared without another word, closing the door behind him.

From the bathing room, Tyr called, "He's not wrong. You are obscenely reckless."

"Shut the fuck up, phantom."

"You're also exceedingly foul-mouthed."

"And you're a stalker who specializes in voyeurism. You can't be seen? That's your power?"

He stepped out from thin air and shrugged, still shirtless. "Sorry about the shirt. You're in enough trouble as it is without him worrying about you having men in your room. I thought I was doing you a favor by staying hidden. Well," he amended, "I was doing us both a favor."

She looked to her feet. "Harland is not going to get me in trouble."

Tyr shrugged. "Maybe that used to be true, but he might be inclined to start reporting your misgivings if he thinks it'll help keep you safe. Maybe you could use a little bit of a spanking."

"You're crude."

"I am. I think our demons would dance well together."

Her face had reacted in notable surprise before she'd had time to conceal her expression.

They heard footsteps in the hall, and Tyr took a backward step into the unknowable space between things, vanishing once more. She kept her eyes narrowed at the empty place where he doubtlessly stood as Harland returned with clean bandages and several more glass bottles. She continued to stare at the blank corner, wondering if there would be any sign, any ripple, any disturbance in the air to give him away. There was nothing.

Harland ordered her to sit on the bed, and she obliged.

"I should be calling a healer for this. I should call your lady in waiting."

"But you won't."

Harland stilled his hands against where they wrapped her wound. His gaze met hers, but his hazel eyes were tight and colored with pain. He sighed as she winced against the bandage. "I know. That's why I'm here doing this myself, isn't it? As if a guard is qualified..." His words trailed off as he forced her leg up to get the bandage around her thigh more fully. Their relationship had abandoned the appropriate boundaries of guard and royal charge long ago. "As soon as I tell someone, they'll report it. And maybe they should, for goddess's sake. When will you stop? When will it be enough for you?"

Ophir's frown came from somewhere deep within herself. She propped herself up on her elbow to look at him. Her soul itself turned the corners of her mouth downward. She didn't know why she was so broken. She didn't know why she couldn't be more like Caris.

With a quiet voice, she opted for honesty. "I went to see if I could do it again."

His fingers stilled against her, hands resting on either side of her leg. Harland's eyes were as tense as the flexed muscles in his jaw. "You didn't."

She quietly said, "I succeeded."

He swallowed, frozen to his place on the bed. Harland closed his eyes slowly and brought a hand to his temple, rubbing it against the early signs of what might have been a headache. He leaned away from the princess. "That's what I wanted to talk about. The serpent. This gift..." He was clearly struggling for his words as he leaned his weight away from the bed, standing fully on his feet. "Dwyn shouldn't have known you might have the potential to manifest. There's no reason she should have believed any such thing about you. She came out of nowhere on the night of your sister's death and suddenly she's eliciting one of the most dangerous magics of the old gods from you? Firi, I..." His voice disconnected as his eyes unfocused.

"Is she..."

"She's still in the castle. Your parents have never questioned her presence. I didn't either, and it was foolish of us. After she arrived, you seemed to calm down. Her friendship appeared to be helping, and we were too happy to question it. Ever since you stopped burning down chambers and began sleeping through the night... You're eating again, Firi. You looked relatively healthy before you got your ass kicked tonight by whoever or whatever did this to you—"

"This would be the handiwork of the high tide."

He dismissed her statement. "Dwyn seems like a nice enough girl. She's strange, she's foreign, she's violent and odd, but nice enough. I don't know shit about Sulgrave, but I also don't care who she is or where she's from. Whether Dwyn was born in Aubade or Yelagin or Raascot or Tarkhany, I think she's a wolf in sheep's clothing. My gut is telling me you shouldn't trust her."

Ophir met his eyes with gravity. She leaned forward and touched his hands. "The damage is already done. What more could she possibly do?"

"Look at yourself."

Ophir studied his hazel eyes for sincerity. She got up from where she'd been sitting and stood in front of the full-length mirror on the wall. The ornate, floral gilding that framed the mirror created a portrait-like effect, but the sight within it was anything but lovely. Purple bruises and rust-colored scrapes covered the half-drowned girl who stared back at her.

"Give the tonics a chance to work," she muttered.

Harland sighed at the young woman in the mirror. Posture heavy with disappointment, he moved to depart. With his back to her, he offered low parting words. "You've never shown particularly good judgment, Firi. It would be great for everyone if you would start."

At least when Dwyn had slapped her, the evidence had been physical. This was much, much worse.

He closed the door behind him, leaving his words to course through her like a poison.

Tyr reappeared with an arrogant smile. "I like him."

She glowered at Tyr, then returned her attention to a pink, puckering welt across her cheek in the mirror as the tonic knit it together. "Why are you still here?"

"Are you asking me, or her?"

"Jackass."

He approached slowly from behind, standing a little too close over her shoulder as he looked at her reflection. "I think I'll do him a favor and help keep you in line. It would kill two birds with one stone if we can keep you put, Ophir. Who knows—maybe Harland and I will become best friends."

She continued to make her displeasure clear from where she stood, her golden eyes slits as she glared at him through the glass. "You're not invited. And unless you start explaining yourself, you can show yourself out."

"What do you want to know?"

His smoldering gaze held hers for a little too long. She was the first to break, looking away as she said, "You came to Farehold because you were following Dwyn because...what were you saying about blood magic?"

He leaned against the wall. Looking up and to the side as if searching his memory like a teacher preparing a lesson, he asked, "There are no Reds in the south. What do the fine people of Farehold know of blood magic?"

Her nose twitched as she fought a sneer. The truth was that she knew very little, save for that blood magic was forbidden, as it led to death. Whispers claimed that moments before perishing, a fae could wield one final power that they'd never accessed before. Little else was said on the subject, as no one was stupid enough to try it and find out.

When she didn't answer, he said, "Sulgrave has a militant branch of the church who have learned how to call upon stolen powers. If they're strong enough, it brings them to the brink of death without pushing them over."

Ophir's lips parted in silent surprise.

"There are fae who have learned how to take it a step

further. Not only do they borrow from the groundwater—is that what you call the world's power in the south?—but they can do it while forcing someone else to die in their stead."

"And..." Ophir searched his face for a tell. He nodded encouragingly until she said what they were both thinking. "That's why you've followed Dwyn?"

"Your guard was wrong about you," he said. "Look how clever you are."

His mocking tone was one step too far. She was tired of being condescended to. She was tired of being underestimated, of being cornered, of being forced to play nice, or be proper, or chastised until she filled the royal hole left by Caris's shoes.

She hated the smug stranger who stared at her from across the room. "Bastard."

"Oh, I hear you, Princess." She stiffened as he lifted a hand, bringing his large palm closer to her face. She continued facing the mirror as she watched the man behind her run a finger along the bruise on her high cheekbone. "Do you know what I see when I look at you?"

Her lips parted at the sudden shift in tone. She didn't know what to do aside from stare at the man in the mirror. His hand dragged from her cheek down along her jaw. She felt her chin lift, inhaling, lungs filling with air as her body nearly betrayed her. It had involuntarily given him a signal to continue. A treacherous craving had wanted his hand to dip. It had been curious to see if it would graze her neck, her collarbone, settle on her throat.

She caught herself in the moment before she could find out. Ophir grabbed his forearm. Her mouth parted in horror. "Surely, you jest. Do you not realize who you're talking to? I'm the lone heir to Farehold. I'm the only surviving princess of Aubade. I don't care what you look at when you see me. Get out, you goddess-damned phantom."

She turned around to show him the conviction of her glare, but he used the motion to roll her hand so that she no longer gripped him. Her entire forearm was easily encircled in his hand. Under different circumstances she would have found the motion sexy. Instead, all she wanted was to punch him in the face. Perhaps she would have tried it if she hadn't been certain that he would have snatched her fist out of the air.

The corner of his mouth tugged in a crooked smile. "Are you kicking me out? Is that really the best way to express gratitude?"

Heat tingled in her palm as she prepared to call on her power. The only thing stopping her was the knowledge that this bastard had pulled her from the sea on the edges of unconsciousness and tended to her wounds.

"You're right," she said.

He raised a single, speculative eyebrow. "I like those words."

"I mean to say you're right: I'm not kicking you out."

His expression flickered. Taunting became caution as he studied her face. His hold slackened as he took a half step closer. "Good, because I'm not going anywhere. Your guard is right. Dwyn is remarkably unsavory. With her down the hall and Berinth on the loose, you'll be much better off—"

She broke free of his hand and cut him off by marching to the door.

"Ophir—"

She ignored her name on his lips as she limped for the hall. Her intentions were clear. He disappeared into the place between things—his final expression a look of duress—as she stormed down the hall.

Her guard jogged after her, releasing a gruff string of protests as she went directly to Dwyn's room, but she waved him away as if he were little more than a troublesome insect.

Ophir didn't bother knocking before twisting the knob and letting herself into Dwyn's room.

She would not be alone tonight.

TWENTY-ONE

* * * *

Amber hearth light coated the room like molasses, banishing shadows as it illuminated the room's occupant. Black button eyes looked at Ophir from a surprised face. Dwyn cocked her head to the side, curtain of hair falling over her shoulder. Her inky locks were the only thing obscuring her nakedness, as Dwyn reclined in her typical state of undress while paging through a leather-bound book from underneath the covers. A proper lady may have yanked the sheets up to cover her stomach and chest, but the princess had never known Dwyn to be proper.

Ophir shut the door quickly to ensure Tyr wouldn't be slipping in behind her. A discomfort pulsed through her the moment the latch clicked. She hoped her urgency to block out the phantom and the guard wouldn't come across as presumptuous. She leaned against the door as her face twisted in apology.

"I hope I'm not interrupting."

"No, no." Dwyn gestured tentatively for Ophir to join her on the bed. "Goddess, Firi, you look terrible. What happened?"

Rather than accept the bid to crawl onto the comfortable

mattress, she found solace in the straight, sturdy wood. It was unlike her to be nervous, but then again, she hadn't been herself in a long, long time. The temptation to let her eyes wander south, from the sculpt of Dwyn's neck and collarbones to her soft arms, the pillows of her breasts, the curve of her waist, or the gentle tummy that should have been beneath the blankets was strong, but she was careful to keep her eyes trained on Dwyn's face.

"Cat got your tongue?" Dwyn asked.

Ophir opened her mouth, then closed it again. Demonic serpent had her tongue, more like.

She was sure Harland was already repositioning himself outside of the room, cursing the princess for her obstinance. Truth be told, Ophir didn't care if Dwyn was the goddess-damned devil herself. Maybe she had let a demon into the castle—so what? The siren was kind, and she'd saved her life in more ways than one. If Tyr was telling the truth, and Dwyn was after some grand power by setting someone else up to take the fall while she survived, then she'd had the chance to do it to Ophir a thousand times over. Yet Dwyn had rescued her from the depths of the black seas, the fires of night terrors, and the powerlessness that had consumed her following her sister's death. Dwyn had shown her how strong she could be. If she had one ally in the castle, it was Dwyn.

If the siren truly was an evil bitch, perhaps they could be evil together. After all, Ophir had a long list of names and a bloodthirst that could not be quenched until every last one of them lay six feet under.

Perhaps it was her newfound respect for Dwyn's power that gave her pause. She'd experienced a number of contradictory emotions surrounding Dwyn, but never before had she been nervous. She attempted to swallow, but it was as if cotton filled her throat. "I don't really want to talk about it. I came to ask..."

Dwyn might have been an owl for how deeply she tilted her head as she waited in curious silence.

Goddess, why did she feel like a schoolboy who'd never spoken to a woman? Unique vulnerability prickled her spine as she struggled to ask for permission. Her lips twisted to the side as she fought to speak her mind. "Can I sleep in here tonight? …With you?" When Dwyn's brows lifted, Ophir added, "My nightmares aren't so bad when I'm next to you."

The tension softened, though Dwyn's eyes remained wide. She lifted the sheets to extend the invitation. Her voice was a soft lullaby as she answered. "Of course, you can."

Ophir's heart squeezed as she stared at the open space on the silken sheets. Her eyes flitted to the hand that lifted the duvet, then dragged her gaze slowly over her arm, her body, her face.

"Oh," Dwyn said softly.

Ophir's pulse skipped painfully as she shrugged out of her robe. It puddled at her feet to reveal that, aside from the bandages, she was similarly nude. She fought to swallow once more against nerves. She slipped beneath the sheets, holding her breath as she folded herself against Dwyn's soft curves. She draped her arm over the fae, forearm settling against her sternum, luxuriating in the warmth between her soft breasts. The exhilarating, wintery rush of mint splashed over her as she inhaled Dwyn's scent.

The urge to cry surprised her as a knot formed in her throat. She hadn't realized just how touch starved she'd been until someone was in her arms. Yet, the answering emotion wasn't sorrow. She'd survived the worst thing that could have befallen her. Her night terrors were steadily lessening. She was healing. And for the first time in a long time, she tasted the distant memory of what it had been like to feel powerful.

"Are you tired?" came Dwyn's whisper.

Yes. No. She didn't know.

She'd come to Dwyn's room with a need to escape Harland's oppressive shadow. She'd needed freedom from Tyr's strange imposition. She'd wanted to be free and had only seen one path forward in taking control. Whether it had been sleep, or friendship, or something else entirely, Ophir didn't care.

She inhaled deeply and smelled something beneath the mint. There was the warmth of body heat, yes. There was the honey and almond soaps and fresh silk sheets and small, homey smoke from the fireplace. But there was something more. Something deeper.

A curl in her stomach blossomed. Blood pumped through the bloom within. A distant, unanticipated throb began to speak to a deeply buried part of her.

They'd been naked together before.

Dwyn had held her in the sea, had gripped at her skin on the beach, and had intertwined with her in the sudsy waters of the bath. The siren had made no efforts to portray modesty under any circumstance. If anything, the Sulgrave fae had done everything to make nudity sexless as she'd desensitized the princess to its presence. She'd stepped out of her clothes and crawled under the covers on more than one occasion, pressing her body into the princess night after night before they'd been separated. She'd draped an arm around Ophir and her flames, holding her slim body, breathing in the gold-brown tufts of her hair, musing as to how the princess always smelled of sunlight.

Tonight was different.

Dwyn's body stilled in her arms as if she'd stopped breathing altogether. Ophir's heart quickened.

In a world before this amalgamation of terrors, the princess had kissed boys and shared stolen kisses with girls, but she'd never fully been with a woman in the ways that clandestine diaries of so-called unsavory women enjoyed sharing. She'd locked lips in opium dens and traded flavors on tongues as wine had flowed freely. It had always been the sort of thing she could excuse to the drug or drink. Perhaps that's what had prevented her from allowing her eyes to linger on Dwyn for too long.

"I'd like…" She tried a sentence and failed.

The siren arched her back ever so slightly. "What would you like?"

"Only if you would…"

Dwyn's voice dropped a register. "I want to hear it."

A vindictive thought rolled around on her tongue before she spoke. Harland hated Dwyn, and Tyr seemed to want to kill her, and Ophir felt a rather headstrong delight at the idea of pissing both of them off in one fell swoop. The men who'd forced their way into her life had no say in how she lived or what she did with her time. She was no child. The things she did and the company she kept were hers and her choices to make. This was truer than ever as her world turned to ash around her.

"I'd like…to feel good. For one night."

Ophir pressed her body into Dwyn's with intent. Her mouth hovered just above the back of the delicate neck in front of her, savoring the goose bumps that rippled down her in response to her breath.

"So would I," Dwyn breathed.

"Dwyn?" The name was spoken on a hope. She dragged her hand where it rested, moving in slow lines up and down the vertical cut that separated Dwyn's middle from her breasts to her navel. Each excruciatingly slow touch summoned more intrigue, more curiosity, more longing. She tantalized the woman's inner thighs, brushing over her stomach, nearing her most sensitive places, growing closer with each daring pass. Dwyn's hips responded to move against the princess's fingers, grinding slightly against her. She allowed the strokes to continue, body rocking with the slow, delicious movements as desire swelled between them.

"Yes, Firi?" she gasped in return.

The hummingbird thrum of the siren's heart mirrored her own.

"Tell me to stop."

"No," Dwyn was quick to respond, still facing away as her body stretched beneath the princess's curves. "I don't want you to stop."

The gentle hand swept up, circling Dwyn's breast before cupping it gently, moving it in a soft, massaging motion before encompassing the other in her the cool grasp of her palm. By the time the princess's fingers moved to explore lower, Dwyn was as soaked as the water she summoned. She twisted beneath the sheets, lifting a knee and locking it over the princess's hips. She pulled her in close. Their lips parted, mouths meeting in sweet pleas as they drank one another in.

"Just for tonight—"

"Shh," the siren hushed, reaching behind herself and wrapping her fingers in the toffee mess of Ophir's hair. Their eyes fluttered closed as their bodies moved, curves and flesh of two perfectly fitting spoons as Ophir continued her steady, pleasurable movements.

Dwyn gasped an honest, sharp inhalation as one finger, then another slipped within her.

Everything began with the gradual slowness of shy, new lovers, before building into the frenzied dance of fingers digging into flesh, mouths against soft, beautiful parts, the pull of hair, the taste of sunshine and honey. They were lost in the maze of tongues, teeth, flesh, throats, shoulders, fingers, breasts, navels, hips, thighs, and toes. Every inch was explored with inhalations, breaths, and the soft escape of involuntary moans. Every sensation dragged out to beautiful, sensual, gasping resolution. Each movement matched the gentle undulation of hips as pleasure flowed between them. Comfort, passion, heat, and release were one in the same as they held one another.

For a moment, Ophir nearly remembered what it meant to feel alive.

Dwyn's back arched, her hips rocking rhythmically with each pump, each soaking, satisfying movement. Her fingers knotted in the cloud of toffee hair behind her as Ophir brought her closer and closer to the edge. It was the tide lapping against the seaside rocks, every intense wave coming in sharper and louder and higher as the ocean rose and rose and rose. Dwyn's breathing hitched, each inhalation growing shallower and faster as she approached the precipice. Her entire body went rigid, back curved, hips locked, toes curled as she released a high, involuntary whimper in the seconds before she shuddered, entire body flexing and collapsing with her climax.

Dwyn let out a nearly feline purr as she rolled in true delight. Rather than being exhausted, she seemed invigorated in the moments following her orgasm. Ophir scarcely had the time to slip her fingers out of the siren before Dwyn flipped the princess onto her back.

"Do you taste like sunshine, too?" The red glow of embers in the dying hearth lit the room in shades of shadow and burgundy. She purred, tracing a scorching path of sensual kisses down Ophir's middle. The wet evidence of her kisses and licks reflected against what remained of the dim, reddish light. She dragged her fingernails on a path from her chest, down her stomach, and clamped them onto her inner thigh.

"Don't stop" was all Ophir needed to say.

The hour hand dropped two places on the grandfather clock between their earliest touches and the end of their exhausted pulls for air against the bed, holding each other, gripping their pillows, pools of pleasure soaking the sheets.

Hair mussed, mouths soaked, bodies tired, flesh tingling, smelling of sex and joy and forbidden desire, their needs for affection had been satiated. Their hearts passed for full, even if the bandages that held them together were a patchwork for whatever greater pain, whatever larger horror haunted them. Tonight was about escape within the four walls of a bedroom. For one night, Ophir was liberated without going anywhere. She was free.

She caught Dwyn's satisfied smile in the afterglow just before the coals winked out into blackness. Just as the beautiful woman nestled into her arms and made the contented sound of someone truly happy, Ophir's returning smile faltered. Sleep took Dwyn beneath its waves, leaving Ophir alone in the dark as the emptiness returned.

TWENTY-TWO

*   *   *   *

OPHIR HAD BEEN AWAKE FOR THE BETTER PART OF AN HOUR before Dwyn poked her head up from the sheets. She rubbed her eyes, stretching as she searched the room for the princess. Ophir sat at the writing desk, leg bouncing as she stared at the same boring tome Dwyn had been reading the night prior. The princess's jittering muscles stilled the moment Dwyn caught her eye.

"Come back to bed." Dwyn yawned.

"I'm ready to do something, and I'm going to need your help."

Dwyn pouted. "Before tea?"

On an exhale, Ophir asked, "You've wanted me to change my sorrow into anger? I've succeeded. I'm furious. You've wanted me to manifest? I've now accomplished it on more than one occasion. I don't know your motives, but if you help me with my agenda, then honestly, I don't care. We can burn down the world together. I just need you to be with me on something first."

"No tea then." Dwyn's lashes fluttered as she absorbed the information. She straightened her posture and ran her hands through her hair while considering Ophir's words. In only a few short sentences, Ophir had made it clear that she suspected Dwyn of ulterior motives on multiple fronts. She'd also kept her tone casual enough to convey that she was pretty damn comfortable with it.

Perhaps Dwyn could have denied it, or interrogated her to ask Ophir what she meant, but she didn't. After the surprise passed, Dwyn nodded. "Name it."

Ophir planted her hands on the bed where she stood and leaned forward with grave seriousness. "Help me kill the men who murdered my sister."

A slow smile spread across her face. "I thought you'd never ask."

"There's one more thing," Ophir began.

Dwyn's body tensed in anticipatory silence.

"Who's Tyr?"

+   +   +   +

Ophir chose her steps carefully in an attempt to evade Harland. The cold, stone floor leached into her bare feet as she maneuvered down the corridor in the flimsy, white material of a nightdress that scarcely grazed the tops of her thighs. She'd borrowed the indecent silky fabric from the clothes provided in Dwyn's armoire—sleeping clothes that the siren had never touched.

She didn't make it far.

Harland was waiting for her. Her guard was stationed at the first intersection when she rounded the corner, so no matter where she'd tried to go, he'd intercept her. He frowned at her state of undress briefly before his expression tightened. "Ophir—"

She brushed past him without turning her head. She had no patience for his opinion on her choices. "Save it."

"Princess Ophir, stop."

She hesitated at his use of her true title. It was too formal. Almost as if he were a proper royal guard.

"King Eero and Queen Darya have requested your company, Princess Ophir. I'm to escort you to the war room immediately. Please, get changed." His voice was unusually strained as he spoke. She was unnerved by his usage of their formal names, feeling the unfamiliar language slither down her spine with an upsetting chill.

She paused mid-step on the rug that ran down the center of the corridor. She turned partway over her shoulder. "My parents?" Her back went rigid. "Do you know what this is about?"

He said nothing. She searched the curve of his hard jaw, the way his tendons seemed too tense in his neck, the way his brow faced off to the side rather than looking directly to her. Harland wasn't meeting her gaze. His face appeared unnatural, as it was so rarely this uneasy.

His silence drove her to an uncomfortable edge. She turned on the corridor's carpet runner to look at him. She didn't care how thin or short her silky nightdress might be. He'd seen her in far more revealing states of undress as the one who'd run into her room as she'd burned her bed to ashes and embers night after night.

"Harland? Do you know why?"

She could have been mistaken, but there was something pained about the way he nearly flinched at her question. "Please, dress and let's go."

She tried to prod him for more, but he shut his eyes as if to conceal whatever it was that his gaze might communicate. Nerves made it nearly impossible to perform grooming tasks as she left Harland in the hall for the few moments it took her to run a brush through her hair and find a dress. Ophir's bruises were almost invisible now, particularly as she'd dusted a bit of coverage on her eyes and cheekbones to help blend the evidence of her brush with death. She wore a crimson dress in Farehold colors for the late fall day. It was long enough to conceal her bandages and any other visible wounds quite well. Her pulse became painful as she stepped into her clothes. Her hands trembled as she attempted to weave her loose, gold-brown strands into a single braid.

She emerged from her room but didn't step a foot beyond the doorway. "Please, tell me."

He shook his head once. It was a single denial through the sideways motion of his chin to tell her that no, he could not say what needed to be said.

She knew in that moment that nothing good awaited her.

Ophir resisted the urge to plead with him and instead lifted her chin and straightened her shoulders. They walked forward like an executioner and his charge making their way to the gallows. There was pain on his face as he walked her down the beige corridor, nearly silent as their feet padded against the red runner that lined the hall. The castle normally hummed with Farehold's reds and golds, from the neutrals of its stones to the crimson of its curtains and carpets to the very color of the eyes of Eero and his youngest daughter. Today, the attendants moved like sodden corpses—little more than neutral stones come to life, the browns and beiges of their linens breaking the scarlet of the fabrics that accented the castle.

This was not the first time she'd been to the war room. It was, however, the first time she'd been summoned without notice.

Harland's silence exacerbated her anxiety thousand fold If only he would look at her. If he would turn his stupid head and just meet her desperation. But he gave her nothing. Maybe they knew each other too well. Surely, he'd break if he looked at her, and they both knew it.

They mounted the several flights of stairs in the winding tower that led to the space typically reserved for generals, diplomats, and meetings. Harland's eyes touched hers briefly, his hazel gaze pained as he grazed over her golden, pleading questions. He opened the door for her once they reached the top of the tower, but he did not enter. He bowed to the king and queen and took his post outside to wait, closing the door behind him.

Ophir hesitated at the entry. The war room was in the

backmost circular tower on one of the castle's four posts. It curved with the same yellow-brown stones and cream mortar that filled the rest of the castle. They were toward the top of the tower so that the sun could fill the space with warm, cheery light without anyone worrying about their maps or plans being seen or intercepted by prying eyes.

"Mother, Father." She nodded at them, dread swelling as she spied the worry on her mother's face. "What is this about?"

"Sit, love," the queen motioned. Her face was controlled in a way that served to deepen her anxiety.

Caris and Queen Darya could have been sisters, they looked so alike. Ophir saw Caris's face in every line and curve of her mother's features, from the scoop of her nose to the arch of her brow. Even Darya's voice was too familiar. Their resemblance was another in a long line of piercing wounds that reminded Ophir as to why she spent so little time with the queen.

She needed more distance than even the walls' corners and tilts and floors of the castle could offer. No stones would be thick enough for the separation required from her pain. The ageless fae exchanged looks and waited for their daughter to take the chair across from them. The map of the continent stretched between them. Something continued to stick in her throat as she eyed her parents.

The queen had the same wet-earth smell that had been Caris's signature perfume. Between her blue eyes, the scent of rain, and her cascading, golden hair, Ophir could scarcely stand to be around her mother. Her voice was gentle as she broke the uncomfortable silence. "There's no easy way to say what must be said. We understand that this will be difficult to hear."

Ophir wanted to feel something else, but only one emotion came to her forefront. Anxiety burned from her stomach to her throat. "Please, just tell me what's happening."

Her father's face was stern. The golden burn of his irises

was as royal as the crown on his head. She'd received her honey eyes from him, and in this moment, they were not kind. He did his best to sound emotionless as he delivered cold, impassive news to his daughter.

"The marriage union between Farehold and Raascot must continue as planned. Caris was promised to Ceneth at birth for the good of the continent. The intent to bring our two sovereign kingdoms together has not changed. In three months, you'll be wed and relocated to Gwydir, where you'll be expected to produce heirs who will rule a single, unified kingdom."

No.

There was a strange, spinning sensation. She was quite certain she'd hallucinated, or misheard, or dreamed the words that had come out of this cold, dispassionate man.

Ophir's mouth hung open, tongue paper-dry. She wasn't sure if she had blinked a single time as the king had spoken. "I'm not seventy-five."

A ceaseless onslaught of horrors assaulted her, and of all the injustices, this was the only thing she could think to say.

"Caris was," her father said, no emotion in his tone. He amended, "Would have been, I mean. The marriage was set for this year. It is time."

She couldn't believe what she was hearing. He spoke like a man discussing the inevitability of taxes. This was not a father who loved his children. This was no man at all.

Her mother attempted to soothe her. "A true utopia is at stake, Ophir. Ceneth and Caris have spent decades in phase one of their plan, but it's all meaningless if we don't reach the second stage. Separation was a temporary relief from immediate violence or threat to the fae's survival. The separation of humans and fae—the discrimination of powers—will make matters worse if things don't move forward. Plans for a borderless kingdom have been in the works since before either of you was born. In the event of..." Her words drifted off. She couldn't bring herself to reference Caris's death. "We waited for as long as we could before telling you. But now that you seem to be getting better..."

Unity could not be chopped in one fell swoop of an axe. The trunk of this complicated tree was thick. The cuts required to fell preconceived notions and rebuild the continent would be no small task. Caris had known this, and her passion overrode any fear of the challenge. Ophir saw it, and...

"I can't marry Ceneth," she said. She tried to swallow again past the knot that continued rising in her throat but found she could not push down the hardened lump of emotion. She remained perfectly still, perfectly calm, though she'd nearly ceased breathing. A monotonous, high-pitched ringing began to sound in the space between her ears as a headache born of oxygen deprivation sang its painful song. She inhaled slowly through her nose, but the ringing did not go away.

"Duty calls to you, Ophir," her father said coolly.

The queen's face rearranged in a complicated stitch of downward motions as she absorbed her daughter, from the shock of her face to the rigidity of her posture. She attempted levity despite her frown, but it did not reach her blue eyes. They were the same bright blue that her eldest princess had inherited. "A winter wedding will be lovely. We'll decorate the castle with Yule trees and fill the halls with fae lights. We can serve whatever you want at the banquet. You used to love those cranberry tarts, didn't you? Cranberry is so festive around the winter holidays. We'll get a lovely stag. We can serve mugs of warm liqueur and lovely little Yule garnishes for every guest. Wouldn't that be nice? I think it could look rather charming. Oh and the pine—of course we'll cut fresh pine. It'll smell divine. We'll have Ceneth bring it down with him from the northern kingdom. The whole hall will be filled with the scent of pine."

She'd been punched in the gut by invisible hands. "You think...you think I'm worried about what food will be served? You want...pine? You want to talk to me about decorations?"

"Ophir," came her father's exasperation. "This is not a matter for discussion. It's my own fault for allowing so much time to pass on Caris's shoulders. We did not prepare you. You were not groomed to take over, and I rest that blame on my shoulders. The fact remains: being born into the monarchy comes with certain obligations. Ceneth is a good man—"

"Does he know about this?" Ophir's question sounded strangled. She wasn't totally convinced hands weren't gripping her throat as she spit out her words. "He was in love with Caris. He truly loved her. He *tolerated* me. Is Raascot's king aware that you're planning to swap us out as if he won't notice?" Every word came out higher and angrier than the one before. She braced her hands against the table, barely clutching sanity.

Darya attempted to reach across the table to comfort her daughter, but Ophir jerked her hands away as if her mother were no more than the very snake she'd summoned.

"Yes, he knows. A love match would have been fortuitous, but, you have to understand, love matches are rare." She tried to soften her expression. "A political arrangement was inevitable. Ceneth did ask if you'd like to see him to speak about anything before the wedding. I told him I'd send a raven with your response."

If she didn't find a way to choke down the knot in her throat, she was pretty sure she was going to throw it up. Her stomach churned violently as she picked through the words. "To be clear—you are asking if I want to talk to Ceneth or if I just want to wait until we're at the end of the aisle and he's lifting my veil before I see him? You're asking if I want to meet the man who's in love with my dead sister before we're wed?" She looked between her parents. "This is absurd. You see how insane this is, don't you?"

"Please try to be reasonable," Darya sighed.

Her mouth opened and closed wordlessly like a fish lofted above the water. "I can't. I won't."

The king slammed his fist and the women closed their eyes tightly against the sudden impact, resisting the painful urge to flinch. Eero rarely showed outbursts of emotions. He was a stoic man, making his anger all the more violent in the wake of their pain. Ophir's lips tightened into a hard line.

The king's voice held no kindness as he spoke a cold truth. "You can and you will, Ophir. Your days of parading around the city are over. It is time for you to live up to your responsibilities. Your sister took up the burden for the kingdom, but she isn't here any longer. If you can't agree to it willingly, I'll see to it that Harland has your rooms closely guarded if you pose any risk of leaving the castle. I'll have fifty men stationed outside of your chambers if that's what it takes to keep you in line."

She searched him for any trace of leniency, of compassion. She stared at the anger etched into her father's face, allowing his resolve to chip at hers like a pickax over ice. "So that's that, then. There's nothing more to say."

She searched his face for a sign of hope, of benevolence, of grace, but found none. The man nodded once in confirmation and relaxed the fist that had been flexed against the table until his palm was flattened. He leaned back ever so slightly into his chair as he waited for any further reaction to come from his child.

The pause stretched into a pregnant silence. The room began to ring with the same high, dizzying sound that only occurred between one's ears. Ophir fell into a deathly calm, folding her hands in her lap as she looked from one parent to the other.

"Fine."

The monarchs sat rigidly as they eyed her.

"I understand," she continued, voice as blank as her expression.

They watched her, tensed with suspicion.

"I'll stay in my rooms."

"You're...you're okay, with everything?" Her mother's blue eyes clouded with worry. They looked too much like Caris's, save for the gentle concern her sister's would have shown. Ophir couldn't meet the intricate shades of robin's egg, deep sea, sky, and gems she saw when she looked at Darya. She hated her mother's eyes.

"No." Ophir's answer was honest enough to assure them she was not intentionally deceitful. "Of course I'm not okay with it. But I'm the heir to Farehold. Raascot is our ally. I don't have to be okay with it to understand the law of the land—the obligations of Gyrradin."

Her mother inhaled sharply through her nose. Something about the way Ophir had cooled so quickly unnerved her. "I know this isn't easy, sweet girl. I'm so sorry to have to tell you in this way. Will you tell us if there's anything you need? Let us know if there's something that will make this transition easier?"

"Yes, I'll do that."

She wasn't surprised at their shared apprehension. They'd undoubtedly expected her to put up more of a fight.

"I'll keep Dwyn with me as a handmaid—for the nightmares. The fire...her water..."

Eero and Darya nodded with clear discomfort. Whether Ophir lived in Aubade or Gwydir, her flame would pose a threat to any who dared lie beside her. No answer aside from a water-summoner had presented itself.

"Are you okay?" her mother asked again, ocean eyes prodding.

"Not even a little bit," she answered honestly. The pregnant pause filled the room before she spoke again. "I haven't been okay since Caris died. Why should it be any different now?"

TWENTY-THREE

* * * *

Her room was a flurry of motion. Ophir held up her middle finger at the closed door the moment Harland locked it behind her. He remained in the hall like an ever-vigilant prison guard trapping her in her cell. The only reprieve she'd been granted was the reasonable request for a handmaiden who could quell her fire. Of course, handmaidens were usually demure ladies of fine breeding and modest clothing. Dwyn, in her daring black velvet dress with a plunging neckline and slit that ran up her hip, was anything but.

"I'm so sorry, Firi." The look of pain on her face made Ophir think Dwyn really meant it.

"I'm only going to ask you one question, and I need you to answer honestly," Ophir replied. She grabbed a leather satchel and began throwing things in it. She yanked any articles of clothing that were muted enough to pass as a commoner's outfits from their various drawers and hanging places, a metallic water flask, and the sharp dagger she'd hidden under her bed long ago. The decorative elements of her room were a blur around her. She wouldn't need beauty or comforts with what she had in mind.

Dwyn's head moved side to side as the princess darted

around the space, almost like a cat watching a caged bird. "Ask it."

Ophir paused to look at the siren, and without any inflection, she asked, "Do you intend to kill me?"

The siren made a face between disgust and bewilderment. "What?"

"Whatever you need me for—whatever brought you to Aubade—I don't care. I don't care why you're here. I don't care why you need me, why you saved me, or why you wanted me to create a snake. I don't care if it's blood magic. I just...I don't care. But I was there. I saw what they did to Caris's body." Ophir became statuesque in her stillness. "I saw how Caris had been cut open and... Dwyn, you've been my friend, and so far you've done more good than harm. This is my only question: do you need to murder me for my organs or whatever it is about royal blood that supposedly lured you here in the first place?"

Dwyn covered her mouth as she drew a sharp breath. Her voice dripped with genuine horror as she said, "Goddess, no."

"Great." Ophir nodded. She shouldered the pack she'd been gathering, then dragged a chair across the room, pinning it against the door to keep Harland out.

If they left now, no one would know they were missing until dinner.

Harland was right, after all. Ophir did pose the greatest threat to her own safety.

If she stayed in the castle, she could get married off to the northern king and live a perfectly safe life, safely dressed in dresses and jewels, safely guarded by armies, safely kept behind shut doors and high walls and moats and borders. Harland was right in one other thing as well: she would have to cut him out. If she was going to succeed, he could not come.

"Let's go." Ophir pushed against the mirror just as Tyr stepped out of the space between things. In addition to his dry expression of disapproval, she noted the clean male clothes he wore that had probably belonged to one of her guards. She spied the tattoo that crawled from his arm to the space over his shoulder and licked the base of his neck, then cast a quick glance to the lines of black ink that peeked through the slit in Dwyn's dress. She wondered if such markings were common among all Sulgrave people but decided it was neither the time nor the place.

Dwyn glared. "What the fuck are you doing here?"

He leaned against the stone wall and ignored Ophir to address Dwyn directly. "I told you to stay away from the princess. You're as bad at listening to instructions as she is."

Ophir wanted to be angry over Tyr's constant invasion of privacy, but she'd have to find time for her emotions later. "Fine. Let's all be bad at listening to instructions together. Are you in, phantom, or are you out?"

Tyr looked between the women as if considering his options. She knew he could yell for her guard, though then he'd have to explain why he was in the room. She dared him to make a move.

The threat lingered between them until at last, he said, "I guess I'm in."

Ophir eased open the mirror without waiting for an answer. She'd had one foot on the staircase beyond the hidden space before the words had left his mouth.

+ + + +

Ophir knew that in a few hours, Harland would check on her only to find her door barricaded by the chair. He'd undoubtedly bust the door down, crumbling the chair beneath it, causing enough noise for other guards in the castle to be alerted to the disturbance and call for aid. They'd search her rooms, but they'd find nothing. Rumors had spread over the years that Ophir might possess the ability to step through walls, though she'd never admitted to any such power. She'd also never dispelled this gossip, preferring to wink anytime someone mentioned that she was a being with multidimensional abilities. Her parents would be informed of her escape, and the entire kingdom would be on high alert. Guards and constables and citizens would be rallied to search for the missing princess. Everyone in the kingdom would be desperate to find the last hope of Farehold.

But their efforts would come too late.

She was gone.

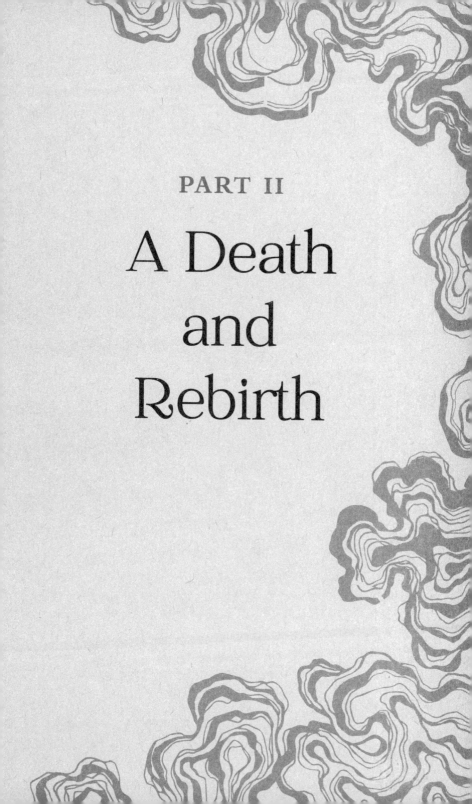

PART II

A Death
and
Rebirth

TWENTY-FOUR

+   +   +   +

MURDER IS BOTH ART AND SCIENCE.

Of course, one must consider the technicalities of homicide—the who, what, when, where, and how required diligence, patience, and intelligence. The "why" was a given, at least for Ophir. The men at Lord Berinth's had worn masks that night, but she'd seen the angles of their jaws, the colors of their irises, the wicked curves of their mouths, the bodies and clothes of the men who had stood in the room while Caris was bound, stripped, humiliated, and gutted like a pig.

Killing is easy.

Vengeance is hard.

To properly avenge someone, the killer would let the target know why they no longer deserved the air they breathed. A certain understanding by the dying was required for justice to be satisfied. Poison is too slow, too impersonal. She thought of beheadings as a royal cliché but liked the stage and audience that a guillotine demanded. The same could be said of many popular modes of execution. She found herself with an abundance of choices on the matter of murder.

Retribution required fear, knowledge, and poetry.

Every man needed to understand why he was hunted. The

comprehension in their eyes would be an essential component. She wanted to witness the twinkle of justice before their life was extinguished with the slow smothering of a cap over flame. The artistry of the act…well, that was where true brilliance was required.

Ophir would be an artist.

TWENTY-FIVE

+   +   +   +

HATE WAS A FUNNY THING IN HOW OFTEN IT BLURRED LINES with love.

It had been just under a month since Tyr had stormed after his watery nemesis and the princess he'd been roped into keeping alive. And goddess, was she difficult to keep alive. From the moment he met her, she'd been at a party where she didn't belong surrounded by people who quite literally wanted to slice her open and scoop out the very parts that kept her alive. Since his hunt for Dwyn had forced him back into Ophir's path, she'd nearly burned the castle down, she'd tried to die at the ocean's hand on more than one occasion, she'd created numerous terrifying serpents, and she'd aligned herself with the most dangerous murderer of all.

His resentment for the princess should have mirrored his loathing for Dwyn.

If anything, he should have been angrier with Ophir for dragging Dwyn—and him by extension—south, to a kingdom so ignorant that it seemed criminal to allow them to maintain their seats on a throne.

And yet...

He stared ahead at the women who walked arm in arm,

sidestepping the trunks and dodging the branches that dangled in their path. Dwyn swatted a rust-colored leaf as if it were an attacking hornet. They'd been locked in what felt like ceaseless conversation for weeks on end. The two never ran out of things to talk about, and fuck did he hate it.

He cast a glance to the road that ran parallel to their hiding place in the forest. A peasant and his mule pulled a wooden cart full of freshly reaped wheat en route to Aubade. They kept to the forest, should a member of the king's guard or a lone knight meet them on the regency's road, but for weeks on end, they'd subjected themselves to exposed roots and mud puddles and untraveled paths for nothing. Of course, he knew the law of luck well enough to understand that the moment they stepped foot from the trees, they'd undoubtedly come upon a legion of soldiers and be forced back to the castle in chains.

Dwyn wanted very much for the women to continue on their own, but for once, it was Tyr who knew something she didn't.

"He was at the party," Ophir had said.

"So? We can get the information we need without him."

"Absolutely not," Ophir had argued. "It was you who told me to crave vengeance. The lone reason my heart continues beating is my need to see the death of every last man who took Caris from me."

Dwyn had made a show of her displeasure. She'd thrown up her hands. "And *Tyr* is who you want to trust with this mission?"

"He was there," Ophir repeated. "He saved me that night."

"I saved you," she argued.

"You saved me in the ocean. He saw Berinth. He spoke with the men. He knows their faces. He has the list."

Dwyn had jutted an accusatory finger at him as if she were brandishing a knife. "If he were a true friend, he'd give you the list in its entirety right now."

That one had stung. He and Ophir had exchanged the

long, broken stalemate looks of two people who knew they were out of options.

Ophir defended him. "He's giving us one name at a time because as soon as we have the whole list, you'll get rid of him."

"Exactly!" Dwyn's fingers twitched as if to grab the princess by the shoulders and shake her.

And while it wasn't a satisfying arrangement by any means, it told him one good thing.

Ophir had listened to him.

She certainly didn't act like someone who distrusted Dwyn, and yet, she must have truly heard him the night he'd rescued her from being bashed against the seaside cliffs. She must have believed him when he'd carried her to her room, healed her, and explained that Dwyn was not her friend. As much as Ophir loved Dwyn, some piece of her, however small, trusted that Tyr had not been lying.

And so, he was allowed to stay.

But by the goddess, the princess was infuriating. She was stubborn, she wielded untamed powers, she refused to listen to reason, and she'd chosen Dwyn—*Dwyn!*—of all people as bedmate and confidant. If it had simply been sex, he might have understood. Everyone needed a good hate fucking now and then. But he didn't miss the way the women's hands brushed, the way they giggled, their shared jokes, or the easy way their bodies fit together night after night as they fell asleep beside one another. His lip pulled back in a sneer as he thought of what an inferior partner Dwyn was. Ophir would feel safer in his arms. If he held her, it wouldn't be with lies and bloodstained hands. If it was him in her bed…

"Where's the dog?"

His head popped up at the way the bitch referred to him. Dwyn continued her forward stride as if she weren't the most offensive woman alive, but Ophir looked over her shoulder to ensure he was still behind them. She offered an apologetic shrug when they locked eyes, and he hated how his anger

205

deflated at the barest of looks from the princess. His eyes softened, mouth moving to the side to offer the returning shrug that his shoulders refused to do.

"He's with us, Dwyn," Ophir chided softly. "We could use the muscle."

"We can handle ourselves just fine," Dwyn said. "Especially with the things you've made! Everything you create gets better and better, Firi. You're magnificent. Soon you'll have a menagerie to do your bidding."

"We're on the same side," Ophir said definitively. She cast another backward glance at Tyr, then one into the deepest part of the woods, as if searching for a trace of her manifestations amidst the brush. "All of us."

They'd carry on together until they found the first name he'd provided: Guryon, a spice merchant, and the very man who'd provided the surgical tools the men had needed for Caris's execution. However, if they had to spend another night beside campfires and counting the stars that peeked between rustling, autumn leaves, he might bow out of the blood race and abandon the women just to sleep in a bed without their goddess-damned giggles, their stifled gasps, the quiet moans, and the countless things they did at night thinking he couldn't hear every single beat of Ophir's heart.

He'd stay with them.

He'd keep Ophir safe, despite how ardently she tried to dance with death.

He'd learn how Dwyn had circumvented the fatal laws of blood magic.

And then he'd bind Dwyn's wrists with iron and leave her at the bottom of the sea. Her siren's proclivity for water would allow her to keep living and breathing, but with any luck, no one would see or hear from the evil bitch for a thousand years.

TWENTY-SIX

✦ ✦ ✦ ✦

H USH, YOU'RE UPSETTING HIM."
    "Him?" Tyr's word was a single, bewildered cough.
It was mingled with humor, as though he hadn't quite learned
to master his emotions.

Ophir hadn't missed how Tyr hadn't looked at her since her
so-called abomination had curled up to her near the fireplace
like any natural-born hound. Instead, he'd made several
grumbling comments about how the last remaining princess
of Farehold cuddled the monster she'd conjured from the pits
of her nightmares. It may have resembled a canine, he'd said
to the room, though its froglike skin refracted shades of black
and gray. She didn't care how he looked. Her creature seemed
perfectly content to lean into the strokes of its mother's touch
as she ran her fingers along its head, just like all dogs enjoyed
the pats of their masters.

Ophir smirked at Tyr's tone. His rough agitation over her
beasts had been a reliable source of banter. It was soothing, in
a way. She could count on his pushback as confidently as one
knew the sun rose and set each day. She looked at him with
challenge in her eyes, and he winked.

Ophir's cheeks heated as she turned away.

He'd gotten very, very good at making her blush.

Tyr was devilishly good-looking, tenacious to a fault, and knew precisely how to get under her skin. The only thing worse than his ability to get a rise out of her was the level of enjoyment she got out of it. She returned her gaze to her perfect pet.

"Sedit is a good boy, aren't you, Sedit?" Ophir slicked her hand along the smooth skin of her canine-adjacent creation. Its black eyes were the large, black beads of nightmares, dotted with three smaller eyes beneath each of its individual orbs. He was as much spider as he was dog, or cat, or demon. "Though I do wish he smelled better. We'll work on that, won't we?" She smiled at her animal.

"I just don't like it around Knight."

"His name is Sedit, and he's a good boy, not an 'it.'"

Dwyn looked up from where she'd been cutting her nails with a sharpened knife. "And how are we spelling your new baby's name? S-E-D-E-T-T-E?"

"I-T," Ophir corrected.

"That should be Said-it," Tyr mumbled.

Dwyn's sigh was for show. "Are you implying she spelled her own creation's name wrong?"

"There are numerous things wrong with it." Tyr grimaced. "Like if Sait-it gets hungry."

Dwyn rolled her eyes. "His name is pronounced Sed-ETTE, and he is a more welcome member of this party than you are. Besides, how long have you had that horse? You've only been in Farehold for a few months. You're acting like it's your damn child."

"You *would* hate animals, psychopath," Tyr scowled.

"Please, give us a reason to kick you out," Dwyn said. "Take your stupid horse with you. We'll get new ones at the next farm we find. Off you go."

Sedit snuggled in closer, warming Ophir's heart. She didn't look away from her sweet angel as she chided the pair. "Don't be territorial, Dwyn. You and I both know that Tyr's abilities are indispensable."

Tyr walked over to where the women rested. He leaned on the back of the couch and placed his hands against the sofa's back, spreading his arms behind the princess. Heat spread through her body at his nearness as he said, "Then, you don't want me to leave, princess?"

She choked down the spike of nerves that lodged in her throat the moment he brushed his lips against her ear. "Maybe I do," she said somewhat unconvincingly. "Leave us be."

He chuckled, lowering his mouth even closer to her ear. "You know, you have a tell. I know when you're lying." Tyr stood from where he'd bent over the couch and watched as pink flushed her entire body. He returned to where he'd lounged against the wall, leaving Ophir to wonder if he took pleasure in the way she squirmed.

As the weeks bled on, Dwyn and Tyr did very little to conceal their competition for Ophir's affections. Ophir enjoyed the attention and leaned into the opportunity for flirtation but found very little time to think of anything other than her plans for revenge.

Tyr made no attempt to conceal his dominant brand of affection, though Ophir knew he did it just as much to antagonize Dwyn as he did as any real attempt to seduce her. She didn't mind any of it—the graze of his rough hands on her hips as he moved behind her, the smell of campfire smoke and leather when he was near her, the unflinching way in which he'd hold her gaze, heavy with intent. Ophir had always enjoyed the release of sex and the clarity that came from a good tumble, but unless Dwyn and Tyr wanted to put aside their differences long enough to join her in the bedroom, she was quite certain she wouldn't be able to truly indulge while she traveled with the pair.

Tyr's primary failure to flirt came with his feelings on Ophir's hellish beasts. He struggled to conceal his displeasure as everything she created seemed birthed directly from the nightmares that so often stirred her from sleep. They learned the hard way that if she wasn't being tightly held each night, they'd be awoken past the midnight hour with a burst of flame.

He'd stated that he didn't see why those night terrors needed to spill out into the physical world. The hound at her feet had peeled back its dark lips at him as if it understood his disapproval, baring its rows of needle-like teeth. Maybe this was part of what made Tyr feel the recurrent need to pull the princess close to him. Perhaps she needed to feel safe so badly that her powers were creating an army of monstrosities just to surround her. Each new layer she revealed about the depths of her pain resulted in a domino cascade of reactions from her companions. Tyr wanted to hold her—he'd said as much. To help. To strip away whatever trauma revealed itself as many-fanged feline-dogs with too many eyes and froglike skin. No one should have to suffer what she had endured.

Maybe someday she'd make something less twisted.

Dwyn, on the other hand, encouraged every feat of manifestation. She'd celebrated each snake, creature, and abomination that Ophir had brought forth from her night-mares into reality, her enthusiasm growing with each innova-tion and new, more horrible addition to the world of night-mares. The latest creation had proven to be something that Ophir could create time and time again until she had enough to fill the royal kennels, should she want. If they weren't careful, they'd become overrun with amphibious dogs before they knew what to do with their pack of hellhounds.

"I think we should keep your hound and get rid of the dog," Dwyn said definitively. She made it very clear which beast was the hound and which monster was the dog as she glared at Tyr.

Perhaps Dwyn's hatred of the man was part of what made his attention so delicious, though she'd never say as much to Dwyn. Instead, Ophir did her best to look bored, glanc-ing idly from where she was stroking her pet near the fire. Venom dripped from Sedit's jowls, which made her smile.

She liked the consistent, needle-like cluster of terrifying teeth in the mouths of all of her beasts and was unwilling to hear an unkind word about her children.

"Your...*dog*...is lovely," Tyr said apologetically.

"Sedit," Ophir chided softly as the hound continued to look up at her appreciatively. His teeth were composed of rows of hundreds, if not thousands, of needles.

"And have you given any thought to Sedit's breed?"

Ophir perked at his question.

"You've made...seven, now? Apart from Sedit, who clearly won't be leaving your side anytime soon. I don't expect you'll be calling all of them Sedit."

"Right, right. You are a rather vague hound, aren't you..." She smiled at that. "Vague. Such a vague representation of a hound."

"What are you doing?" Tyr furrowed his brows disapprovingly.

"Wait. I'm naming his breed."

"I don't like where this is going. Names are important, Princess. Names hold meaning and power. Don't just—"

"Vageth."

"No."

"They're vague hounds."

"You can't call it a—"

Ophir clucked her tongue as she cut him off. "If you invent a species, you can call it whatever you like. Would you like me to make another hound? Sedit could use a friend."

Dwyn grinned at their exchange, lifting her head from where she'd focused on her nails. "Yes, please make another. Maybe it won't be as docile as Sedit. In fact, do me a favor just for my own curiosity: focus on creating a vageth who wants to tear out Tyr's jugular."

"I don't like that you're already calling it a 'vageth.' That's not a word," Ophir retorted.

"Nothing is a word until you speak it into existence," Dwyn defended, returning to her nails. "You wouldn't know

211

that, though, would you. You have no power for creation. What's your power? Disappearing? Go ahead and utilize that."

"And your power, witch? Water?"

Dwyn's eyes narrowed. "You wish that was all I could do."

Ophir looked up lazily. "Pick new fights. I'm bored of this one."

She made a sharp noise, not dissimilar from a whistle, and Sedit was up on his sharp talons. She motioned for the hound to leave, and he was more than happy to head for the exit. Tyr opened the door and seemed relieved as the hound escaped into the woods to hunt whatever unsuspecting creature might await the thorny needles of his teeth.

Dwyn used the opportunity to cross the room and settle tightly into the space near Ophir on the sofa, lying down. She rested her head on Ophir's lap and continued to pick at her nails. The princess ran her fingers absently through Dwyn's glossy locks.

They'd come across a cabin that had not been left empty for more than a day or two. The freshness of the eggs gathered from the country home's clucking chickens and the ripe fruits resting on the table assured them that its owner hadn't been away for long. When no one had answered Ophir's knock, she'd let herself in. Tyr had been prepared to shift into a less visible form, should it have been a farmer more comfortable with accepting women into his home, but no such extremes had been required of him.

"How far are we from Henares?" Dwyn asked.

Ophir sighed. "I have no idea. We took the most indirect route known to man. We followed no proper roads, we didn't ask directions, we consulted no map—"

Dwyn set down her knife and sat up, twisting until she was eye level. The princess's toffee hair was yellowed against the crackle of the fire within the hearth. The siren tucked her feet underneath her, cutting off Ophir's train of thought.

"I have an idea."

Ophir hadn't meant to reach out and touch her, but her

hand had moved of its own volition. She'd found the siren's posture endearing. "You always have ideas."

Dwyn's teeth were white and clean in the firelight as she smiled. "This is a new idea."

Tyr remained silent from the far side of the room.

"We haven't made anything inanimate," Dwyn said.

"We?" Ophir asked speculatively, though her question was in jest. Truthfully, she knew that her power was just as much Dwyn's as it was hers. Without her friend, she wouldn't have unlocked her ability to manifest. She would never have created her enormous, black serpent. Her breed of demon hounds now roaming Farehold's forests were thanks to a prompt from the depths of Dwyn's mind. They really were in this together.

"Have you considered an object?"

Ophir's lips puckered as she thought. "What sort of object?"

Tyr made a dismissive sound from the other side of the room.

Dwyn's bitter tone cut through the room. "Please, share your thoughts, oh Great One. Or do we need to remind the princess that you're only in Sulgrave because you're a thug in a blood gang?" She turned conspiratorially to Ophir. "You could kick him out, you know. You could build a stone case around him with no exit. You could—"

"Quiet, witch." His tone remained impassive. "No one is here because goodness and morality have driven us. You want power? Great—good for you. Ophir wants vengeance? Perfect, couldn't be happier to help. I want answers? Incredible. Look how everyone wins."

Dwyn had been quick to divulge Tyr's ties to the Blood Pact, probably hoping Ophir would banish him. He'd had no trouble sharing that she'd also been a member of the same group, which had cooled the power of her argument substantially. Ophir didn't care either way. She'd made it quite clear that as long as no one planned to disembowel her, their motives weren't her concern.

The corner of Ophir's lips twitched upward in the wake of their argument. In many ways, she was grateful for their rivalry. It was a much-needed distraction. Their tension had drawn her attention away from her own pain on more occasions than one. She returned her attention to the siren who sat at her feet. "What object did you have in mind?"

Dwyn's eyes twinkled. "We're in need of directions, aren't we? We suspect your target is in Henares? If we've wandered away from any knowable point on a map, then perhaps..." She allowed her sentence to drift, as if hoping the princess would take the prompt to complete it on her own.

"You do come up with the cleverest ideas."

"I do, don't I."

Tyr didn't appear to be trying very hard to conceal his expression at their affectionate exchanges. He'd win no favors by openly expressing jealousy or distaste.

Ophir closed her eyes and lifted one hand before her, palm flat. The other two eyed her curiously as they watched her process. She pushed thought and intention into her palm. Air, minerals, and particles begin to wield into a single object. When she opened her eyes, a round shape as golden as her irises rested in the center of her hand. Ophir's gold-brown brows puckered in the middle as she looked at the thing she'd made.

"What's wrong?" Dwyn asked.

She fought her disappointment. "Things just don't quite...turn out the way I think they might."

Dwyn took the object from Ophir's hand before she had the opportunity to examine it. "It's a watch?"

Ophir sagged. "It's meant to be a compass. I wanted it to show us wherever we wanted to go. I guess my thoughts may have mixed with how much time had passed in our journey... how long it's been since Caris passed...how long—"

"Yes." Dwyn made an intentional sound to cut off Ophir's train of thought before it could veer toward sorrow. "That's okay! Life is complicated. Thoughts and emotion and intentions are deeply intertwined. So, here we have a watch. Shall we see if it does anything?" The golden pocket watch was on a rather elegant chain, but otherwise it was terribly simple. Dwyn snatched it, watching the clock's hands tick unceremoniously as they measured the passage of time.

Tyr pushed away from the wall once more, despite himself. He peered down over Ophir's back from where she lounged on the couch. He let a hand slide along her shoulder as he looked at the pocket watch.

She stiffened under his touch, but he gave her arm a squeeze to calm her fears. "Let's see what you made, Princess." His voice was low.

"How do we make it work?" Ophir asked, looking at her watch.

Dwyn shrugged. "Your hounds and creatures listen to you fine. Why don't you ask it something, and see if it listens to you, too?" She passed the pocket watch back to Ophir. Dwyn's eyes didn't miss Tyr's presence on the princess's arm. Her eyes seemed to linger with a telling, burning intent on his hand.

She palmed the watch. "Just ask it a question?"

Dwyn struggled to arrange her face into a look of patience. "You made it, Firi. Don't ask us how it works."

Tyr slid a second hand down her opposite arm. "Maybe it will take our princess a little bit more encouragement to believe in herself."

"Fuck off." Ophir motioned as if to shake him off, but he only smiled at her halfhearted rejection. He did not relent, clearly enjoying the way she wiggled under his hands. If she was truly angry, there'd be fire to accompany her words. She'd demonstrated on more than one occasion that she had no trouble underscoring her emotions with flame. The firelight from the hearth had to have betrayed the red blush that crept up her neck whenever he touched her, and she knew he could tell precisely how he heated her blood.

Tyr didn't relinquish his touch. He settled close to her face from over her shoulder, hands sliding down her arms, feigning interest in the watch. His breath was warm next to her cheek. His lips moved against her ear. "Tell it what you want to see."

Ophir's heart squeezed. Tyr made no attempt to conceal his ever-growing closeness, and she knew Dwyn had seen it all. Dwyn was not ignorant to the way he'd touch Ophir's hip, brush her hair away from her face, guide her by placing his hand on her back, or cause her to redden time after time.

The game played among the three was one no one spoke, yet everyone understood.

Ophir swallowed as she stared at the small mechanism in her hand. "Where is Henares?" she asked the watch. Without waiting a moment, it began to spin. The hour hand, minute hand, and second hand swung as they narrowed into a tiny, acute angle, before homing in on a singular point. They remained in their arrow-like directions for a moment before the pocket watch abandoned its guiding point and resumed ticking the appropriate time.

Ophir frowned. "How do we know if it was right?"

Both Dwyn and Tyr seemed to make an amused face at this.

"Because you made it." Tyr spoke for both of them.

"Do you want to go tonight?" Dwyn asked.

Ophir looked out the window at the lateness of the hour. "What if we eat the rest of this man's food and leave by morning? I'm sure he's on a hunting trip—it would all be spoiled by the time he returned, anyway."

"My thoughts exactly," Dwyn agreed.

They left the fire crackling as they crawled into bed. Dwyn made the executive decision that Tyr would remain on the sofa. He hadn't protested too much, given that he'd be closer to the fire. Dwyn crawled into bed first, her body pressing into the space closest to the wall and its window. She faced the princess in the moments before sleep, taking off her clothes and draping her leg possessively over Ophir's hip. The princess began to fall asleep while entangled in Dwyn's limbs, pleasant scent of mint comforting her as she relaxed. The soothing sound of the siren's deep, steady breathing as she fell under the waters of sleep was a comforting lullaby.

Her lids fluttered to a close as she felt the fabric of the bed begin to tug and lift. Heat spiked through her as she realized who was joining them in the bed.

TWENTY-SEVEN

✦ ✦ ✦ ✦

OPHIR TRIED NOT TO MOVE. SHE RESISTED THE URGE TO make any noise. She didn't want to wake Dwyn. With extreme caution, she swallowed and looked over her shoulder to see…nothing.

"I think there's room in the bed for three, Princess," Tyr whispered in her ear, his bodyweight pressing down into the mattress behind her. "The sofa isn't particularly comfortable." His arm draped against her front, forearm settling into the space between her breasts as his hand cupped the space near her face. His hips pressed into her backside, and she could feel, in no uncertain terms, that he was wide awake.

"It seemed comfortable enough to me," she whispered, heart skipping several beats.

"Yes, but you're not there."

Her breathing hitched. She wondered if he could feel the way her entire body warmed as if she'd unwillingly summoned her gift for flame. Damn, traitorous body. It wanted what it wanted.

"Shh," he whispered. "You'll wake her." Tyr squeezed Ophir to him ever so slightly, without stirring Dwyn where she slept. He brushed his thumb against Ophir's lips, then lowered the tips of his fingers lower to rest against her thundering heart.

"Are you nervous, princess?"

She struggled to remain calm. Yes, he did make her nervous. Not because he was a man, and not because he was in her bed, but because he was a phantom mere inches away from the space she shared with Dwyn. His disregard for taboo had her heart thundering, which he could doubtlessly feel from where his arm rested. He seemed to like playing with fire, and she was flame personified.

"Do you want me to go?"

"Yes," she said, hoping he'd hear the blatant untruth in her word.

"You know...I can tell when you're lying."

Ophir bit her lower lip, hard. His hand slid up from where it had monitored her heart. It gently clasped over her mouth to silence her.

Tyr remained in the space between things, likely enjoying the pleasure of remaining unseen. She couldn't anticipate his movements, nor would the siren awaken to spot him. Ophir's breath caught as he explored her body with a careful, teasing hand. A finger dragged along her spine, drawing its way down her back; it traced along the crease down her center as it sought her warm, tender center. Her hips rocked slightly, pushing into him.

"Do you want to know what I have on my mind?" he asked in her ear.

"No," she whispered back.

"Liar."

Dwyn rolled away in her sleep, dead to the world.

Ophir swallowed, and he continued to whisper against her hair. "One of these nights, I'd love to slip inside you with your favorite witch an inch away from us, Princess. How fun." His words released a rush of water into the space between her thighs. She felt her body heat, her hips rocking again instinctively. The wall of his back pushed against her.

Tyr moved his arms so that his underarm could slip beneath her head, keeping her face in gentle control in case she might be at risk of making noise.

With a cruel dismissal, he gave a quiet command as his lips brushed her ear.

"Go to bed, Firi."

His game was clever. Dangle, and deny. She wasn't naïve. She knew what he was doing. And part of her admired him for how well it was working. It did make her want. She sighed in frustration.

Good for him.

She wiggled her hips against him ever so slowly, moving in a way that encouraged his hand to move farther south. He slipped his fully cupped hand into the space between her thighs, leaving it there while she throbbed, wanting more.

Tyr stilled against her with an unmistakable smile on his mouth, leaving his hand cupped against her to feel her ready warmth soaking his fingers, though he denied her what she wanted. His fingertips possessed saintly control as he refused to slip a single finger beyond her entrance, no matter how her eagerness flooded his hand. She stifled an impatient sound. In return, he moaned appreciatively against her neck, which only made her hips rock more greedily against him. She could feel from the hard length of him that his body was just as hungry for intimacy as hers, but he made no moves to satiate his hunger.

"You'll wake Dwyn if you keep moving like that."

"Let her wake up," she challenged.

He left his hands draped so that one pinned her to him from beneath her head, and the other cupped the hot, sensitive place between her thighs. He'd inferred precisely what she'd meant and smiled. "Goodnight, Princess."

Her frustrated grasp elicited a soft, appreciative chuckle from the man.

"Soon." He kissed her neck once more.

"I still hate you," she whispered.

"I told you"—he smiled—"I can tell when you're lying."

Ophir hadn't thought she'd be able to fall asleep, but she'd been wrong. Between the pressed warmth of their bodies, she drifted off into a deep, dreamless rest. She may have slept well into the morning if it hadn't been for the angered shriek that shook her violently from her slumber.

While she'd remained comfortably trapped between Dwyn and Tyr, the opposing Sulgrave fae had rather unintentionally draped themselves in such a way so that Tyr's arm was over Dwyn's back and her foot was resting on his calf. To say she was displeased when she opened her eyes to find the man in their bed would have been an understatement.

"Get out, dog!" Dwyn had to shove Ophir to shake Tyr off of them.

"Is someone angry that we all slept well? Let me guess, Dwynie, best night you've had in months?" Tyr mocked.

"Fuck off." She was already jumping out of bed and dressing for the day, grabbing her shirt and pants with more fury than should have been acceptable at such an early hour. "I will *never* want you in our bed."

"Never say never." He winked.

Ophir took her time gathering her things and getting her clothes on while they fought. The Sulgrave pair had never made the slightest attempt at camaraderie. Dwyn seemed to get more and more hostile toward Tyr as their time on the road progressed. They continued yelling at one another in the cabin. Ophir's eyes flitted from the siren to the still-shirtless man. He had slipped his arms through the sleeves of his shirt but had not yet pulled it over his head. His chest, shoulder, and neck still bore the looping curls of his black tattoo.

"I've been meaning to ask…" Ophir laced the front of her tunic over her chest as she looked over her shoulder. "Your tattoos. They're so similar. Does everyone from Sulgrave have something like that?"

They stilled in their fight a bit too quickly. Dwyn had appeared to be in the midst of raising her fist to douse Tyr with water when her hand went motionless above her head. She lowered it slowly as they both looked at the princess.

"What?" Suspicion surged through Ophir. "What is it?"

"Yes," Dwyn answered coolly, addressing the question. She relaxed from where she'd tensed mid-fight. Her words came out wooden at first, finding their stride as she worked her way through the sentence. "It's tradition to get them once you reach adulthood in Sulgrave. I would say that most of Sulgrave's citizens have them."

Disbelief pricked the back of Ophir's neck. Something about the way they'd both acted as though cold water had been dumped over their heads made it seem like she'd struck a chord that she hadn't been meant to pluck. The princess's brow twitched as she fought the urge to arch it skeptically. If it was true, they would have brushed it off and continued their verbal battle, wouldn't they?

"You don't get a lot of exposure to Sulgrave fae, so I'm not surprised that you haven't seen it before," Dwyn continued, keeping her voice too easy, too light.

"Is this your gang?" Ophir asked, looking from one to the other. "This tattoo?" Her eyes trained on Tyr. "You did say that Dwyn was in it once, didn't you? Why would you lie about it?"

"Shit." Tyr heard a sound at the same time as the women. They paused amid their discussion to turn to the noise.

"Let me do it." Ophir grumbled as she moved toward the door. The others made sounds and moves to stop her, but she was already reaching for the handle. "Stay out of sight. At least I look like I'm from Farehold. This will go down more easily if I talk to him."

Dwyn peered out the window at the approaching shape. "I think he's human."

"Even easier." She smiled. "Go out the back. I can do this."

TWENTY-EIGHT

+   +   +   +

O PHIR STEPPED OUT OF THE CABIN AND A PALE, MIDDLE-
aged man skidded to a halt the moment the long hair
and thin frame of a fae woman populated his vision. He
wouldn't have expected anyone to be in his home, let alone
a beautiful fae girl. Shock was clear on his face. One hand
was filled with rabbits that had been caught and snared in the
woods. The other went immediately to the hilt of his sword.

The weather was warm considering the lateness of the
season, and the remaining red-brown leaves on the trees
danced cheerily behind him with the gentlest of breezes. The
scent of dying grass and falling leaves filtered through the air.
The sun beamed down, catching in Ophir's toffee hair to
make it lighten to a vibrant shade of gold. Misdeeds should
happen in the dead of night or rainy weather, not under happy
sunlight. The pleasant conditions felt a tad disrespectful.

"I'm sorry!" Ophir was quick to speak. Her eyes scanned
the space behind him for hunting companions amidst the
trees but settled on the human. "I was on the road late last
night. I only sought shelter and a place to sleep. I didn't mean
to startle you, and I apologize for using your bed. When no
one was home…"

"You're her," the man breathed. Her face struggled against the urge to scrunch as he mumbled out two words she had not wanted to hear. Ophir could see recognition as it painted itself onto his otherwise unremarkable features. He was rather plainly dressed and looked like any hermit one might find in the country. While they'd been pillaging his kitchen for dried goods and drinks, there had been no paintings or evidence of the royal family within his simple home to suggest that he'd be familiar with the appearance of Farehold's monarchs. Having lived for more than six decades, Ophir supposed knowledge of her description would have been around for longer than this human male had been alive.

Ophir felt the muscles in her back go rigid as she attempted to fruitlessly deflect. "I'm just a traveler..."

"No," said the man, dropping the rabbits to the ground. He unsheathed a rusted, rather blunt sword. What he thought he'd accomplish with such a weapon, she'd never know. The blade's only applicable use would have been sawing through the snares of his fur traps. "There's a high reward for anyone who has information on the princess. I'm afraid I can't let you leave."

Ophir made a sad sound as she eyed the man. "You're right. I am the princess. And do you know what I can do?" She took a step toward him.

He stumbled backward. "Don't come any closer, Princess Ophir. I need to get you back to the castle. The whole kingdom has been looking for you—"

"I don't have to come closer." She lifted a hand and procured a small orb of fire. "I'm afraid I'm going to need you to lower your sword. I am sorry for sleeping in your bed last night. Though, out of curiosity, how did you plan to get me back to the castle? Particularly if I can't step any closer?"

"You're going to have to come with me," he said, shakily ignoring her questions. "I have to bring you back to Aubade."

She made a long, weary exhalation as she eyed the

human. "Alternatively, you can step aside, let me leave, and keep your life."

He looked over his shoulder and began to shout names. The words were sharp, scared sounds on the man's lip, demanding assistance. Ophir stiffened when she realized the man was not alone. His yelling continued as her eyes shot back to the trees. He was awaiting companions.

"Be quiet!" she hissed.

He shouted the names again, urging others forward. She could spot the moment the men broke from the tree line that he was the only human in the group. "Goddess dammit," she murmured.

"It's her!" the man yelled to the companions. "It's Princess Ophir!"

"Shut up, you fool!" she snarled.

"Get her!" The farmer went one step too far with his command.

She felt no fear, only agitation. It was deeply annoying that such a simple man was causing troubles larger and deeper than he could possibly comprehend. She released the air from her lungs as she tried to decide how she'd deal with the nuisance.

Two men were advancing—one full-blooded fae and the other a faeling of mixed origins. They both had the telltale ears of the fair folk. She didn't have time to find out if they could wield powers that might neutralize her. She couldn't allow herself to be taken back to the castle, nor could word reach her parents as to her location. Her face crinkled in irritation as they ran for her.

"Stop!" she warned, raising her fireball. They slowed, but they did not come to a halt.

Over their shoulders, she saw another shape from the shadows of the forest. It was the gray, lithe shadow of an unnatural canine. It prowled like a large, agile cave cat, its many eyes blinking from the gloom between branches and trunks.

"This is your last chance," Ophir warned, allowing the fire in her palm to grow into a menacing, orange orb.

The men did not stop.

"Sedit!" She cried for her hound. It let out a bloodcurdling howl, a sound that was too throaty for anything other than a legion of demons. Sedit's sharp talons tore through the earth as it covered the distance between them in seconds. The vageth sprinted for the nearest man, launching itself through the air. It sank its needle-like teeth into the throat of the human's flesh. Ophir thrust her ball of fire toward the nearest fae and watched as he screamed, his clothes catching fire as her power enveloped him. The human's life had been forfeited the moment Sedit had ripped his jugular from where it was meant to stay. The demifae turned and began to run.

"Go!" she urged her hound, and the canine turned on sharp talons to tear after the man. The screaming of the fae on fire had ebbed as he fell to the ground. She looked over her shoulder with puckered brows, wondering why neither of her companions had come to help.

+ + + +

The moment Ophir left the door, Tyr and Dwyn locked in a quiet, angry battle.

"You're on thin ice, witch."

"I will kill you where you stand, dog," Dwyn hissed.

"You can't, and we both know it."

He anticipated her next move. Tyr stepped into the place between things, shifting out of visible sight as she hurled water toward him. An entire pitcher overturned as she threw it toward his mouth, as if hoping to drown him on dry land. It missed its mark, soaking the wood of the floor as it splashed against nothingness.

"You think you're clever?" Dwyn's eyes were wild as she looked around the empty space for clues as to the man's presence. "You think I don't know what you're doing with her?"

He stepped back into view, an arrogant grin curving his

mouth upward and bringing his eyes to a twinkle. She'd wasted the water before she'd been able to find him. "It was your idea, wasn't it? More than one way to possess a royal heart?"

She narrowed her eyes. "What were you doing before that, Tyr? I know you were at the party the night Caris was killed—oh yes, Firi and I have talked about it. We've discussed it all. I know her hopes, her fears, her crushes. I know how she tastes." He hated the flicker of jealousy he couldn't conceal and despised the slow, savory smile it elicited from Dwyn even more. "You didn't know? The princess you held last night? The one you're attempting to seduce? I've made her scream for the goddess. She trusts me. She's told me everything."

"She trusts a lie."

"I saved her."

"So did I," came his bitter response.

She lowered her voice further, curling her fingers into a fist as she searched for answers. "You think I don't know you saved her from the room where her sister died? I know you were at that party. What I don't know is *why*. Why would you steal her away before you understood my game? Before you even knew I'd found Ophir?"

He managed to work through whatever jealousy had claimed him, forcing himself to relax against the wall. He wasn't interested in satisfying the siren's curiosity. "How deeply can she trust you if she lets me stay even though she knows how much you detest me? If she loved you like you so desperately want, she'd respect your loathing for me. Your enemies would be her enemies. It sounds to me like you don't have the grip on her that you think you do."

Dwyn looked as though she possessed the powers of fire rather than water as she burned from within. Her face twitched as she controlled her anger. They could hear shouts from beyond the cabin but were too locked in on their anger to adhere to Ophir now. The princess was capable of handling a simple human farmer on her own.

"You know you can't kill me, as much as you want to. Why not hog-tie me and leave me in the forest so you and the princess can continue on your merry way?"

He made a contemplative face.

"Goddess, dog, I'm not trying to give you ideas for how to get around the conditions of the bond."

More noises and shouts rose from beyond the cabin, snagging Tyr's gaze once more as his eyes drifted to the window a second time. He leaned against a table and looked over his shoulder to where he could see Sedit near the tree line. "Our princess has her hound, in case you were worried."

"I wasn't."

"Does she know you don't care about her?"

"I'm not worried because I know she's capable. I've trained her, Tyr. *I* did that." She thrust her hand toward the window. "I'm the reason she can defend herself. I *do* care about her. You're the one toying with her feelings when you hold someone else in your heart."

He laughed, but the sound was as black as the charcoal from the dead fire. "You care about what you can get from her. You care about what you're grooming her to be. You don't care about her."

"Oh, I forgot. Tyr the Red, Tyr the Altruist, Tyr the Saint is here in Farehold for noble purposes. Tyr the Noble is only with the lovely Princess Ophir because he's a good, good man." She laughed in a dark, cruel sound. "Only one of us will win, you know. You're nothing more than Tyr of the Blood Pact, and all I have to do is outlast you."

"None of it will matter if Berinth beats us to it."

"You know he can't. You know as well as I that he was only able to leave with Caris's liver."

Tyr's lips pulled back in a snarl. "Berinth only left with Caris's liver because I was there. I was in the room. Why don't you thank me for keeping his hands off Caris's heart? Why don't you try a little gratitude that your precious princess is here at all?"

"You don't care about her," Dwyn bit once more.

"You know nothing of how I feel."

The sounds of argument from outside of the cabin stopped.

"She'll never love you—not if you do anything to get rid of me," Dwyn said, voice singed with her anger. "That's why you know you can't touch me, isn't it? You know you don't stand a chance if you take me from her. She wouldn't forgive you."

Tyr looked toward the window again. "She's coming."

"I saved her," Dwyn said again, voice low.

"So did I," he repeated once more as his final words.

Ophir opened the door, flinging it on its hinges with anger. She burned hotly as she looked from one face to the other. "Thanks for the help, you two."

Tyr conjured an easy smile. "You looked like you had it handled. Besides, I wouldn't have left you alone if I hadn't seen Sedit. Your monster breed is wildly effective in battle."

"Vageth."

He grimaced. "Are you sure that's what you want to call them? Are you sticking with that? Vague hound? That's…"

"It's great," Dwyn finished.

"Kiss ass," he muttered.

"Dog," she replied.

TWENTY-NINE

*   +   +   +

I S THIS HER WORK?" ONE OF THE MEN ASKED, NUDGING THE charred remains of a corpse with his foot. The late warmth of autumn shined down on the country home, but despite the corpse's grilled appearance, the body was cold. The other two fallen men and their blood loss helped him to establish a timeline. It had been hours since this slaughter had occurred.

Harland took a knee by the body and looked at the sight around him. While one was clearly the product of fire, the other two had been mutilated by some unholy power. It almost looked like the product of a wolf, but something about the bites and claws was unnatural. An intrusive thought crept into his mind at the idea of unnatural creations. The guard pictured the snake on the edge of the cliff and brought a hand to his eyes, rubbing his temple. At this point, he had no idea what Ophir was capable of, though he hadn't expected it to be murder.

"Maybe they deserved it?" one of the men offered, voice mingled unconvincingly with hope and some indiscernible emotion.

Harland and his men were tired. They'd been on the road for weeks. A few centurions had stayed at the castle to guard the king and queen, while others had been posted at all of Ophir's preferred entrances and exits to Aubade, should she try to sneak back into the castle. The rest of them had dispersed among the cardinal directions surrounding the royal city in search of Farehold's last remaining heir.

A pleasant breeze rubbed the nearly naked autumn branches together, scattering a few reddish leaves to the ground. It rustled his hair. On the wind came a distinct sadness. The day was too lovely for such horrors. Harland's chest tightened. It wasn't just the bucolic setting of the cabin near the trees, nor the distance from the surrounding villages. It was the snared rabbits that had been left, untouched, fallen by the man's feet.

These men had not deserved what had been done to them.

Harland knew exactly why Ophir had run.

She'd lost Caris, and he'd stood guard outside of her door after she was told that her freedom, kingdom, autonomy were to be taken as well. She'd been informed she was to be married off to King Ceneth, and she did the only natural thing she could have done: she'd fled. He blamed himself every bit as much as he blamed Dwyn. He knew little about the Sulgrave fae, save for her arrival bringing on new and terrible changes for all of Aubade, if not the entire continent. The ominous legends connecting blood magic to royal hearts had seemed like little more than ghost stories. He'd been a fool to believe that the timing between Caris's slaughter and Dwyn's arrival was a coincidence. Caris's death had left a gaping wound just big enough for an opportunistic snake to slither in, only this one was more deadly than the serpent on the cliffs. It was true that she'd spared Ophir from drowning, but the princess she pulled from the waves was no longer the one he recognized. Dwyn's influence had not only twisted all he knew to be true of Ophir's character but had threatened their alliance with Raascot.

He'd love a chance to get his hands around the throat of the wicked water fae, just once.

"I think we're on the right track" was all Harland said. "Do what you need to do to see these men are buried. I'll meet you in the next village," he announced. The guard returned to his stallion and swung his legs up into the saddle. He urged his horse onward before they could argue. When they finally found Ophir, Harland wanted to be the one to confront her.

THIRTY

+   +   +   +

A RE YOU SURE YOU'LL RECOGNIZE HIM?" DWYN ASKED IN A whisper. The air was colder in the first hours of night. The bushes that concealed them had browned for the season, ruffling slightly against the wind. The night was clear, but moonless. Only the silver sting of stars burned the sky, allowing them the coverage of shadow and darkness.

Memories assaulted Ophir. She tasted the copper tang of blood in the back of her mouth as if drowning in the thought of Caris's blood. The thick scent of roses wove its way from her memory directly into her nose, nearly causing her to gag. She shoved down the waves of visuals that splashed through her mind, flooding her from within. She forced herself to focus on only the faces and their masks. They'd been burned into her thoughts, both waking and sleeping. The princess had been shaken awake and doused in water, surrounded by ember and ash from her angry flame as the men from that night had pursued her even in her nightmares. She'd seen the cruel shapes of their jaws, their noses, their eyes, their teeth, their shoulders, their hair behind her closed eyelids for months.

"I'll recognize him," she promised.

Tyr had been at the fated party long enough to learn the names and identities of several partygoers. He continued to prove himself extensively useful. Lord Berinth may have fled, but he had not been a lone actor in the unspeakable pursuits of that night.

Tyr slid his hand onto Ophir's arm, completely ignoring the way Dwyn's face scrunched in disgust. "You don't have to do this," he said. His voice was strangely calm.

Ophir began to object, but he went on.

"Don't mistake me, princess. They'll get their vengeance, and you'll be the one to give it to them. They deserve to die, and they will. Let me go in and secure him. I can have him in ropes and on his knees before you so much as set your foot in the door."

Ophir swallowed at the seriousness in his voice. He wasn't telling her to be forgiving, or to be ladylike, or to let it go. He wasn't telling her to let him handle it. He was offering to neutralize the immediate threat so her avenging spirit might be swift and easy.

"No." Ophir shook her head. "I want to do this. I want to do it all."

"She can handle herself," Dwyn said, shooting him a glare. He returned the narrowed eyes.

"Sedit will come in with me. And if things go south..."

"We'll be right behind you." Dwyn nodded in agreement. Perhaps she hadn't meant to use the plural of the word, but as much as she hated Tyr, some part of Ophir suspected that Dwyn knew it was better to present a united front.

"Guryon?" Ophir asked, looking at Tyr.

"Guryon." He dipped his chin in agreement. He told Ophir that he'd met the merchant at the party in the hour preceding the fateful events. The man was no lord, knight, or duke. He held no titles. He was a man of little importance, save for his crumbling empire as the baron of spices for the southern kingdom. The merchant Guryon was once a man who had mattered. His trips across, up, and down the continent's coast and its seaside ports had come to a screeching halt as storms had brutalized his ships, dashing his empire of peppers and cinnamons and salts.

Tonight, the three knelt with little dignity in the once-manicured bushes at the edges of the merchant's garden. It was clear that his estate had fallen into something of disrepair over the past few years. Though late fall had made the grasses die after the season's first frost and the trees turn into shades of oranges and browns, it was clear that his lawn had been filled with weeds and brambles long before autumn's onset.

It wasn't hard to imagine what the man might want with blood magic. Guryon would want his fortune returned. He'd want ships, and wealth, and power. He'd seek a way back into the life in which he'd grown so comfortable before it had been snatched from him.

One question that had plagued their minds was why there would be multiple actors in Caris's mutilation. Whatever the late princess could offer, Berinth should have wanted for himself.

It had been a matter of debate what the team of malicious intent may have hoped to accomplish, unless they'd planned to divide Caris's blood and sweetmeats among one another, each taking what they'd needed. As their ritual had been woefully interrupted, it had seemed as though few had profited from her death. The fact remained: they had killed her. Whether or not they achieved what they'd set out to find was of little consequence.

"You're sure this is him?" she asked again.

His gaze was steadying. There was no condemnation in his repetition as he asked once again, "I am. Are you certain you want to do this?"

Ophir wet her lips once as she straightened from where they'd crouched behind the bushes, leaving her Sulgrave companions behind. Sedit trotted beside her as she walked with specter-like grace down the once-lovely path that led from the road to the estate. There was no sign of gardeners, servants, or groundskeepers as she moved forward. Her chin stayed high with regal control as if she floated rather than walked.

She didn't glance over her shoulder as she reached the door, even if a swelling urge begged her to look to ensure that they were there. She knew that Tyr and Dwyn would enter at the first sign of trouble. As it stood, she hadn't been deceived in a long, long time. She knew that neither of them had come into her life by accident. It was no coincidence that the same night other men had taken her sister, others had entered her own. Why they'd traversed the Frozen Straits, battled through the crowds of Lord Berinth's party, or swum through the waves seemed unimportant. It was their story to lead, not hers. If they planned her no harm, she could only benefit from their presence.

Before leaving the castle in Aubade, Ophir had asked Dwyn in no uncertain terms whether the siren had planned to kill her, and when the girl had said no, she'd believed her. The rest didn't matter.

Her attempt to swallow stuck in her throat like dry bread. No matter how hard she struggled, the anxiety wouldn't leave her airway. Her feet remained glued to the landing as she examined her options. She raised her knuckles to rap against the front door but hesitated. Ophir took a step backward and looked at the house. In her concentrated forward motion, she'd failed to truly consider the space before her.

The lower levels were dark with the early hours of night. Only one light flickered in the upper right corner of the estate, suggesting that Guryon was home alone. She quietly tried the front door but was unsurprised to find it bolted. Ophir abandoned the path and began to move along the home's perimeter, Sedit at her side. She brushed her fingers against the stones and mortar of his home as she passed by the windows, over the bushes, and rounded the corner. The handle to a back door opened easily under her twist as she stepped into the home's kitchen.

It was cold.

There was no scent of bread, stew, or nice things on the air. There was no sign that a cook had been on the premises in a long while.

"In, Sedit," she whispered, opening the door for her hound. His talons clicked against the stones with more noise than she would have liked, but seeing as how the man within was about to perish whether or not he heard them, she figured her silence wasn't particularly important. Sedit wriggled his amphibious hindquarters the way a bloodhound fresh from the kill might've, blinking his many black eyes at his master.

"Shh," she hushed her creature. He stilled to the best of his abilities, though his talons continued to clack noisily with every step. It was a relief when they left the kitchen and his paws could sink into the fibers of a rug's carpeting rather than cold stones.

Ophir navigated through the rapidly darkening house as she crept down the hall. The last glimpses of evening light filtered through grimy windows, but no candles or fireplaces had been lit on the lower levels of the home. Shadows filled the space, their looming presence almost a separate entity entirely.

She began to mount the stairs and flinched when the first step creaked under her weight. After a pause, she relaxed her face from its responsive flinch and began to walk upward toward the lone candle light she'd seen in the windows. The corridor wasn't particularly long, and the silence of the home suggested that no one else was present to thwart her mission. She would soon be alone with the merchant.

There were roughly three rooms on either side of the hall, but she knew with some certainty that they'd all been empty for a long time. This man lived alone. After several muted steps on the plush, dusty rug that stretched throughout the hall, her hand wrapped around the brass knob that would lead her into the only room that had shown evidence of life. Ophir breathed in through her nose, closing her eyes for final moments of courage. Then, she opened the door.

A man turned from where he'd been sitting at his desk, hunched over ledgers, quill in hand.

She froze studiously as she searched his face for recognition. Visions of the men and their hair, their jaws, their noses and exposed features against the man appeared before her as she recognized the man behind the mask. Guryon had hovered in the back corner as she'd thrown open the door. He hadn't fought. He'd stood behind the man holding the sword that had been plunged into August's torso, antagonizing her sister's personal guard in his final moments of life. This man was no warrior—he was a coward.

"Guryon." She said his name.

He blinked at her. "Are you...?" His question drifted off as he released the quill in his hands. The man stood from where he'd been sitting at his desk. Somehow, he hadn't looked surprised at her entrance. His face looked deeply haunted, as though the ghosts of his soul had not allotted him rest in a long time. Perhaps he'd been expecting a phantom to claim him.

She pushed open the door further to reveal the presence of her hound. "Sit, Sedit," she commanded. The vageth obeyed.

The man was clean, but his clothes were not new. He looked like he'd kept himself tidy, while allowing the world around him to fall into disarray. When his eyes settled on Sedit, he appeared to know that she'd come to collect a life debt.

"You're Ophir."

Her lips twitched with the ghost of a smile. "You know why I'm here, then."

He closed his eyes slowly. "I didn't..."

She took a step into the room, his hint at a denial emboldening her. "You didn't what? You didn't...mean to kill her? You didn't...profit from her death, as you thought you might? Go ahead, Guryon. What *didn't* you do?"

He opened his eyes again, but there was no fight behind them. His words may have been a question, but his tone did not retain the essential upward tilt of inquiry. He spoke with flat acceptance. "You're here to kill me, aren't you?"

Ophir was put out by his resolve. She crossed her arms over her chest. "Why are you so ready to die? Is it because you committed both murder and treason, contributing to the loss of a woman's life, but then didn't benefit from her slaughter? Would you be as willing to stand down if you'd gotten... what would it have been? Riches? Titles? Tell me, Guryon."

The gaunt man shook his head. "It wasn't like that."

"What was it like?" She took another step toward him.

"I wouldn't have killed a monarch for money," he promised, eyes searching hers. "I don't expect you to understand. She was your sister."

Ophir wanted to gag, but it came out as a cough. Rage rose within her. "Was! That's right! She was!" Another step. "Tell me. Make me understand."

To his credit, he hadn't flinched. He hadn't tried to run. He stared with deflated acceptance at the presence of the princess and her hellhound. "What does it matter?" he asked, his voice quiet.

Her volume surprised her as she shouted back, "Everything!" Ophir's fists balled at her sides, glowing with the impending embers. "It means everything!"

The merchant shook his head, but she took the three remaining steps to close the space between them. Guryon was no fae. He was human, as the farmer had been. She grabbed him by the throat and forced him up. She allowed the barest edges of her flames to lick his throat. She was neither strong nor tall enough to bring him off of his toes, but she'd forced him to his feet, and he hadn't fought.

"Just kill me," he groaned against the blisters that were forming on his neck.

She released him with a sharp, cruel laugh. He fell to the ground, his body collapsing against the floor with the sound of potato sacks and dead meat. "Kill you!" Her eyes widened. She was growing wilder by the second, her emotions roiling within her. "Of course I'm going to kill you! There is no situation wherein you survive, Guryon. There is no future where in you walk out of this room. You get to decide one of two things. Are you ready to hear your options?"

He'd remained where he'd crumbled on the floor, pushed up by only one arm. Another hand came to his throat to feel the blisters she'd given him.

"The first is that we take hours, or days, or weeks to slowly maim and cauterize. I'll call my flame each and every time you're bitten or wounded or gored by my hound so that you don't bleed out, ensuring you stay alive for all of it. You'll feel every pain. You'll beg for death, but it won't come. You'll wish your heart would stop coursing its blood through your body, but the fire won't allow it. I'll keep you alive until you tell me what I need to know. Does that sound like a good option?"

He turned his head away from her, eyes unseeing as he looked to the stones in the gloom of his room. His candle created deep, unforgiving shadows against the corners and furniture of his room. His face was half-illuminated, half-concealed by the flickering candle. The hollow spaces beneath his eyes meant nothing to her. His soul may have left him long ago, but it was time for his reckoning.

"The second is that you tell me quickly, and I will mark the pace of your information. However quickly you explain yourself is how fast I will permit your death. If you draw it out, I will match your pain step for step. If you answer with speed, so will I. Sedit can ensure you're dead before you've had the chance to blink. He goes for the jugular. It's a mercy. A kindness that you don't deserve. A kindness that wasn't given to Caris."

"I'm sorry," he said, still on the floor in his wormy cowardice.

"I don't care!" She almost screamed. "I don't give a fuck how sorry you are!" Her voice continued to rise until the words tore at her throat with the same angry, ragged exertion of her night terrors. "Cry for me, Guryon! Sob at my feet! Beat your chest! Tear your tunic! I feel nothing." She bent on one knee, kneeling nearer to him. It was a move she wouldn't have dared if Sedit hadn't been waiting hungrily over her shoulder. "I don't need your apologies, Guryon. I need your reasons."

"Blood magic—"

"So, I've heard," she bit. "The blood of a royal is particularly potent. Let's pretend I know the basics. Get to it."

He looked up at her. "It's not just potency. It's not money, or titles, or gifts. It's…everything."

Ophir's fists flexed.

"It's the gift of the divine, Princess Ophir. What we stood to gain from Caris was…godhood."

She blinked, then controlled her emotions. "How?"

He shook his head. "I don't know. I wasn't the leader—"

"Lord Berinth was," she finished for him. "How did he recruit you? How did he find out that you'd be willing to sacrifice Farehold's princess?" She raised a ball of fire, threatening the first of her blows.

"There's a clan!" he said, raising his forearm in a cowardly flinch.

"A clan?" she demanded.

"Yes. Berinth didn't find me, I found him! I knew there was a clan looking for how to ascend, to surpass mere humans and fae—deities, Princess Ophir. They seek to be like the old gods."

She shook her head, uncomprehending.

"He wasn't the first clan member." The man babbled on. "They've existed all over the continent since the beginning of time. They're in Raascot, in Farehold, in Sulgrave—it's those who seek the power of gods."

She lowered her fire and stared at the man beneath her. "It's a cult?"

"It's not a cult," he defended. "Their powers are real. They've been wielding blood magics to access new and unnatural powers without it hurting themselves or drawing from their own blood. We've seen others do it. Berinth brought…"

"Berinth brought what?"

Guryon sounded like he might cry, but his whimpering only annoyed her. "He would bring people in sometimes—usually women. Peasants, women from the pleasure houses, women who didn't know why they'd come to his home… He'd show us a new power he'd accessed without it harming him. He'd drain them instead, leaving him whole."

Dizziness made it hard for Ophir to focus, but the anger brought her back.

Women.

Vulnerable women who worked in brothels, who were impoverished, who trusted too much, who were princesses and heirs to the throne. It didn't matter. Women. No one woman was safe from those who took and took and took. She swallowed again, still feeling dry bread in her throat. "And Caris?"

"Royal blood…royal organs, a royal heart…it's the power of gods, Princess. There's no other way for me to say it. This was no simple blood magic. This was not the borrowed power of some peasant. We thought we'd be accessing abilities as great as the All Mother's."

Her mouth was in a hard line as she brought her fire to her fist once again. "And what power is that?"

He shook his head, looking at the floor. He was prepared to die. "Everything."

THIRTY-ONE

✦   ✦   ✦   ✦

D WYN AND TYR WAITED OUTSIDE WITH FIDGETY IMPATIENCE. Whether they'd heard the conversation or simply been confident in her abilities, it was unclear.

"So?" Dwyn asked.

Sedit trotted at her side as Ophir passed the two without speaking.

"Firi—"

"Don't." She spun on them. "Don't call me that."

Dwyn raised her hands, eyes wide with true surprise. "What happened in there?"

Ophir looked from one, then to the other. "I'll be moving forward on my own."

Dwyn's eyebrows puckered in the center, but Tyr remained unbothered. He took two steps forward, looping his arm around the princess's. "No, you won't."

"Hey!" She called her fire, and the moment he grabbed her wrist, the fireball stopped short in her palm. It smoked out, leaving her hand empty.

Ophir groaned with her exertion and thrust it forward with her mind alone, but much to her surprise, Dwyn quenched the flame that had been intended for the Sulgrave man.

"Firi, I'm happy to let you kill Tyr. Tell me why, and I'll be the first to see him die."

Her jaw clenched. "Sedit?" She looked to her hound. The beast let a low growl rumble through its throat.

"Don't," Dwyn breathed, genuine fear flashing through the single syllable.

"Tell me why you're here," Ophir demanded.

Dwyn's hair shook around her in a cloud as dark as the night. The surprised whites around her eyes could be discerned despite the late hour. "We're here to support—"

"Tell me why you're *here*! Why did you cross the Frozen Straits? Why are you in Farehold? Why were you in the water that night? Why did you come to find me?"

Tyr released her wrist, holding his hands flat as if he hoped to pacify her. "What did Guryon say?"

"Firi—" Dwyn tried again.

"Stop lying!" She brought her hands up and summoned a large black serpent. Both Dwyn and Tyr tensed against the presence of her beast. "Tell me another lie. Tell me!" She threw out her hand and a second vageth sprung into place, adding to her demonic pack of hellhounds as they slowly populated the shadows of the continent. "Lie to me again!"

Her army of nightmares filled the space, too many black eyes, too many dripping teeth all focused on the bewildered Sulgrave fae. The snake's tongue tasted the air before them as if licking the sweet nectar of their fear. A noxious wave of rotten meat rolled off of the creatures as their horrible odor filled the air around them.

"What happened in there?" Dwyn demanded, eyes shooting between the new vageth and the enormous serpent.

Ophir was flanked by her pitch-black creations. The snake's mouth widened, allowing venom to glisten from its fangs. Its tail wriggled as it coiled itself to strike. Her demons of night were tightly knit to her emotions, tensed with her anger as they stared at her target.

"For you!" Dwyn said honestly, eyes earnest, face pleading.

"What about me?"

Dwyn flinched against her next words, holding her hand up defensively. "I didn't lie to you, Firi."

"Don't call me that."

"I didn't lie to you!" she cried back, taking a half step away from the princess. It was clear from the flit of her eyes that she was searching for an exit strategy—a source of water. "I'm not going to hurt you. I'm not like them. I want to help you, not hurt you. Since the beginning I've been helping you!"

Ophir was unmoved.

"I did this for you," Dwyn practically cried. "*I* did this! Your vageth? Your snake? I helped you find them. Why would I do that for you if I intended you harm?"

The new vageth dragged a single paw on the ground in front of it, flexing its talons and dragging them across the ground.

When Ophir looked unmoved, she changed tactics. "You said you didn't care. You said as long as I wished you no harm, you didn't care why I'd come."

"I care now."

Dwyn looked at her counterpart. "What about him?"

"I'd also like to hear Dwyn explain herself," Tyr said.

Bitterness rolled over Ophir's tongue. "Tyr followed you here from Sulgrave. He said it himself, and you've never denied it. We both know why he's here—*you*. Why are *you* here, Dwyn."

"What did Guryon—"

"This isn't about Guryon. This is about you."

Dwyn threw up her hands in exasperation. "For goddess's sake, Firi—"

"That's exactly right."

Dwyn went rigid.

Ophir met her gaze with a challenging stare until she was certain Dwyn had hinged on the same word. "A god?" Ophir snarled. "You think I can make you a god? That's what they wanted from Caris, isn't it? It sure as fuck doesn't seem like you'll get what you want while my heart's still beating."

"You wanted to die," Dwyn said, tears in her eyes. "If I wanted your dead heart, I could have let that happen. I've helped you every step of the way. Why would I do that?"

Ophir's lips remained pulled back in a snarl. "It appears that whatever they did with Caris didn't work. Maybe I have to unlock my powers before you can steal them from me? I don't know your game, Dwyn. You want to be the All Mother? I'd say 'over my dead body', but honestly, I'd like to see you try. Sedit?"

The hound snapped, drool pooling on the floor beneath its maw.

Dwyn shrieked. She brought her hands in front of herself defensively, practically wringing her fingers together. Her voice rose with ever-increasing panic as the shrill worry of bells tinkled in her typically musical voice. "I swear to you, that's not what this is. Will you please trust me? Please believe when I swear an oath that I will never hurt you? I'll cut my wrists here and now and swear my fealty, Firi. I only want what's best for you. Will you believe me when I say I want to help you uncover your power, to stay close to you, to protect you?"

Ophir lowered her fist slowly. She stared at Dwyn for a long time before her hand dropped fully to her side. She relaxed her shoulder. "No, I can't."

"Can you call off your snake? Your hounds?"

She looked to Dwyn, then to her monsters, then to the house behind her. "Come, Sedit," she said. She flicked her hand, dismissing the new demons to the forest with her other discarded creations. Ophir began to walk back to the house but raised her hand. "Tyr can come. You can decide whether or not you want to be honest with me before you dare to knock on this door. And then I'll decide whether or not I believe you."

Ophir was nearly to the front door before Dwyn cried, "Tyr is here for the same reason I am! The only difference is you know me—you know I care about you! We've shared everything, Firi! We've shared a bed! We've shared a life! I've been at your side for months! I save you from your night-mares! I've held you through your sleep! I pulled you from the waves! I helped you when no one else could!"

"You were no friend to me, Dwyn. You wanted borrowed power? Sure, fine. You want to dabble in forbidden blood magic? I supported you. Who doesn't love a little anarchy? But that's not why you're here, is it? And it's certainly not why you chose *me*."

Dwyn begged, "But, Firi..."

"It's Princess Ophir to you, and it's a higher title than you'll ever attain. I want you out of my kingdom, and out of my life."

"What do you know of him?" Dwyn's eyes danced with tears. "What do you know of Tyr?"

The princess had already opened the door as she looked over her shoulder at the screaming fae. She'd lost her fire. Her parting statement held no fight, only chill. "I know he isn't you."

THIRTY-TWO

◆　◆　◆　◆

D WYN?"
   She recognized the unwelcome voice instantly. Her eyes flew open as she looked up at yet another man who despised her. She remained as still as possible, but frustrated surprise escaped her lips before she could control it. "Fuck."

Harland looked to where she lay in the bushes, then up to the estate. He'd already drawn his blade, holding it from where he sat atop his horse. "What are you doing here? What are you doing...outside?"

She wondered if he could see the mechanisms behind her eyes turn. She knew her hesitancy made one thing clear: she was not forthcoming. He had been right not to trust her, but she couldn't tell him that. Instead, she got to her feet as she looked up to the guard who'd pined after the princess from the moment she met him.

"Is Ophir inside?"

Dwyn tensed. "She's with someone."

The guard dismounted from his steed and looked over his shoulder. Had he come alone? Perhaps if he'd followed Ophir's sloppy trail of corpses, Dwyn assumed any men accompanying him must still be burying the bodies of the countryfolk they'd found. If she was lucky, they could be hours behind.

"Who?" he asked.

Dwyn blinked. "We were traveling together," she admitted. A story wove itself together composed mostly of honesty. She'd never get anywhere with Harland if her words rang too false. "We fled after her meeting with her parents when they told her she was going to be sent to Raascot. She needed to get away from her marriage to Ceneth. I knew no one would support her running, but I did. I still do. I wanted to be there for her if she was truly only trying to escape a forced marriage. It's her right." Dwyn emphasized the final word. She searched Harland's hazel eyes for any sense of relief, but his face held none. She continued, "She's been safe for weeks, and then she met a man. I've seen him before. I think he followed me here from Sulgrave. He has Sulgrave features."

His face tensed, a tendon in his neck moving at the information—part distrust, part jealousy. Harland hesitated as he looked from Dwyn to the estate. The reins remained bundled in his hand. "He's a Sulgrave man?"

She nodded tentatively, hands held in front of her to pacify him. "He traveled with us at first for a few days. I hate him," she said with honest vitriol, "but the princess finds him very fucking charming."

Dwyn's words caused Harland's face to flicker. His eyes tightened. A muscle in his jaw ticked, joining the tendon in his neck that flexed once more. These were honest words.

"I don't know his intent," Dwyn continued, watching her message find purchase. She'd primed the soil. It was time to help the seed grow. "They're in there now. All I want is for her to be safe."

He looked to the dark estate again before his eyes returned to the siren. "Ophir is in there right now and has forced you to sleep outside?" His question was thick with disbelief. "That doesn't sound like her."

Dwyn was quick to nod. "It's not her. The princess I've

known would never have kicked me out to be alone with a man. It's this new traveler. His abilities—he can step into the place between things. It's like a dampening spell, but he cannot be perceived. You won't be able to see him even if he stands before you. Deceit is his first nature."

"He has the power to go unseen?"

"Be extremely careful."

She held her breath as she waited for him to take the bait, breathing only when Harland urged his horse forward and tethered it to a nearby tree.

"She won't be happy to see me," Dwyn said, following him quietly. "He's poisoned her against me."

Harland's shoulders slumped. "She won't be happy to see me, either."

"The newcomer is dangerous," Dwyn whispered.

"Stay out here."

Dwyn fought the urge to scrunch her face. Her lips twitched. "I should go in with you."

"No," Harland gestured. "I'll go. Stay with the horse."

Dwyn nodded and watched Harland walk toward the house. He made the same decision Ophir had made earlier, forgoing the front door in search of a side entrance. The siren waited until he rounded the corner and then she followed, hugging the shadows as she moved silently near the guard. Harland opened the door to the kitchen and slipped in, leaving the back entrance open behind him. Closing it would have been an unnecessary risk in noise when all he needed to do was secure his princess.

Dwyn tiptoed into the house, following the guard from several paces behind. Harland was as fae as she, but his ears had been tuned specifically to hear his princess. He listened as he crept through the kitchen and into the hall, ascending the stairs. Dwyn waited until Harland had reached the door at the end of the hall, silently hugging the stairwell as his hand gripped the knob.

Dwyn watched as Harland leaned into the door and

listened for a moment, hearing Ophir's voice behind the door. He swallowed once before twisting the handle, opening the door to where Ophir was leaning against the desk in the room, a large, dark-haired man leaning onto the space next to her, his bodyweight on one arm as he pressed into her personal space.

Harland's eyes widened. His mouth opened to comment, but before he could say a word, Dwyn was behind him.

She brought one hand over his mouth, the other to his throat. He crumpled before he had a chance to realize anyone else was in the hall.

Ophir was caught in the middle of her exclamation. She'd barely begun to gasp his name when she turned to Dwyn. "What did you do!"

Dwyn shrugged. "You're welcome."

Ophir crossed over to him, kneeling to check his pulse. Her golden eyes burned a molten shade of melted gold as she stared up at the siren. "What did you do to him!?"

"I stopped him from dragging you back to the castle."

"I'm asking—"

"You're asking what power I used?" Dwyn crossed her arms. "You're asking if I called on a borrowed power? Yes. I did. I used a bit of his blood so that I could summon an unfamiliar ability. You want to know why I came to Farehold? It was because this is what I do. I've used the bloods—the lives—of others to tap into borrowed powers. The old gods spoke of ways to secure borrowed powers so that they were no longer…borrowed. It's how they became the old gods. The legends say that they were little more than fae who'd elevated themselves to deities."

"The All Mother—"

"This isn't the All Mother." Dwyn shook her head. "These are men, women, and fae who became gods."

Ophir shook from where she knelt on the ground, hand still against Harland's throat. She had run from the castle, but she'd never wanted harm to come to him. "And… You want to make stolen powers permanent?"

"Yes."

Their eye contact was unbroken, underlining the honesty of her answer. She had not come to lie. Across the room, Tyr had remained completely still. Whatever Dwyn chose to say next could change everything for the man.

"What do you need from me? To use me like you used Harland?"

"Harland will be fine. He'll wake up with a headache and little more."

Ophir stood and stumbled to the middle of the room, backing toward the wall. Her face was painted with the night's turmoil. Exhaustion mingled with her anger as she demanded, "What aren't you telling me?"

Dwyn closed her eyes slowly as she lowered her arms. She leaned against the doorframe; Harland's strong, powerful shape was little more than a pile of muscles and armor on the ground. "Don't worry about Harland," she said again. "What do you know of blood magic? What do you know of those who borrow power?"

Ophir shook her head wordlessly, but the movement of her hair and the set of her jaw indicated rejection rather than curiosity.

She went on. "Do you know of the Reds? I don't believe they operate outside of Sulgrave, so there's a chance nothing like it exists in the south. The Reds are a powerful arm of the church, serving the All Mother with their magic and swords alike."

Ophir pulled in ragged breaths. Dwyn knew from the spark of recognition that she'd heard of the assassins trained to fight for the goddess.

"Your dog here was a Red." She gestured to Tyr. "He might be best qualified to speak on the topic. The religious nutjobs are trained how to pull on unnatural powers. For example, a fae who has the inborn gift of changing the weather might be able to call upon the ability to influence moods or walk through dreams. These powerful fae know it's a trade one makes at great risk. Nothing comes for free. Whatever you take, you must give. With the Reds, their own blood is the penance for the use of abilities that don't belong to them."

Tyr spoke for the first time. "It's the price of magic."

Ophir took another step backward. She positioned herself so that she was farther from each of them, creating a triangle with their bodies. "My magic..."

"Your magic comes at a price, too," Dwyn said quietly. "Royal hearts are the most powerful, as they draw on the blood of their kingdom. You don't have the heart of one fae, Firi; you have the hearts of millions. Sulgrave has no monarchs for this reason precisely. Our mountains are ruled by seven equally powerful Comtes, all selected democratically. Sulgrave didn't used to be this way. We had an Imperator long ago, until it became clear that our royal family would face what Farehold is undergoing now. Our imperator's final act was to step down after his royal children were served up like piglets on a silver platter. We've had no royal bloodline for a millennium. There's no succession in the north. The southern kingdoms, however..."

Dwyn chewed on her lip as she looked at the princess. It appeared from the unsteady pulls of air that Ophir's lungs would not fill completely. She trembled as she asked, "It's true, then? That's why my sister is dead?"

"Yes. They killed Caris for her power. They took as much as they could of her blood, and if they hadn't been interrupted, I'm certain they would have harvested everything. They wanted her heart. Tell me: Caris was a virgin?"

Ophir's face twisted in disgust at the question. "Why does that matter?"

Dwyn sighed heavily, but there was no use in lying. She spoke slowly, but none of her message came out with condescension. Dwyn was choosing each word carefully not because Ophir lacked comprehension but because understanding might be too terrible to swallow. "Because, once

you've claimed your own autonomy, you're more…*yourself.*
Your willingness to take lovers brings you into your own body.
You don't belong to others, to society, to the kingdom…not
in the same way she did. She was saving herself for others.
She didn't belong to herself the same way that you belong to
yourself."

Ophir was speechless. Her pink lips parted wordlessly as
she gaped at Dwyn.

"Well thank goddess I'm a whore, then?" Ophir finally
said, sputtering the words with both disgust and confusion.

"You're still royal, and you still have the heart of your
people. Caris was their preferred target, but in the wrong
hands, you'd do just fine."

She looked from Dwyn to Tyr.

"You're safe," Tyr said quickly, raising his hands. "We're
not the wrong hands. Well, *I'm* not the wrong hands. The
witch is a little less trustworthy. Goddess, Dwyn, could you
do a worse job explaining the situation?"

"At least I'm being honest."

Ophir's lips moved noiselessly as if struggling to find
words that wouldn't come. She struggled to ask, "What do
you want with me?"

"Power," Dwyn said. She said it so Ophir would know
beyond a shadow of a doubt that she did not lie.

"But you said…"

"I meant what I said. I have no intentions of hurting you,
and I never will. There are violent methods to achieve these
means. Berinth's tactic may work. Perhaps gutting you would
yield the results he might want. But once he slaps you on the
table and takes a dagger to your stomach, what if he fails?
Then what? He's taken his one chance at power and squan-
dered it. You're the only princess left. They only get one
more shot at this."

"I—"

"But what if you're alive, Firi?" Dwyn moved farther
into the room. "What if you live, if you thrive, if you come

into your own? What if you become wholly yourself, if your heart—beating with the blood of millions—courses through your veins? What if you fully own your power?"

"What would you gain?" Ophir asked. "What would you gain from me finding my own power?"

"You said you knew," Dwyn said quietly. "You said that you knew I wasn't here altruistically, and that it didn't matter, as long as I wasn't going to hurt you. I never will, Firi. I swear it."

Tyr spoke for both of them. He didn't enjoy collaborating with Dwyn, but it was clear that his allegiance with Ophir faced equal fragility unless this was untangled with delicacy. "I first encountered Dwyn in Sulgrave using blood magic. I've followed her for years. She's discovered what none of us have, and the bitch won't share her knowledge." He cast her a sour look, and she pulled her lips back from her teeth in a noiseless snarl. Tyr finished, "She's the key to blood magic that doesn't injure the user."

"So, you're just as power hungry?" Ophir clarified numbly.

Dwyn deflated at the sight of the princess. The vibrant, beautiful fae so full of life usually had eyes as gold as the family crown. They'd dimmed to a flat shade of ochre, shoulders slumping, heartbroken as she looked at Tyr for answers. Dwyn's fists flexed at her side as she begged Tyr not to fuck this up.

The phantom shook his head. "We have very different motives, trust me. Dwyn's an elusive sprite and the continent would benefit from her death, but she's clever. There is a clan—the blood gang she's referred to..." He redirected his words. "Well, I followed her here to Farehold with the intent of bringing her back to Sulgrave. They—the Blood Pact, that is—want to be able to do what she does. And yes, Ophir, I want to know how she does it every bit as badly as they do. Dwyn funnels power through others. The selfish witch won't tell a soul."

"Fuck off," Dwyn growled.

Tyr exhaled through his nose, nostrils flaring as he waited a moment for his patience to return. "Once I got here, I realized what a beacon you and your sister had been for those seeking blood magic. Raascot's king has no children—you and Caris are the only heirs in all of Gyrradin, which has drawn a few unsavory figures to Farehold. While trying to locate this plague of a siren, I found Berinth. Fortunately for everyone, Dwyn seems to believe that your heart is more valuable while beating."

Dwyn shot him a warning look.

"But…" Ophir's word was a breath. Sedit had been lying curiously on the ground, eyeing the party while they spoke. As his master's emotions shifted, so did his body. He sat up and crossed to Ophir, crouching at her feet. He seemed to sense her distress well enough to position himself against the Sulgrave fae. "I met you first," she said to Tyr. "I met you at the party before I met Dwyn. You tried to stop the man called Aemon from drugging me. You carried me to the castle."

Dwyn smirked. She pushed away from the doorway and went to sit on the bed. "Your turn," she said to Tyr.

He spoke through his teeth. "The world would be a better place if you died, witch."

"So you've said." She shrugged and reclined against a stack of pillows, picking at her nails with all of the idleness in the world. She was doing her best to communicate that she did not fear the outcome of the conversation.

Ophir looked to Tyr like he was a life raft in a storm.

"They're not secretive, princess. The people who want power…well, I wanted Berinth to meet his end just as badly as I continue to desire Dwyn dead," he said. "I was at the party to intervene. Removing you from their hands was the best I could do."

Dwyn wanted so badly to comfort the princess, but she forced herself to remain still as she watched their exchange. Tears threatened Ophir as she blinked at him. "Why?"

His face twisted against a complicated emotion. He ran a

hand over his face, raking it from his brows to his chin. "Races for power don't get to tie for first prize," he said. "Whether it's Berinth or Dwyn, I'm more invested in keeping power out of their hands than I am in taking it for myself. I won't lie to you, Firi: I want it. But not as badly as I want *them* to not have it."

Ophir looked at her at long last. Dwyn did her best to remain cool and reassuring as she said, "He may or may not be telling the truth. All I know is: he's a bastard, and I don't like him."

Ophir backed into the wall until her spine was flush against the stones. Her hand flew to her heart, covering its beating with her fingertips. From down the hall, the clip-clop of another set of talons approached. Her other hound had let itself into the room, presumably entering from the open kitchen door. She didn't even look at the vageth as it eyed the fae. It rested its stomach on the stones beside Harland's limp body, reclining so as to block the exit.

"I still don't understand." Ophir's expressive, amber brows collected in the center as she looked to Dwyn. "If you don't want to hurt me, or cut out my heart, how could you stand to profit? What can you gain from this?"

Tyr seemed just as interested in the answer as Ophir was.

Dwyn struggled to look relaxed. She couldn't dare to lose her cool now. She pushed up from where she'd leaned against the bed and threw her legs over its edge. She set her delicate feet on the stones and began to cross to Ophir. The hellhound at Ophir's feet began to growl, but she paid it no mind. She clasped Ophir's hands in her own as she leaned in closely.

"I care about you, and I want you to care about me. I want to *be* with you, Ophir. I understand—sure, I could have killed you. I could have let you drown on the waves, hauled your body to shore, and taken your blood or heart then. I could have, but I didn't. I swear to you, Firi, I would never hurt you. You'd be gone. I'd be alone." Dwyn ran a hand up her arm until it cupped the princess's face. "If we rule together, we have the power of two. I didn't mean to lie to you. But together…we have so much potential, Firi."

"I—"

Dwyn dared to brush her lips over Ophir's—the gentle, tempting graze of a kiss. Ophir's eyes remained open. Her heart flittered with the speed of a hummingbird's wings out of alarm, not pleasure. She was not soothed by the gesture.

"Don't do that." Ophir tried to pull away. "Don't try to kiss me now like everything is fine."

"You liked it, once."

"That was before."

"It's okay if you don't trust me. I saved you on the waves, I've held you, I've doused your flames night after night, I've shared your bed in more ways than one, I've traveled with you, and I've even put up with him." She threw a single vulgar finger over her shoulder to Tyr. "It doesn't bother me, because I'm in this for it all. I'm not going anywhere. As angry as you might be, I know that you see the truth in my words: I've been there for you. I've been there for you, protected you, and stood beside you. I helped you become who you were *meant* to be. And I'm willing to wait until you're ready to see me as I am."

"Don't touch me," she said, freeing herself from Dwyn.

"Are you okay?"

Ophir searched her expression. After an eternity, she said, "No, I'm not. I haven't been okay in a long time."

Dwyn studied her face carefully.

With the sort of pained carefulness as if picking over broken glass, Ophir said, "I'd like to be alone tonight. You two can find another room. I don't care. Just…don't be here."

Dwyn surged with emotion. "Please, Firi—"

Tyr reached out to stop her, and for once, she did not fight him. She watched the princess helplessly. The sudden end to the meeting was chilling. Everyone seemed acutely aware of the night's temperature and disquieted by Ophir's sudden stillness. They began to nod with some hesitancy, but Tyr looked down at Harland's crumpled shape.

Ophir's voice was flat as she looked at Tyr. "If you could set Harland by his horse, I'd consider it a great favor."

✦   ✦   ✦   ✦

Tyr agreed wordlessly and had already begun to loop his grip under the guard's arms, dragging his unconscious form backward down the hall. Ophir did not meet their eyes as they departed into the hall. She did not look to them as she closed the door. She did not look at them as she blew out the candle, or as she watched out the window to ensure Harland's sleeping shape was left safely by his mount. She did not look for them as she created her second inanimate object, manifesting a ladder from little more than breath and thought. She didn't look over her shoulder as she climbed out the window and crept across the lawn, save to ensure that her very lithe beast had not only the power of a canine but also the feline agility that allowed him to follow her. She didn't look for them as she called a twisting, knotting pit of vipers to smother the lawn, their rope-like bodies so thick and intertwined that they'd never be able to run after her. She didn't look to Harland as she passed his fallen body, or to the house as she created her first steed—a gaunt, bony, terrible thing that seemed more ghost than mount. She didn't look to them as she took off down the regent's road, and she didn't look over her shoulder at the high-pitched scream of her name cried over the horizon, barely reaching her ears in the distance she'd already covered.

She vowed to never look back again.

PART III

A Trail of Blood and Beasts

THIRTY-THREE

+   +   +   +

Harland wished his king would speak. He wanted to be yelled at, to have furniture thrown, to be caned or sent to the dungeon. Instead, Eero had absorbed his message and sank into a chair. He'd rested his hands in his face, concealing the eyes that he shared with the honey-colored features of his missing daughter. Queen Darya had been present at the beginning of the meeting, but she'd wordlessly excused herself. Her unceremonious departure had left the men in the world's longest uncomfortable silence.

"Your majesty…" He looked at where the king sat at the war room table. The bright windows lit the beige, circular room without the aid of fire or torches.

Eero looked up from his hands. "I don't blame you, if disapproval is what you fear."

Harland's chest tightened painfully. His king's heart was so saturated with anguish that his words had been more of a punishment than a comfort. He wanted to take his ruler's pain. King Eero had been a good and fair ruler for three hundred years. He'd birthed two beautiful, intelligent, powerful daughters. He had seen his kingdom prosper and had been ready to hand it over to Caris and her betrothed as he aided the royal visionaries in their efforts to change the world. Everything had been at the tips of his fingers, and then with the plunge of a dagger, it had been dashed.

Harland knew Ophir better than anyone else in the castle. As her personal guard, he was not only responsible for her, but he'd become Aubade's foremost expert on the wayward princess. He'd requested that the other guards be dismissed as he relayed his findings, and the king and queen had listened. He didn't want other people to know that Ophir had become a murderer, though it was surely only a matter of time before word of her actions began to spread.

Harland remained at full attention. He hadn't relaxed his posture in nearly an hour, and his body ached from the rigidity of his stance. His legs were shoulder-width apart, and his hands were clasped behind his back. He couldn't very well lean against the wall, or recline in a chair. He'd returned to Aubade to inform his king that Ophir had been found and lost once more. What was more: their worst fears had been confirmed. Ophir was seeking vengeance on those who'd taken Caris's life, and she was succeeding.

"Dwyn…" Harland began to say the name of the fae, and the king shook his head.

"I don't blame you, or anyone, for her, either," the king said. "Ophir hadn't slept in months. She was burning down the castle. My daughter was falling apart. When Dwyn came into the castle, I didn't want to know more. I was unwilling to learn anything that might lessen my favor for the girl. She had the power to summon water, and she was a friend to my only surviving child. Ophir began sleeping through the night. The castle was spared from her flame. It was a salvation."

"But she was from Sulgrave—"

"And perhaps I liked her for the same reason you distrusted her. Neither of our reasons was acceptable. She was from Sulgrave, and we know nothing of Sulgrave. You should not find someone suspicious simply because they are from an unknown land, nor should I have given her the benefit of the doubt as wise or benevolent for simply her exoticism. She was a fae woman. Her nation of origin seems unimportant compared to the reality we face. We were ignorant in equal proportion, but in truth, Harland, I would do it again."

The guard's brows pinched. His back continued to ache from his stance, but he couldn't relax. "Your Majesty?"

Eero stood and began to walk toward the war table. "We were losing Ophir, one way or another. She'd attempted to take her own life, hadn't she? Isn't that how Dwyn found her in the first place?"

Harland was speechless. He hadn't told anyone what he'd seen the day after the party. He hadn't spoken of the pools of salt and sand in her room, nor of the way Dwyn had flippantly revealed that she'd thwarted Ophir's attempt at suicide. He'd kept it to himself, hoping that he'd be able to get her the help she needed on his own. Secrecy had been a mistake.

"Yes, I'd thought as much. Those were the rumors. The servants reported her entering the castle from the beach with a stranger. I didn't put the pieces together until much later." He leaned two hands on the map and looked at the continent that stretched before him. "She tried to drown herself. I would have buried both of my only children in the same year. It bears repeating: we were already losing Ophir. Allowing Dwyn into our home may have just helped us to lose her in a way that kept her alive, rather than lose her in a way that united her with the All Mother."

Harland shifted closer to the war table, muscles rejoicing at the movement. They'd grown so stiff in his unwillingness to waiver.

"You saw her here?" King Eero pointed on the map to the neighboring city of Henares.

"Five days past," he confirmed.

"And came directly back to the castle?"

"No, your majesty. I would have been back in only two if I'd returned immediately. I attempted to follow her trail, but the tracks were...unintelligible. I tried for several days before returning to inform you. I apologize for not coming back sooner."

"None of that," Eero chided softly. "Self-flagellation will get us nowhere."

Harland failed to stifle his heavy breathing. He had always been grateful for his king. Eero was the ruler that Farehold deserved. Caris would have been just as wonderful serving on the throne. Now instead they were thrust to the hounds as Gyrradin fell into turmoil. All he could do was offer one piece of disappointing information after the other. "She was with another—a man from Sulgrave. I don't know his name, nor do I know anything about him. Dwyn didn't care for him, so I have no reason to believe they're working together. That being said, she and I didn't get the chance to speak more than a few words.' As I said, by the time I was rendered unconscious…"

He eyed the map. "If Ophir is pursuing Berinth and his collaborators, then that's what we must do as well."

"Your Highness? Haven't we been doing just that?"

Eero released his hands from where they'd been resting on the table. He folded them across his chest and rested one hand beneath his chin. "We have been using the constabulary and traditional means of investigation, including all of the resources available to the southern kingdom. We need to scry."

The tempo of Harland's heart increased. His lips turned downward as he searched his king's face. "But the dark powers—"

"Ceneth is our ally," he said calmly. "He deserves to know why his betrothed has gone missing. I believe him to be a good man, and that he, too, desires vengeance on whoever took Caris's life. If there are fae in Raascot's courts with the power to scry, he will have access to them. I'm confident he would supply us with the abilities we need to find Ophir."

Harland made a face, shifting uncomfortably.

"Please, speak freely."

"I'm not sure…"

"Harland." Eero eyed him seriously. "You remained Ophir's guard longer than any man before you. She's chased away guards and maidservants and suitors alike, but she trusts you. You know her well. You know as well as I that Ophir is a complicated puzzle. If you have an opinion on the matter, I will hear it."

Harland inhaled through his nose, feeling his nostrils flare as he did his best to control his face into a mask of respect. "Sir, if we bring in a dark fae so that we might scry to find Ophir, she will run again. Your daughter seeks vengeance. Dragging her back to the castle with her mission unresolved will be little more than watching the clock until we see her escape once more."

The look King Eero leveled was grave and empty all at once.

"If you're going to bring in someone who can scry, then we can't use their power to find Ophir. We must do it to bring Caris's murders to justice, once and for all. Don't give Ophir a reason to flee. Eliminate the reason she needed to run in the first place."

THIRTY-FOUR

· · · ·

"STOP LOOKING AT ME LIKE YOU'RE GOING TO KILL ME." Dwyn's eyes narrowed into bitter slits. Tyr met her challenging stare until her gaze waivered to the true evidence of death at their feet.

Tyr struggled to control his breathing. He hated Dwyn, sure, but had to hand it to her: she was perceptive. Not a moment went by where he didn't want to see her dead.

"I'm trying to keep my body count lower than yours. In the meantime"—he gestured to the ground—"can you not do things like this in the house?"

Dwyn scrunched her nose disapprovingly. Perhaps she didn't find much pleasure in eyeing the fallen. "They're as light as paper. You should be able to carry them into the woods without an issue."

"If they're so light, you do it."

She sighed and made a point of turning her back on the mummified husks of the husband and wife who'd owned the farm home they now occupied. They'd answered the door with a mixture of confusion and skepticism, but Dwyn had given them no time to feel fear or pain. She'd placed her hands on them and sapped them just as she had on the icy, western shores of Sulgrave so many decades prior. It had unnerved him to see then but only bothered him to see it now.

Tyr felt a surge of irritation as she moved toward the fire to warm herself.

"You're really just going to leave them?"

She looked over her shoulder at the husks. "They won't smell, if that's your fear," she assured him. "Their blood and flesh and the normal elements of rot don't pose a problem when they've been drained. It just"—she made a small, explosive gesture with her fingers as she finished her sentence—"evaporates."

He was pretty sure he caught her moving to warm herself by the hearth as he carried the belated countryfolk out the door to bury them in the garden. He may have abandoned the Reds long ago, but his noble sense of decency had nothing to do with the church and its moral code. Maybe that was why, even as he muttered last rites to the fresh-turned earthy mounds that were a happy husband and wife only minutes ago, he knew Dwyn would continue to have the upper hand. Her absence of a moral compass allowed her to play chess while he remained confined to checkers.

He returned to the house exhausted and covered in dirt to the homey smells of jam and eggs. Fresh bread sat atop the kitchen table, buttered knife abandoned halfway through its task. A still-hot skillet sizzled on the window sill.

"Do you need help with washing?" Dwyn asked, making a gesture with her hand to indicate that she'd be willing to call whatever water he might need from the trough.

He picked up the sandwich with earthy hands and bit into it. His eyes lifted appreciatively. "I'm shocked you cooked dinner for me."

"I didn't," she said between bites, speaking with her mouth still full. "I cooked for me. There just happened to be enough food for two." She made a disgusted face as she watched him, eyeing the dirt that smudged his body. "I can't believe you're holding that sandwich with your hands after touching dead bodies."

He didn't want to let the amusement tug his mouth up at the corners but couldn't help it. "You were the one who killed them. You're the reason the bodies were dead in the first place."

She shrugged, returning to her final bites. "Fair enough."

Tyr looked around for the water pitcher but landed on the assorted jars and bottles of wines, ales, and spirits in the corner. "Is the only fresh water for their farm animals?" He'd made sure that Knight had enough to eat and drink before he'd taken care of himself.

Of course, riding Knight had meant sharing a saddle with Dwyn, which had been equal parts terrible and amusing. He enjoyed causing her displeasure, which made it a win to hear her bitch every time she brushed against him or felt his chest against her back on the horse.

"They have a well," she said.

"And?" he asked. "Will you be doing the honors?"

She brushed the crumbs off her hands. "No. I'm in the mood for wine. Go pump the well yourself." Dwyn fetched one of the tall green bottles and found a small silver cup. He watched as she poured the wine in, swirled it once, and inhaled the full-bodied scent before drinking it.

"Kill the farmers, eat their food, but then sniff their wine to be sure it's up to your standards?"

She rolled her eyes but didn't take his bait. If he hadn't continued staring at her expectantly, there's a chance she wouldn't have said anything at all. Finally, with another appreciative sip of the rich, red liquid, she said, "I can do this without you, Tyr. I've just absorbed the life I'll need for whatever ability I might require to find Ophir. You're the one who can't move forward without me. You wouldn't know where to go, where to look, or how to even begin to find the princess. I'm only keeping you around because..." Her voice trailed off with distinct hints of sadness.

He leaned back in his chair, wetting his lips. The glass of water called to him, but something else was on his mind. Her shift in tone had scratched his mind with a thirst greater than the need for a cool drink. "Can I ask you something?"

"I'm sure you will anyway," she said, taking a generous swallow of the wine. She tipped the green bottle up once more and refilled her silver cup.

He made a speculative face, eyeing her as if studying a caged animal. He'd spent years hunting her. Once he'd found her, she'd uniquely positioned herself so that catching her would be disadvantageous. Now that he was only an arm's length away, he wasn't sure if he even looked at a woman or if she was another creature entirely. Her heart did not seem to tick with the mechanisms that wound within the chests of men and fae. "Are you genuinely sad that Ophir doesn't like you at the moment? Or are you just upset that your plan to manipulate her isn't going smoothly?"

She looked with icy calculation. "I like her."

He stared back. "That's not what I asked."

She tilted her head slowly. "I want her to like me."

"Now I'm wondering one of two things. Either you're being intentionally vague because you're a narcissist who's disappointed everyone isn't playing by her rules, or you're not emotionally intelligent enough to understand your own feelings."

"Two things. Go fuck yourself, and know that I hate you."

"But alas." He grinned somewhat humorlessly, tugging at the collar of his tunic to reveal his tattoo. "There's little you can do about that hate, is there."

Dwyn's gaze shot to where a similar, complex swirl of ink wrapped around her leg and over her hip. It was always hidden below whatever pants or tunic or dresses she wore, but it marred her just as it did him. He'd watched her eyes fill with rage every time she caught the way the darkened edges of his tattoo licked above his collar, impossible to truly conceal. Neither of them needed the constant reminder of the single biggest mistake they'd ever made.

"Her royal guard," Tyr began, changing the subject as his mind wandered to the man he'd set beside his horse in the yard nearly one week prior. He'd been able to find them when no one else had.

"Harland," Dwyn supplied.

He grunted his acknowledgment. "Will he pose any problem?"

Dwyn shook her head. "No, I don't think so. He's already tried his best, after all. I've known him for some time. He doesn't like me very much, but he'd die for Ophir. I can't be sure, but something about the way he looks at her leads me to believe they've shared a bed. He loves her," she said, ruing the word with a tinge of jealousy. "Even if we come across him, I think we'd be able to win him to our cause if it means reuniting them. He's uptight, but he wouldn't make the worst traveling companion."

"You wouldn't kill him?"

The siren's chuckle reminded him of belladonna blossoms and brightly colored serpents and other poisonous things that came in pretty packages. "I'm trying to get Ophir on my good side, remember? Even when they fight, it's like a spat between family. Besides, you'd run and tell her what I'd done immediately. If you knew how, anyway."

"Right," he said, voice as dry as the crusted earth he dusted from his palms. "And you can, because of the farmers you slaughtered so you...what, exactly? Why did they need to die?"

"Nice try" came her deadpan reply. "You know that I can borrow any ability I want from the well of power that flows through the earth. It's why you followed me across the Straits. If I wanted to find Ophir right now, I'd just"—she snapped her fingers to underscore her point—"and there you have it, I'd be a natural-born tracker."

"Then do it."

"I've only borrowed two lives," she said. "And I have far more than two things to accomplish if I want to help Ophir.

Finding her is a quarter of the battle at best. Can't go wasting good blood, now, can we?"

He drummed his fingers against his bicep. "Why don't you show me how to borrow powers like you do, and then we can double our efforts to help her?"

"Your selfishness betrays you," she said. "You'd get what you want, and you'd disappear to do goddess-knows-what with your newfound powers. You don't care about Ophir."

"She won't love you," he replied. He hadn't meant for it to come out as quietly as it had. His words felt both too heavy and too quiet for the small country home and its crackling fire. There was a sadness and weight to the simple statement. It soured the room that had been filled with the warm, hearty smells of fire, ash, cooked ham, and eggs only moments before.

"She may yet," Dwyn said quietly.

"Why do you need it?" he asked, knowing she wouldn't answer.

"No." She refilled her glass. "Why I need it isn't the question. You're not unintelligent. You've discerned my motives."

"Power for the sake of power?"

"If it were as simple as that. But yes. The true question is, oh noble Tyr, why do *you*?"

Revenge. But he wouldn't tell her that. If she knew about Svea…if she knew of his weaknesses…well, he didn't need anyone else to see his weak spots. They'd been his undoing. He looked away and could see Dwyn smile.

"It's a woman, isn't it? Your secret?"

He didn't look at her.

"It is," she pushed. "I knew it. I've always known it. Let's see…you weren't high status enough for her? Something to prove? A heart to win? A lover scorned?" She leaned forward on her elbows, testing each question against his impassive expression. "No, that's not it… Was she family? A sister? A mother?" Dwyn stood and wandered nearer to him, still holding her wineglass. "I'm getting warmer, aren't I? Something happened to her."

His face tightened in a way that would have been utterly imperceptible to anyone else.

"That's it, isn't it. Did she die? They always die."

He closed his eyes slowly.

"Yes? No? Let's try again... Did someone hurt her?"

"Stop speaking of things you don't know. It's not for you to understand, Dwyn. We'll get Ophir back. You can continue whatever game you're playing for her heart, though I have to say, I think she'll see through it. She kept me in Guryon's house when she kicked you out, remember?"

"You don't know what she will and won't do."

He reached up and took the wineglass out of her hand, draining it. "What, because you fucked her you think you've cemented a place with the heir of Aubade? You want to rise to power alongside the last remaining hope of Farehold? Please, you should know the difference between sex and love. She slept with her guard, didn't she? Does she love him?"

"Are you saying she's easy?" Dwyn's posture tightened as if ready to spring into defense.

"I'm saying, she slept with you because she doesn't respect you. She saw you as an opportunity for fun, or escape, or rebellion. Not because she views you as an equal."

Dwyn's mouth dropped open in offense. Her brows lowered. She raised her palms, hands filling with fire.

"Don't go draining your abilities before we've used them on anything good just because you can't keep your legs closed."

She threw a punch that he caught, staring at her as she lit her fist on fire. He didn't flinch as the flame consumed his hand, crackling with shades of white, orange, and yellow. The small home filled with the scent of roasted meat as smoke billowed from his grasp.

She cried out in pain, buckling under the dually inflicted wound as it consumed her. The sound was a high, sharp, guttural noise as if it had wrenched itself up directly from her belly. He felt every crackle of skin, every boil of blood, every splinter of bone that she felt, but all he had to do was remain conscious while they shared the unspeakable pain she'd intended to inflict only on him. She grunted through the pain, intensifying her flame in a final burst of energy as if she'd forgotten even for a moment that, for her, he was untouchable.

Finally, she released the call on the flame, blinking at him in shock and disgust. Her face turned a greenish shade of sick. Sweat danced on her brow as she struggled to maintain her angered expression. Her small fist remained in the blackened, cooked remains of his scorched hand, but he'd endured it all without a single reaction.

"You sick fuck!" She gagged, staggering to the side as she failed to jostle her fist loose from his grasp. "Why did you let me do that?"

He refused to break his challenging stare. "I think you underestimate your opponent, Dwyn. You want power for power's sake? Your life, your future, your prospects, your happiness, everything is at stake for you. Me? I have nothing to lose."

"Are you going to let go of my hand?"

"Oh, I can't. My fingers are absolutely fused together. Make yourself useful, would you?"

She tried to jerk her fist free of his grasp. He gleaned some satisfaction from the way her expression changed when she realized he was right. He'd made a horrific, unconscionable gamble, and won. His heart was still racing against the exchange. Tyr had undergone excruciating torture without flinching to prove, what, that he wasn't afraid of her? She called magic to her fist once more, but this time it was a healer's touch coursing through her until his flesh was pink and healthy once more, allowing him to relax his hold and disengage.

"You're so much more fucked up than I realized."

He arched a brow as he emptied the bottle of wine into the glass. "And that's why I'm going to win."

THIRTY-FIVE

✦ ✦ ✦ ✦

W HAT ARE THEY ASKING FOR?" CENETH RUBBED HIS temples, hunched over his war room table. The room was windowless, midnight blue with the captured refraction of labradorite on which the castle was built, as if the night sky glittered in every precious stone. If it weren't for the oil-soaked rags and torches, the room could have been utterly black.

"Eero has been very forthcoming, Your Majesty. He's shared that Ophir is missing of her own volition, and that they're hoping we might provide someone with the ability to scry."

For years, the Castle of Gwydir had been undergoing the beautification process necessary to house its impending queen. Loving touches had filled every corridor. Luxurious curtains, latticed windows, ornate carvings in the once-plain pillars of the throne room, paintings of landscapes, planting of bushes and trees and flowers throughout the castle grounds. Now the blue-black stones of Gwydir seemed hauntingly cold. All efforts for renovation had ceased with the news of her passing. Scores of decorators, gardeners, landscapers, seamstresses, upholsters, painters, and the like had lost their stations in the castle overnight. Now it was a place where a heartbroken king would sit over his map and strategize, throwing himself into how to fulfill Caris's vision for a better world even in her absence. He rarely left his war room, save for eating and sleeping. He had little reason to carry on without her.

The king's hands slipped into his hair. "They'd have someone with the ability to scry in Farehold if they hadn't spent hundreds of years demonizing powers they deemed 'dark.'"

"You know as well as I that Eero and Darya are not to blame."

He did know that. King Eero and Queen Darya had inherited a kingdom of systemic injustice. He also knew that passivity in the face of injustice was as good as condoning its continuity, and their daughter was the first to do something about it. Caris was a revolutionary. She wanted to use her power and privilege to make a change in the world. She wanted safety, she wanted education, she wanted not just tolerance, but peace, understanding, and appreciation among the people of the continent. Her heart had been too good for this world, and the world had killed her for it.

Ophir had killed her.

"Do we want to find Ophir?" Ceneth's voice was tired. He hadn't slept in months. He didn't want the younger princess in Gwydir any more than she wanted to be there.

"The plan for the alliance has been in place before Eero and Darya even had children. The fact that they had daughters was advantageous, but irrelevant to the need for the alliance. It's what's right for Raascot."

"Substantially harder to birth an heir to both thrones if they'd had sons, I suppose." He wanted to smile but didn't have it in him. He'd loved Caris. He'd loved her more than he'd thought possible. He'd wanted to tear down the world and make it new for her. He would have ripped out the hearts of her enemies, baked her ten thousand cakes, picked her flowers every day, given her the heads of her enemies, and made the world a new, beautiful place as they ruled. He would have given her every piece of himself every day for the rest of his life.

But Ophir had taken the most perfect treasure in this wretched world and dragged her to a viper's den. And now he was supposed to marry his beloved's murderer.

"I know you don't care for Ophir, Your Majesty, but—"

Ceneth scoffed.

"The fact remains, she is your betrothed now."

"Call a medium."

"Your Highness?"

He continued to rub at his temples. "I don't have one in the courts, and I'd like to appoint one to reside within the castle. Please inform whoever you find that I hope for them to take up residence in our guest wing. I need to speak with Caris."

The man shook his head. "I have to disagree. There are some powers—"

"Some powers that what?" His voice was thick with challenge. "Some powers that are evil? Some powers that should be forced out of the south and sequestered to the north, where all evil things reside? Some powers that are only for the wicked, dark fae of Raascot?" He looked disgusted with the man. "Find a medium and put them in my employ. Give them whatever rooms in the castle they'd like. Pay them whatever they ask."

"And of one who can scry, Your Majesty?"

"Eero can wait. If Farehold's princess is missing now, either she'll still be missing by the time we respond to his raven, or they'll have found her and the problem will have resolved itself. Or maybe she'll be eaten by wolves, and then once again, the problem will resolve itself."

The man frowned disapprovingly.

He clucked his tongue. "Come, now. I wouldn't hurt Ophir. Do I blame her? Yes. Do I think she should have died instead of Caris? Yes. Every day of the year my answer to that will be yes. For as long as I live, my answer is yes. Am I angry with her? I think you know that response as well. But would I harm her?" He paused as if considering the question. "...No. It would upset Caris."

"Caris is dead, Your Highness."

Ceneth's eyes flashed, burning with a dark, angry fire. The man flinched, understanding precisely what he'd done wrong. "And why are you wasting time telling me what I already know when you should be finding me a medium? Don't come back until you have one."

He didn't want to sit alone in the war room with the smell of oil and fire.

When the advisor left, he took a rare stroll around the castle. *Stroll* may not have been the right word. Perhaps *sulk* would better suit his disposition. He wandered the grounds, looking at everything through the lens of what would never be. He and his golden, elfin bride had been meant to rule for one thousand years, madly in love. The castle grounds would have been filled with blossoming bushes. The yard may have had happy children, half him, half their beautiful mother, playing with well-loved puppies and bringing smiles to all of Gwydir. Instead, he'd be wed to her murderer.

But Ophir wasn't the only one to blame.

No, the list of those who needed to pay was long and written in blood.

✦   ✦   ✦   ✦

Even among the Raascot fae, there were a few gifts considered more terrible than others.

The wisdom of the kingdom was that an ability was no more good nor evil than the one wielding it. Surely that was true of all gifts, including mediums. Surely families were healed when they could learn their loved ones had forgiven them. A mother could hear that their child was safe and whole. A soldier might learn that the friend who'd fallen on

279

the battlefield had passed on to drink pints in the great halls of the afterlife. Surely, there was good that could come from it.

Ceneth wasn't sure why he was sweating.

He'd told his people for centuries that powers were morally neutral, as had his father before him. How could he believe that if he feared the gifts of the one visiting him now?

The war-room door opened and a somewhat androgynous fae stepped into the windowless room. A silk, copper-colored scarf was wound tightly around the fae's hair, concealing it entirely, nearly matching the bronze of their skin. The medium examined the war room, then shook their head.

"I'm sorry," said Ceneth. "I was expecting a woman."

The medium waved a hand. "Such titles are constrictive and useless. Call me neither, for I am none."

Ceneth nodded quickly. "You're right. I'm sorry."

He was king. He shouldn't be apologizing to anyone, but he was nervous. Yet, this individual might be the only person in his kingdom that might allow him to speak to Caris. He'd signed over whatever authority or respect he had the moment he'd recognized their power to connect him to the one he'd loved.

"This won't do," they said. "You're in this room to avoid your emotions, Your Majesty, not to connect with them. Bring me to wherever you had the strongest connection to your loved one."

He knew exactly where he felt most connected to his beloved—the bride who would never be.

Caris had been to Gwydir twice. The first time had been on an ambassador mission with the entire royal family. She'd been escorted by an entourage of guards. The King and Queen of Farehold had been ushered through the kingdom, waited on hand and foot. While the first night had come with its uncomfortable cordial interactions, by the second night, they'd had a chance interaction in the corridor.

"Oh, I'm sorry." The fair princess shook her head, her blond hair cascading around her bare shoulders. "I was just looking for your gardens. You seem to have so much space between the castle and the river, but where are your flowers?"

He'd laughed, and then immediately stopped himself when he caught her expression. "No, I'm the one who's sorry. I didn't mean to laugh at you. I suppose the last woman on the grounds was my mother, and she wasn't particularly interested in aesthetics. The castle really could use a lady's touch." He'd watched her blue eyes as she listened intently, nodding as he spoke to let him know she was engaged with his every word. "What would you do with it?"

It had been like breathing.

They'd stepped into one another's lives as if they'd always existed there. Their stories had begun somewhere in the middle, as if it were quite by accident that the author of life and time had left out the first part of their lives, too tired to write how their souls had been born together, grown up together, known each other on a level deeper than blood and bones. Ceneth had accompanied her through the grounds as she commented on what she'd fix or change, all while showering Gwydir in sincere compliments every time she saw a lovely bend in the river, glisten in the stone, tall tree, or friendly face. He hadn't faked a moment of sincerity with her. Everything between them had been so easy.

He'd known his heart belonged to her before they'd left the gardens.

They wanted as one. They planned as one. They even dreamed as one.

Ceneth blinked away from the memory. "My bedchambers, I suppose. No, no, nothing untoward. I won't have you thinking a single improper thought of her. She was perfect and peerless in every way. It was me. I used to dream of her all the time while she lived. Almost every night, in fact. And now..."

The medium turned from the war room as if they were leading the way, even though they had no idea where the king slumbered. Fortunately, Ceneth's advisor was still present to escort the medium through the halls. The castle had its twists and turns, but after a few winding flights of stairs, they found themselves in the king's room. It was ostentatiously large, with a wall of floor-to-ceiling latticed windows that opened onto an enormous balcony overlooking Gwydir.

"Your bed?" the medium asked, their expression heavy with implication, though not of judgment.

Ceneth felt a compulsion toward honesty. Caris had passed, and there were no secrets worth protecting if they might cost him the ability to reunite with her once more. "We weren't intimate. Not in the flesh. But my dreams knew only her nearly every night after we met. I haven't dreamed of her since she passed, and it's like I've lost her all over again."

The medium took it upon themself to drag the desk from where it had rested against the wall closer to the fireplace. The grating sounds of wood and stone disrupted any sense of peace and decorum, but after the curtains were drawn and candles were lit, a deeper, more ominous energy filled the room. The medium sat on one side of the desk with their back to the fire, becoming a dark silhouette as the flames licked behind them. They extended their hands across the table and made a sweeping gesture for Ceneth to take a seat.

The advisor had remained idling in the doorway, but with one pointed look from the medium, the man was dismissed. He closed the door behind him to give them privacy.

"Sit," the medium said.

Ceneth knew exactly why nervous adrenaline coursed through him. He wasn't afraid of what he might meet. He was afraid of disappointment. Caris's absence would be yet another loss in a string of acute, painful streams of mourning. He was afraid that she would not answer his call. He was afraid to face the reality that perhaps the spirit did not live on after death. A greater fear seized him that even if there was, she wouldn't want to see him.

The medium's hands remained extended until Ceneth placed his palms in each of the medium's hands, clasping them loosely.

"Let your mind go blank," the medium said, voice low.

Ceneth silently obeyed.

"Picture her."

He did.

"Listen to my voice as I take you to her. Listen as I count backward from ten. When I reach one, you will be reunited with your beloved. Ten"—the medium's voice continued in a slow, steady pattern—"nine, your heart feels light. Eight, your mind is empty. Seven, your body is relaxing. Six."

They continued to count down, and with each number, Ceneth felt himself disconnect further and further from the chair, the desk, the bedchamber, and the mortal plane. He heard the number two, and then opened his eyes when the number one failed to come.

The medium wasn't there.

"Caris?" His voice caught in his throat as he stared into the ocean eyes of his beloved. The outline of her hair, her shoulders, her slim frame caught against the flickering backlight of the fire. The smell of newly budding flowers and the petrichor just after a spring rain filled the room. Her hands were soft yet strong as she held him.

She smiled sadly back at him, squeezing his hands. "I'm so sorry we never get our wedding."

A hot, violent spike of tears stung his eyes, but he didn't dare release her hands to wipe them away. "Are you really here?"

"Yes, and no," she said, testing each word for accuracy. She spoke slowly, carefully. "Time is blurry here. I'm with you. I'm before you. I'm thousands of years beyond you. Things have never been and will always be. Threads, tangled and interwoven. Tapestries and patterns and lines between then and now and next. All of it, and none of it, and yet I still wish you could have seen me in white. I have the loveliest dress picked for our day. Had. Will have. It's hard to say."

The tears spilled over his lids as he looked at her, cheeks pink and healthy, hair as golden as the sun. Her lips puckered in a sympathetic pout, as if she knew that nothing she could say or do would ever ease this pain. There was no comfort. She tried, releasing the grip from one hand so that she could use her gentle fingers to run soothing pats and traces along the king's giant, calloused hands.

"I'm to marry Ophir." He closed his eyes as he delivered the news.

"I know." She nodded. "It's already happened."

Rejection and denial bubbled through him, horrified at her words. "No, she's missing, she—"

"You'll marry her, but she won't be your bride. There's no betrayal. I won't feel hurt or wronged. You'll need to do it to save her. From what could be, for her, for you, for the world. It doesn't work. It does. It hasn't. It will. The threads, the fabric, it's still being woven. It's already finished. It hasn't begun."

Half of what she said didn't make sense. It was garbled and nonsensical, though her voice was bright, curious, and clear. "You speak of fabric? Time?"

"Yes, my love. The fabric of time. You understand. You don't. You haven't. You will. And you'll marry her. I know you will, because you know I love her, and you love me. Loved me. Will love me. I loved her before we were born, and in one thousand years I love her still, though she breaks. Raascot breaks. Has broken. The gods will break it."

"Raascot?" He looked at her, confused.

"It's fuzzy, almost as if I'm looking through curtains, or hair, or as if the quilt is still on the loom. Sometimes I see it so clearly, and then it shifts. Sometimes it's complete. It is complete. I see five generations of broken hearts on Raascot's throne, then three, then ten. I see pain. I see terror and darkness. I see..." The lines across her forehead deepened.

"Caris? What? Are you safe? Where are you? What's it like? Are you okay?"

She shook her head. "I'm yesterday, and one hundred years before that. It's all a ball of yarn that's been unraveled and put together again by careless hands. In some futures, I see you smile. You can smile again. You can have a child—he shares your wings."

"That's impossible." He shook his head. "If I'm to marry your sister—"

"And you will. You already have."

Frustration and sorrow collided as they seeped into him. He shook his head. "Caris, we were going to change the world. We were going to break the wheel. The people, the kingdoms…"

"Five generations," she repeated. "I see it now, the threads, the stitching, the fabric. Things will get so much worse before they get better. An army. A league. A brotherhood. A tragedy. A war."

"Caris… Are you seeing the future?" He was hurt and confused and nearly frantic as he held her small hands more tightly. He didn't know how to make sense of any of her words. "What do I do?"

"No." She shook her head. "It isn't the future. It's now. It's then. It's maybe. But so much of the maybe is dark. So much is pain. So much is…" She looked around. "Why am I here? Do you have a question for me?"

"What is the afterlife?"

She tilted her head slightly to the side as if she didn't understand the question. "After?"

He swallowed, deciding it didn't matter. Maybe this was not something he was meant to know or understand. Maybe that's why the goddess saw fit to scramble her words, to jumble her meaning. "I don't dream of you anymore."

"You never dreamed of me," she responded.

"I did. Every night. Every—"

"Wings, dreams, and heartache will be your family's legacy, and blood, talons, and pain will be mine." The words sounded like a witch's curse, a horrible prophecy, an unhinged fate. They were said on a mouth so lovely, on a voice like a song. "Will you do something for me?"

Tears filled his eyes as he dug into hers as if prodding her bright, ocean-blue gaze with a shovel, burrowing himself into her gaze. "Anything."

"Don't call on me again."

He nearly flinched. "Caris, how could you ask that of me? How could I...?"

"Because some futures have light, and joy, and kindness. That's the one I see, and the one that changes. You won't find them if you cling to the past. The one on the loom is dark, Ceneth. Threads of wild and shadow. You won't be the one to see our dream, my love, my heart, my then, my next. But you can set the wheel in motion. One day the kingdoms can be united by the daughter of Raascot and Farehold—though she is not ours. Not our daughter. It wasn't our time. It was. It did."

"Who killed you? Please, goddess, tell me who did this?"

"In some ways, it was the All Mother. Ophir will know— she does and she doesn't. Help her, and when you help her, you'll have helped me. Will help me? Had helped me."

He loved her so much that his hatred for this false representative, this incomplete version of her burned through him. She was almost his Caris. She was nearly his beloved. But it was wrong. It was off. It hurt.

He couldn't stop staring at her. She was so real, so solid. The slope of her nose, the flower-petal pink of her lips, the cream of her skin were so unbearably vivid. Every breath he took filled him with the devastatingly lovely, delicate scent of springtime rain. And yet, this wasn't how Caris spoke. She'd always been always so articulate, so clever. Now her words twisted with each new sentence, fading in and out like a wandering mind. She was herself, and she wasn't.

"I don't want to let you go."

She squeezed his hands again. "We shared more love than most people have in a lifetime. Everything we did was real. We're lucky, Ceneth. And now Ophir needs you. I need you. Raascot needs you. The continent needs you. And when you find her—"

"Ophir?"

"No." Her voice softened. "When you find your bride, I need you to know that I'm happy for you. Your son is beautiful, and strong, and kind. His son and the son after them are children of the sky in your kingdom of wings. And none of it will happen if you don't help Ophir. If she's left alone...she'll unmake the world."

"Don't go," he said quietly, knowing she couldn't stay. He wanted to say she was wrong. That he'd never have children with Ophir. That everything she said was impossible. But he couldn't.

"I was never here, and I always will be."

✦   ✦   ✦   ✦

"Your Highness?"

Ceneth continued to stare blankly forward. He'd died all over again. His body entombed the void of his heart as he stared blankly forward.

"Your Majesty?" the medium attempted once more.

His eyes slid to the medium, blinking against the stark contrast from the woman who'd been sitting there only moments before. The silk of their scarf, their androgynous features, their larger hands. Ceneth slipped his hands out of the medium's. He smelled the smoke from his hearth and the medium's spiced scent, but a lingering perfume of fresh spring rain remained faintly in the air.

"Thank you." Ceneth cleared his throat, shaking his head as if to remove the cobwebs from where they'd knit within his mind.

"Did you learn all you sought?"

He stood from the table and took a few steps toward the door. "I don't know. I didn't know what I needed to learn when I began, and I'm perhaps more confused than I was before. May I ask you something?"

The medium dipped their chin.

"Time?"

They clucked their tongue knowingly. "You asked her about the afterlife, and she spoke of past and future, correct?"

Ceneth shook his head, uncomprehending. He began to pace around his room, walking from wall to wall with the carpeted rug, amidst the candles and paintings and four-post bed painting a striking, royal scene around him. "Do they all do that? She referred to a loom."

The medium stood as well, straightening their shirt and pants and adjusting their scarf. "I've heard others speak of the loom. I cannot know anything for certain, except that they are not gone, even though they are. They depart from our moment in time, but they continue to exist in the past, in the future, just not in the present."

"So, I'll see her in the future?"

"No, for you, every moment is always the present. For all of us, each second, each minute is the present, no matter how old, or how gray, or how long."

"She is always one second out of my grasp in either direction?"

"I cannot say for certain, Your Majesty." They were apologetic, but their voice was firm.

"Every time but now?" His question was flat, empty, and hopeless.

The medium looked at him sadly. Ceneth's emotion must have been familiar. This was a reaction they'd seen before.

He nodded, rubbing his temple as if fighting off an early headache. "Right, right. Thank you for your help. I'll be sure you're fairly compensated."

The medium shook their head. "When the King of Raascot requests your natural wellspring of abilities, you do not ask for something in return. It was my pleasure to serve you. When your advisor met me, they asked me to move onto the castle grounds. Will you be calling on me again?"

Ceneth inhaled slowly through his nose. "She asked me not to."

The medium nodded. "Yes, I expect she did. But that was

not my question. Her will and your will may not be one in the same. For now, I will stay." They offered a subtle bow as they departed from the room, leaving Ceneth alone, always one second out of Caris's reach.

THIRTY-SIX

✦   ✦   ✦   ✦

S HE'S GOING TO BE MAD ABOUT THIS."
Dwyn drummed her fingers against her arm
impatiently. "No, she isn't. She hates snakes."

"Then why did you force her to picture a snake?" Tyr
demanded, sword dripping with a sticky, tar-like blood as he
stood over the slain body of an enormous serpent. The sulfuric
stench of spoiled meat and rotten eggs wafted from its steam-
ing corpse. His lips pulled back in a snarl as he shot a glance to
the bits of the regency's road he could spy between the trees.
They'd been running parallel to the road, picking their way
through the woods just out of eyesight from passersby until
he came upon a snakelike abomination. A goddess-sent gust
of wind rustled the branches, moving their hair and clothes as
it brushed the leaves together, sending the demonic cloud of
noxious odor as far from them as possible.

"Because she—" Dwyn stopped in the middle of her
sentence. "Wait, how did you know? Goddess, dog, how
long have you been spying?"

He wiped the black substance on his pants as he shrugged.
"It'll be good for you to keep in mind that the walls have
ears."

"You're disgusting." Her eyes widened. "She and I have shared a bed! We've—"

He leveled an unamused stare and leaned against the same tree that tethered Knight. "While I'd like you to keep in mind that, yes, I do have the power to have been there watching your every intimate touch, I prefer for the partners to perform consensually if they're putting on a show for me."

Her nose twitched. "You are repulsive."

Tyr lifted a shoulder. "You say that now, but you look like the kind of person who'd enjoy an audience. Most narcissists do."

"Is this why your woman left you?"

He cast his gaze to the trees once more. "You have no idea what you're talking about."

Dwyn's words took on razor-sharp accusation. "No. No, noble Tyr. This isn't lovelorn, this is love lost. She was killed, right? Is that it? Is that why you've crossed the Straits—you're on a righteous mission to avenge your...what? Betrothed? Your wife? Your lover?"

His face wrinkled in a flash of disgust. "The words of a witch who's never known love."

"Fuck off and make yourself useful." She gestured to the grass, the trees, the pressed road beyond. Dwyn abandoned her torment and returned to the task at hand. "If her snake is here, how far off is she?"

He glared. "Make *myself* useful? I just killed a hell-snake the size of an ox. Why don't *you* make yourself useful? You have the ability to find her, don't you? Unless calling on fire wasted what you took from the farmers."

She looked at her hand, flexing and unflexing her fist. "It wasn't just the fire. You also made me heal you."

He raised a single brow. "I made you fix what you'd broken. I'm sorry if you don't enjoy the consequences of your actions."

Dark hair danced around her shoulders as she shook her head. "I'll need new blood, but I have an idea."

Tyr's mouth turned down. "I'm guessing if you're going

to try to replicate what Ophir did for finding things, you'll want a manufacturer. There should be one in the next town. You can find them everywhere in Sulgrave."

"First: no, I don't want to copy Firi's compass-watch. Second: this isn't Sulgrave. The continent is backwater once you get south of the Straits. Which I should be grateful for, I suppose. If they had evolved beyond monarchs, we wouldn't be chasing a princess across the world, would we? But no, I don't need a manufacturer."

"You need a tracker's abilities, don't you?"

"I used that farmer husband's life to char the palm of your hand, but the wife will do just fine when it comes to tracking power. I can still feel her blood humming within me,"

It was a struggle not to sneer whenever she spoke. "You're disgusting."

She'd been ignoring him completely, eyes trained on the snake's body when she said, "Did it just move?"

"It's probably an involuntary reflex. Some cadavers spasm."

"It's not dead!" Dwyn leapt backward, half of her body careening into the trunk of a tree as she stumbled out of the way. The snake's tongue flicked out of its mouth. She held her hands out in front of her as she continued to back away, but there was no water on which she could call. Its body twitched, then began to worm toward its severed head.

"What the fuck?" Tyr balked, shaking his head at the snake. He swung his sword on instinct, chopping the wriggling torso. Three disconnected parts paused for only a moment as corpses should before they began to move.

"This isn't possible." He gaped at the horror, then lofted his sword overhead once more.

"Wait."

"Wait for what?!"

"I want to see…" Dwyn took several cautious steps toward the man to stop his butchering. "Let's see what it does."

"What could it possibly do?" His words came out in sputtered repulsion. Knight whinnied uncomfortably beside him, pulling on its tether to try to put as much distance between itself and the snake as possible.

"Shh, boy." Tyr tried to calm the horse, but its fright was clear as it yanked its head against its constraint.

Dwyn's tone changed, words hitching with excitement. "It's not dead! This is goddess-damned incredible. Look at its blood, Tyr. The thing doesn't bleed red. Look!"

The pieces of the snake twisted and moved as if searching for their missing pieces. A second wave of sulfur and meat hit them as the wind stilled. Grass and leaves crunched beneath its enormous body as one severed part found the other. The bisected sections of its smooth, black body rolled into one another. Smoky tendrils began to reach from one side of the body to the disconnected piece like a sweater unraveling in reverse. Tyr swore as Dwyn gasped. The snake was knitting itself together.

Abject horror leached down his spine. "If it reaches its head…"

"It can't die."

"It can't die," he repeated. "Holy fucking shit."

Dwyn's face flickered with pride, her mouth slowly turning up into a smile. "Well, well, well. Look at that, Firi. What on earth have you done?"

+ + + +

Being near Dwyn was a lot like being infected with repulsion. Tyr couldn't get his top lip to stop sneering, as if it had settled into a permanent, disgusted disapproval. He watched her wave prettily at a commoner in simple clothes while he stood with his arms crossed, watching from the space between things.

He hated this. He hated her. He hated himself.

Navigating Farehold with the distinctly foreign features of Sulgrave fae made it difficult to remain inconspicuous. Tyr didn't struggle, as he could always slip undetected to be one with the air, but it would leave the rather peculiar sight of a saddled horse sauntering unattended. Instead, he hung back while Dwyn closed her approach on a man tilling a garden, feigning the need for directions. Moments later, a papery husk remained where the healthy peasant had been. She'd expressed certainty that she would need at least three stolen lives under her belt before she'd be ready to enter town. She left the garden and let herself into the farmhouse. There was a brief shout of confusion at the intruder, followed by a second, louder voice who called out in terror. Then silence.

He didn't enjoy watching her do it, both because it was wrong, and because it was frustrating that she'd found a way to drain and channel blood long before anyone in the Blood Pact. It was a secret she would not share.

She returned a few moments later. "I'm ready."

He fought an unwinnable war with his expression. It was impossible not to glare at her. "Get in, get the supplies, get out."

"Don't tell me what to do. And keep yourself scarce. No one wants to see you."

"Fortunately, staying out of sight is my gift."

She painted her face with existential exhaustion. "I'm aware, phantom."

Dwyn insisted that their plan was both simple and foolproof, which had made him uncomfortable. "Foolproof" was the sort of word you used when you were ready for the universe to make a fool out of you. She'd explained that she would use her first borrowed blood to call upon the power to shape-shift, wielding the gift to disguise her features so that she could pass for a Farehold commoner—someone pretty enough by Farehold standards, but with the rounded eyes of the southern kingdom, pinkish skin, and colorless hair. Next, she'd spend her second stolen life using the gift of persuasion to get a vendor to fill a sack with traveling supplies without requiring coin in return. The third was her margin for error. She never knew if she'd need to call on an additional ability, she said, and didn't want to risk pitting her back against the wall and needing to draw on her own blood.

"Because that's how you die?" he asked.

She pursed her lips. "Don't sound so hopeful."

"I'll be here," he said quietly as she turned to go.

"Please don't be. I won't need you once I have supplies and a tracker's power."

A growl colored his words. "Are you implying that I need you more than you need me?"

"How sweet, to hear the dog learn to speak. You followed me here from Sulgrave. That's some flattering obsessive behavior, Tyr. I *know* you need me more than I need you, because I don't need you at all." He heard the change in her pitch before he saw her shift. The woman's voice belonged to someone else. Her hair lost its nightlike quality, rippling into something hay-colored and wavy. Rosy, freckled cheeks and rain-blue eyes looked back at him.

"Then get rid of me," he said to the strange face Dwyn wore.

"Don't you think I've been trying? Off with you. You're bothering me, and you're going to draw attention. Let the master work." Dwyn, wearing the face of the blond stranger, lifted her hood as she entered Henares on foot in search of a manufacturer.

Hostility throbbed within him. He did need her, and he loathed it. She'd unlocked the secrets of blood magic and made it look so damn easy, like siphoning water from a spigot, redirecting it from its intended source to her. She was a parasite, but a dreadfully clever one. Even if he could have killed her, he wouldn't. He needed her alive to teach him how to access her abilities.

If it weren't for the motherfucking bond.

He'd love to torture it out of her. He'd fantasized about strapping her to a chair and playing with a variety of tools and weapons until that psychopathic bitch loosened her lips. He still might. He thought perhaps his demonstration with withstanding the fire was the first time she could see that he might be able to take pain without flinching. He hoped it made her worry. It should. Maybe he could cut her open and pick her apart and withstand what it would do to him.

But no. She had no interest in sharing—and why would she? Spying had proven useless. He'd seen her flex her witchcraft countless times and had no inclination as to how she was doing it. He'd followed her. He'd stalked her. He'd despised her. He'd attempted to copy her. And none of it had worked.

For now, they remained at a stalemate.

The sounds of grass crunching underfoot faded as he watched her walk away. His mind drifted to the game of hearts she played with the princess, and his shoulders slumped at the thought. Cutting was easy. Hacking, slashing, and being violent for the sake of violence, thoughtless, sloppy, and required little by way of cunning or intelligence. Perhaps this was the real lesson Dwyn was teaching him without even trying. Maybe she needed to possess a royal heart for the power she craved. And maybe if he had any hope of learning her secrets, he'd have to find a way to win hers.

✦   ✦   ✦   ✦

Tyr thrust a hand to the empty horizon. The tendon in his neck strained as he swallowed his urge to yell. "There's nothing to the south, Dwyn."

"I'm telling you," she responded calmly, clipping the bags together and draping a blanket over the horse's back before saddling it. "She's southwest."

"And I'm supposed to trust, what, the farmer's wife's blood that you stole so that you can play the role of tracker? She wasn't even fae."

"Any life, for any power. I don't expect you to understand" came her irritated reply.

Tyr remained firm. "We got supplies for the road. We didn't get supplies for the goddess-damned desert."

"You keep saying *we*. There is no 'we.' Stay here. Live in Henares. Find yourself a good wife and settle down. Have little invisible babies. Or get eaten by a wolf. I don't care. I'm going to Tarkhany." Dwyn shouldered her bag and put her foot in the stirrup. She'd managed to persuade more than just food, clothes, a broad-rimmed veil to shield herself from the sun, and healing tonics from the vendors of the market. Her charm had been so effective that despite having no money, she was now in possession of a tawny mount, two weeks' worth of provisions, and enough water to keep her alive for at least the next several days. Her horse wouldn't love the weight of her supplies, she knew, but the mount would have to adapt. At the very least, her acquisition of a steed meant that if they were to travel together, they would no longer need to share a saddle.

"Bye, dog," she said as she swung into the saddle.

"There's no way she's in Tarkhany!" He balled his hands in his hair from where he remained on the ground, shouting after her. "How would she have gotten to the desert kingdom! Why would she go there!"

Dwyn didn't need to raise her voice. She called back in mocking singsong. "She's a manifester, Tyr. She can do whatever she wants."

His heart turned to stone. "And once you get her..."

"I'll be able to do whatever I want."

THIRTY-SEVEN

＊　＊　＊　＊

HARLAND'S FINGERS FLEXED AGAINST THE WAR-ROOM TABLE. It was too hot, then too cold. Job and title be damned, he was a shit royal guard. He hadn't just failed at his mission. He'd burned it to the ground.

"This doesn't make any sense." King Eero bumped against his crown as he stuck his fingers in his hair, holding his head against what may have been the early signs of a headache. He wasn't sure how the news could get worse, but then again, he'd never met a scryer before.

Harland's brows knit in reluctant agreement. He shot a desperate look at the scryer. "Can you try again? They can't be at the same place."

The fae who looked back at him was a void of disapproval. There was a general agelessness to those kissed with immortality, but every once in a while, a fae entered the room with an aura that felt thousands of years old. The scryer had been escorted from Raascot to aid Farehold's monarchs at the behest of her king. If Ceneth hadn't offered generations of her family sanctuary from the southern kingdom after they'd been forced to uproot from their ancestral lands, she would have denied the request altogether. Though her face had no lines, and her hair no grays, she was very, very old. The air around her was heavy, as though time itself dragged behind her like a cape around her shoulders, filling the room with her presence.

Perhaps the exodus of fae was not Eero's fault, but he hadn't stopped it, either. Harland kept his eyes on the fae woman, battling the unwise urge to drag a gaze of treasonous disapproval over his king.

The scryer looked as though she couldn't be bothered to fully arch a brow. Her dark eyes were nearly bored as her head lolled from the guard to the king. Everything about her was terribly, if not laughably, informal. She wore a loose, black dress that may as well have been stitched from shadows and cobwebs. The gossamer gown was a product of comfort rather than fashion, and not a fit, shape, or fabric he'd seen in any kingdom. Perhaps she'd been on the earth long enough to value the gentle brush of whisper-thin material on the skin far more than the opinions of peers. Her dark hair was entirely unbound, which was also out of fashion. Most of the women wore braids, even if they only adorned half of their hair. Perhaps the rubbing or twisting of braids and ties was just as unimaginable as the discomfort of fashionable clothes. The woman looked tired, not in a way that denoted sleeplessness or stress, but with an overall fatigue at the world and her role in it.

"If you know better than the spirits, then you know better, Your Majesty," she said, a lip pulling back ever so slightly, showing the barest hint of her pointed teeth.

Harland fidgeted, looking to Eero.

The king's grip on his temple tightened. "First, we ask you where Berinth is, and you send us to the desert. The man is *clearly* of Farehold blood. He's *not* a Tarkhany man. Then we ask you where Ophir is—the daughter of Farehold—and you point us to the same desert! Are we to believe they're together?"

She inclined her chin. "That is an entirely separate question. Shall I?"

His crown tilted over the press of his fingers as he nodded. He pushed back from the table and moved from one side of the room to the other as he waited for the woman to act.

"Stillness would be preferable."

Eero stopped his pacing. Speechlessness seized his tongue. The man was a king all right, Harland thought. Perhaps the occasional serving of indifference was good for his humility.

The scryer closed her eyes and rested her hands on the map that covered the war room table, palms facing toward the ceiling. The fae inhaled through her nose slowly, breathing the dense quality of eternity into her body, letting it fill her lungs. Her hands slowly began to turn over as the spirits guided them once more to Tarkhany, fingertips landing near one another, but not touching. Her fingertips dragged left to right and right to left, one scratching from The Shining Wilds, written in both the Farehold tongue and in the two unpronounceable languages of the southern kingdom, and the other from The Dying Sunset, which shared the same three-name process so common to the regions of the desert kingdom. One finger landed on the border town of Amurah, while the other stopped just shy of the capital city of Midnah.

"It would seem," she said, slowly opening her eyes, "that though they're separated by stretches of sand at present, the two will end in the same destination, though they do not share the same journey."

"And what are they doing there?" Eero asked.

She slowly allowed a single brow to rise. "It would *seem*," she drawled, "that you're mistaking me for one with omniscience, *Your Majesty*."

Another man would have snapped. Anger would have been an understandable response. Instead, King Eero grew still as he soaked in the information. This was a quality Harland had both loved and hated. Eero was a fair, level-headed monarch, but it would have been easier to understand his emotions if he would yell. His benevolence made his disappointment so much more poignant.

"We knew she'd pursue those responsible." Harland lost himself in the map. "She must have learned of his whereabouts before we did."

"I understand," Eero said slowly. He turned to Harland. "But how did she cross the desert? And more importantly: why? We barely trade with Tarkhany. We've only received them on one ambassador mission in the last hundred years. Aubade and Midnah do not speak."

Harland frowned. "By design?"

"By geography!" He gestured to the map, making a broad gesture toward where the fae woman's hands still rested. "There's no known water between Farehold's border and Tarkhany's capital. There's rumored to be an oasis near Zatra, but those who've made it back alive swear it's seasonable and cannot be depended upon. Besides, I don't believe my father left things on particularly good terms with their ruler."

"Your father was on the throne four hundred years ago," Harland offered. "The desert king at the time was human, was he not? Those in power might not even know the tales. Things went smoothly on the ambassador visit, or am I mistaken?"

Eero resumed his pacing. "I have no way of knowing if those in power are human or fae right now. We hear nothing from Tarkhany, nor do we send word. But the appropriate time to offer my condolences has long since come and gone. After my father…"

"What happened, Your Highness? The books don't—"

"I was a child." He shook his head, halting his stride to grip the back of the chair with both hands. He looked down at the map, eyes flitting between the words that may have shared Farehold's letters, though their vowels had new, strange marks and dashes, and the artistic, unreadable dots and lines of a slithering language that twisted and turned over the dunes. "It was a different time. My parents and their parents before them ruled with iron fists. Our lineage has not been known for fostering peace relations."

Harland pursed his lips, eyes grazing the fae woman who continued to sit at the war room table. The bright, circular room in the tower always allowed for natural light, which somehow felt improper given the solemnity of scrying. He studied her features—she was not quite the rich bronze of Raascot, but also not the pale pink of Farehold. She was probably from the borderlands between kingdoms. Perhaps Farehold had been her home once, long before the division of the world. His mother and brother had been forced north due to the hostility toward certain magics in Farehold, just as hers undoubtedly had. Farehold hadn't been known as a kingdom of tolerance. While Eero was good, he was also benign in the face of generations of injustice. Caris had been the continent's first hope in shifting the tide.

The woman looked up at the man from where she remained at the table, growing more disinterested with every second that passed. "Will there be anything else?" She didn't bother using his honorific this time.

Eero frowned at her. "Midnah? You're sure of it?"

She looked at him in a way that conveyed deep disapproval over his question. Of course, she was sure of it. This was her power. She'd been doing this for millennia. This ancient fae had been scrying since before the king of Farehold had been in his mother's belly.

Her look was answer enough.

"Okay. Thank you. That will be all."

She stood from the table and reached into a bag, extending an object to the king.

He frowned. Pinched between her fingers was the plume of a long, blue-green peacock quill. "What's this?"

"Convenience," she said. "Don't make me travel across the continent to answer simple inquiries. Write your questions to Ceneth, and I will have them answered from the comfort of my kingdom."

Eero turned the feathered quill over in his hand. "What do I do with it?"

Once again, the deadened, bone-tired look of a headmistress frowning at a misbehaving student overcame her emotions. "You write with it, Your Majesty. It's a quill."

Harland sucked in a breath of air at her disrespect. He knew enough of his king to know that he was relatively toothless, and he expected there'd be no recourse for her back talk. Still, it was incredibly bold to speak to a monarch as though he were an uneducated child. Perhaps she'd lived long enough and was simply poking bears, hoping one would bring her days to an end.

"My sister is a manufacturer," she said with infinite boredom. "Her quills are particularly popular among young lovers, as they never seem to run out of things to say when separated. This one, however, will be for you and King Ceneth exclusively, as he owns its twin. Anything you write with this quill will appear in his castle. If you have a question for me, he can fetch me in Gwydir. And if that's all"—she stood eyeing them for a long, judgmental moment—"I will begin the three-week trek back to Gwydir."

The king looked surprised at this. "They're not flying you back?"

She'd reached the end of patience that had never existed in the first place as she said, "I was brought under the urgency of a king summoning me. No one cares how long it will take me to return. Now, if you'll excuse me."

The scryer didn't wait to be dismissed. Her loose, black dress floated out of the room—the material existing as the only buoyant thing about her. The room seemed smaller with her gone, as if her presence had been holding the cream-colored stones at bay. They pressed in on the men as they stood around the map.

"She lacked decorum," Harland said politely as the tower door closed.

Eero laughed, though the sound was not happy. "I admired her apathy. I can't tell you how comforting it would be to feel indifferent when facing such things."

"Your Highness?"

Eero closed his eyes, perhaps shutting out the too-small room like Harland wished he could. It wasn't just his missing daughter, nor was it the one who'd been taken from him. It wasn't just his people, or the kingdom, or the direction of the continent. It was his crippling inability to do anything about it. It was supposed to be Caris. She had been meant to succeed where he'd failed.

Instead, that's all he'd leave.

A legacy of failure.

"Shall I leave today?" Harland asked.

Eero looked at him with eyes as bright and golden as Ophir's. "You're a good man, Harland. You've done a good job taking care of Ophir. If anyone has a hope of getting her back, it's you. I know you'll do right by this kingdom. Have you spent much time with our spymaster? He's rather young—still in his first century of life, but he's a discreet and powerful asset with an impressive skillset. I'm confident he's picked up more than a few languages as a hobby."

Harland made a face. "You trust him?"

"As surely as I believe in the heavens, yes. I put my faith in him as I trust you with Ophir's. You shouldn't go on this mission alone. It's important that we keep our efforts contained. Relations with Tarkhany are strained, and sending an army to retrieve her and slay Berinth might start a war, for which Aubade is not prepared. This kingdom will not survive more loss."

"I'll leave tomorrow," Harland promised.

"Make it tonight," Eero said. "I'll send word for Samael to meet you by the stables."

PART IV

The Puppet Master

THIRTY-EIGHT

✦ ✦ ✦ ✦

I T WAS HOT.

It was so fucking hot.

Goddess, she'd never been this hot in her life.

Ophir sucked in a scalding breath, coughing and choking on the dry air. She squinted at the taunting, yellow ball of light and cursed it from the bottom of her heart. It was meant to be the middle of autumn, not the torment of high summer. The princess had long since shed her extra layers, scattering clothes and coverups and bits of cloth about the meandering southbound paths, then regretted it, wishing she'd kept her shawl to keep the scorching rays off her baking skin.

She was going to die. She knew it. Her skin would be fried before the sun set. She'd be able to eat her fully cooked arm for dinner under the sizzling heat of the sun. The moment Ophir realized she had to cross the desert, she'd been categorically unwilling to remain on the sand. The baking rays reflected off the dunes as if they were glass, intensifying the blistering heat from all angles. How many words were there for hot? It was scalding, blazing, sweltering, feverish, broiling, fiery, goddess fucking miserable.

Sedit whimpered.

"I know, boy," she said, "I don't want to be here either. But this stupid compass insists he's…" She looked from the pocket watch to the rolling dunes beyond. "Honestly, I have no idea. This goddess-damned thing is probably broken. There's no reason for him to have fled to Tarkhany. Why would he seek asylum in a country where he'd stand out as the only fae paler than the sand?"

Sedit's bony, lizard-like tail wagged from side to side as if he was just happy to be included.

"Does he have some safe house in the dunes? Could it be a trap? What if he…" She stopped herself from saying it was crazy, as she reminded herself that she was talking to a demon hound she'd created.

He looked at her with his too-many eyes. They glimmered with the suffering pout of any pet who'd been denied a treat. As she stared into her beloved hound's face, something within her began to shift. She had made this vile, wonderful, utterly unique, terrifying thing. Sedit was born of her whims and raw power. She was not the same woman she'd been the last time she'd encountered the man.

"You're right, boy," she said with a nod. "There's nothing he can throw at me that I can't handle."

She would have remained roasting in her self-congratulatory thoughts, had Sedit not begun flinching as each step forced him to place his paws on the blistering sand. She loved her vageth far too much to let him suffer. "I'll fix this," she promised.

So, she tried.

It was hard not to feel like her craft grew markedly worse with each and every monster.

"It's okay, boy," she said unconvincingly. Ophir reached forward to stroke the mane of her latest creation. She'd attempted to make a horse for her and Sedit alike. They needed to get their feet off the sand and cross the unforgiving wastelands far more quickly than she and her hound could on their own. But the moment she brought the cursed horse into the world, she knew she'd never be able to take it on a main road. Not only did the steed look like the decaying remains of a reanimated stallion, but reptilian scales clung to the knobby bumps of its ribs and spine, ending in a serpent's tail. Disappointment settled in her stomach like stones, but Sedit didn't mind the horse.

"You're not much of a looker, are you?" she asked the undead horse. Her face fell as the creature carried her forward, and she couldn't help but wonder why all of her creatures were born into the world with goddess-awful needles for teeth.

Sedit was born to be her protector, so the vageth's mouthful of prickly, venomous thorns was both blessing and marvel. Her first creation, the snake, was also intended to have fangs, so its horrid, pointed teeth hadn't been a surprise. This was her first attempt to make a gentle, grazing creature, and she'd failed miserably. She winced when the horse pulled back its lips to reveal rows upon rows of glistening, ivory weapons, as though she was looking at the bone-white jaws that sailors hung on their mantles from predators of the deep. She reached a hand for its nose, touching the scales below its sunken eyes, and decided she loved it.

It hadn't been what she'd intended, but perhaps it was what she needed. A docile steed would not serve her.

"You knew what I needed for you before I did, didn't you." She softened, patting her new horse with all the tenderness she could muster. Well, "horse" wasn't quite right, but it was certainly horse-adjacent. She would prefer to find a way to create things that didn't smell quite so bad, but maybe that was part of it. The creations birthed from her subconscious created a protective barrier for all the senses. Terrifying to look at, horrible to breathe in, and deadly to touch. She wouldn't dare try to eat one of them but was confident that they'd be poisonous in one's belly.

After bringing her mount into the world, Ophir created a saddle, which also didn't turn out quite like it was supposed to.

She wasn't confident enough in her riding or in the comfort of the steed's bony spine to want to ride it bareback. She took the horse all the way from her escape beyond Henares to the desert's edge, where she realized her plan would have to change. She couldn't stay on the horse, nor did she want Sedit to burn his paws.

She slapped the corpse-like rump and set it free into the wild as she looked at her hound. "What can I possibly make that would get me across the Tarkhany Desert?"

Sedit's pitiful whine pierced the desert air.

"Trust me, I'm as hot as you are. A horse won't serve us across an ocean on fire. If only we could fly…" Her eyes stayed fixed on Sedit and his pathetic state before they dragged over the horizon, then up into the aquamarine of the cloudless sky. "Why couldn't we fly?" she asked the dog.

He tilted his head, his numerous insect-like eyes sparkling up at her.

"Don't worry, Sedit. I'd make something big enough for both of us. It would have to be something that could cover ground quickly, and suit two riders. A very large bird, don't you think? Or a horse with wings! But a bigger horse, one where you could sit with me. A…"

Sedit whined again, and she created bowls of water for each of them. He didn't drink from his obsidian basin but dipped his amphibious paws into the bowl. She winced apologetically as the sizzling sound of steam wafted up from where his feet met the water. A string of apologies and curses wove together as she created a blanket for Sedit to get safely off the sand, as well as a canvas to protect his skin from burning. She didn't know much about her sweet, strange dog, but at present, Sedit was her only friend in the world.

"Okay, hands." Ophir wiggled her fingers expectantly. "Let's make something with wings."

She had an idea in mind, though the fictional beast only existed in the distant reaches of nursery rhymes and children's stories. She meditated on the infantile fantasy of a creature made by mothers and nannies and storytellers to tantalize little ones into falling asleep. Ophir knew exactly what she needed.

Focusing her intention, the princess cast her palms before her and birthed a dragon.

✦   ✦   ✦   ✦

Ophir was lucky it was night. Not only could she spot the glow of the Tarkhany capital from the air, but the dark, enormous shape of her quadrupedal winged beast would be little more than a smudge against the black sky—a peculiar place in the dark where the stars seemed to blot out of focus.

She touched down outside of Midnah but found it difficult to part with her winged serpent, neck and tail nearly twice as long as its spindly torso. It was her favorite thing she'd ever made—save for Sedit, of course. She frowned at it from her place on the sand, eyeing its wormlike neck, the rows of endless teeth, the enormity of its wings. "I don't know that I can just set you free, my friend." Her frown deepened. "You're too frightening for the world, and far too powerful for its citizens. I crave violence as much as the next, but I want to be the one who doles out the justice. I can't have you eating my enemies before I find them."

It looked down at her curiously, head twisting like a semi-intelligent lizard, tasting the air as she spoke. It used one of its terrible talons to scratch at the sand dunes as if to respond, kicking up a tiny cloud of dust in the chill of the desert night. This poor dumb beast would know only hunger and the gnashing of teeth. It would have no herd, no nest, none of its kind, no one in the world to love or find or stay with.

It belonged nowhere.

Maybe it didn't know better. Perhaps it couldn't hold the capacity for sorrow. Or a third possibility: she was projecting her loss and loneliness onto the gargantuan, winged serpent before her.

She sighed at the monster knowing that, like her vageth,

it would offer patience and curiosity only for her. The world would be its orchard as it plucked its fruits from the ground in the form of humans and animals, wicked and innocent alike. The bird-snake monstrosity was not something made for mercy. Yet, she didn't want to kill it. It was the best thing she'd made.

"I have an idea, friend. I don't know if it will work, as things never seem to turn out the way I want them to, but let's give it a shot, shall we?"

Its serpentine neck coiled unnaturally to look at her from different angles, trying to understand her words, though it lacked comprehension of language. It was trying, the poor thing. Her eyes raked over it from head to tail, examining the taut skin of its bat wings, its talons the size of axes, its needle teeth. The monster with the gift for flight was bigger than a house and had the serpentine length of trees stacked one on top of the other. She was quite sure that nothing so enormous had ever existed on the continent—until now, that is.

The corner of her mouth tugged up in a smile as she admired her creation once more. She might have gone on smiling had the answering silence not tugged her face downward. Dwyn would have been proud, too. Joy lost some of its sparkle when she had no one to share it with. The creature deflated at her sorrow, chuffing as it nuzzled her.

Ophir leaned into its snout, patting the stretch of black skin between its eyes. "You need someone who can keep you under control. Someone with wings, in case you get away. Someone who can tell you what is and is not good to eat. I can't have you vanquishing my enemies for me. Not yet, at least. Not until they know exactly why they're dying."

I'm a manifester, for fuck's sake. I made this fairy book thing, didn't I? I brought a fiction into the world. Why can't I make a fae? Something smart, something good?

She pictured a friend—something that could speak, something that could fly, something that could rein in the monster when it needed control. She closed her eyes and pictured a winged fae, something powerful, something resilient, something that could soar through the sky, two unique and perfect bats in the world that she had created all by herself. Ophir dropped her hands to her sides as she let her intention fill her, visualizing an intelligent creature, picturing a face, a torso, arms, legs, hands, feet, and wings. She lifted her hands and pushed her intention into the world, opening her eyes to see what she'd made.

Fuck.

"What the hell are you supposed to be?" She frowned at the abomination, a familiar stench roiling off its flesh.

It hissed back at her, hunching its shoulders as it squatted, flaring its membranous wings behind it. Enormous horns twisted from its head, mirroring the spines of her black dragon. It opened its mouth to show matching teeth, truly her dragon in a near-human body. It slowly rose from the crouching position, and a spike of fire jolted through Ophir as it stared at her. It was so much bigger than she'd expected. Its gray-black flesh ripped with a warrior's muscles. It flexed talons at her. Of course, she couldn't make a fae. She'd been insane to try. She rolled her eyes, hands on her hips as she pondered what to do with the monstrosity.

"Youuu…" it hissed.

She took a half step back, fingers flying to her heart. It picked up with an intensity she hadn't felt in weeks—her first true jolt of fear since abandoning her companions. She swallowed against the lump of fear in her throat. "You speak! You do speak!" The breath left her lungs as she looked around the empty expanse of the desert. There was no one to see her hound, her winged serpent, or the demonic, male human shape she'd crafted.

"I can't believe I did it," she breathed again, pride and terror coursing through her in equal portions. The confused spike of anxiety and satisfaction tingled in her fingertips like cold water.

The creature took a step toward her.

"Stop," she commanded breathlessly, and it listened.

She knew she shouldn't be afraid. Every creation had heeded her will with blind obedience, but she'd never created something with the intent of it talking, thinking, or making decisions. She swallowed again, feeling her mouth go dry. It was as if the dust of the entire desert coated her tongue and throat, making swallowing impossible. It was as though she'd swallowed chalk.

"You're in Tarkhany," she said carefully. "Can you say Tarkhany?"

The fae-beast hissed again, testing the word slowly as it stretched the vowels, elongating the final sound. She shuddered against the chill of its word but rallied herself for bravery.

"Good, good. Look at this. Look what I've made." She gestured at her serpent, urging the abomination to drink in its features, to acquaint itself with the winged snake on the sand. "This is why you're here. This creation needs someone to keep an eye on him. You will be his master. It will answer to none but you and me, do you understand?"

The new demon did not move toward her, but it dipped its head in a similar curiosity, not knowing why it had been brought into the world, understanding little of the earth or its purpose. All it knew was that it existed, and it listened to Ophir.

"Yesss," it responded, hunching its shoulders once more. She noticed a smoke-like quality begin to spill from the demon as it spoke, as if each word created tendrils of mist that crawled into the world.

"I need you to keep it out of sight. You should do your best to remain hidden, too. Don't bring it into cities or villages, okay? Especially not in full daylight. The forests, the wilds, the desert, the sea are all fine, but I can't let people know about my creature. Not this one. It would give too much away. Can you do that?"

Yes, it confirmed. It could.

"One more thing?" She arched a brow at the human-adjacent monstrosity. It opened its mouth, smoky tendrils of sulfur and rancid meat emanating from its depths. It looked at her with its terrible, sunken eyes. "You have one other purpose, and I don't care what you have to do to accomplish it. Use your gift for speech to spread a message. Tell Berinth, wherever he is, that I've already killed his cohort, and I'm coming for him next. I believe he's in hiding now, so you may have to wait until he's in public. I don't just want him afraid: I want to bury him. When the moment is right, spread the message so that everyone, everywhere, can know exactly how evil he is. He's a murderer, but he deserves more than murder. Revenge needs to be so much more thorough to be meaningful." Ophir realized she was monologuing to an abomination that could barely string a sentence together. She shook her head, cutting herself off. She returned her eyes to the black, beady eyes of the monster and emphasized her final point. "I want him afraid—I want this monster *terrified*. Do whatever it takes to scare the ones who did this to my sister. They should never know peace again. It's what they deserve."

It was a half-truth. She'd killed one pathetic human outside of Henares, after all. But the fearmongering she might achieve with the help of her slippery-tongued creation would make her vengeance so much sweeter. Make him tremble. Give him nightmares. Make him wet his britches at the sight of her monstrosity and the carrion of its smoke-like words.

She smiled to herself as she turned toward its new beast.

It flapped its wings once, then twice as it tested its gift for flight. With a beckon, the winged serpent reared up onto its two hind legs, long black tail twisting on the sand behind it. It began to flap its wings, joining the demon as it became airborne, bound for anywhere that it might stay hidden from prying eyes.

She watched them go before turning her eyes to the glowing lights of Midnah.

THIRTY-NINE

+   +   +   +

D O YOU WANT TO PLAY A GAME?" DWYN ASKED, SWEAT dripping from her head onto her tawny horse.

"Not even a little bit." Tyr was too tired for her games on the best of days. This was not the best of days. The unwashed scent of dirt, travel, fur, and animal joined the thick, distorted quality to the air as visible heat undulated around them.

Each word came out with burned, sluggish exhaustion as she tried to rally their spirits. "Over there? In the distance? Let's play a game where we guess whether that lake is a mirage or an oasis. Whoever wins has to tell the other a secret."

"It's a mirage. They've all been mirages. This is the fourth time we've played this game."

"Four? No. It can't already be four."

He glanced at her to see if she was wilting from heat stroke and winced at what he saw. Her forehead and cheeks had taken on a sizzling, tomato quality. He didn't want to be empathetic but couldn't help the uncomfortable feeling at clear signs of suffering. "How are you holding up over there? Am I losing you to the sun?"

She blinked her eyes hard, perhaps trying to summon

moisture. "Well then, why don't you guess mirage and win the game? Then I'll tell you."

He sighed. It was his fourth day in the desert, and if they ran out of water, their bones would soon join the drifting sand. Every once in a while the hot, dry wind would pick up, flinging the sand against any exposed bits of skin, stinging them with the force of hundreds of tiny glass daggers. He'd love for it to be an oasis in the desert, just as much for Knight as for him. There was so little water left, and if they didn't find a fresh source soon, well…

He wasn't sure he could handle his horse dying in the desert because they'd gone on a fool's errand after a princess who didn't want to be found. He tried to swallow, but there was no saliva left to soothe his throat.

"Fine. It's a mirage."

"And I guess oasis."

"How do you have the energy to talk? Can't we just shut up and die in peace?"

He expected another wise retort, but Dwyn didn't respond. They wandered toward the glimmering silver in the distance, allowing their horses to plod forward at the slowest of paces. They couldn't risk their mounts expending any unnecessary energy. So they pointed them toward the distant, metallic shimmer and clung to whatever remaining drops of hope sloshed in their nearly-empty waterskins.

Forty minutes later, he didn't have the energy to be disappointed that he was wrong. He was thrilled to be wrong. Excitement bubbled through him the moment he realized they were in fact approaching a watering hole dotted with fresh vegetation. It filled him with the sort of unspeakable joy that one gets to experience only a few times in one's life. He jumped off of Knight's back, immediately taking care of his mount so that it could wade into the pool and cool itself.

Dwyn appeared proud of herself but too tired to properly gloat. She didn't bother to take care of her horse first, which was precisely the behavior he expected from someone so selfish. Tyr's disapproving scowl became a permanent fixture as he tended to her mount while she waded into the water.

"You're such a bleeding heart," she said from where she knelt on the banks of the pool, hair dripping from the water. Tyr still hadn't made it to the water's edge as he busied himself unsaddling the horse she'd abandoned. She began to strip at the water's edge, dropping her clothes in a pile on the bank as she dove into the pond.

He wanted to roll his eyes at her, but he was too relieved at the sight of water, and genuinely eager to do the same. It was Dwyn who cried out in surprise as he pulled his shirt over his head and began to tug at his pants. He'd expected her to use the opportunity to express disgust, but she was something of a nudist, and too sun-touched at present to antagonize him.

One moment later, he jumped into the small lake, grateful for its cooling waters. They gave each other a wide berth while their body temperatures lowered, enjoying the healing sensation of the pool. He gulped directly from the pond, savoring sweet relief over his burning throat.

Eventually, he found a place where the pond was both shallow enough to stand and deep enough to continue covering most of his chest. The bottom of the pond was hard and compact, which made standing easy.

"How did you know it was an oasis?" he asked.

She looked at him deviously and wiggled her fingers.

His jaw dropped open. "No."

She took a mouthful of water and spit it at him.

"But you'd guessed oasis so many times! You were always wrong! You were..." He let the realization hit him. She could sense water. Of course. "You were hustling me."

"You owe me a secret."

"You goddess-damned bitch."

"A bitch owed a secret."

He dunked his head under the water, shaking it like a dog when he reemerged. At least Knight was happy. Their mounts had cooled themselves and now rested comfortably on the banks, looking to all the world like they'd died as they napped beneath the shade of a tall, thin tree with odd, fanning leaves clustered at the top.

"Fine. What do you want to know?"

She considered her price and kicked up from the bottom of the pond, floating on her back and looking into the sky. "What will you do with the power if you get it?"

He deflated, heart heavy. Of course, this was her question. It could have been worse. It could have been any number of things that he'd been less willing to answer. All things considered, it might feel good to get this off his chest.

"I'll return to Sulgrave and use ice, shadow, and flame to kill three men."

Her eyes widened. "What? You're doing this for…three people?"

He nodded, not bothering to elaborate.

"Come on." She moved the water slightly in his direction, not quite splashing him. "There's a story there. Three gifts, three men, a trip across the continent, an unhealthy obsession with a stunning young woman. I'm referring to me, of course."

He chose not to nibble on her narcissism. He was doing his best to get on her…better side. Gaining her favor might be out of his reach, but perhaps they could hate each other a little less. "There is a story, but your bet was for one secret, and you got it."

"These are three specific men, right? You're not just attracted to the number three and have an itch for the murder of your people, correct?"

He closed his eyes before he could roll them, lips twitching in a half smile. He could tell from her quiet chuckle her taunt was intended to make him laugh. She grinned at the success of her joke. "Yes. These are three specific men, with three specific powers that deserve to be used against them."

"It's for the woman, isn't it? The one you refuse to talk about?"

319

Tyr said nothing.

She made a low, appreciative sound to revel in the tension. "Well, next time I make a bet, I know what I'll ask you."

He chuckled. "You think I'm going to fall for the same hustle twice?"

She dunked her head once more, splashing upward with more exuberance than the occasion called for. "I have other tricks up my sleeve."

"I don't doubt that." Their bickers were so commonplace, it nearly passed for kindness. "Can I ask you something?"

She turned and began walking toward the shore, now cool enough to enjoy eating the provisions in her saddlebag. He averted his gaze with some irritation that she insisted on being so blatantly immodest.

"That depends. Can you stop being a prude? It's just a body." She wrung the water droplets from her hair and reached for the saddle that had been left to dry out on a fallen member of the peculiar, thin, branchless trees. She chose a handful of dried figs and began to pop them into her mouth, relaxing in the shade with her toes still in the water. "You want to know how I learned to drain people?"

He ran a hand through his wet hair. "Well, yes, everyone does, but it's more than that. Why do you need Ophir's power if you already take whatever you want?"

"Oh, I'm sorry, were you not in the room when Ophir was yelling at me and kicking me out of her life? Apparently, none of you think I would make a very good All Mother. It's hardly your fault. Why would mice ever love a lion?"

He bit down on his tongue to block his retort. Once the first wave of irritation passed, he said, "I'm not asking why you want a royal heart. I'm asking about your end game with Ophir. If you were going to kill her, you would have done it already. So, if you aren't going to finish the job, what are you doing with her?"

She frowned at a small piece of stem that had stayed in her date, picking it out of her mouth with her thumb and forefinger and flicking it into the pond. "Figs are a little too sweet, don't you think? They're more like candy than fruit."

"I take that as a no, you won't answer my question."

"You won't like the answer." She popped another one in her mouth, grimacing at the overpowering sugars and washing her mouth out with the freshly refilled waterskin.

Now that was intriguing. "What could you possibly say that could make me like you less than I already do?"

She winked. "You make a good point."

Tyr joined her on the shore. She made a bored look at the space between his legs, then looked up at his eyes, unimpressed. It was a joke, sure, but a good one. She was excellent at getting under people's skin. "So?"

She sighed, chewing on the answer more than she had on her food. She offered him a fig, and he took it, always surprised when she extended him simple courtesies like food. Her answer would win her no favors, but there was no reason to put it off any longer. "The same reason Anwir doesn't care who gets the prize, so long as one of us does. The same reason I won't hurt her. The same reason you won't kill me."

He turned his head to look at her, mouth open in a mixture of surprise, admiration, and disgust. His eyes shot to the tattooed vine that crawled from her knee to her hip. From where he sat, shirtless and dripping, it nearly looked as though the ink on her hip ended where the markings on his bare chest began, as if they'd been woven together with ink. He knew she was brilliant, though it was a truth he held with both resentment and disdain. She was clever and resourceful and patient and tenacious and so fucking awful. He studied her now in the heat of the late afternoon as the fanning leaves overhead filtered their shade over her prone form. She really was pretty and probably could have done any number of things with her life. She was talented and witty and... "You really are a bitch."

"Yes, but, if you're going to be a bitch, you might as well be the best at it."

The city smells of hot food and unwashed bodies and refuse hit them long before they entered the Tarkhany capital of Midnah. Tyr had always hated cities. Getting in undetected would be impossible.

"Well, shit."

Dwyn sucked in the hot late evening air with a steading breath. "I'll handle the city folk, just like I handle *everything*."

"Pull your hood up," Tyr said, eyes darting nervously at how impossible it would be for them to slip through the city unnoticed.

"It's hotter than the goddess-damned sun!" she protested. She muttered to herself about how much she hated how sweat collected around her sternum and pooled in the center of her back, saying something or other about how she was much more comfortable naked.

"Look around," he insisted. Many citizens had covered the exposed parts of their skin. Hoods were the norm. The sun was more like an oven when wearing thin, flowing cloaks, and head coverings. Its rays sizzled like a frying pan when they hit exposed flesh. The oven of cotton cloaks and clothing was hot, yes, but it was more sustainable than the bare-skinned alternative.

"Disappear!" she commanded.

"I'm completely in the open right now," he hissed back at her. "I can't vanish while people are looking at me. It defeats the purpose."

While Tyr and Dwyn had gilded undertones darker than the average pink skin in Farehold, they were ashen compared to the rich dark browns of the citizens of Midnah. There'd be no chance of maneuvering through the streets undetected.

They'd barely stepped foot into the city's outskirts before he knew they were out of their depth. From the burbling conversation of the public to the signs above shops, neither he nor Dwyn had any idea how to make sense of their surroundings.

He'd been a fool to assume anything about the tongues of the desert kingdom, regardless of how adept he'd been at learning languages in the past. Those from Sulgrave had the luxury of never choosing to learn the common tongue, should they desire. While it was spoken in Raascot and Farehold, the Frozen Straits created enough of a separation to keep the continent's citizens from stumbling into their kingdom. Education was abundant, opportunities were available, and life was long. Most of Sulgrave's citizens learned the common tongue as a fun hobby of sorts, enjoying the peculiar way that vowels and consonants rolled on their tongue, tasting new words, and lording superiority over any monolingual peers.

They hadn't expanded their linguistic studies to other parts of the continent. He'd never met anyone from Tarkhany, or the Etal Isles. Information was surely available, had he sought it out, but ignorance was much like a blind spot. It was challenging to know what you were missing when you'd yet to see it.

Dwyn slid off her horse and approached the first person who made eye contact. Their eyes widened, bewildered at her appearance, but she flashed a friendly smile as she gestured to the alley. It took her a moment to step just out of the public eye before she left a husk in her wake.

"And now, I'm an omnilinguist." She stuck her foot in the stirrup and swung herself back onto her fawn-colored horse.

"And a murderer," he murmured disapprovingly.

"Oh, but such a cute murderer!"

"Can you be cute in a better disguise? I can easily slip out of sight, but if we get caught because you stick out..."

She looked at him with steely disapproval. Dwyn tugged at her hood, pulling it so it covered more of her face. "Isn't that always the case? Someone chastises you for killing a person and then it's '*Oh, Dwyn, can you please murder someone else for me in order to make disguises? Feel bad about it, though, so I can maintain my superiority complex.*'"

"That's a terrible impression of me."

"It was spot on, and you know it."

"Could you expand your power, if I didn't have the ability to step into the place between things? Could you shape-shift both of us if you needed to?"

She sucked in a thoughtful breath. "I've never tried to do it to someone else, but probably. It's not a good idea, though. We can't pick miscellaneous civilians and take their identity. We don't know who they are, or their reputation, and we're on a specific mission to get close to a princess. It was fine in Henares when I just snagged the closest village girl's face to get supplies. It wouldn't serve us if we become commoners who are no better off than we were before. At least if we're ourselves, maybe we'll get dragged to whatever authorities as intruders, who've probably seen a very pale princess wandering their streets. All that to say, yes. I could. I can do anything."

"It's amazing how you manage to stay so humble."

"It really is, isn't it?"

He tugged on Knight's reins, bringing them deeper into the shadowed alley. They'd need to wait for nightfall before moving around if they had any hope of remaining undetected.

"Do you still have your tracker's ability?" he said quietly, looking over his shoulder as he dismounted.

"What do you think?"

"Well, how are we supposed to find her?"

Dwyn rubbed her temples. "Can you do me a favor?"

Tyr frowned, resting his elbow on his horse's saddle from where he stood. Knight shook his hide, swatting his tail to remove a stray fly that tickled him. He patted Knight twice on the neck before returning his look to Dwyn. "Name it."

"You're either in, or you're out. Get on board with my brand of blood magic right now, and be appreciative with my usage, or don't get on board, but then never, *ever* ask favors of my magical abilities."

He sucked on his teeth. She was right.

"You know what I think?"

He looked at her, equal parts exhausted from the sun and her company. "What."

"I think your problem with me is a reflection of your own journey. You want Ophir. You want her power. And obviously you want revenge. Those are fine goals, Tyr, but do you know what they don't align with? Your self-righteousness and bleeding-heart bravado. Either you'll do what it takes, or you won't. And at the end of the day, you're here because you will. It's time for you to let your perception of self catch up with reality."

FORTY

✦   ✦   ✦   ✦

9:00 PM

OPHIR STOOD ON MIDNAH SOIL FOR SEVENTEEN MINUTES and thirty-seven seconds according to her pocket watch before she was intercepted by a cloud of thundering guards on horseback.

It was probably for the best.

A miserable anxiety had filled her while she approached the city. Not only was she alone, but she'd told Sedit to stay outside of city limits so that he wasn't harmed. She could call on another beast to aid her at a moment's notice in her time of need, but every step bringing her closer to the orange, vibrant glow of life in the midst of a night-darkened desert made her nerves swell.

She'd barely had time to take in her unfamiliar surroundings before the clattering of hooves greeted her with a universal truth: trouble was approaching. She couldn't read the signs, she didn't know the language, and she'd drawn more than a few stares for looking like a phantom. She'd been an ignorant fool to barrel southward without thinking twice about how different one kingdom would be from the next. Perhaps the late hour and the moonless night aided in her aura of mystery, but she wasn't sure if it was helping or hurting her cause.

Four men sat atop glossy mounts in lightweight, leather armor. It was probably more appropriate for the climate than the metallic breastplates common to Farehold. They peered down at where she stood, an unaccompanied foreigner on foot.

The first thing the guard said to her had Ophir blinking up at him in helpless bewilderment. He waited expectantly for an answer, but none came. The guard looked around, perhaps wondering if his words had been in any way unclear. An idea struck her and she held up a finger—a known signal for him to wait for just a moment. She put her hands into her bag as if she were fetching something, but instead she closed her eyes and focused her intention. The cool weight of a metallic cuff settled in her hands and she closed her fingers around it, lifting it from the bag as if she'd intended to find it all along. She slipped the cuff over her ear. Its curve and points fit perfectly, though it was quite flowery and more ornamental than she'd intended, which was a nice change from the terrors of the night she so often created. The cuff ended with a small, metallic curl that looped into her ear.

She smiled, dipping her head in a nod.

He repeated his question, and to her delight, her device worked. He'd asked her to speak her name and business. The ornamental cuff translated his words, funneling his message directly into her ear.

Shit. How was she supposed to respond?

She offered her most apologetic frown. "My name is Ophir—Princess Ophir, from Farehold."

The man looked over his shoulder at a second guard, who stepped forward. His brows were low and heavy, as if weighed down with their suspicion, as he inspected her. The night was dark enough that she wasn't sure how much they could discern from her expression, but from the torches they held, she could see their skepticism.

"You're a princess?" He responded in the common tongue, his words curving as curiously as her ornamental device, the lilting, unfamiliar accent compared to the flat sounds of the citizens of Aubade.

Surprise and relief colored her cheeks in return. "Yes, I am. I'm the daughter of King Eero and Queen Darya of Farehold. I'm looking for someone who I think is taking refuge in your city."

He turned to the first guard and translated her message, which, thanks to her device, she received with perfect clarity.

"Another one?" The first guard's tone was more unnerved than surprised.

"Two is hardly an invasion," the translator replied in his native tongue.

The four exchanged uncomfortable looks, their horses shifting with impatience.

"Two too many," the first guard muttered. "Will this one also go to the dungeons?"

The dungeons. They'd already stumbled upon another foreigner in the city. Berinth. It had to be. Her heart raced at the picture of Berinth caught behind bars like a rat in a cage.

"No, no," the second replied, "this one claims to be royalty. A princess."

She hung on every word, ascertaining that she was to be taken to the palace so that their king might decide what to do with her—they hadn't used the word "king," but she gathered his position of power from the context.

To her surprise, the one who'd translated dismounted from his horse and offered it to her. She expected him to swing back into the saddle, but instead he led the horse while remaining on foot. It may have only taken seventeen minutes for the guards to find her, but it was another hour of escorting her through the city before the first otherworldly firefly dance of fae lights illuminated the world surrounding the enormous, vase-shaped tops of the palace. The gates were opened, and they were ushered in, but Ophir had little attention to spare on the minutiae of city life while her eyes were busy drinking in the golden palace—at least, the tops seemed to be made of gold. The body of the palace was made of an unfamiliar light-colored stone, not quite marble, but not the cream or custards of Aubade. The same tall, branchless trees she'd noticed in the city grew in rows here, their leaves gathered at the top like a feathered plume on a hat. The greatest display of wealth and opulence in the desert was the wastefulness of water that flowed freely from decorative fountains and reflective pools before the palace doors.

They left the horses behind as she stepped into the surreal, out-of-body experience of having lived decades of life, been to so many parties, seen countless things, and yet had the hubris to assume she'd seen most of what the world had to offer. Meeting Dwyn and Tyr had made her starkly aware of how little she knew of Sulgrave. Arriving in Tarkhany was a wakeup call to her narrow exposure to the world. She thought of all of this, and none of it as her eyes scanned the tall pillars that held up unfathomably high ceilings—doubtlessly for the heat, allowing it to rise while the humans and fae below remained comfortable.

Ophir kept an eye on the bodies around her as she entered the palace, trying to see if there were any manner-isms or practices she could perceive and adopt before making a fool out of herself. Instead, she was too distracted by the loveliness of the intricately designed fabrics in the flowing swaths of clothes, much of it loosely draped and leaving little to the imagination. A curious bird nearly the height of a fae wandered about the castle on two thin legs. Its body was an interesting combination of white, black, and gray, but its face was the vibrant orange and yellow of sunset. Elaborate tufts of black feathers looked like a spectacular halo, almost as if the bird was wearing a crown. It turned to look at her, cocking its head curiously to the side.

She turned to inquire about the unusual bird, but the guards were whispering to one another. She kept her mouth quiet as she listened.

"Let's take her to the king."

"No, we'll let her decide what to do with the princess."

"Is that wise? Should she—"

"She'll want to see the girl."

Ophir's earpiece translated each message rapidly as her eyes darted from person to person. The man who'd given her his horse knocked on a door and whispered to the answering servant. Ophir stood stoically behind the guards, wondering who she would meet and what might unfold.

I'm a snake.

She repeated Dwyn's affirmation until she believed it. She had nothing to fear. She had power. She could strike. Ophir's fingernails bit into the flesh of her palms nervously, wishing Dwyn were here now. It was a foolish wish—no different from wishing there had been poison in her wine or hoping a storm might capsize your ship. Wanting Tyr or Dwyn was no different from desiring your own demise.

She knew it to be true. And yet.

The servant returned and exchanged a few more whispered words to the guard. Their voices were too low for her to discern what was being said, though she tried. The guard gestured for Ophir to follow the servant as he took a step backward, ushering her into the long, pillar-lined palatial space beyond.

Aubade's castle was huge by all measures of the imagination, but the vaulted ceilings of the palace made it seem larger than life itself. Rooms in Aubade were half of the size of the halls and foyers in Tarkhany, and she assumed it was by design. Her bedchambers at home needed to be small enough to capture the heat from the fireplace. Similarly, these rooms needed to be large enough to allow the heat to dissipate, rather than suffocate the resident. Ophir attempted to ask the servant where she was going, then her name, then what they were going to do with her, but the woman did not respond. Either she didn't speak the common tongue, or she *did* and preferred not to answer.

No matter where Ophir looked, a new, vibrantly colored,

brightly scented object, flower-filled vase, incense-laden pendulum, or elegant bust decorated the large, open rooms.

"Here you are," said the servant with flawless command of the common tongue.

Ophir's eyes became unappreciative slits. How rude.

They led her to a fae woman with close-cropped black hair in a loose gown that would have matched the burned- orange desert sands in daylight, contrasting beautifully against the rich depth of her skin. It wrapped around her neck, covering her chest, but with a daringly low cut in the back. When she turned to lead the group farther into the room, Ophir could see the entire divot of her spine as it ran from her neck all the way to the small of her back where the dress scooped, fabric gathering once more just below the dimples of her hip bones.

Ophir wondered if this was the *"she"* the soldiers had referred to.

10:00 PM

"I assume you haven't learned our language before coming to our lands?" The Tarkhany woman spoke the common tongue with the same melodic accent Ophir had heard with the guards. It was technically a question, but it was clear she knew the answer.

"I'm sorry," Ophir apologized, "though I am grateful you possess more skill and education for language than I do. I'm not here on a diplomatic mission, I'm afraid. I'm looking for someone. My name is Ophir."

The woman's eyes grazed slowly from the top of Ophir's head down to her toes. While all fae had irises larger than that of a human, the coal-dark depths of her eyes almost made it appear as though they were composed entirely of pupil, with only the barest hints of white at the outer corners. It was almost owl-like. A slow smile spread across her mouth, revealing her pronounced canines. "Are you really? Do I look upon the Princess of Flame?"

Ophir straightened her shoulders, though it was shame that made her do so. "Please, accept my apologies. You know my name, my title, and my power. With whom do I have the pleasure of speaking?"

Ophir waited for a name. She fidgeted uncomfortably, reminding herself that she could call hounds into existence at any moment. She thought of Sedit, wishing he were with her. Hell, she wished Tyr and Dwyn were beside her. Alas, she was alone. She'd come alone by design and would have to live with such consequences.

"Leave us." The woman waved to the servant. Once she exited the room, the woman crossed to a long, thin table covered in foods and drinks. She'd brushed past Ophir in her pursuit of the table, and a citrus scent radiated from her. "Are you hungry from your travels? Of course, I'll set you up to have you bathed, but please, Princess Ophir of the Middle Kingdom, share a meal with me."

"Farehold," Ophir corrected. "I'm from Aubade."

"The Middle Kingdom," she said with feigned gravity. "The kingdom that sees itself at the center of the world."

Ophir wasn't sure if she'd been insulted or if this was merely a show of geography. She stood uncertainly for a moment, scanning the room. She was confident she'd been brought to the stranger's private quarters, though she wasn't sure why she'd be escorted to a bedroom. After an uncomfortable silence, Ophir walked tentatively to the table and eyed the unfamiliar fruits. Many were brightly colored, fragrant, and utterly foreign to her. She selected a magenta fruit that looked to be covered in soft, green needles, frowning at it. "How do I eat this?" she asked.

The woman's smile broadened, teeth brilliantly white. She plucked one for herself and demonstrated how to peel it, sucking out the sweet, white fruit inside.

"You don't look filthy enough for someone who's crossed our desert and wandered into my kingdom alone and on foot. Your hair is tangled, but your presence is…curious."

Ophir's hand flew self-consciously to her hair. She scanned her clothes, knowing exactly what the woman meant. She should have been caked in orange-red dust from the sand. She should have been coated in dirt, drenched in sweat, and half-mad with heat stroke. Instead, thanks to her winged mount, her hair had only twisted into snarls in the wind after a day and a half of flight. She could use a hairbrush, but she did not look fresh off the trail.

"Will you tell me your name?" Ophir asked finally.

"I suppose it's only fair, though I find it insulting that you've entered my palace without knowing of my existence. I'm Zita." She extended her hand.

Ophir clasped it, and Zita chuckled.

"You're meant to kiss it."

"But, I'm..."

"A princess? Yes, I'm aware. And I am queen of this land. These kisses are born of neither fealty nor subservience. They're merely polite. You've made no effort to educate yourself beyond your bubble, have you? Such a pity." Zita relaxed onto a lounging chaise and pulled a small bowl of fruits to her. "Princess of Flame, sit with me, Queen of the Desert, and rest beneath my shield. Tell me why you've come, and if I find your story worthy, I'll tell you who I am. Is that a fair trade?"

"And by shield—"

Zita's amusement colored her face. "I know one of your abilities, do I not? You know one of mine."

The queen spoke in riddles steeped with consequence. Despite her grime and exhaustion, Ophir did her best to reorient herself as she would before royalty. She pitched her voice for due reverence.

"All right, then. I suppose I don't know what you might consider worthy, but yes," Ophir agreed, "I'm looking for someone who I believe to be hiding in your city. He goes by Lord Berinth. Do you know of anyone by that name?"

"That name? No. A pale fae in Tarkhany who doesn't

belong, however—that I do. Such a man resides in my dungeons as we speak."

It didn't surprise her that he'd used an alternate name. What did surprise her was how easy it had been to confirm his whereabouts.

"Did he commit a crime?" Ophir nearly gagged on her question. *Aside from slaughtering Farehold's firstborn heir, robbing Raascot of a queen, and gouging out royal organs,* she amended within the acidity of her heart. "I mean to ask: why did the man I'm pursing travel to Midnah only to be thrown behind bars?"

"He wasn't arrested for the crime of hailing from foreign lands, if that's your question," Zita said, sarcasm balanced on the razor's edge of bitterness. "He was a raving lunatic, and I do mean that in the most dangerous way. Your—Berinth, was his name?—was screaming obscenities, hurling stolen objects, and violently attacking anyone who attempted to subdue him. Truly, I'm pleased to hear he's a criminal. I refuse to punish the indigent, and madness is a consequence of a world without the food and shelter due to all mankind, human and fae alike. Midnah is an asylum with numerous shelters and support for those in need. We do not, however, tolerate violence and hatefulness by those who perceive themselves to be above the law."

"He deserves to die," Ophir said.

"So he shall."

"And I need to be the one who does it."

The queen tutted her tongue, propping her head up with an arm as she leaned more deeply into the elegantly turfed furniture. "You're meant to be telling me a worthy story, are you not?"

Ophir looked for a place to sit, but the room was so spread out, it was hard to decide upon a location. Zita sensed as much and gestured lazily for Ophir to sit beside her on the chaise. She took a seat and made an honest expression of her discomfort. "Again, I extend my regrets. I don't know if this is common practice in Tarkhany, but—"

"Common practice in Tarkhany?" The woman raised her eyebrows. "This is common practice amidst royalty! Tell me, Princess Ophir, if I were in your shoes: would you not be entitled to explanations from someone who wandered into your castle?"

She thought of how both Dwyn and Tyr had wandered quite confidently and disrespectfully into her room, setting up camp in her life. Her title and its entrapments hadn't meant much to them.

"Do you want to know what I know of Farehold?"

"I..."

"I know that King Eero and Queen Darya have ruled for the last three hundred and forty-two years. I know that two daughters were born to them, one of whom claims to sit here beside me. I know your language, your seasons, the names of your cities, and of your religious expression. Do you know why I know these things?"

Ophir did not.

"Because I understand that the world is composed of more than one kingdom. Does Farehold know the same?"

"I'm sorry," she apologized, and she was.

Zita waved her hand. "Apologies are useless. Now, I'm owed a story. Please proceed."

"My sister was murdered," she said, spilling the venom that had sloshed behind her teeth until her anger filled the room. Caris's death was common knowledge throughout Farehold, and not a secret she needed to grip with both hands. The second half of her rather brief story may have been a gamble to share, but she was a manifester—what did she possibly have to lose? "The man called Berinth—the one I believe is in your dungeon—must pay for what he's done."

From the expression on Zita's face, it was clear this was delectable information, tasted and savored as if it were a rather decadent sweet. "You've crossed the desert alone, unaided, unguarded, for revenge? My, my." She positively sparkled, sitting up and leaning in with true entertainment. "Well in

335

that case, you are most welcome. I do love a strong woman, almost as much as I love a tale of vengeance. Let's get you set up in a room, run a comb through your hair, and I'll see about tracking down the location of your nemesis, shall I?"

"How soon?"

The queen's head tilted to the side as if amused by the informality of the question.

"How soon can I kill him," Ophir reiterated.

"You're on Midnah's soil. I expect you will not be so brazen as to disrespect Tarkhany law?"

Ophir's fingers clenched into fists. Her flash of emotion was not anger with the queen but fear that justice may be slipping between her fingers like desert sand.

"Once you've confirmed his identity, I'll confirm with my advisors regarding your testimony and his subsequent fate."

"How long?" Ophir repeated, impatience bleeding into defiance.

"Assuming he's found guilty? We'll need a day to erect the scaffolding while the city's criers proclaim his sentence."

"How long?"

The queen had every reason to find her repetitive line of questions annoying. Instead, her lips flicked upward in a wicked smile. "After our meeting concludes? You will be shown to your chambers, and you will sleep. Then there will be one full day, and one full night," Zita replied. "In scarcely more than thirty hours' time, you'll have your justice, Princess Ophir."

Zita stood and called for her servant in their native tongue. Quick instructions were given, all of which Ophir was able to understand with perfect clarity. With her hair over her ears, they might not even be aware that she was in possession of such a device. A detailed sketch was sent to their chambers within the hour, each prisoner's portrait strewn before them with excruciating accuracy. Ophir pointed to Berinth in no uncertain terms, identifying him amidst the array of artfully done profiles of humans and fae with Farehold features, ensuring that Ophir had indeed located Berinth. Everything was going better than Ophir could have hoped. Maybe everything would be okay, after all.

FORTY-ONE

✦   ✦   ✦   ✦

11:00 AM
19 HOURS AND 45 MINUTES UNTIL EXECUTION

Y OU CAN'T BE SERIOUS."
Dwyn shook her head in smiling awe as they pressed themselves into the wall, eavesdropping on excited muttering going on beyond the palace walls. "Oh, is there nothing she can't do?"

It had taken them the night to gather their bearings and gain the intelligence necessary to learn that Ophir had been in the capital for a day or so, comfortably residing within the palace walls. It was also brought to their attention that they'd arrived just in time for what was to be the very public execution of a foreign fugitive: Lord Berinth.

"I can't believe she found him," Tyr breathed, keeping his voice low while they remained in earshot of others.

"I can."

"She can't hear you. You don't have to kiss her ass when she's not around."

Dwyn turned from where she'd kept her cheek to the wall, glaring. "Is it so hard to believe that my emotions are genuine?"

"Yes."

"Well, they are. She's gone from the most fragile, direction

-less thing on the continent, to an unstoppable force. She fears nothing and accomplishes everything. There's no one I'd rather have as a partner. Now shut the fuck up. I'm trying to listen."

He pressed into her a little too close in the shaded alley as they arched their ears toward the gossiping going on just around the corner. She threw an elbow for him to get back, but he did not.

"...four of them!"

"All from Farehold?"

"Yes! But two..."

Tyr whispered, "What is she saying?"

Dwyn spun on him, shoving him with two hands so he created space. She fumed back at him. "You just spoke over what *may* have been valuable information. Why don't you disappear and go down there! Use your ghost power and make yourself useful!"

"Because I don't speak the language!" he bit back, keeping his words to an angry whisper. "You're the one who keeps sucking civilians dry so you can understand what they're saying!"

She waved a hand to shush him.

"Which I *appreciate*—" he tried to amend, remembering their conversation.

"Appreciate me later!"

By then, the bystanders had moved on to other topics. Dwyn was visibly annoyed, but they'd learned enough. The courtyard in front of the palace would host a beheading at sunrise. Given the city's heat, she was grateful everything seemed to close around midday. She wasn't sure if she would have been able to stand in the crowd to watch Berinth's justice while baking to death, pressed against thousands of bodies.

"What do you mean, beheaded at sunrise?" Tyr asked.

Her face remained utterly expressionless as she met his gaze. "I mean they're beheading him at sunrise."

"But Ophir is the one who wants revenge. Why would she want someone else to do it? Why would Tarkhany get involved? Why would—"

"I'm sorry, do you have a fundamental misunderstanding for translation? I'm relaying the message. Their queen gave some decree last night, they're spending a day informing the people and overseeing labor, and other than that, I have exactly as much information as you do."

Dwyn had killed no fewer than six people since their arrival in Tarkhany, three of whom had unwillingly given up both their lives and their home so that the Sulgrave fae had a place to hide. Their horses now had a shaded place to stay, which had made Tyr happy. He didn't like the idea of subjecting Knight to the heat just because he was on a foolhardy mission through the desert. Tyr had asked why she didn't kill hundreds and stockpile blood but inferred from her answer that she'd tried something of the sort once, only to find borrowed abilities to be rather time-sensitive. He stopped himself from commenting on the mass murder of what had undoubtedly been a helpless village in the name of her experimental pursuit for power. He was trying to get on her better side, after all.

✦   ✦   ✦   ✦

They'd been in the house for scarcely a minute before Dwyn stepped out of her clothes, leaving them in a pile by the door the moment it latched behind her. She collapsed onto the middle of the bed, dark hair sticking with sweat to her neck and part of her back.

"Move over."

"Sleep on the floor," she murmured into the pillow, voice muffled.

He made a face, looking at the rock-hard floor. It was cool, which was nice, but he couldn't imagine a less comfortable night's sleep. "The floor is stone while the bed is big enough for three."

Three who remained were mummified husks in their very room, watching them with dehydrated, lifeless eyes. They had no place to bury the bodies in the sand, stone, and clay of Tarkhany's capital. They'd remain in the room as dead sentinels, monuments to Dwyn's callous theft of life.

Dwyn sighed and moved from her place comfortably in the middle to the far side of the bed. It was too hot to sleep under the sheets, but the family had barrels of water set aside. She'd been able to call to it in the form of a mist, cooling them intermittently to keep their body temperatures low. Tyr took off his shoes, then his shirt as he lay down next to her. He—as did most people on the continent—possessed a modicum of modesty more prevalent than the siren's.

"You got an answer from me in the desert," he said, folding his hands behind his head as he stared at the ceiling. "I want a secret."

She rolled to her side. "Fine. It's too hot to fall asleep. What do you want to know?"

"It's something I've been thinking of for a while. The more I've been around you, the more I've seen your power, the more confused I am."

It was clear from her expression that he'd tickled her curiosity. "Go on," she prompted, propping herself up on her elbow as she looked at him, black curtain of hair falling over her shoulder, gaps between tendrils of hair revealing the curves of her breasts. From her navel, to her hips, to her toes, she was far too comfortable being naked.

"You can do anything," he said.

"Is that the question?"

He shook his head. "Can you manifest?"

"Is *that* the question?"

Tyr met her eyes at last. "Why haven't you broken the bond?"

Her expression tightened. "You're asking why I haven't removed my tattoo so I can kill you," she reiterated flatly. Ah, yes. The siren understood him just fine.

He didn't bother nodding, just continued to look at her.

"The Blood Pact doesn't use a natural power for the bond. You know that. Their namesake has appropriate connotations. It's unbreakable."

"But surely—"

"It's not magic. It's not a power. It's a curse, Tyr. We're cursed. We willingly submitted ourselves to a fucking blood curse. Surely, if there were a way, I would have done it. The removal, that is. Not the killing you."

His eyebrows lowered, lips twitching as if fighting the urge to smile.

"No—"

"You don't want to kill me." His smile began to spread.

"I didn't say—"

He was certain his eyes sparkled. "You don't hate me."

"Tyr, I hate your guts."

He shook his head, still grinning. "You don't want me dead. You said so yourself."

"Fuck off." She plopped back down on the bed, allowing the arm that had been supporting her to relax at her side. She covered her eyes with both hands. "Now I have to kill you again just out of spite."

Though her eyes were covered, he hoped she could hear the smile in his voice. "Sure, sure." Then on a more serious note, his voice dropped. "It really can't be removed? There's nothing that can be done? Even with Ophir's power?"

She released her palms from where the heels of her hands dug into her eyes, allowing them to thumb to her sides with irritation. "Our Blood Pact is a curse, Tyr. It breaks when we die. Ophir can manifest. Only death breaks the curse. We could kill Anwir to break it—"

"Then we'd all die."

"Precisely."

There was a simple elegance to the Blood Pact's cleverness. Mutually assured destruction kept them in line. It was much like a witch's poppet created to be stuck with pins, except the object was the giver, and the subject was the receiver. If Dwyn killed Tyr, she would die. When she'd burned his hand, her own had melted into his. Tit for tat, no action could be committed from one member of the gang by another without reciprocal consequence. This was why she hadn't taken Ophir's power directly. It hadn't been altruism. It hadn't been love or affection or kindness. It was because Dwyn feared that if she carved out Ophir's heart and ascended, everyone in the Blood Pact might stand to benefit. It was a risk she wasn't willing to take. Anwir seemed to believe it to be true, and she would be damned if she gave him the chance to be right. The curse that bonded her with every member in their fucking blood gang reminded her of it every time she looked at her leg.

In the race for blood magic, there would be no tying for first.

If she and Ophir reigned as partners, Dwyn could possess a heart by proxy. Anwir and his Sulgrave Blood Pact gained nothing.

"You didn't even try other methods?" he prodded. "You could have trapped Anwir in a cave for ten thousand years—"

"And if he got sick? If he starved to death? Since I was the one who enacted the trapping—"

"I get it." A long pause stretched between them. "Dwyn?"

"Hmm?" She didn't look at him.

"Put some clothes on."

"You're such a prude." Her eyes then landed on him, widening. Her hand flew to her mouth just as it dropped open. "You're attracted to me!"

He closed his eyes and faced the ceiling again. "You're a naked woman next to me in bed. And learning you wouldn't murder me is pretty much your equivalent of a compliment. It's not my fault that your foreplay is twisted."

She punched him, and he smiled, keeping his eyes closed. "Go to bed, dog."

"See you at dawn, witch."

FORTY-TWO

· · · ·

3:00 PM
15 HOURS AND 45 MINUTES UNTIL EXECUTION

Guests have arrived for you." The servant knocked on Ophir's door and called to her.

Ophir looked up from where she'd been relaxing on the bed. She wore gauzy, loose-fitting clothing that matched the fashions of the palace. Her dress was the same blue Caris's eyes had been. Zita had treated her as an honored guest following their conversation, and it had taken no time to track down the fugitive in question. Ophir's time in Tarkhany would come to an end.

She twitched in confusion, face bunching together, confident she'd misheard the young woman. She'd left her earpiece on, but the girl had been speaking the common tongue. "What guests would be here for me?"

The servant exhaled. "They're from Farehold—arrived several hours ago. They've already spoken to the queen. She had them bathed from their travels and determined it appropriate that they hold an audience with you before tomorrow's events."

Ophir stood, dress so airy that it floated on a nonexistent wind in her wake. Outside the palace, people had been practically bundled against the sun, leaving little skin exposed to its scorching rays. In the shade, however, they remained in an ongoing state of near-nakedness.

Wearing gauze had been the norm since she'd arrived in Midnah, as had napping during the hottest times of the day, eating chilled, brightly colored fruits, and watching the strange, tall bird as it wandered around the palace as if it owned the place, skinny legs with knobby knees angled in the wrong direction, enormous black eyes always sparkling with avian curiosity as it looked for food. She supposed she would have let Sedit do the same, if it had been her palace. She hoped he was okay.

"Are you looking at the bird?" It was the same servant who'd refused to speak to her in the common tongue when she'd arrived. Ophir hadn't been surprised that she'd come to check on the princess as she'd sat near the fountain under the setting sun. "He's beautiful, isn't he?"

"Is he a pet?"

The woman made a half-shrug. "He's more of a guardian. This type of bird is known for their relationship to snakes. They have a rather curious hunting technique. They strike with their talons before they peck."

Ophir cast a nervous glance at her feet. "Are snakes a problem here?"

"In Tarkhany? Yes, of course. Cobras, vipers, mambas, all variety of venomous serpents. In the palace, however? No. And you can thank him for that."

And so, she did. She silently thanked the tall, peculiar bird every time she passed the gardens. She wondered if she needed a bird on her side now that she was about to receive unexpected guests. Perhaps there would be snakes that needed stomping out.

She approached the middle of the room, each footstep slower than the one before until she came to a complete halt. Her time in Midnah had been so utterly removed from the horrors of Aubade that she'd nearly forgotten why she'd fled. A northern king, a white gown, a bridal veil, and a life in chains to duty awaited her. Anxiety was a cold, thumping thing as she waited to see who'd come to drag her back to Farehold. Her heart skipped arrhythmically as she looked for aid, wishing Sedit was there.

Sedit...

It was as if she'd looked in the mirror, then immediately forgotten her appearance upon turning her back. She possessed an emotional impermanence, born from a life of deeming herself the auxiliary sister, the unworthy heir, the failed daughter. But she was a motherfucking manifester. The truth of her power was as real and innumerable as the sands between Midnah and Aubade, yet her belief in her abilities was as thin and fragile as the gauzy gown she wore.

She became immediately self-conscious of how the cloud of fabric settled around her, hugging her curves, draping with such a thin, sheer covering that it peaked at her nipples, dipped with her navel, and pressed into the outline between her thighs. She hadn't minded in the slightest while wandering about the palace, as everyone was dressed in similar garb within palace walls, but she wasn't sure how it would appear to someone from her kingdom.

She clasped her hands in front of her and fidgeted with her fingers until an all-too-familiar face appeared at her door.

"Are you fucking kidding me?"

"Ophir," Harland practically cried in relief. He rushed to her as if to hug her, but her standoffish posture stopped him just short of the embrace. Instead, he snatched her hands from where they'd been folded delicately in front of her, scooping them into his own. His joyful reunion caught on a snag as his eyes dropped from her face and grazed over her practically exposed body. "What are you wearing?"

She shook her hands loose and took a step back, voice a mix between confusion and irritation. "You've come all the way to Tarkhany to ask me about fashion?" The truth was, it did feel good to see him. She'd felt very alone in the palace and would have taken anyone's company. Berinth was already kept securely in shackles in the dungeon, and now all that was left was to dole out bloody, cathartic justice. It was the sort of thing Harland could be present for.

She looked over her shoulder. "Who did you bring?"

Ophir scanned the dark hair, the pointed ears, the gorgeous features of an entirely unfamiliar fae male. He was muscular, but not in the way Harland was strong. His jaw was sharper, while Harland's was square. This new man was built for agility, for silence. Something about him sang to her of shadows and secrets. She lifted a single brow as she regarded him. He remained impressively expressionless, despite his exhausting journey, her practical nudity, and his presence in a foreign land. Perhaps he was one of the rare beings who could not be fazed.

The fae waved two fingers in idly greeting. "I'm Samael. I'm—"

"Oh!" Her eyes lit at the name. Her entire posture changed in a moment as her eyes trained on him with more purpose, reacting in both surprise and excitement. "Yes, I know you! You saved my father's life." She stepped away from Harland toward the stranger, shaking his hand. She may be angry with her parents, but she loved them and hadn't wanted her father dead. The assassination attempt had been a close-guarded secret within the royal family. It wouldn't serve them to let the world know how easy it had been to infiltrate their walls, or how King Eero would already be with Caris in the afterlife if a lowly guard hadn't sensed trouble and gone to investigate. "Thank you. I'm sure he'll spend his life in gratitude, as will we all. Your promotion to spymaster was well deserved."

She dropped Samael's hand and turned to Harland, only to find his eyes were still trained on her a little too intently. How revealing *was* this dress?

The column of Harland's throat worked as if struggling to speak. "Ophir, we've been told about the execution. How did you find him? How did you get to Tarkhany? How—"

She attempted to make a face as if to communicate to Harland that now, in front of their new friend, was not the time. "I have ways" was all she said.

He released an exasperated breath, face betraying his displeasure. He was clearly exhausted. He'd traveled through ungodly conditions, skin pinked by the baking oven of hell itself—which would have undoubtedly been a cherry shade of red with white and purple blisters had they not packed the tonics necessary to knit their cells back together—only to find a princess who didn't want to be found. She was handling things just fine on her own.

"Samael." Harland pursed his lips, words coming out with thinly veiled control. "Can you wait outside for a moment?"

Samael and Harland were of separate but equal ranks. Harland could not command him, but Farehold's spymaster didn't seem to mind. His gesture wasn't quite a shrug. It was almost a curious disinterest, as if both amused and indifferent to the world around him. A few moments later, they were alone. Harland ushered her to the bed to sit, but she remained on her feet. She knew he was used to them sitting side by side, with their familiarity, with their intimacy. She expected him to find the subtle gesture of distance was unsettling. Still, he shook his head and searched her eyes for answers.

"You found him?" he said, voice hushed.

"I have."

"And..." This time when his gaze darted between her breasts and her eyes, she ensured he would see the disappointment on her face. He cleared his throat for what must have been the nine thousandth time in their short reunion. He said, "You've come all this way and you're okay with the justice of another nation's due process? I have to say, I'm surprised."

"It's better this way," Ophir said. "If I'd caught him alone, I would have locked him in a root cellar and spent years peeling him apart one strip at a time. It would have been satisfying, but no one would have known. Queen Zita's way is superior."

He rubbed his chin, and she saw the doubt in his gesture.

"Every kingdom must know of his guilt. The corners of the earth should hear his crimes and see him suffer. I want every man, woman, and child to know what happened to the man who killed my sister. I'd love nothing more than to see Caris's vision for unity come together in her death."

"I don't think this was what she meant," Harland muttered.

"Then she should have stuck around and done it herself," Ophir snapped. "I'm building a relationship with Tarkhany, avenging my sister, and ensuring her murderer pisses himself in front of thousands before I'm the one who swings the ax. Before my head hits the pillow tomorrow night, this will be a deeply satisfying memory."

His hazel eyes used to sparkle when they looked at her. They'd reminded her of all things green and rich and alive once upon a time. There was something flat about the greens and browns as he looked at her now, as if disappointment came with its own opaque sheen.

"Perhaps you shouldn't say it with such pride," Harland said quietly.

Ophir didn't bother lowering her voice. "You've brought Samael with you from Aubade. Isn't it his job to know everything? Why the secrecy now?"

He extended his hand for her arm. The obstinate pieces of her wanted to create space, but she'd been so touch starved. She didn't want to be alone. She allowed the contact, submitting to the pressure as he pulled her to the space beside him. "It's not Samael I'm hiding from. You know nothing of this kingdom. I've only asked him to step outside because I know you won't talk about your…"

"Manifesting?"

His command for her to hush was sharp and cutting.

Her lip pulled back in an involuntary show of her fangs. In that moment, she wished it had been Dwyn who'd found her rather than Harland. "So, we *are* hiding things from Samael, just to be clear?"

"It's not that, Firi. Don't be foolish. Nothing is hidden from *him*. Your manifestation is something we're hiding this from the *world*. If they knew what you could do..." His face collapsed, hazel eyes catching on her features like a sweater snagging on a nail. It was as if he were searching for ways in which she'd become someone entirely new, an unfamiliar creature, something as wild and wicked as the serpent he'd seen her conjure on the cliffs.

+ + + +

Harland knew a few things.

He knew that one should never put his sword away wet. He knew that most of one's body heat was lost through the ground, and so it was more important to sleep on top of something than beneath something when slumbering on the forest floor. He knew that the juice from citrus fruits made milk curdle. And he knew that Ophir would never do anything she didn't want to do. He couldn't cross-examine her. He couldn't force answers from her. He couldn't do anything unless she, too, felt it was what she wanted for herself. He didn't just know this; he accepted it. It was part of why he'd remained her guard for so long while others had failed. He understood her.

Instead of pressing the issue further, wondering how Berinth had been caught, what the conditions had been, how she'd been certain, he attempted support instead. "I know Berinth didn't act alone. Have you gotten other names from him? So that the information doesn't die with him?"

Ophir tilted her head ever so slightly.

He understood her, but she couldn't say the same of him. He hated that she was consistently surprised when he showed patience—always impressed when he was practical, supportive, and restrained. It was an uncommon reaction within the castle walls.

Her pause told him that no, she had not.

He tried again. Rather than asking her in a way that

might seem condescending, he chose his words to empha-size the belief that she'd already done the correct, intelligent thing. "When you affirmatively identified him, did he say anything?"

She perked at this, recognizing his tactic. He knew it was why he'd outlasted the others, just as he knew it was why she hadn't chased him away.

"Yes," she said, relaxing slightly. She put her hands behind her, propping her weight up in a more comfortable position. "He was feral when we spoke, but I expected as much. How would anyone act when they'd been caught on the run? How does any dishonorable man behave when they're about to meet justice? He was incoherent. Nothing he said made sense."

Harland allowed her a moment to process, knowing she'd get there in the next thirty seconds without him saying anything. He watched her face as her lips moved together. It almost looked as if she were rolling something over her tongue, testing an idea, tasting a thought.

"We should go speak to him before the execution," she said.

Yes, this was why they worked together. He didn't tell her what to do, and he didn't underestimate her intelligence. He knew that she was perfectly capable and that sometimes the best thing he could do was play a facilitating role. "Do you have access to him? I'm ready now if you are. Though I do think Samael should come. He doesn't need to know anything about your manifestation. He's special in a way none of us have seen. It's hard to place. He has...intuition. He'll be an asset."

"Intuition? What kind of gift is that?"

Harland's cheeks puffed as he pushed out a slow breath. "He just knows what needs to be done. It's an inborn judgement. He trusts when he knows what needs to be done. Of course, he has incredible skill in battle, or he wouldn't have made it in the king's guard. But when it comes to his intuition... Farehold would be without its king if it weren't for Samael. Your father trusts him with his life."

He wasn't sure what Ophir knew of Samael, though, to be fair, her limited understanding perhaps matched his own knowledge of his colleague. He'd gained something of a mythical reputation for having saved King Eero's life only a decade prior. Farehold's king never spoke of it, save to sing the fae's praises. Samael had bypassed thousands of years of convention with his instant promotion to spymaster. Despite his devotion to proving himself steadfast and trustworthy, the bizarre nature of his arrival and instantaneous rise to his station gave even the most open-hearted among them pause.

Still, Samael had yet to let anyone in Farehold down.

Neither Harland nor Ophir could say the same.

"Fine, fine," she said, as if she didn't have the energy to argue. "But I don't want the attention I'll draw in broad daylight."

"You? Draw attention?" He regretted it the moment her lips flattened into a straight line. He took on the stance of a proper member of the royal guard, straightening his shoulders and dipping his chin as he said, "Come nightfall, we find the dungeons."

+   +   +   +

7:00 PM
11 HOURS AND 45 MINUTES UNTIL EXECUTION

Ophir had only been to the dungeons once, but Tarkhany's layout was unforgettable. As with many dungeons, theirs was underground. It only required stepping into the palace gardens encased by the inner pillars of the palace walls. She led the way, baby-blue gown floating behind her as if she were made of little more than clear, daylight air. The evening hour had already allowed for a stark drop in temperature, which hadn't ceased to amaze her. No matter how blistering the noon hour was, the nights were incomprehensibly chilly. At present, it was the crimson hour before dusk. Still warm, but no longer unbearably hot. Ophir breezed beyond the final pillar and stepped into the courtyard, walking nearly to the middle. The rectangular fountain had a curious illusion effect, where it appeared to have a permanent shadow on one side.

She led them to a sinking set of stairs beneath the fountain. It unfurled into a large, circular room the size of the courtyard above them. It would have been dark, had it not been for the dim, crimson fae lights dotted above every cell.

Their jail was intermittently populated—perhaps emptier than the dungeons of Aubade, though she'd never had cause to go down there herself. Her brief appearance in Tarkhany's dungeons the night prior had only served to confirm the identity of the criminal while he screamed rabid, frothing lies of his innocence. She hadn't turned her head that night as he'd wailed after them, allowing herself to walk back to her room, heart warmed with vengeance.

Vengeance.

Dwyn would have wanted to be there.

Ophir shook her head of thoughts of the Sulgrave girl, focusing on the present moment. Dwyn. Fucking Dwyn. She wasn't sure who she hated more—Dwyn, or herself for wanting to trust someone so badly. She looked over her shoulder at Harland and Samael, who didn't rush her but seemed to wait for her to signal their forward movements. She'd trusted Harland once—before he'd escorted her away to be married off to Ceneth.

She held Harland's eyes for one breath, then two. He dipped his chin slightly, encouraging her forward. The desert was arid, which prevented a musty scent from developing, but a stale, unwashed smell of bodies and sweat filled their noses instead. It made her miss the smell of sulfur and spoiled meat. She could trust her creatures. Sedit would never betray her. Nothing she made would harm her. She wanted her hound. Instead, she had a guard, a spymaster, and a captive to confront.

Ophir stepped up to his jail cell and watched as Berinth's eyes lifted slowly. Her stomach turned in disgust. She wanted to kill him now. She wanted to summon a demon within his cell, or to cook him on an open flame between the stones of his prison. The public execution would send a better message. She needed the world to know that they could not touch Caris without consequence. Ophir was the consequence.

The moment their eyes locked, he scrambled for her. His hands, smudged and filthy, wrapped around the bars.

"Please!" he began, words tumbling over each other like water over stones. "Please, you were there that night! You know me!"

She almost vomited in her mouth. "Yes, I was there, you sick fuck. I was there when you led her away. I was there when you—"

He shook his head. "Led who away?"

She scowled. "Don't you *dare* play this game with me. Give me a reason to end you now, Berinth."

"My name isn't Berinth!" His pathetic attempts at deceit were a disgusting plea. He gripped the bars like a rat trying to dig its way out of a cage. A hand shot through the space between the bars, clawing at them as if they might reach out to comfort him. "You have to help me! I'm an innocent man. I don't know why I'm here. I don't even know where I am!"

Ophir opened her mouth to scream at him but felt a shoulder on her hand.

It was meant to be a calming gesture, but she turned the flame of her fury on Samael instead. If Harland hadn't been there to absorb her blow, to intercept the moment he recognized her wrath, Samael may have left the dungeon with third degree burns. Harland was no stranger to being scorched by her fire. Her fire quelled within her palm as she glared up at Harland, teeth bared in a snarl, eyes hard.

"Don't touch me!" She tried to shake free, but he kept a heavy hand on her shoulders.

Instead of addressing her, he looked to Samael.

The fae said nothing; he merely shook his head. It was one swift motion to the side, an abrupt cut of denial, that said everything he needed to say. *No.*

"What!" Ophir demanded. "What's '*no*'!? No, don't kill him, it's immoral to murder? Is that it? Because guess what?!" She didn't care if her yelling was unseemly. She saw the whites of the eyes as the other prisoners pressed themselves to the bars to watch. "I'm killing him in the morning. That's right, Harland. Come tomorrow morning, I'll be the one who kills him."

Harland remained silent, looking to Ophir, then back to Samael.

Her anger spiked higher, somehow. She hadn't thought it was capable of growing.

Samael's expression was unreadable, though somewhat amused. "What an interesting gift."

She looked between them, relaxing enough so that Harland released his bruising grasp. "Flame?"

He pursed his lips. He was not speaking to her. Turning to the prisoner, he asked, "What's your last memory? Before being dragged to the cell?"

Berinth continued his despicable, clawing motion against the bars. The iron slid beneath his palms, forcing him to adjust his grip time and time again. The smell of piss hit her once more. She could barely keep herself from gagging on the putrid scent, particularly mingled with her overall revulsion for the man. She scowled at the exchange as he spun idiotic lies about his family, his life, his village.

Samael turned back to Ophir. With no emotion, he said, "You knew his name was not Berinth, correct? You expected it was a pseudonym?"

She frowned. Yes, it had been suggested that he'd been using a false name. "Why do you ask?"

Samael arched a brow. He looked at Harland as if asking whether he should speak his mind, but Harland nodded.

"He did everything you accuse him of," Samael confirmed.

"I'm certain you've correctly identified the man who killed your sister. But this man is innocent."

Perhaps she'd kill Samael instead. "Listen. I don't care if you saved my father," she growled, taking a step closer to him, "I'll—"

Harland quelled her temper, putting his hands on her shoulders once more.

"Samael." Harland's eyes flared with urgency. "Can you explain?"

Farehold's spymaster shook his head. He could not.

Harland's frown deepened, but now Ophir's expression was mirroring his.

"What are you saying?" she asked. "Someone *made* Berinth kill my sister?"

Samael appeared unbothered, as if this were any unimportant weekday afternoon. "I'm saying, he is not responsible for what happened. He doesn't remember it. He has no recognition of you before your encounter in these dungeons. I know that to be true. And if this man was at the estate the night of Caris's murder, he wouldn't be able to effectively conceal his recognition. He couldn't fake knowing you."

"He was…what? What could you be implying?" Ophir prompted.

"He was threatened? Forced? Coerced?" Harland offered.

"He was hypnotized."

FORTY-THREE

+ + + +

IMPORTANT MILESTONES WERE OFTEN MARKED WITH FANFARE—cakes on birthdays, gowns and blushing maidens and parties for weddings, banquets for coronations, hand-whittled bassinets for newborn babes, solemn blood oaths under the dying, crimson light of sunset. Then there were the things that happened in the quiet of the night, the events behind closed doors, the moments between whispers. Some changes took place in seconds, whether the heartbeats before and after someone called themselves a maiden, or the single inhalation as a dagger slipped between ribs. Others started so slowly, so softly, that day by day everything seemed the same, and then one day you looked around and systemic injustices had grown around you like thorny vines sealing in a garden. One false promise, one implication, one right at a time, things became stripped away until nothing remained.

Zita had been there for them all.

She'd worn the beautiful white gown when she'd married her husband—human, though he was. She'd loved him with the brightness and intensity of the sun, giving him her moments, her heartbeats, her milestones and monuments. She'd given him sons, raising their faelings with crowns on their heads and pride in their hearts, leading her kingdom by example. She'd hosted events at the seaside summer palace—a beautiful home where her father and father's father and family for generations before had lived in the hottest months to escape the heat of the desert. She'd graciously extended the invitation for their friends and allies from the colder climates to make themselves comfortable and employ her servants, sleep in her bed, and look upon the ocean at sunset in the winter when she was away. She'd arrived to meet her friends and allies only to be met with an army of thousands and the announcement that no, they would not be leaving the summer palace, and that she and her royal caravan should turn around and go back to the desert. The middle kingdom, the Farehold fae, had staked their claimed in the land she and her kin had owned for thousands upon thousands of years.

Shielding was her secondary ability, and attempts to protect her loved ones from the sun nearly cost her life. She'd been on the trek, clutching her heart against the pain of betrayal, weeks and miles and sunsets away from the nearest healer, when her husband succumbed to heatstroke. They'd only had supplies for one direction of the journey, but were forced to march back empty-handed, their lands taken, their seat of power on the coast stripped.

She'd been there as word of fae forced north into Raascot filtered into her ears.

She'd been there as her demi-fae children, not blessed with immortality, had grown old and succumbed to death while the virus called Farehold spread. She'd been in her throne room when their king announced the birth of a son called Eero, and in her dining room when word came of his marriage to Darya.

And she'd been there when the king of Farehold's only remaining daughter stumbled unaccompanied into Tarkhany, asking her for help.

FORTY-FOUR

✦ ✦ ✦ ✦

6:00 PM
12 HOURS AND 45 MINUTES UNTIL EXECUTION

Tyr opened his eyes. He held his breath as he dared a glimpse of the woman who shared his bed. He'd been prepared to wait until the earliest hours of morning but was immensely relieved that the sun's baking rays had joined the ocean of travel fatigue to pull Dwyn into a deep and corpse-like sleep long before the supper bell's toll.

Dwyn's deep slumber resembled the comfortable peace of someone who rested with a clear conscience. She'd remained above the covers, the soft cloud of her dark hair the only modicum of covering on her still-naked shape. The barest hints of crescent moonlight filtered in from the window, casting their room in deep shades of muted grays and midnight blues. While he knew it would take a lot to wake her, he still moved with painstaking slowness as he slid out of bed and tugged his shirt over his head. Grabbing his boots, he tiptoed to the door before slipping them on. The second before opening the door, he stepped into the place between things, unseen by all the world.

Dwyn would be angry when she awoke, but he didn't imagine she'd be surprised. He didn't love leaving Knight behind, but the horse was in a shaded shelter with plenty of food and water. It was a vast improvement over the endless stretches of sand dunes that the beast had endured. Two horses and a beautiful, sleeping monster in a woman's body stayed behind as he set off toward the palace.

Ophir was in the royal palace, and that was all he needed to know. Dwyn had been privy to the same information he had, but she'd chosen to go to sleep. She'd always had more patience than him. Maybe she planned to let Ophir work out her rage through a sunrise execution before trying to ingratiate herself once more. Her path forward was of little concern. Maybe if he did his job well, Dwyn wouldn't need a path forward at all.

He'd win.

If there was one thing he was good at, it was slipping into places he wasn't meant to be.

Given that they'd taken over a home as close to the palace walls as possible, all he needed to do was walk past the guards and through the front gates to enter the palace grounds. The centurions were none the wiser, and within a matter of moments, he was in the orange-scented mist of the incense-laden palace. He'd never been anywhere with ceilings so high. While he knew he needed to focus, it was hard not to gape at the pillars, the overflowing potted vines and moon blossoms, the statues and gauzy curtains that separated parts of the enormous room to offer privacy without restricting the airflow in such a hot climate. It was a work of art. He wished he had more time to appreciate it, but he was on a mission.

This next part would be challenging. Entering the palace was easy, but finding the princess was a bit like looking for a blueberry in a barrel of poison berries. Everything looked the same and choosing wrong meant trouble. He couldn't simply open doors and poke his head in without alerting every resident to the presence of a ghost. He scanned for clues, for something, for anything that might indicate where in the palace the bedrooms might be. The palace grounds were enormous, and he could just as easily find his way to a ballroom, any number of kitchens, the servants' wing, or a royal menagerie before he stumbled across the princess.

He took a few more cautious steps toward the center-most area, where the pillars gave way to a large, circular garden. Fountains, lush, tropical vegetation, and an exotic bird wandered about the courtyard. His eyes snagged on an odd dip near the fountain. It appeared to be a pool of shadow, but something about it didn't look quite right. The fae lights twinkling about the garden should have cast a dim, even lighting—there shouldn't be consistent shadows gathered to one side. Tyr approached the shadow near the fountain, realizing with each passing step that he wasn't seeing a shadow at all. The courtyard gave way to a sinking set of stairs.

The fountain's burble had covered the voices initially, but as he drew closer, he could distinctly make out the sounds of conversation. Tyr wasn't sure what he expected to find as he slipped quietly down the staircase. Perhaps a treasure trove, or a collection of art, or maybe this was where the royal tiger slept whenever it didn't have a prisoner to devour. Instead, he stepped into what was unmistakably the dungeon, seeing none other than Ophir, her personal guard, a strange fae male, and the unmistakable face of Lord Berinth.

The gaunt, bedraggled lord was not alone.

+   +   +   +

7:15 PM
11 HOURS AND 30 MINUTES UNTIL EXECUTION

It was hard not to smile. Tyr supposed it didn't matter, as Ophir and her compatriots couldn't see him, but it didn't feel entirely wholesome to grin at the chaos unfolding in the princess's allotted chambers. Harland, ever the white knight of the moral high ground, stood firmly in the camp of belief that the one they'd believed to be Berinth was innocent and should be spared. Ophir, true to her temper, didn't give a fuck whether or not he'd been in his right mind—it had been this man's hands stained with Caris's blood, and he deserved to die. Perhaps it was the third fae making him smile. The man leaned against the wall with one shoulder, inspecting his clothes for signs of dust as if the conversation were of little interest to him. It was relatively comical when contrasted against the princess's furious pacing and Harland's expressive gestures.

"Isn't your gift god-tier judgment? What do you have to say about this?" Ophir spun on the new fae.

The newcomer sighed, still dusting his clothes as if they were infinitely more interesting than the princess's mood. Tyr studied the man for any familiar traits, but he did not look like a citizen of Farehold. Still, he spoke to Princess Ophir as if he were a natural born subject as he said, "More often than not, good judgment is realizing you don't have enough information to make a decision."

"And?" she pressed, angry. "What would you have me do?"

He looked at her with a taciturn expression. "If Berinth is killed at dawn, will Caris have been avenged?"

"Of course not!" she fumed. "If he's a puppet, that means I have more questions than answers. Where are the puppeteers? Who do I have to blame?"

"Then," Harland attempted to clarify, "you won't execute him tomorrow?"

Ophir made a show of her offense. "What would make you say that? Of course, I'm going to kill him."

"Why?" Harland's eyes were so wild with a cocktail of disappointment, anger, and surprise that the whites of his eyes could be seen all around his irises.

She shrugged. "Catharsis."

It was truly an effort for Tyr not to laugh. Ophir made staying hidden rather hard. He steeled himself as he listened.

"Help me out here, Samael." Harland turned to the third man, exasperated. So, the stranger had a name after all.

The man called Samael offered a dispassionate cross of his arms, leaning against the nearby wall. "I don't think the princess is looking for input."

"I already like him better than you."

Harland glared, looking between them. "But if she *were*?"

Samael appeared to consider this. "Who else have you met in the palace? What else has transpired since you've been in Tarkhany?"

Not many, she admitted. She'd been met by guards when she'd entered the city. She'd been escorted to the dungeon when she'd first confirmed Berinth's identity for Tarkhany's royal authorities. She'd interacted with the servants as they'd brought her meals and helped her bathe and dress. Other than that, she'd only had a few peculiar exchanges with Zita.

The barest curiosities sparkled in Samael's expression. "Peculiar how?"

She amended that she didn't know whether or not the exchanges were typical for Tarkhany culture, seeming rather embarrassed as she recalled the scolding she'd received on her ignorance of the other kingdoms.

"And the prince?"

Ophir's eyebrows bunched in a confused frown. Her eyes unfocused into the middle distance, scanning as if she were reading lines from a tome as she scanned her memories. She'd told Tyr once of an ambassador mission between their kingdoms and her playtime with a boy who'd called himself the Prince of the Desert. She used to tell him everything. That seemed like another life, now.

"No, I haven't met a prince. The queen hasn't mentioned one, either. The guards did mention something when I arrived about who they were bringing me to see, but they decided that Zita should be the one to receive me. I don't know anyone else from the royal family, or if there is one at all." Her sentence drifted away at the end, not unlike the wind taking the sand from the tops of the dunes and scattering it to the night sky.

The men didn't need to press her further to ask if she found it unusual, because of course the answer was yes. It was hard to blame her. She'd been focused on the capture and pending execution of the man who murdered her sister. It was understandable that little else had been on her mind.

"Are you swinging the axe?" Harland asked. "Even if he wasn't in his right mind when he committed the crime?"

Unruffled, she said, "Whether he's mad or sane makes no difference to me. The man is stained with my sister's blood. And, I assume you mean the metaphorical axe? Because yes, I will be the one who kills him. Tarkhany's executioner needs no more blood on his hands. This is my fight." She would burn him in front of all who'd gathered. It was her death to avenge.

From the placement of the mirror on the wall, Tyr could see the guard's very transparent emotions, even though his back was to Tyr. Harland tilted his chin forward ever so slightly, meeting her gaze and hoping she heard him when he said no, it wasn't her fight. If Berinth was little more than a puppet, he was not responsible for Caris's death.

Ophir's eyes bore two rebounding words: *fuck you.*

Tyr debated stepping into the light, mostly because he was concerned that if he waited too much longer, he'd chuckle in sheer delight of their absurdities and give himself away. Fortunately, it was decided that the men would return to their assigned rooms and Ophir would go speak with Zita. Samael had a gift for language and promised to do whatever reconnaissance he was able, and Harland more or less said he'd be brooding until dawn, should she need him.

Tyr knew she wouldn't be pleased to see him, but the time had come.

The moment the men closed the door, he took three quick steps and put himself behind her to cover her mouth. He didn't need her to call out in surprise when he appeared. He stepped out from the place between things in the same moment his hand clamped down on her mouth.

As anticipated, a startled cry bubbled from her throat.

Muffled by his hand, the sound was absorbed, and he turned her to look into the mirror. "It's me," he said, voice low. He saw her eyes meet his in the mirror and watched her shift from fear to fury. "I'm going to let go now. Don't scream."

The moment he removed his hand she spun on him. "Every time you—"

He put a hand to her mouth once more, then brought a single finger to his own lips, shushing her. He gestured to the door, arching a conspiratorial brow. Ophir's face flushed with a familiar shade of pink at his nearness, which he appreciated. He kept his voice barely above a whisper. "A bird told me you might be in need of a spy."

She shook her head in disbelief, toffee-colored curls moving about her shoulders as they spilled down her back. Her eyes were an even brighter gold than normal when she was angry, almost as if they were iron-scorched and heated in the fire until they were a blinding shade of yellow. "How is it that I can never get rid of you?"

He smiled. "To your credit, you do try. Don't think I've forgiven you. Crossing the desert was astoundingly unpleasant, and I plan to hold it against you forever."

She peeked over his shoulder. "Is Dwyn with you?"

"In Tarkhany, yes. At the palace? No. She doesn't know I'm here. She also claims I'm particularly hard to shake."

"Has anyone compared you to a venereal disease? If not, allow me to be the first."

He pursed his lips for the third time that night to keep himself from smiling. Maybe it was a laugh threatening to bubble over due to being reunited after she'd put an entire desert between them, or just a general glee at her temper, but he found her endlessly amusing.

"How did you cross the desert?"

His amusement faded. "With substantial difficulty, a touch of heat stroke, and what Dwyn swears are third-degree burns."

"I assume she used a healer's magic, since you're not horribly disfigured from your skin melting off under the sun?"

"You assume correctly. And am I hearing things, or are you calling me handsome?"

"You're hearing things. And yes," she sighed, losing much of her steam. "I'd love if you could spy for me, but you don't speak the language. There is so much I need to uncover, and next to no time to learn it. I don't think Zita will expect me to stay once Berinth is killed, but if he's little more than a puppet, then there's a reason he came back to Tarkhany. It's safe to assume his puppet master is here."

He frowned. "Yes, my inability to speak the local language has been a recurrent theme regarding my lack of usefulness."

He'd scarcely finished his sentence when Ophir's face lit. It hadn't been the candle of an idea but the bonfire sort of light that erupted when brilliance struck. Her hand flew to the side of her face, creeping up to where her hair hid her ears. She winced as if pained with the somewhat indelicate action of whatever she was doing, but moments later, she procured a metallic ear cuff. She extended it to him, and he took it.

"I made it!" she said proudly.

He rolled it over between his fingers, examining the rather ornate look of the metallic shape. It arched and pointed as if to follow the elfin points of the fae ear, surrounding it perfectly. "And it's beautiful, Firi, but I fail to see—"

She tried to hit him, but he caught her wrist with his free hand before she made contact. She shook like she would have if she'd received a chill down the spine, as if her body couldn't physically contain her burst of rage. She suppressed it into silence. "It's a translator, smart ass. I made it on my first night and I haven't taken it off. It doesn't work both ways, so I haven't been able to speak to anyone, but I can hear what they're saying no matter what language they're speaking. Perfect for a ghost. Go ahead, put it on. Let me see how it looks when you disappear."

He continued speaking while he fitted it to his ear. "I was with you in the dungeon toward the end. I'd only just arrived to hear what the newest member of your party was saying. It seemed like a far-fetched conclusion. I'd sooner believe Berinth was lying."

Tyr turned his head to the left and right, then shook it like a dog, intent on ensuring it wouldn't fall off. Satisfied that it was securely attached, he turned his inquisitive gaze to Ophir.

Ophir chewed the inside of her cheek. "It's his thing—Samael's, that is. I don't know if it's his power or just a knack, but he's in possession of the sort of gut instincts that saved the kingdom. My father has never told us the whole story, but he was convinced enough by the man's gift that he appointed him as our spymaster."

Tyr considered this information. "Perhaps the spymaster should be the one with the translator."

She made a face. "Perhaps the spymaster should be the one with the gift for invisibility. Now, let me see it."

He obliged, taking a step into the space between things. Ophir's face changed the moment he disappeared, searching the air for any hint, any trace of him.

"I think if I look hard enough, I can see evidence of your eyes," she said finally.

He stepped back into the light. "Yes, it's the one thing I can't fully conceal. It's never caused me any trouble. If someone catches a pair of eyes out of their peripherals, they usually convince themselves their vision is playing tricks on them. We tell ourselves little lies all the time to downplay our intuition when the truth would be too terrible. It helps keep us sane."

"I feel like there's a lesson in there somewhere."

He nodded. "There is, but few learn it. Your spymaster, Samael, may possess the gift of intuition or judgment or spectacular hunches or whatever it is you believe him to have, but it's ignoring our own that gets us killed. Trust it." He extended the tips of his fingers, grazing her abdomen.

She gave him a shove toward the door. "Well, right now my gut is telling me that you have the chance to be useful. Please, go do that."

"Fine," he said, disappearing once more. Her hands remained pressed to his chest, eyebrows shooting up when she could no longer see him. "But when I return victorious, I expect a reward."

Ophir remained in stunned silence as he brushed his lips over hers. A hand went to her lower back, the other cupping the back of her neck. His fingers flexed the moment she relaxed into the kiss, melting into him. In his arms was the single most precious thing in all the kingdoms. Princess Ophir, the only living heir to the southern throne, the final hope of Farehold, a motherfucking manifester.

"I hate you, you know," she murmured.

"I don't think you do," he replied. She didn't open her eyes until he broke the kiss. The last thing he saw as he stepped from the room was her searching the air for a trace of phantom eyes.

FORTY-FIVE

✦ ✦ ✦ ✦

7:30 PM
11 HOURS AND 15 MINUTES UNTIL EXECUTION

WHEN YOU DIDN'T KNOW WHERE TO GO, EVERY PATH was equally wrong. It was quite different from not *caring* where you went, in which case, every step would have been equally right. Tyr returned to the courtyard, if only because he'd had luck there once before. Who was to say it couldn't happen again? Additionally, its circular, centralized nature offered an equal advantage to the various points of the palace. Pillars supported cathedral-high ceilings on all sides, halls and rooms and things of importance and mundanity in all directions.

It was familiar, knowing what he wanted with no idea how to achieve it. He knew he needed Dwyn in order to figure out how to use borrowed powers, but he had no clue how to get her to give up her secrets without incurring the wrath of the bond they shared. Before he'd needed to know her secrets, he'd needed to find her in the first place. And before it all came the need to see the men who'd hurt Svea brought to a violent and terrible justice.

Kings, generals, and militaries would probably disagree, but Tyr was quite certain there was no such thing as a foolproof plan. All anyone could do—particularly a lone actor—was the next right thing, one step at a time, while hoping for the best.

The All Mother must favor him, he thought, as his luck sparkled within a few moments.

He'd been in the courtyard for no more than two minutes when a woman floated out from behind the pillars near the opposite end of the courtyard. He'd spent enough time in Tarkhany to know the posture of peasants and enough time lurking about the castle in Aubade to spy the way nobility carried themselves.

This woman was no commoner.

He marveled at the woman, skin darker than Odessa calla lilies, cloudlike dress stitched of night itself. Twilight-deep, jewel-toned purples and blues rippled behind her as she walked. While some of the attendants in the castle had been human, this woman's arched ears were easy to spot from the close crop of her hair. From the quick, intentional pace of her stride, he'd expected her to cross the courtyard into a separate part of the palace. Instead, she came to an abrupt halt near the fountain.

Tyr took a few careful steps toward her, wondering if she was going to descend into the dungeon.

The woman exhaled slowly, nostrils flaring in a clear sign of anger. Her fists flexed at her sides. Before long, the bird took several careful steps toward her.

"I won't insult you by asking you if you did this," she said to the bird. He could hear enough from his free ear to know she wasn't speaking the common tongue. The translation device was terribly useful. He wasn't confident he'd give it back. "Because I know the answer. There's no reason for those men to be here. This was handled."

The bird cocked its head from one side to the other.

"No one's here," she said through her teeth.

With one step forward, the bird's foot transitioned into the step of a man. She matched his height almost exactly, shoulders straightening as if to emphasize her anger. Whoever this was, she was not here to show a sign of weakness.

"I didn't bring them here," he answered, voice low and irritated.

As with Tyr and his ability to step between things fully clothed, the shapeshifter before him was dressed in finery both loose enough for the climate and brilliant enough to portray his status. His tunic and pants resembled the same blacks, oranges, reds, and yellows belonging to the bird moments before. This was an important man.

"You did, Tempus. You've been bringing them here for sixty years. You shouldn't have gone to Farehold. You started this when—"

He looked to the side, crestfallen. "I didn't know you knew about that."

She looked as if he had slapped her. The insult to her intelligence was as violent as any physical blow. "When I brought you in to this palace, you understood what you were getting yourself into. You knew who I was, and what I—"

"I've known that you will not bloody your hands with the justice you crave, Zita."

"This isn't justice!"

"Lower your voice. No one knows I'm here."

Her hands flexed again as if controlling a great and powerful storm within her. Tyr idly wondered what abilities she might possess and whether or not he might be at risk of harm, should her wrath win.

Zita made a controlled expression. "If you're seen, we'll say you've arrived in the night. It's well known: you've been on an extended trip away. I'd prefer that we keep it that way."

The man she'd called Tempus showed a combination of frustration and defeat. "Why did you marry me, if I never stood a chance in your court? Why would you agree to this union? Hundreds of years have passed, Zita. He's been gone for—"

Her expression changed in an instant. "Don't you dare speak of him."

"This! This is why! This has to happen. You won't let him go. You won't let any of them go. You won't—"

"I'm not the one who needs to lower my voice," she said, spinning on her heels as she returned the way she'd come. Tempus jogged after her, and Tyr responded by picking his way carefully across the courtyard. He hugged them tightly enough to slip into her room, undetected, as the door closed behind them.

Her room was not so much different from the one Ophir had been assigned, save for a few personal touches. Zita's was thick with the same bright citrus scent that permeated the palace. He'd thought it had come from the incense that smoked from the pendulous fixtures around the halls and rooms, but perhaps it was as much from its queen as from the decorations.

Tempus ran a hand over his face. "Zita—"

"I didn't confront you on your little ambassador mission because no blood was shed. You needed to see them for yourself, and you did. You came back and we never spoke of it. It was over."

His face was ripe with incredulity. "You want Farehold to get away with this? With nearly a millennium of injustice? You want—"

"Of course not!" Full-bodied anger tore through her, irrespective of the late hour. Tyr looked over his shoulder for something he suspected he might see: rune etchings on the doors. They'd been engraved by a manufacturer for their dampening ability. No one would be able to hear what happened within these rooms. "But do I blame the grandmothers and the children and the feeble and the poor of Aubade? Do I blame the ignorant princess stumbling around here with little more education on the world than a toddler? Am I any better if I take their land? If I rain terror down on the citizens, don't I match their monstrosity?"

There was a tinny quality to his high, mocking laugh. "Where is the accountability? Where is the justice?"

"You'd have me rush into battle and risk my people's safety after all we've endured? You've always been shortsighted," Zita replied.

Tempus's hands clenched into fists. "It's been six hundred years!"

Her reply was a gentle desert breeze. "And if I'd taken your council, the regents who sit upon their stolen throne would have been ready for retaliation. Revenge, dear husband, is a dish best served cold."

"Goddess damn it, Zita. There's cold, and then there's whatever the hell *this* is."

She didn't dignify his petulance with a response.

He was unmoved. "You have a plan, then?"

The bored stare she gave him could have frozen every drop of water in the palace. "You gave up the privilege of knowing long ago, Tempus."

Tyr touched a finger to his lips, leaning into his silence as he listened. He'd been right. The All Mother had favored him indeed.

Tempus stomped to the far side of the room. Something told Tyr these were fights the walls knew well. The shape-shifting man cast an exasperated arm as he made a sweeping gesture to the world at large. "The humans who were forced to evacuate the coast don't even know the names of the ancestors who died in the pilgrimage. Many of the fae who held your grudge have died. If you had planned to stay alone in the desert—"

"I should have," she bit. "I was happier alone."

His eyes went wild and pleading as he crossed the room. His tone softened as he reached for her hands. "You don't mean that."

She jerked them free. "I do. You'll never be half the man he was. Now, leave me be. I have an execution to prepare."

Tempus turned away, but not in anger. This was pain. Tyr recognized the broken emotion painted from his wounded face to the slump of his shoulders. He was looking into the fractured heart of a man in the sort of love that would never be returned. Despite the tumultuous conversation before him, he couldn't ignore the thrum of excited adrenaline. This was a fist-sized diamond of finds in the world of espionage. He'd uncovered more in thirty minutes than any of the Farehold parties could have hoped to discern if they'd remained in Midnah for years.

Tyr had witnessed many gifts and powers throughout his years and couldn't help but find his superior. Shapeshifting? Yes, a clever way to hide in plain sight, but a more effective gift for hiding was the ability to step into the place between things. Harland possessed supernatural strength? Good for him, but what good was brute force if the enemy spotted him a mile away? Tyr had developed his own hardened muscles and skillsets and could deliver punches and dodge similar blows without ever being seen. Samael had excellent intuition? That sounded wonderful, but if he was discovered the moment he followed his hunch, how useful was his power? Ophir could manifest? Well…okay, she had him beat on that one. It was the superior gift.

And Dwyn? She was infuriating. He hated that the irreverent, too-often-naked witch, her stolen powers, and her unconscionable trail of victims took residence in his mind. She did not deserve the thought he gave her.

Now what was he to make of the two before him? Zita, the clear royal of the palace, and the fae male called Tempus— was he truly her husband? A late-in-life marriage to a man who lived in the shadow of her resentment? Tyr supposed it was possible he was jumping to conclusions, but the angst, brokenness, and context allowed him to fill in some gaps whether he had some goddess granted gift for wisdom. Tyr leaned against the marbled wall and waited. If he gave them ten more minutes to talk, perhaps they'd spell out everything he needed to know about Berinth, Farehold, blood magic, and if he was lucky, maybe they'd stop fighting and give a detailed lesson on how to drain people and steal power.

"What was your plan?" Zita asked with a sort of resigned softness. "After the princess killed him?"

Tempus cupped his face once more, fingers rubbing over the ghost of a beard. "Now, that part I didn't do."

Zita's eyebrows knit together. "What?"

"I don't know the man in our dungeons."

Her eyes were sharp. "I don't believe you."

"I can't tell you what you are and are not allowed to believe. You know I've orchestrated several moving pawns in this game. I *did* go to Farehold decades ago to see them and speak to them myself, and you're right: Eero and his family were toothless. Between the two of us, I seem to be the only one invested in righting the wrongs done to the continent. But I do not know that man in your dungeon."

She took a careful step back. "You swear it?"

The man must have seen his opening and took it. This time when he grabbed Zita by the elbow, it was with the gentleness of a lover craving only acceptance. "I swear it on my life, on the All Mother, on the souls of my ancestors. I've been to Aubade. I've been in the castle that once belonged to your family. I've met their king. I've seen the lands they've claimed as their own. I've put my nose where it doesn't belong. I've wanted to help you close this chapter so that you can begin to heal. But I am not responsible for the man in your dungeons, nor do I claim responsibility for the vengeance that brought Eero's daughter here."

Her face puckered everywhere from her brows to her lips. It was confusion, it was distrust, it was pain. "I never thought you'd admit to going to Aubade."

Tempus brought her in close, holding her tightly as he breathed his answer against her neck. "I shouldn't have gone. I learned very little. Ophir was a child at the time, so that's what I became. She knew nothing, and her father was as useless as a sack of flour. I don't blame Eero directly, though he certainly hasn't done anything to right the wrongs. Caris, however..."

She pulled away. "The slain princess?"

Tempus sank from somewhere in his middle, like a building whose pillars had cracked. Sweat glistened on his brow from both the heat and the stress of their fight. If the light had caught his eye in any other way, Tyr would have thought the man was about to cry. "She would have been on our side, Zita. She wasn't just a pretty monarch set to marry Raascot's king. She didn't just want peace. She sought justice. Caris desired unity for all the right reasons."

Zita considered the information, chewing on each word as if it were a particularly tough piece of meat. After a prolonged silence, she asked, "And his second born? The princess with us now?"

He shrugged. "The girl desires singular vengeance for her sibling. I believe she knows Caris was her superior in every way, and the best contribution she could make to this world would be to end the life of whoever killed her. She isn't our enemy. She isn't anything."

Tyr closed his eyes against the assertion. It was hard to hear, even for him. He leaned his head back against the cool marble of the stone, breathing in the smell of freshly juiced oranges and limes as he digested what Tempus had said. No one on the continent believed in Ophir. They didn't know her. They didn't know what she could do. Even if they did, would it matter? Maybe that was part of what he liked about her. Nothing about her was obvious. Her underestimation was gift and curse. It was the continent's preconceptions and folly that made them unable to see what she was capable of—that was no failure of hers.

It was odd, this feeling. Almost like an itch within a wound, the healing stitch beneath a scab that would reopen and be more painful if one contacted it. He wanted to tear at it, to alleviate the discomfort, but he knew it was inherently unwise to do so. He didn't prod. Tonight wasn't about perplexing, invisible injuries and indefinable sensations, no matter how much they bothered him. It was about information.

Focus.

"But tomorrow..." Tempus prodded.

"I know."

"So, what do we—"

"We do nothing."

Zita pulled away from the embrace, and Tyr saw the pained look again. It was the face of a man in love. Such a dangerous, treacherous thing. Love wasn't an emotion, not really. It was a verb. It was the force that shaped his life. A feeling was the least of Tempus's worries—clearly his feelings fluctuated greatly, as Zita's contradictory tugs on his heart pushed and pulled him with equal intensity. Whether he went to Farehold, shaped the kingdoms, influenced criminals, or lured princesses was perhaps inconsequential contrasted against his reason for doing it.

"Do you have a plan, Zita? What have you brewed for six hundred years?"

She wilted. "It hasn't been six hundred."

He looked to his feet. "I know. I know the first few years…and with your children…"

"I don't want revenge."

Tempus dared to return her gaze. "Maybe you should."

She swallowed. "It wouldn't serve us. It wouldn't serve Midnah, or Tarkhany. It wouldn't serve the people of Farehold who are no more guilty of the atrocities than our own citizens. The poor shouldn't suffer for the disputes of monarchs."

"They took everything. They took what didn't belong to them. They—"

The powerful woman before him remained downcast, as if whatever fury and strength that fueled her had smoked out. "They didn't take everything. That's the tactic, isn't it? You offer two options, one in which your heart is cut out, the other in which it's merely broken. Isn't that why the shop boy stays with his cruel employer? Why the woman remains with her wicked husband? Why we live on in Midnah without outright war? Our hearts are cracked, yes, but they're ours."

Tempus didn't argue.

It was a terrible fight. It was wrong—surely the man could concede that much. He couldn't have agreed, but he must

377

not have known how to form a rebuttal. She was describing abuse. Whether from the assistant, the wife, or the kingdom, it was lose-lose. This couldn't have been the first time they'd had his conversation. Or the second. Or the tenth. It was clear from the slump of his shoulders and the way he headed for the door that he was a man who'd lost this fight long ago.

"What do you want?" he asked finally.

She looked at him in a way that showed the entirety of her soul. Even Tyr could see the crushed powder of her heart from where she stood. "I want them to do the right thing."

Tempus's lips became a flat line. "Waiting on someone else to come around for justice—"

"Is like waiting for rain in the desert. I know."

"You could do it. You have a power unlike any the world has seen. You could bring Aubade—no, Farehold—to their knees. You should have done it then."

"I won't use it."

Exasperation choked Tempus. "But now we have their princess. It's his last remaining daughter. If we—"

"No," she said, voice low but firm. "Ophir is not a hostage. She's not leverage. I'd rather have her as an ally. If Caris truly would have been an agent for justice…"

"Keep holding your breath, Zita. Maybe it will only take another six hundred years."

Tyr saw from the posture, from the step, from the subtle shake of the head that Tempus was resigned to his inability to win her heart through any feat of logic or strategy when it came to regaining the lands they'd lost or the royals he deemed their enemies. Tyr couldn't know that marrying Zita had been the best day of Tempus's life and a relatively calm weekend for her. He didn't know that the sun over Midnah had been bright as it shone over their union, but not too hot, or that the kingdom had been receptive, but there had been no gay joyousness in their celebrations. She was a good queen, of that Tyr was sure after only knowing her for a moment. She was one who had moved on, it seemed—at least, she had for public appearances. She'd found someone who loved her. He couldn't know the man before him with lands and titles and a good heart who would bring his armies and passion to the palace and battlefield.

And then there was the list of things that only Zita knew.

She did not want to give her new husband children, for example.

It had been a scandal to the kingdom and a tragic, heart-breaking honor to their mother. She'd had children, after all. Three sons born to her late husband, the joy of Tarkhany, the lights of her life. Their father's name would die with them, they'd declared. Their wives hadn't understood, nor had the kingdom. Tempus hadn't understood. The only thing he knew, a truth he gripped with miserable fingers, was that they were in an unhappy marriage. Not because they didn't care for each other, not because they'd done anything wrong, not because they weren't a good fit, but because they were two beings whose paths had intersected at the wrong time.

And what if they'd met before she'd ever fallen into the arms of her human? Perhaps Tempus would have been a marvelous king. Maybe he should have been her first and only love. They might still hold the coastal shores, own the fruitful lands, bear fae children who still lived, have a beautiful legacy of kindness and peaceable relations with their neighboring kingdoms. Perhaps if Tempus had been the king of Tarkhany when Farehold's king had made a play for their lands, he would have intervened. Maybe their presence closer to the shore could have positioned them to help the fae who'd been forced north to Raascot. Perhaps Farehold could have been kept in check, balanced by forces from both the north and the south.

Farehold—the middle kingdom, as the continent called it—hadn't won from superior strategy or better armies.

The victory had come from betrayal, subtlety, and time.

Brick by brick they'd built their empire of stolen

supremacy. One stone went unnoticed. Two, then twenty, then ten thousand. Before the neighboring kingdoms had been willing to accept the atrocities implied by the fortress around them, Farehold had created an empire of violence. Move, or be moved.

Tyr thought of his miserable journey across the Tarkhany Desert, wondering if it would have been manageable at all without the intermittent clusters of trees, the pools of water with firm bedrock that refused to let it evaporate. The Frozen Straits had no such luxury. There was no fresh water, no reprieve, no shelter or break or moment of calm. Human and fae alike died on the ice, their bodies frozen into infinitely preserved icicles, their flesh and blood never decaying, never decomposing, trapped forever in an endless winter. Maybe geography was the only thing that had kept Sulgrave safe from Farehold's interference. Thank the All Mother and the frigid torment of her blizzards from the south and their colonization.

He wanted to believe that Sulgrave would have fought back, that they would have bested Farehold in a battle and left their conquerors in rubble. From his time in Tarkhany and the palace, he'd developed a few opinions about reasons one might win or lose in a war. Defending your territory was much easier if you saw the enemy coming from a distance. Inviting the enemy into your home under the banner of goodness and hospitality and not realizing they were a cockroach until they'd infested your home posed an entirely new set of problems. Perhaps Sulgrave would have been no different. Hopefully they'd never need to find out.

"Go, Tempus."

"Once upon a time, I shared your bed. You used to let me stay with you."

She looked at him sadly, all of the fight in her evaporated like water on the sizzling marble. "I did try. I wanted to love you."

When Tempus transitioned, it wasn't into the tall, familiar bird Tyr had seen before. He became a vulture, enormous, threatening, and ready for flight. She opened the door for him, and Tyr slipped out the second before Tempus exited. It was disconcerting to see a man become a creature that looked so much like death. Perhaps if he hadn't seen Ophir's atrocities, he would have considered vultures to be among the ugliest things on the planet. Now he knew better.

Tempus spread his wings and took off into the star-studded black of the night sky above the gardens, leaving Zita in her room and Tyr in the open air between the pillars. He wasn't sure exactly what he'd learned. The more he knew, the more questions he had. He wasn't sure Ophir would be entirely happy.

Tyr crossed the courtyard considering how he might tell her, what he might say, what he might do to explain what he'd heard. Perhaps it wouldn't change anything for her execution. Maybe Ophir would be able to make more sense than he had. Maybe she'd learn something that he hadn't been able to discern. Maybe—

The air left his lungs.

A strangulation hold gripped him around the throat from an invisible assailant.

He clawed at the unseen enemy and made contact with something that seemed to be made of stone. It didn't feel like the flesh of human or fae. Unseen? And the power of a vice-like grip? And the...

Dwyn.

She snarled as her ability to stay in the space between things slipped out of her control. Her grip on his throat was weakening. Her borrowed powers wouldn't be of use to her much longer. His face flashed from surprise to fury as he looked into the black eyes of his assailant. Raising his fist, he brought it down with all his might to hit her, but she lifted her other hand to block him. Strength. Shield. How many borrowed abilities was she using? How quickly was she burning through them? What could she withstand before it affected her? Whatever remaining siphoned power she used for strength remained. One hand on his throat and the other on his fist, she drove her forehead into his face and knocked Tyr to the ground. He saw her head swim with the impact, but she had the benefit of healing on her side. Had she leveled a village in preparation for this fight? His last moments of vision before the world slipped into dizzying darkness were Dwyn's pretty face twisted in the satisfaction of victory and violence.

FORTY-SIX

+   +   +   +

7:30 PM
11 HOURS AND 15 MINUTES UNTIL EXECUTION

DWYN WAS FUCKING FURIOUS. VENOM DRIPPED FROM HER every movement as she aimed to maim, to wound, to come as close to killing as she could. She'd see his body in a withered husk before he could blink, were it not for this piece-of-shit dog and his piece-of-shit tattoo and her piece-of-shit terrible goddess-damned judgment that had led her to ever inking her skin in the first place.

Shame at having been not only discovered but tricked burned hotter than the princess's flame ever had.

Dwyn had lowered her guard for the barest of moments thinking that the two of them could work together, could collaborate, might even be on the same side, and the moment she closed her eyes, he'd vanished. She'd yawned into consciousness that morning with a smile on her lips and the naive belief that, for the first time in decades, she had an ally.

Of course, he'd been playing her for a fool.

Of course, he'd only pretended to be kind, to be her friend, to be on her side because he'd already learned what she'd fought so hard to hide.

She'd looked at the cold rumple in the sheets where he'd lain only hours prior and known why he'd left. She'd let her guard down for scarcely more than an hour and he'd betrayed her. An hour during which she'd rested and recovered because she had done the hard work, she had exerted herself to the extents of her limit, she had carried him to the corners of the world and taken the barest of reprieves in order to recuperate. He'd deciphered the plan she'd so cleverly disguised. She thought he'd been tracking her for all these years like a stray dog without a master, all the while he'd been piecing together the most glorious plan Gyrradin had ever known.

His dash to Ophir had given him away.

She'd gag him by any means necessary to keep him from ruining what she had with Ophir, if it was the last thing she did.

Her mistake had been in trusting him, if even for a second.

His mistake had been not letting the prisoner finish the job.

Dwyn had her borrowed strength long enough to drag Tyr across the courtyard and halfway down the stairs into the dungeon before the stolen ability evaporated from her arms. He wasn't fully unconscious, and for that she was grateful. She wasn't sure if she'd still be standing if she'd successfully knocked him out.

Fuck.

She cried out the moment the pain of his weight crashed into her arms. The dog was awake. *Fuck, fuck, fuck.*

Dwyn was unable to stifle the grunt the moment his full weight hit her, barely jumping out of the way in time for gravity to take him the rest of the way down the stairs. She pressed herself into the wall of the stairwell as she watched him hit the bumps, the curve, the twist in the stairs as it curved just out of sight. The sounds came to an end the moment he hit the landing.

She just needed to figure out how to get him into a cell. She had to stay conscious, stay strong, stay present just long enough to lock him away.

The noxious cloud of unwashed bodies, piss, and waste

washed over her. The heat exacerbated the unbearable scents of the dungeon. She sucked in a breath with her mouth, refusing to breathe through her nose as she looked around for a solution.

Her head still buzzed from the blow she'd landed against him.

Her plan wasn't working. She was still feeling every hit, every move, every fucking connection. Even with her shield, her healing, and the strength she'd stolen, the Blood Pact's binding seal reverberated through her, threatening to drag her under. If she was this affected from striking him in the nose even with her arsenal of rapidly expended power, she didn't dare wound him further. *Come on, come on*, she willed herself, desperate to shove him into a cell and slam the iron bars behind him.

The dungeons were dimly lit—the fae lights being a kindness rather than the sort of torches that might add heat to an already sweltering space. Dwyn hurried down the stairs and eyed the prisoners. Several of them clambered to be closer to the bars, desperate for pity, for sympathy, for a chance at release. One man leaned against the slots of his cage and whistled. It took two seconds and one vulgar word for her to know exactly who she was draining.

The disgusting, predatory prisoner sparkled with delight when she approached him. Her eyes had twinkled for an entirely separate reason. She extended her slender fingers toward his face and he raised an eyebrow, as if in any universe a beautiful woman would saunter into a dungeon and be sexually interested by a strange prisoner. He was stupid enough to deserve the withering death that befell him.

The others in the prison screamed as they watched her suck him dry with her prolonged touch. She whirled on them, telling them that if they weren't silent, she'd come for them next. One cried out with righteous indignation that he knew a witch when he saw one. Her eyes burned, but he did not look away. She didn't have time to bother with him now.

It had been the only threat she needed to buy their compliance. No one made a sound. Now to get Tyr—

Shit.

He was gone. Could she not catch a fucking break? She gritted her teeth, scanning the jail frantically for any nook, any cranny he could have used to hide. If he'd stepped into the place between things...

That was it. She used the life she'd stolen from the prisoner and called upon the ability to rightly see. The moment they made eye contact, he smiled, and she realized her mistake.

She'd used her borrowed ability too soon.

She was useless.

There was no water down here. She had nothing in her reserves. She was as helpless as every other goddess-forsaken prisoner in this dungeon as she waited for Tyr to deliver her fate.

+   +   +   +

Tyr closed the space between them in three seconds flat. Dwyn barely had time to react as he grabbed her, twisting her away so that her back was pressed into his chest. He pinned her throat between his forearm and bicep, pinching off her blood flow. She'd be unconscious in a matter of seconds.

"Stop!" she gasped.

Dizziness overtook him, just as he'd known it would. The bond was the only reason she'd lived this long, but she'd survived one breath too many. He only needed to outlast the curse a single second longer than Dwyn.

An idea struck him. Tyr made eye contact with the lone prisoner who'd dared to defy her. They were united for a single moment against a witch. Nothing else mattered. Perhaps he couldn't kill her, but a hateful stranger sure as hell could.

Tyr slammed Dwyn backward into the metal. Her head struck the iron, reverberating as stars filled her vision—an impact he knew was successful because of the white and orange dots that clouded his ability to see. The prisoner grabbed her in the same moment Tyr released her throat. All he needed to do was hold her wrists. He wasn't responsible for her death, just for her inability to drain him. The scourge of their bond was magically sealed, but everything had a loophole.

So he thought.

The prisoner's arm wrapped around her neck as Tyr held her wrists tightly.

He watched as Dwyn's eyes popped in fear.

He saw the life drain from her face.

He saw the moment she realized she was going to die.

And he knew that Dwyn couldn't tell that he was losing consciousness just as quickly.

Of course.

He was still responsible for her death. But if he could stay on his feet until the last possible second... It was Dwyn calling the flame and fusing his fingers together all over again—he could tolerate whatever she could take. If he could just outlast her.

She managed to sputter three final words. "I'll teach you!"

"What?" He grunted against the hold, struggling to sound stable.

She thrashed, fighting him with everything she possessed. Her shoulder blades rolled off the iron. Her hips thrust up and away from the bars. She attempted to kick, but he pressed himself into her, preventing her from moving away from where the prisoner held her in his death grip. He could see it in her dark, panicked eyes: she thought he'd finally found a loophole. She couldn't even gasp for air. A few more moments, and she'd be on the ground.

Dwyn said it again, each word weaker than the one before, as if her sentence were being pulled under the depths of the sea into the blackened pits of its trenches. "I'll teach you to drain."

He knew he had less than ten seconds before he joined

her on the floor. He'd die the moment she took her last breath. But she didn't know that.

He released her wrists, and her hands flew to the crease between his arm and hers where the prisoner held her in a chokehold, fingers digging into her skin as she drained him. The shock on the imprisoned man's face disappeared along with his blood, his flesh, his soul. Soon he was little more than a mummified memory. Dwyn panted as she looked at Tyr. He knew from the frenzied panic on her face that she fully believed he'd found a way to kill her.

He held the upper hand for a second longer.

Tyr eyed her with lethal stillness, knowing that if he wavered, if he showed a single hint that he'd been a moment from death, their deal would be off.

He hadn't understood it when Zita and Tempus had fought in her room. He hadn't known at the party, or when he'd watched Ophir and her guards in the dungeon, but the moment Dwyn had populated into his vision with deadly intent, he knew precisely what she'd done. He understood Berinth, he understood the hypnosis, he understood Caris's mutilation and blood magic and manipulation and villainy and every horrible thing all at once.

His mouth began working before he'd let it sink in. He met Dwyn's still-frantic gaze with cool gravity as he cast his final piece of leverage.

"You teach me to drain, and I won't tell Ophir that you're the puppet master."

FORTY-SEVEN

+   +   +   +

12:15 AM
6 HOURS AND 30 MINUTES UNTIL EXECUTION

So?" Ophir's heart skipped. She leapt from the bed the moment her door cracked open and padded toward the center of the room. Relief was overdue. She'd been unable to relax as Tyr wandered about the palace with her translation cuff. It was impossible to know what he would or wouldn't learn, but her imagination played an infinite loop of worst-case scenarios. She'd almost made a new vageth just to have something to play with that might distract her, but she didn't know how she'd get rid of it when someone other than Tyr entered her room. She'd struggled to pass the time, nibbling on a few of the crescent-shaped cookies filled with cinnamon, nuts, sugar, and a tart orange marmalade, but rather than finishing any of them, she just took singular bites out of three separate pastries to see if they'd all taste the same. Her table was now a graveyard dedicated to abandoned, half-eaten cookies. Her throat knotted when she saw that Tyr was not alone.

"Dwyn?"

"Firi!" Dwyn's face lit with delight. She ran to the princess and threw her arms around her. Ophir blinked in surprise, failing to return the hug. The wave of mint hit her along with a bucket of memories, of being slapped on a windswept cliff, of being doused with water when night terrors had engulfed her in flame, of being told she'd tasted like sunshine between the sheets. Dwyn seemed unbothered by her disconnect. The fae gripped both of Ophir's shoulders and observed her at arm's length. "Oh my goddess, I don't know much about the fashion in Tarkhany, but please tell me you'll start to wear this dress when we get back to Farehold. Have one made in every color."

Ophir was once again very aware of just how exposed she felt in the sheer fabric. She gathered her thoughts. "But, nothing has changed. You still lied."

Dwyn straightened her shoulders. "You're right."

The admission caught Ophir utterly off kilter.

"I wouldn't have saved you from drowning if you'd been a random maiden swimming beneath the moonlight," Dwyn went on. "I traveled to Farehold because I was motivated by power, and for no other reason. But then I met you, Ophir, and I've meant everything I've said since our night on the beach. I'm committed to keeping you safe. I'm determined to help you step into your magic. If I told you I didn't care about you, it would be the only outright lie to leave my lips. Let me be here for you, Firi, however you need me."

Her words struggled to keep up with her thoughts. "So, you aren't..."

"I'm not pretending to be anything I'm not. Tyr thinks I'm a power-hungry bitch? He spoke the truth. I came for your potential. I stayed for the woman who possessed it. Now, have we crossed the desert to make Tarkhany our bitch, or what's the plan?" Dwyn winked.

Ophir pressed her index fingers into her temples. "I thought Tyr—"

"Tyr came to the palace without me because he's a dickhead. Please get rid of him. I have a laundry list of reasons he doesn't deserve to stay. But in the meantime, you know me. I'm not one to be left behind." She changed the topic, releasing Ophir in pursuit of a pitcher of water. She wrapped her fingers around a crystal glass and filled it to the brim.

"So"—her voice stayed bright—"the buzz around the city is that some beautiful foreign princess is set to execute a traitor at dawn! You're amazing. Tell me everything."

Ophir couldn't quite place the separation she felt. She rested a hand on one of the bed's posts as if to steady herself. She looked at Tyr to search his face for an answer, but his gaze remained fixed on Dwyn. It was odd. He was usually so quick to insult her, to push back. Perhaps it was his expression that aided in her unease.

"Tyr?" Ophir prompted.

Dwyn stiffened, slowly turning to include the third in their conversation.

He inhaled through his nose before turning to face Ophir. A slow smile tugged his mouth upward, though it didn't reach his eyes. "I wish I could say I was surprised to find her in the court-yard, but what did you compare her to? A venereal disease?"

Ophir fought the edges of a smile. "I'm pretty sure that was *you*."

"No." He pinched his chin between his thumb and forefinger, looking up and to the side as he moved forward. His smile grew with every second. "I'm confident you said it about her. You'd never say such a thing about me."

Tension began to melt at their familiar banter. She missed them even when she hated them. They didn't judge her. Dwyn was her advocate, her champion for chaos and violence. Tyr was markedly less supportive, but it was nothing compared to the bottomless well of disapproval that poured out from Harland every time he looked at her. And even though they'd followed her across the desert just as Harland had, their arrival was entirely different. They did not come with judgment or tradition or disapproval. They were here to support her to the bloody end.

Harland had chased her down because duty compelled him.

Dwyn and Tyr had followed because they were her friends. She learned something new when she looked at them. Despite her need to run, to hide, to push anyone and everything away, the true friends were ones who looked "the monster of her self-loathing" in the eyes, planted their feet, and remained steadfast.

If she thought about it any longer, she'd begin to cry, and she had far too much to do to allow the emotion.

"Your room is fabulous, Firi. I've always said there aren't enough pillars in Farehold's architecture."

"You've always said that?" Ophir quirked a brow.

"Ever since I developed the opinion, which was roughly ten seconds ago, yes, I always have. But my, the fabrics are so luxurious! The translucent curtains, the airy fashion within the palace, the chandeliers of incense and fae lights, everything in Midnah is so beautiful! Are there gardens? Can I see them? I want a tour. Wait." Dwyn slowed. "Never mind. Now is perhaps not the best time. I guess I'm just excited to see you."

Ophir wasn't sure how to categorize Dwyn's energy. She expected Dwyn to be angry with her, to resent her, to demand apologies and explanations. Instead, she wanted a tour of the gardens and six dresses in this style? It was unsettling, even if Ophir didn't know why.

"Tyr?" Ophir called to him again, which irritated Dwyn to no end.

"Firi, stop. Forget about him."

Ophir shook her head. "I'm talking to him, Dwyn. You're not the only one I care about."

Tyr's eyebrows rose noticeably enough to set Dwyn ablaze. She snapped with an unpredictable thoroughness. She'd been a tinderbox ready to ignite, and this was the match she needed. With an uncontrolled rage, she spit out, "For fuck's sake! You want to keep your pet, that's fine. Let the mongrel stay. But I hate it, and I need you to like him a little less. It's annoying."

Ophir's lips twitched.

"I'm serious!" Dwyn balled her fists in irritation. She thrust her finger at Tyr. "He and I have called a temporary ceasefire, so I'll tell my archers to stand down, but you don't have to like him. Stop showing him favoritism."

"Dwyn, are you jealous?" he teased.

It was the wrong move.

"*Jealous?*" She sounded as if she'd been punched in the stomach. "He's still in love with the memory of whomever he left behind in Sulgrave! I can't be jealous of someone who doesn't deserve your affection."

Ophir stiffened. She didn't mean to look at him with so much hurt, but she couldn't help it.

"Excuse you?" Tyr asked, teeth clenched together in disgust as he stared daggers at Dwyn.

Dwyn crossed toward the middle of the room. Her words tasted of poison. "Stay! Clearly Ophir doesn't want to get rid of you, and I'm resigned to give her what she wants because I care about her. You're my horrible teammate, no matter how much I'd prefer to have you killed. So, stay. Be here with us, Tyr. Remain and learn and be a friend, but don't continue this charade. This bit you do where you act like you like Firi, where she keeps giving you attention under this false pretense of yours? You came down from Sulgrave for another woman. Admit it."

"I didn't—"

"Admit it!"

The air had been knocked from Ophir's lungs. She didn't understand the gaping hole punched through her center at the thought that Tyr was here for another woman. Her world had been tipped upside down for months, each new horror worse than the last. She wasn't sure how much upending turmoil she could stand before she broke altogether.

Ophir hadn't realized a hand had unconsciously gone to her chest. She fought to reconcile the thorn protruding from her heart with the facts laid before her. She brushed at her sternum as if her fingers might snag against the thorn and pluck it free. She looked at Tyr, then quickly away. She shouldn't be feeling this way, reacting this way, looking at him with this well of pain in her eyes. So what if he didn't care about her? So what if he loved someone else?

"Ophir—" Tyr moved toward her, but Dwyn put herself in his path.

She stared him down, teeth bared like she was Ophir's guard dog. "I've known for months that you came for someone else. You need three powers to avenge the woman you love. You've said so yourself. This entire fucking mission for you is for ice, fire, and shadow. Tell her! Tell the princess you've been toying with her, and stop playing games with her heart. Remain in Midnah, do what you have to do, learn what you have to learn, but cease your cruel charade."

The underlying implication was clear to everyone in the room. Dwyn may as well have said it out loud. The words left unspoken were: *She's mine. Leave her to me.*

If Ophir had looked up, she would have seen the rage that poured from Tyr with a thick, near-tangible stickiness. It was a fury as dark and horrid as the black, tar-like blood they'd witnessed from Ophir's monsters. If Ophir had opened her eyes, maybe she would have seen how victoriously Dwyn crossed her arms, or how Tyr looked like he was ready to rip Dwyn's head from her body.

Ophir felt the thorn in her heart grow as each new pulse forced it to bleed. The unmistakable wound throbbed with every breath. She'd been foolish. She'd been betrayed. She'd been so stupid.

Tyr wasn't denying it. The man's silence was as good as a confession. He remained seething from halfway across the chamber. If Dwyn was claiming possession, he was declaring to the room that it took everything within him not to murder the siren.

After an infinitely long pause, he spoke.

"She's not a person."

Ophir looked at him then, face scrunched. "What?"

"No! Not you, I mean..." He closed his eyes, pinching the place between his eyes. Hatred still radiated from him like a physical heat. "Dwyn, you're an absolute cunt. Have I told you that lately?" Tyr sucked on his teeth as he tried to take several other calming breaths. She'd never seen him lose his temper. Even now he was angry, but he had a handle on it, even if it was clearly a struggle not to tear her tongue out from where it rested between her teeth. He opened his eyes and lowered his hands. "Dwyn is right about one thing. I've spent years looking for three powers. I need flame, ice, and shadow, that much is true. I need to kill three men using the same powers that they used against Svea."

The thorn tore at her once more with another woman's name on his lips. "They killed your partner?"

He rubbed at what might have been a budding headache, then looked at her with deadly seriousness. When he spoke, his voice was grave but was free from its hate. "No, Svea wasn't my partner. She was my family, my best friend, my everything. I know what you're going to say. I know what you're going to think. And honestly, I understand how it sounds. I'd had her for six years, and it was she and I against the world. And I had no skills, no powers when I needed to defend her. I was so weak. I was just a teenager, and they were so cruel. I…"

She scoured his face, seeing only his pain.

"Svea was my dog."

Dwyn's jaw dropped open.

Tyr looked at his feet. "She was not just a dog. She was all I had. She deserved the world. She was smart, perfect, and loyal, and innocent. And those bastards deserve so much more than what's coming for them."

Ophir's eyebrows shot high, shoulders straightening.

Cord-taut silence strung between the three.

Dwyn's eyes and lips mirrored one another in near-perfect circles of shock. "There's no way…"

His lips pulled back in a sneer. He spun on her. "Shut your goddess-damned mouth, you absolute bitch. You want to play with fire? Try me."

Ophir reeled. "You want the power because…"

He pressed his eyes together as he thought about the best way to respond. He looked at her finally, choosing honesty.

."Vengeance fuels a lot of us, princess. Spite is as good a reason as any, don't you think? Because I don't think those men deserve to draw breath. The psychopaths who held me down and tortured and killed a dog for no reason other than fucked-up cruelty? They deserve to meet the fate they doled out. They've sealed their fate, and I'm on a mission to deliver it. Don't you think the people responsible for Caris's death deserve the same?"

"I do, but..."

"I don't have a sister," he said. "I don't have parents or siblings or anyone I care about. I don't have a community. I had a dog, and she was my goddess-damned world. Yes, that's why I want to be able to do what your stupid witch does. And no, I don't talk about it. I don't think my vengeance is Dwyn's, or Anwir's, or anyone's business. They shouldn't get to determine whether the men deserve to die. I know they do. She'll be avenged. I want to be the one to do it. I want to look in their eyes when they die the same way they killed her."

"For your dog?"

His challenging glare remained. "For my dog."

The silence that stretched was one of the single most uncomfortable pauses in the history of the written word. Ophir didn't know how to categorize any of the information she'd been given. She knew why Dwyn had tried to alienate her affections for Tyr—the girl was openly possessive. That part didn't shock her. What did surprise her was the way the thorn had dislodged, healing itself as if it had never been there in the first place. The idea that Tyr loved another woman had injured her more than she'd been able to absorb. The knowledge that his murderous rage was fueled by man's best friend was...well, she knew neither what to think nor how to feel.

"Say you're sorry," Ophir said quietly, looking at Dwyn.

Dwyn swallowed, lips twisting off to the side as if fighting the urge to argue. She balled her fists at her side, visibly struggling against whatever it was she wanted to say.

Ophir repeated, "Apologize. You did this to hurt him

because you were treating me like I'm a toy that only one of you gets to play with. That was cruel, Dwyn. Both to him, and to me. Now, tell him you're sorry, and stop being a bitch."

Dwyn inhaled sharply, searching Tyr's face. She shook her head, black hair dancing around her shoulders like a ghost haunting her. "You're telling the truth, aren't you?" Her voice dropped to the register barely above a whisper. "All this over a fucking dog."

"Dwyn!" Ophir repeated.

She closed her eyes against the scold. She wouldn't have let anyone else speak to her this way, but she had a vested interest in maintaining Ophir's favor, and Ophir knew it. The room had seen Dwyn go all in when she should have folded. She'd gambled in an attempt to regain the high ground between herself and Tyr in the princess's eyes, and she'd lost, badly. All of this and more was clear on her face. It wasn't guilt. It wasn't shame. It was the brand of regret that only came from someone who'd been punished.

Dwyn's eyes dropped to the floor. Silence stretched between the three of them, triangulating their positions around the room while discomfort hugged its points. "It's wrong, what they did to your dog. I'm sorry."

"...and?"

Dwyn exhaled slowly. "And I shouldn't have jumped to conclusions." She raised her eyes, then asked "But can you blame me? How was I supposed to guess this woman he was avenging was a dog? How could I—"

"Dwyn!"

"Right, right." She returned her sights to Tyr, and for the first time, there was no hate in her large, dark eyes. They weren't exactly kind, but a lack of enmity was a major improvement. Her posture softened as she did her best to conjure sincerity. "I've said and done a lot of things to you that I don't regret. And I do still usually wish I could kill you. I think you're the worst. But...I would have wanted to murder anyone who had hurt my dog, too. And I'm..." She struggled with the last word, rolling it around her tongue like a child unable to swallow their vegetables. "Sorry."

"Wow, Dwyn," he said, voice tart with vinegar. "That was convincing."

"I tried."

Ophir remained trained on Dwyn. "Well, could you try not being a bitch in the first place? I'm not trying to get rid of either of you anymore. It would mean a lot to me if you stopped trying to rip each other's throats out. I hate to pull the trump card, but isn't tonight supposed to be about comforting me? I have something of a major life event in six hours. I'm not going to get enough sleep as it is. Can the two of you try to hold it together?"

Tyr relaxed into the wall. This wasn't a secret he would have shared willingly, Ophir knew, but it was out. They knew. Perhaps he understood that the same sensitivity that made him a target for three dead fae walking might very well be the same sensitivity that earned him judgment now, but he was who he was. It was injustice against something innocent. It wasn't fair, and the men deserved to pay.

"Where's Sedit?" Dwyn asked suddenly.

Ophir's lips parted, mind flying to her own beloved hound. She pouted, looking around the room that was empty without her hound. "I didn't think it would be safe for him in the city, but he crossed the desert with me. I hope he's okay." She winced as she returned to Tyr. "I'm sorry. I didn't mean…"

He waved her away. "You don't have to apologize for worrying about your…vague hound. I know you care about it, and I won't get between you and your pet. Even if I do think it's a nightmare embodied."

Dwyn made it clear she was ready to stop talking about Tyr. They all knew it would win her no more friends if they remained on the topic. Her tone stayed dry as she spoke of Sedit. "If he's anything like your snake, he's going to be just fine."

"What do you mean?"

They explained how they'd tried to kill her serpent, only

to watch it knit itself together. Ophir was just as shocked to hear this as they had been to witness it. Dwyn began to make a comment about how, if Ophir made all the dogs, then Svea would still be alive.

Tyr looked like he'd been slapped.

"For fuck's sake, Dwyn." Ophir gaped at the woman.

Genuine regret rearranged her features. The joke had presumably been born of good intentions for winning favoritism, but it had promptly backfired. She was on a losing streak. Instead, she redirected to painting a very graphic visual of the enormous, black-blooded snake they'd tried to kill in the woods.

"But on the cliff!" Ophir protested. "Harland beheaded the thing. Didn't he?"

Dwyn cast her an apologetic look. "We rolled it immediately into the ocean, remember? We didn't give it the chance to self-heal. We could try a few experiments with one of your creatures if you want?"

Ophir recoiled. "Are you suggesting I make something just so we can cut it up? That's sadistic, even for you."

"It's for science."

"Science can wait." Ophir sat down on the bed, the world's gravity pushing down on her with exhausting intensity. "Do either of you need something to eat? Should I get anything? You'll have to forgive me, but this is all uncharted territory. Tyr, I have no idea how to comfort you. Dwyn, you have been a bitch. He's right. I don't really know what to do or how to play hostess in someone else's palace on the eve of my debut as executioner. I'm sorry if I'm not on my best behavior."

"Were these not good?" Tyr picked up one of the half-eaten cookies. There was something off about his voice, though she assumed it was something to do with having his shattered heart strewn on display for all to see.

"They were fine. I just wasn't sure if they'd all have the same filling. They do. I'm not in the mood for orange marmalade."

No one knew how to proceed, but perhaps that was okay. Maybe there was no right way to act the night before one was set to kill a man. Dwyn sat next to her, looping her arm around the princess's back. She ignored the idle chatter and returned to the pending execution. "Are you tired? Nervous?"

"Anxious, mostly. I want to do it. I want to scrub him off the face of the earth, no matter how big or small his role in Caris's death was. He's still a part of it." She rubbed her arms almost as if she were cold, despite the warmth of the night. "I doubt I'll be able to sleep tonight."

Dwyn pressed in closely. "I can help with that."

Ophir's eyes widened as she looked to where Tyr still stood. She hoped Dwyn was talking about how she used to hold her in order to help her with her nightmares. She wasn't sure if she was ready to tackle the inappropriateness of the siren implying anything else while Tyr stood arms' lengths away.

He made a face telling them that he'd understood exactly what Dwyn meant. "I'll give you two some, um, privacy. I'll go find the kitchen. I could use a few minutes to myself anyway. Maybe I'll bring something that isn't orange-flavored."

"Tyr," Dwyn began, frowning, "I am sorry. About…"

"I get it."

"Great." She smiled. "Bygones? Over that whole thing? With the…With your, I mean…"

"Stop talking about it, please."

"Super. Don't come back," Dwyn called after him with her light, singsong voice as he stepped into the place between things.

✦   ✦   ✦   ✦

Food was the last thing on Tyr's mind.

Dwyn's pettiness clung to him with sticky, tar-like insistence. Her attempt to alienate Ophir from him over Svea had been cruel, but it was hardly the most dangerous thing about her. If anything, fighting offered the bit of normalcy he'd needed to distract himself from outing her. He needed to focus on the issue at hand.

No, not there. He eased another door shut. *Goddess dammit, how many rooms does this place have?*

It took him several tries and pressing his ear into numerous doors before he found what he was looking for. Tyr quietly opened the bedroom door and slipped in just in time to see Harland go rigid. The guard scanned the empty air in search of the disturbance. Samael stood near him against the wall, hands in his pockets as the men discussed Berinth. If they'd been asleep, he wasn't sure if he would have had any hope of finding them.

Their gazes flew to the opened door, eyes straining against the dim, flameless fae lights for evidence of an intruder.

Though Harland's room was far smaller and more sparsely decorated, it maintained the high ceilings throughout the palace. If Ophir was nervous, then Harland was a wreck. Tyr looked at the doorframe but was dismayed to find a lack of runes. They'd have to stay quiet.

He closed the door behind him before stepping back into visibility.

Harland was on his feet in an instant. Tyr wasn't sure what kept him quiet, but the man didn't go for his sword, nor did he cry out. Perhaps it was Samael's lack of reaction that kept the guard from lunging for him. Harland's hand stilled against the hilt at his waist, tense and ready.

"Nice to officially meet you," Tyr said, wondering if Harland recognized him from their brief meeting at Guryon's estate. His guess was yes a Sulgrave fae who'd escaped with his princess moments before he was knocked unconscious was hard to forget. "My name is Tyr. We have a problem."

FORTY-EIGHT

+   +   +   +

12:30 AM
6 HOURS AND 15 MINUTES UNTIL EXECUTION

I KNEW IT."

Tyr's laugh was humorless. "I very much doubt that. I didn't figure it out myself until about twenty minutes ago." He knew he was at a disadvantage. These men neither knew nor trusted him, and Harland certainly didn't like him. Tyr walked to the desk and turned the chair around, swinging his leg over it to straddle it while he continued facing them. It was meant to put them at ease, posing in a way that would leave him disadvantaged in a fight. This was not how one sat if they needed to throw a punch.

He did his best to look relaxed, but his ears hadn't stopped ringing since taking a bow from Dwyn in the dungeon. They'd barely survived their attacks on one another, and his adrenaline wouldn't let him forget it. He wondered if her heart was also thundering, if her stress hummed through her body, if she felt hot and cold at the same time as if under the threat of an oncoming flu, if her eyes danced with the dizzying stars of nauseating, impending unconsciousness. Probably not. He was beginning to doubt she felt anything at all.

Harland stood firm. "I *did* know it. I knew from the moment I met Dwyn that she was not Ophir's friend. She knew what Firi could do. Somehow, she knew. She was behind this. I just couldn't have fathomed..."

"How deep the rabbit hole went?"

Samael followed suit and took a seat. Harland shot an uncertain look at his companion, then relaxed, though not fully. Samael leaned back in his chair, twisting his lips as he considered the information. "If this Dwyn person is behind Berinth, why is he in Tarkhany? Why isn't he in Sulgrave?"

"Because Tarkhany has motive for revenge. Not only did she create and frame so-called Lord Berinth, but she crafted a failsafe. Tarkhany was primed to be framed for Caris's murder, should her Berinth scheme be discovered. It's why she sent him to the farthest corner of the desert before her hold on him came to an end," Tyr said.

Samael pressed further. "You're saying this with certainty. What do you know?"

With little to lose and Ophir's life at stake, Tyr told them everything.

He explained that he could disappear into the space between things. He told them of the Blood Pact, of the tattooed bond and its restraints, of following Dwyn down across the Frozen Straits. He told them of the shapeshifter in the gardens and the conversation of stolen lands. He told them that he knew beyond a shadow of a doubt that Dwyn wanted power enough to do anything. The others looked on with abject horror as he explained her borrowed powers, her ability to drain, and the trail of husks she left in her wake.

He'd known she was a witch, but he'd made one critical error. He'd severely underestimated just how wicked she was. Dwyn wasn't just motivated to win Ophir's heart. She was conniving enough to create the situation that had required Ophir's need for hope, for a friend, for a lifeline in the first place. Ophir had been in dire need of salvation, and Dwyn had offered it.

She wouldn't get her own hands dirty, of course. It would have been too easy to cut her out if someone had seen a girl from Sulgrave plunging a dagger into Caris's abdomen. But what if someone were clever? What if they were smart enough to understand that Berinth wasn't a lone actor? What if they traced him back and found that such a name had existed for only two years, that such a title, such a man was entirely new to the continent? Had she really thought no one would check?

...had no one checked?

Tyr had been thinking it through in the moments he'd seen her panic, in the minutes when she thought she was about to die. He'd assembled the puzzle pieces when she'd offered her power and when she hadn't denied her role as puppet master. He hadn't given her enough credit, but she'd given him too much. She thought he'd figured it out and had snuck away to inform Ophir.

She'd been wrong.

Her powers had their limits, of course. She could brainwash a man to a point. But she'd have to either eliminate anyone who'd ever known Berinth before he took on his new name or come up with a contingency plan, should he be discovered. Alas, their journey had led them to Tarkhany. Two Sulgrave fae on two horses traipsing across the blistering desert—a woman who always knew it was where she'd end up, and a man who was just along for the ride because she couldn't kill him, and he wanted the powers of shadow, flame, and ice.

"You have to go back," Samael said to Tyr.

"What?" Harland's brows nearly disappeared into his hair. His first word came out a bit too loud before he controlled his temper. "No! We need to go in there and secure Ophir. If she's still with the witch—"

"You need to know," Tyr said, cutting Harland off. "Ophir is not helpless. I know you see in her a certain light because you're her guard, but she is immensely powerful. I don't just mean that she can manifest. She crossed the desert on her own. She survived the worst horror a person can endure. Perhaps vengeance isn't the most noble of fuels, but she isn't defenseless, and she isn't weak. She's resilient and more competent than you or anyone around her gives her credit for."

Harland sucked his teeth. It was clear from the hostile tick of his jaw that he did not appreciate the correction. He quickly learned there was more to it, as Harland said, "We were trying to conceal that she was a manifester. Thanks for that, Tyr."

Tyr flicked away the criticism like raindrops on metal. "You can't expect your people to act to the best of their abilities while keeping them in the dark."

Harland tensed. "Aren't you lying to both Dwyn and Ophir?"

"Rules are meant to be broken," Tyr said.

Samael was unfazed by the information. He might as well have been informed that Ophir was the secondborn princess. Even the crackling tension between Tyr and Harland left the astute fae unruffled, and Tyr suspected he knew why. It no longer seemed like men arguing over how to neutralize Dwyn. This was going to become a territorial pissing contest if someone didn't redirect their attentions.

"Dwyn needs her alive," Samael said. "She is powerful enough to do whatever it takes to keep her that way. Ophir is probably safer with her right now than anywhere else on the continent. And if what you say is true—about Dwyn's use of blood magic, that is—then it sounds like she has an unused power up her sleeve. We can't go in there until she expends it. We'd get ourselves killed and put the princess in danger of exposure. At least for now, the safest place for Ophir is in the dark. It will ensure that Dwyn stays calm. It would be a mistake to put her on high alert."

Harland twisted his hands in his hair. "She's in her room right now with the person responsible for Caris's murder, and you want us to act like nothing happened? To let her sleep next to a killer?"

"Tyr can't let on that anything has changed," Samael insisted.

Harland's face demanded explanation, wordlessly begging the others to see reason.

Samael flattened his palms, displaying their options. "Ophir won't be able to act the same around Dwyn once she's informed. If Tyr does anything to tip Dwyn off, who knows how volatile she might be? The one thing we *do* know is what she's capable of. Tyr is most effective when he's present as a first line of defense."

"He's right," Tyr agreed. "I hate Dwyn more than any of you, but he's right. Ophir is safe with her...though not for the reasons a person should be safe with someone." He inhaled slowly though his nose, both seeing the wisdom in their plan and struggling with acceptance. "I can keep her in the dark, only because it will ensure her safety. Dwyn's defenses will be down tomorrow because we'll be in public. Her attention will stay on Ophir during the execution. If you don't mind attacking a woman in broad daylight in front of a crowd, you'll have a much better chance of taking her out."

"There's something I don't understand," Harland began to pace. Tyr wished he would sit back down. Their room didn't have any dampeners, and even the sounds of Harland's shoes on the floor put him on edge. "She killed Caris to get to Ophir—why didn't she take Caris's heart? Why let Caris's blood, heart, and vital pieces go to waste? Why did Berinth only leave with a liver?"

Samael answered for all of them. "Not only did it make Ophir vulnerable, but it eliminated the possibility of anyone else getting their hands on a princess. Dwyn doesn't want anyone to share her power."

"And if she'd just taken Caris's heart directly..."

Tyr tugged on the collar of his shirt, revealing the tattoo that licked up the edge of his neck like a black flame. "She won't chance direct ascension to that kind of power. Not if it means anyone else might benefit."

"How can she know? How can she know that anyone else in the Blood Pact would gain the power?"

Samael frowned. "Maybe they wouldn't, but how can she be certain when it's never been done? Perhaps she's unnecessarily cautious. But if the Blood Pact *did* ascend with her, it would be too late to undo once she'd realized her mistake. Why risk sharing godhood?"

"She's evil," said Harland.

"She's brilliant," answered Samael.

FORTY-NINE

+ + + +

12:45 AM
6 HOURS UNTIL EXECUTION

TYR STEELED HIMSELF AGAINST LIFE'S GREATEST NEW challenge.

"I thought I told you not to come back." Dwyn draped her nude form over the bed while Ophir remained in the near-nude state provided by her sheer gown, which was nothing new. Dwyn lacked clothes as often as she lacked a conscience. She was objectively beautiful, the same way that a venomous cobra or brightly colored spider is beautiful. Her hair was the black, glossy iridescent of raven feathers and spilled ink. Her chest and hips curved generously, which had been a refreshing testament of confidence in a world that glorified starving itself for social norms. She owned the rooms she entered, she loved her body, her skin, the words that came out of her mouth. Her eyes were large, her lips were berry-dark, and she was all the things that might be okay to see if it was your last moment on earth as she murdered you. In so many ways, she could have been interesting, or admirable, or clever.

She was beautiful, yes. And she was profoundly, and irredeemably, evil.

Dwyn spoke to the invisible space where the door had opened and closed, propped up against the pillows on the far side of the bed while Tyr let the thoughts flit through his mind. He realized with some idleness that she almost always slept to Ophir's right side. He'd never thought much of it, but he'd also vastly underestimated how conniving she was. Perhaps it had been a subtle way to tell Ophir that she was her right-hand man. Or fae. Or witch. Or whatever it was she wanted to be called that day.

The time to reappear had come and gone. He couldn't put it off any longer.

Tyr sucked in a single, steadying breath. He put on his most disarming smile before stepping back into the light. "Yes, but I've never been good at taking orders. I prefer to be the one giving them."

The room was already dark, save for two dim lights on either bedside. Hopefully it would help to conceal any traitorous emotions on his face. Truth be told, he wasn't sure that his feelings toward Dwyn had changed at all. He'd hated her before and hated her now. If anything, it felt good to be right.

He didn't expect what happened next.

Ophir extended her hand for him from where she sat on the bed. Her fingers wiggled to emphasize her unspoken request, which surprised him.

"What are you doing?" Dwyn asked, eyes flashing as she looked between them. She made no effort to conceal her horror. "Make him sleep on the floor."

Ophir shook her head, unbothered. "I have an execution in the morning, and I'm nervous. I think I should get to sleep sandwiched between you two lunatics if it makes me feel any better. Next time you put someone to death in a foreign city at dawn, you can call the shots. Deal?"

She made a convincing argument.

He struggled to move toward her while he juggled painful truths. Keeping things from her didn't feel right. It was dishonest. It was cruel. Yet, if he told her, he would be putting Ophir at extreme risk. There was no way to keep Dwyn relaxed and in the dark if Ophir knew what he did.

But if he stayed close…if he kept her as close as physically possible…

Tyr approached, begging his heart to slow down. Its arrhythmic thunder wasn't only from what he'd learned, or what it meant. It wasn't just his conversation with Harland and Samael, or their plans for the morning. It was also seeing the princess reach out for him. She wanted him there. She wanted him.

He wondered if the women could hear the way his treacherous organ skipped and pounded within the cage of his chest. Perhaps if they did, they'd mistake his nerves for being invited to sleep beside her. He'd snuck in a time or two because he enjoyed irritating Dwyn and causing trouble, and Ophir had found him equally charming, which emboldened him. This was his first time entering her bed truly invited. It wouldn't serve him to act like anything was different, but in that moment, he lost the capacity for thought. He had no idea what he would normally do in this situation. Would he have a smartass remark? Would he antagonize Dwyn? Would he compliment Ophir? Goddess, she'd broken him simply by wanting him there.

Perhaps the reason he couldn't think of an ordinary reaction was that there was no bar for normal. A beautiful princess inviting you into her bed with a naked, possessive villain at her side was no commonplace occurrence. Maybe he was right to be nervous.

Perhaps he wouldn't be able to do the only thing that was asked of him—he couldn't act like nothing had changed, because it had. He couldn't keep the smile on his face as he pulled the shirt off over his head. He'd be lying if he said Ophir's appreciative murmur hadn't set his world on fire. He sat on the edge of the bed, his back to the women as he took off his boots. He wasn't afraid of Dwyn—not in the slightest. He'd been ready to die for a long time, if it meant rejoining his dog in the afterlife. But he was afraid for Ophir and wouldn't rest peacefully until he'd brought justice upon the men who'd harmed the perfect, happy pup who hadn't deserved her fate. The princess was no helpless animal. She could handle herself, of course. She was fierce and terrifying or a force of gods and nature alike. But he was afraid because there was no merit in the betrayal happening right in front of her. Nothing in her life warranted having her closest ally be her worst enemy.

They both deserved better.

He couldn't help Svea. But he would die to ensure Ophir's fate was better.

Ophir's intuition must have pricked. Her brown-gold eyebrows met in the middle as she looked at him, searching his face for an explanation. It was dark in the room, but not so dark that he couldn't see the way her eyes always sparkled, as if she wore the gilded crown around her irises rather than atop her head. Fuck, she was beautiful.

But she was so much more than that.

She was rebellious and independent and funny and brave. She didn't give a damn about convention or tradition or what was expected of her. She did what she wanted when she wanted, and she did it so damn well. She was a highborn noble who'd traipsed across the desert alone to avenge her sister. She was a true, living goddess.

Their eyes held for a moment too long.

The energy exchanged was too sincere.

His intention reached for her, and hers reached back.

He wasn't sure what made him do it, but he pressed his hand against her cheek, sliding his fingers into her hair, cupping the back of her head. He wanted her to know that she was safe, that he was with her, that she wasn't alone. He wanted to use his body as a physical barrier between Ophir and the witch. He wanted to build a wall composed of flesh, bone, and safety. Her breath caught in her throat. He knew it the same moment that Dwyn saw it, and Ophir realized precisely what was happening. While he could see Dwyn's dark eyes widen in horror from his peripheral vision, it was the way Ophir's began to flutter closed, the way she leaned into his hand, the way her lips parted ever so slightly that sealed his fate.

He was going to kiss her.

It was less like an urge and more like an inevitability. He knew he would find her skin. He knew the current that ran between them would be like a mountain river. His pulse thrummed in his chest, behind his eyes, his fingertips, to the consistent, desperate throb deep within him. His ears rang, lightheaded as every drop of blood in his body found a new, singular purpose. He wouldn't have said no to this moment even if he'd had a choice—but he didn't. It was fated, as if it had already happened, as if it would happen again.

If he couldn't kill Dwyn, if he couldn't remove Ophir safely from the room, then he could create a world where Dwyn didn't exist. That part of him didn't care that Dwyn was there—she was nothing to him, nothing to Ophir. He could have been in front of an audience. This may as well have been on the platform outside of the palace before the citizens of Midnah. It didn't matter. The moment was theirs.

Pure sunlight dripped from her tongue. He drank deeply the moment their lips connected. The hand not tangled in her hair found her back, pulling her as close to him as she could be. It took three seconds, two hands, one shared heartbeat to let him know that she wanted it as badly as he did. He drank her in, kissing her so deeply that he nearly lost her breath, feeling the moment she struggled to catch hers. He could feel every inch of her skin through the barely there gauze of fabric that separated his bare chest from the soft pillows of her breasts. When she knotted a hand in his hair, he knew it was over.

He had to be stronger.

"Ophir. I don't think—"

"I want this," she said.

He swallowed, desperate to pull her closer, to yank her away from Dwyn. "Firi, it's not—"

Ophir rested a finger against his lips, silencing him. She inclined her chin toward the third party in their room. Never to be outdone, Dwyn rose to the occasion. She kissed Ophir's temple, then her jaw. Then Ophir twisted out of his arms just enough to offer her mouth.

He tightened his hand where it remained in Ophir's hair, as if securing the physical barrier between Ophir and Dwyn. If he couldn't keep his emotions off his face, he might have to slip into the place between things. For now, all he wanted was for Ophir to know he was here with her—*for* her.

He should stop this.

"But Dwyn—"

"Is a witch," Ophir completed, hands abandoning him completely as they ran over the bare shoulders of Dwyn's skin. She shot a wry look to Dwyn, who winked at their acknowledgement but didn't bother breaking her contact. "I know."

It took everything in him not to shove Dwyn off her. "You know she's a sociopath," Tyr muttered through gritted teeth against her throat as he continued moving along her skin. He'd just as soon stab Dwyn through the heart as share a bed with her. Maybe that was Ophir's one fault. She had terrible taste in women.

Everyone was allowed at least one flaw.

Dwyn had no power here. This moment wasn't about her. It belonged to Ophir.

+   +   +   +

Weightless was never something Ophir had been afforded.

Joy and lust and want and need were the sort of escapes she chased, always slipping between her fingers like sand. Then sometimes, if only for a moment, she caught them. Instead of sand, the silken strands of Dwyn's hair balled in her fists. Ophir pulled her close, loving the petal-soft feel of her lips, the way her breasts pressed into her own, the way they peaked with desire and her skin flushed red and hot and chilled with goose flesh all at once.

Dwyn is a sociopath, Tyr had said. Sure, sure. But didn't they all have their shortcomings?

"A sociopath who's great in bed," Ophir responded through her kiss, still facing away from Tyr. She was so glad he was here, and she didn't care what it meant. She'd missed them. She'd wanted them. She'd known it from the moment she'd entered the desert and wished they'd been by her side.

"The crazy ones are the best lays," Dwyn agreed with wicked ease.

Dwyn smiled against her cheeky remark as the siren soaked in each word that came out of her mouth. She tasted the mint, possession, and greed on Dwyn's lips. Ophir turned the fullness of her body toward the young woman to her right, which Dwyn took as a victory. She didn't want the night to end. She didn't want the moment to break.

Tyr could have refused to participate. He could have left her, abandoning them to their passions.

He didn't.

Sitting upright had been a luxury afforded to her before she was drunk on the moment. It rushed through her veins stronger than wine, its dizzying, overpowering sensation knocking her to her side. When she let her head hit the pillow to absorb each kiss, each touch, each soft fingertip, each tug of the hair, each brush and movement, his strong arm pinned her to his chest. She arched her back, hips seeking him. He pressed into her and she knew there was no turning back. She wanted him. She'd wanted this for a long time.

Ophir's mouth broke away from Dwyn as she looked over her shoulder to where Tyr continued to hold her, to kiss her. He squeezed her tighter. His unwillingness to release her set her body on fire. He clung to her like she was a lifeline. Her back arched again, but her chest moved forward, rolling toward Dwyn.

Dwyn tugged the gauzy dress down over her shoulders, allowing the fabric to pool around her navel. She felt the wet, cool sensation of a tongue on the most sensitive parts of her breasts. She gasped, savoring the tingle that ran from her nipples to her toes at the gentle, luxurious sucking. Dwyn, to her credit, didn't seem to brim with the same hate that generally possessed her. Perhaps sex was her break from fury—her escape from the misery that consumed her. This was about fun. From the electric tip of every nerve and the quiver of her heart to the pulse of water between her legs. This was ecstasy.

Tyr's fingertips pressed into her jaw, urging her to turn away from Dwyn. Her mouth found his, lost in how he consumed her. Soft fingers slipped down to help him out of his pants. His eyes rolled back the moment her fingers grazed his hardened, throbbing place. Their kiss broke against his savoring noises, but her focus was stolen away from him in a fraction of a second. Ophir gasped, the sharp, high sound one of both pleasure and surprise, as Dwyn had not waited. She'd continued licking and kissing her way down the middle of Ophir's body, pushing the gauzy dress up to uncover her knees, her thighs, her hips, every part of her, laying claim to the princess the moment her mouth made contact with where her thighs met, connecting at her very center.

The explosion of stars before her eyes was the birth of the universe, the moon, the night, the world around her swirling. Each slow, claiming circle of Dwyn's tongue, each arch of her hips against Tyr, each wet, sensual lick resulted in a new rush of water.

Ophir's fingers tightened where they'd stayed in contact with Tyr's shaft. He kissed her neck as she rolled from the pleasure. She knew Dwyn wasn't good at sharing, but tonight their bed was meant for more than two.

The moan she made was one she'd never heard escape from her throat before, but then again, this was something she'd never done before. These sensations were utterly new. This was a fullness, a worship, an excitement, a pleasure too delicious for the disrespect of silence. This was not making love. This was not sex. This was glorious, beautiful, toe-curling, luxurious, debaucherous fucking.

More hands. More mouths. More breath and oxytocin and sensation and pure, unadulterated indulgence. More electric than the static in the air before a lightning storm. More intense than the sharp, breathtaking pain of falling to your back so hard that the wind was knocked from your lungs. More beautiful than a field of spring blossoms or scrolls of poetry or secret smiles between loves. More depraved than theft or violence or murder.

More, more, more.

Dwyn lifted the front of her dress, and Tyr gathered the back of the material, bunching it higher until her ass pressed against his hips.

She guided him in like a hot knife through butter, melting at the low growl of pleasure that reverberated through him as he entered her. She couldn't help the way her body arched, the way her hips moved, the sounds she made, the pleasure she felt as he finished pulling the crumbled material of her dress up and over her head from where it had collected.

The way Tyr held her, so firmly, so unrelentingly as he moved within her made her both completely safe and utterly surrendered all at once. Dwyn was another creature entirely, one composed of chaos and decadence, one created for anarchy, thrill, and satisfaction. It was an orchestra of sensation, the harmonies and melodies ranging from high strings to deep basses as the music swelled.

Tyr kept her pinned with one arm, but his hand crept up until his calloused hands held her throat. She threw her head back as his forehead bent forward, nestling into the curve of her neck. His speed increased to match the throbbing musical tempo. She was a symphony of passion. In that moment, the world was hers.

She didn't care how loud she was. She didn't care if the palace listened, if Harland could hear her scream, if the queen or Tarkhany herself stirred from her bed as Ophir came up against the cliff of pleasure just as she had stood on the edge of the seaside cliffs so many months ago. This time when she was pushed over, she didn't go alone. Tyr snapped behind her, his jolt of pleasure echoing her own. Strong arms caught her as she fell, tumbling down the edge of the cliff and into the sea. A mouth continued to move on her, as relentless as the breaking waves on the rocky beaches outside of Aubade. Her cries raked through her, body shivering as she was carried under. It was like drowning, like being born, like the first taste of chocolate, falling in love, the sing of a blade, and the spinning buzz of trying the opium in poppy dens all at once.

She didn't know the meaning of life.

She didn't know why she'd been put on the earth, why she existed, or why anything meant anything.

But she did know those few moments of euphoria made it all worth it.

The ecstasy achieved in the few, gloriously high moments after orgasm were some of the only true seconds of bliss this world had to offer. Dwyn's mouth stopped, but she kissed her way up slowly, gently, almost lovingly until she rested her forehead against Ophir's. She returned the kiss, tasting her own wet sunshine on the siren's lips. Tyr held her more tightly, staying inside her after the moment had passed. He held her close, pressing her into him as if she were adrift in the sea, at risk of floating away.

The sweat and silk and warmth of the night were everything she could have wanted. Dwyn's forehead touching her own, the stunning woman's hands in her hair, and Tyr's arm wrapped around her, still deeply inside of her, the three fell into a dark and dreamless sleep.

FIFTY

✦   ✦   ✦   ✦

4:45 AM
2 HOURS UNTIL EXECUTION

*H*OW CURIOUS, SHE THOUGHT. ONE CORNER OF OPHIR'S LIP quirked upward, while the other tugged down. She wasn't sure how long she'd been asleep, but her first thought was one of disappointment that Tyr's manhood hadn't remained inside her throughout the night. *How curious, indeed.*

His arm remained draped over her chest, just as Dwyn's leg stayed over her hip.

She was no stranger to group sex. She was, however, brand fucking new to sex at the edge of the world. On the eve of her vengeance, trapped between rivals, she wasn't sure if she'd ever feel this again.

The nightmares had ceased to take hold of her after Dwyn and Tyr entered her life. As it were, she didn't care if they were friends or foes. Maybe that was selfish, but she decided that there was a level of greed afforded to women whose sisters had been slain. Blood magic and nefarious intentions aside, she was safe, she was whole, and for the first time in a long time, she belonged to herself. It was more than an added benefit that the sex was transcendent. She knew they hated each other and wasn't sure if she'd be willing to finesse last night into a recurrence, but a girl could dream.

She stayed as quiet as possible, moving slowly as she maneuvered her way out of the bed, tiptoeing to where her failed compass rested on the desk. Fortunately, it served as a rather useful pocket watch when she needed to be mindful of the hour. It was too dark to see the hands of the clock, so she crept toward the curtain, parting it ever so briefly to let the crescent moon illuminate the pocket watch. It would be more than an hour before the first grays of dawn.

This would not be a morning for relaxing.

She wasn't sure where Tyr had tossed the torn remnants of her dress in the night, so she walked soundlessly to the bathing room without a stitch of clothing. The climate lent itself to nudity. When she returned to the room, she frowned at the sight of the bed. Dwyn was there alone.

"Shh." An unseen hand slipped around her waist, pulling her close. Tyr kept his voice low as he whispered in her ear. "I'm going to stay out of sight today, but I'll be right there. Don't feel alone, not even for a moment. Wherever you are, know that I'm there for you. No matter what happens."

"Tyr—"

The same rough fingers that had gently scraped against her skin last night pushed her hair back from her ears, tangling themselves near the nape of her neck as he guided her into a kiss goodbye.

A lump formed in her throat, though she didn't know why. He slid a hand down her arm, squeezing her hand before his presence disappeared. Logic told her he hadn't gone far, but she wished he'd stayed. She saw the wisdom in his choice. He was from Sulgrave. It was challenging enough explaining the presence of three Farehold fae and their Farehold prisoner. If Dwyn was to be at her side, maybe Ophir had enough on her plate for foreign emissaries. Besides, she didn't have to be one for warfare or strategy to understand the advantage that came from having someone undetected on your side.

He'd said he wouldn't abandon her, and she believed him.

The door opened and closed silently. She wouldn't have

seen it at all if she hadn't been staring after the door for exactly such an occasion. It was little more than a darker shade of black against the gray gloom.

Ophir decided that it was her morning, and she should get to decide when the curtains were opened and when the remaining partner in her bed was awake. She slipped the curtains to the side, allowing the very first lights of deep, dark gray to break over the dark sands of the desert. Ophir returned to the bed, crawling onto her knees as she gently shook Dwyn awake.

Dwyn was surprisingly happy to see her. She reached for Ophir the same way that the princess had reached for Tyr the night before, and Ophir accepted the offer. She tucked her body in closely, snuggling into the intimacy of the early morning hour.

"Are you afraid?" Dwyn asked. Her tone wasn't judgmental. Merely curious.

"A little."

Dwyn pressed a gentle kiss to her forehead. "I think that's okay. Everything new is scary the first time."

Ophir moved away just enough to see the silhouette of Dwyn's shape against the early hour. "Do you get used to killing?"

Her face muddled into a soft frown. Dwyn asked, "Can I answer your question with a question?"

Ophir nodded.

"Did you feel bad when you killed Guryon?"

She didn't have to think of her answer. Her voice stayed low in respect of the early hour. "Not at all."

Dwyn ran her fingers through her hair. It was comforting, almost the way her mother used to do when she was a child, or the way her sister would do on their sleepovers. She closed her eyes, leaning into the sensation. Each individual strand of hair tingled as it moved, the gentle scrape of nails feeling so good with each stroke. "And the farmer and his friends when they were going to drag you back to the castle?"

Her eyes stayed closed, lulled by the steady stroking of fingers in her hair. She knew that on some social and moral level, she was supposed to feel guilty, but she didn't. "I asked them to stop, and they didn't. They had their chance," she said, fully relaxed by the soothing stroke of Dwyn's hand.

Dwyn agreed. "Some people *have* to die. It isn't always for the greater good. Sometimes it's for personal gain, and that's enough. The farmer had to die for you, Firi. That's enough. Your life is reason enough. There needn't be any grander meaning than that."

Ophir exhaled slowly, then breathed in the palace's citrus. She was tired of the scent of oranges but was quite sure she'd never get sick of the way Dwyn smelled. She leaned into her hair, inhaling mint by the breathful. It was such a bright, comforting, unique scent. It was perfumed and nourishing, exotic and familiar all at once. Such a unique, sharp, lovely smell.

Dwyn's hands continued to work against her scalp, each comforting line having a more relaxing power than the one before. "What if I had to kill for you, Firi?"

Perhaps the question should have alarmed her, but the sudden rush of mint set her muscles at ease. Had Midnah enchanted its mattresses to make all who rested upon them disoriented and groggy? She hadn't noticed it the other mornings, but there was something new... Something... heavy... Something...

The haze of Dwyn's scent was overpowering and calming all at once. Ophir shrugged, too relaxed to feel any emotional attachment. She succumbed to the mint, the peace, the serenity. "I'm sure you have."

"What if I had to kill Tyr? Or Harland?"

Goddess, she was so sleepy. What a lovely trick. She'd have to thank Zita later. And perhaps ask her why the Queen of Tarkhany and her lovely servants hadn't offered this hypnotic slumber before. It was like sucking in bowls of opium in her favorite haunts in Aubade. Why was she so, so sleepy, unless someone in Midnah had granted her a supernatural sleep before the grand execution?

It didn't matter. It was fucking delicious. Ophir yawned. "Would they deserve it?"

"What if I said yes? That they deserved it because you are the greater good, and they stood between you and the future you wanted."

She opened her eyes, looking into the shadow. Her vision rippled with blissful, lovely, drunken comfort. "You can't kill Tyr though, can you." It wasn't a question. She knew the answer. She knew enough from their exchanges, enough from the odd way they worded things, from their peculiar alliance, that something resentful existed between them. Dwyn would have drained him eons ago if she could have.

"And Harland? If he dragged you off to marry Ceneth?"

Ophir struggled to form thoughts. Goddess, drugs were so nice. Why had she stopped doing them? She'd ask Harland to bring more to her room when she returned to Aubade. Would she return to Aubade? Would she talk to Harland again? She was amazed that she didn't care. Truly, nothing mattered. Fuck, whatever this was, it was so damn pleasurable. A spell? A recipe? A pillow mist she could bottle and pocket and carry with her to every mattress for the rest of her days? Mmm, it didn't matter. It did. Not. Matter.

Was this conversation important? She didn't know. She didn't remember. Maybe they'd been talking about the weather, or whose kingdoms had the softest beds. Damn, wow, for fuck's sake, for the love of the goddess, this feather-soft bed was everything. Mint pressed into her throat, filling her lungs with the gloriously choking perfume of her companion. Whatever Dwyn was saying, it didn't matter.

Ophir meant to make a full-bodied, apathetic expression, but it resulted in an unfeeling shrug against the pillow. "I'd prefer for him not to die, but not as much as I'd prefer to not be shipped to Raascot against my will. I guess you're right. I would choose my path over any universally accepted greater good."

Dwyn's hands felt so good against her body. Her soft arms tucked Ophir in more closely, squeezing one arm around her while the fingers of her opposite hand continued working against the back of her hair. Ophir rested her cheek against Dwyn's chest. "Keep that in mind today when you kill Berinth."

Ophir made a small, agreeable noise against the soft pillow.

"Ophir, you know I'd do anything for you, right? That I've been here for you, on your side, helping you through everything? You know I'd kill for you?"

Ophir was quiet as she wondered whether or not any thoughts were worth voicing in this delightful mist of calm and joy, but she knew the answer. She believed it. She didn't care, though. The stroke of fingers, the mist of mint, the thick, heavy press of love and sleep may as well have been hypnotic swallows of a healer's numbing drug. Dwyn had her back in a way so insane, so troubling, so unconventional and terrifying and beautiful and wild that it should have been forbidden by the All Mother herself. Ophir wasn't sure how long it had taken her to know it, or believe it, or understand it, but for better or for worse, Dwyn was on her side. She could have said all of this, but instead she just said, "Yes, I'm aware."

"You know Tyr and Harland hate me. It's not an uncommon response. I'm an uncommon person, after all. So are you. I do things that make people hate me." Her words were meant to be important. Ophir knew it from the gravity of the message, the intentional weight of each word, the pause between each sentence. Dwyn was telling her something meaningful, something she needed to pay attention to. Her eyes stayed closed against the growing gray of dawn, knowing that soon, she'd have to face Berinth and the crowd. Soon, she'd be the very piper that needed to be paid. Soon, her time would come.

For now, she'd savor this moment. She'd remain in this drunken stupor, whatever its marvelous, curious source. For now, she'd answer Dwyn. Yes, she knew they didn't like her. Yes, she knew Dwyn was a reclusive murderer with a propensity for violence. Yes, she knew all of these things, but she also knew that Dwyn wouldn't hurt her. She believed it with the sort of fullness that others believed in the All Mother. Maybe that's what love was. It was trust, it was understanding, it was stupid, inexplicable belief. But again, now was not the time to say all that. Instead, she answered with two words.

"I know."

"Firi?"

"Hmm?"

"I have something I need to tell you. Something important. Something that, once it leaves my lips, will have no power over you. Something that will never hurt you again."

FIFTY-ONE

✦   ✦   ✦   ✦

6:30 AM
15 MINUTES UNTIL EXECUTION

OPHIR DIDN'T KNOW WHAT TO EXPECT, BUT IT WASN'T THIS. The morning light in the desert was infinitely prettier than any she'd seen in Farehold. Maybe it was the dry clarity of the air, or the infinite expanse of the dunes on all sides, but the gentle pastel gradients were unmatched. Perhaps it was because she was used to sunsets on the western coast, rather than the endless horizons in all directions provided by the desert. Midnah's enveloping warmth helped. It was much easier to enjoy a morning when the air was perfectly pleasant, its dawn climate too early to be anything lovely.

A low scaffolding of sorts had been constructed over the fountain that stretched in front of the palace. It elevated the entire party onto a platform above the crowd, safely removed from reaching hands or the wayward daggers of the particularly rebellious, while still within their line of sight. She had pictured it, of course. She'd seen beheadings, hangings, and magical executions in Aubade. They didn't happen often, but life was long, and justice had a way of finding its target.

Executions in Aubade weren't an entirely solemn event. Occasional street vendors would sell food from their carts, and crowds would gather for the excitement. But it certainly wasn't the banquet thrown in Tarkhany.

Dressed in the finest, airy lavender gown she'd ever seen, face painted for royalty, hair half up, Ophir held her chin high as she exited the palace into the first light of morning. She gripped Dwyn's hand for comfort, unwilling to let go. Ophir was escorted by several guards from the palace to the platform where the crowd waited. The moment she'd exited the palace, she'd been greeted by the music of what may have been a harp or maybe a lute.

Loud, bright, lavender, wonderful.

She wiped the residual effects of minty, relaxing rest from her eyes. Dwyn squeezed her hand, sending an electric bolt of resolution through her. In lieu of pillow talk common to lovers basking in morning glow, Dwyn offered the peace and reassurance Ophir needed to get through the morning. Berinth was to blame, and she was here to deliver justice. There was no looking back.

She scanned for the musician, seeing a man sitting upon the platform with a large instrument that looked like an upright cello, with the stretched leather of a drum for a covering between his legs. He played it masterfully, the music quiet and respectful enough for the occasion, while still bright and lovely. A cornucopia of breakfast foods stretched out across the platform. It was lined with chairs intended for Ophir, her guests, Zita, and her retinue. Street vendors were out in full force, with breads and fruits distributed among the onlookers and the guards alike.

Among the newness, there was one thing that Aubade and Tarkhany had in common.

At the center of the platform, the man she'd known as Lord Berinth knelt, shackled.

Good. She resisted the urge to spit. Rage crackled through her, flame threatening her palms. *Let him grovel. Let him see me coming. Let him sob as the wrath of kingdoms presses down on him.*

She wasn't sure who would be accompanying her that

morning but was relieved to see Zita approaching. The woman wasn't as friendly-looking as she remembered, but perhaps they were both just nervous. Ophir did her best to smile, though she wasn't sure that was the appropriate reaction. At least Zita looked pretty, if not familiar. She wondered if the queen had chosen her orange, black, and gray dress intentionally. She was dressed like the same long-legged bird that stomped about the garden, poised against vipers, cobras, mambas, and the like.

There was one final serpent in the palace, and this one could not be killed. Ophir straightened her shoulders, lifted her chin, and envisioned herself as the big, black snake, ready to strike.

The seats to either side remained empty. The desert queen mounted the steps to the platform, gesturing for Ophir—the middle kingdom's princess, so she'd been called—to sit beside her. Ophir looked over her shoulder to see Harland and Samael trailing behind her with the other guards. She met Harland's eyes for the briefest of moments before facing forward. She didn't have the emotional space for his disapproval. He could handle his revenge however he wanted if his sister was murdered at a party. Ophir was here to do whatever was necessary.

The bubbling voices and faces rippled with surprise over Dwyn's presence. Ophir was the foreigner they'd expected, not someone from Sulgrave. She hadn't been introduced, expected, or invited. No one seemed to know what to do with the way Ophir gripped her hand, unwilling to be separated from her unusual guest. They made space for the unexpected companion as Ophir took a seat with Zita on one side, Dwyn on the other. She looked at the food in front of her, unsure if she'd be able to eat. She scanned the sea of faces, merry chatter, eyes floating to her over and over again—the stranger from Farehold, the first time in centuries someone from Aubade had come to visit, and it was for an execution.

She mustn't overthink it.

Berinth, the murderer, the traitor, the villainous scum, remained on the platform. She'd call her flame. He'd scream. She'd get to watch him die as her fire engulfed the man whose hands had plunged the knife into Caris's body. She could call her fire in her sleep. She'd done it a dozen times, usually without intending to. Summoning flame was as easy as breathing. It would be one moment of power, then a lifetime of knowing that he no longer stalked the earth. He would die. His life would smoke out, and she'd know the barest edges of peace.

It would be easy. She could do it. There was nothing to worry about.

Soon, it would be over. Soon, this would all be a memory.

She continued to look about, wondering where Tyr might be. He'd promised he'd be here, and she had to believe he was only steps away. She knew she wouldn't see any evidence of him thanks to his frustrating, useful, wonderful, miserable gift, but she thought it would be comforting to at least know he was there. She wished he had the power to speak mind to mind. Dwyn was an excellent support system, but her cup was only half full. She longed to be flanked by the two who'd gone on this journey with her in all senses of the word.

Her eyes snagged on someone. It wasn't Tyr, but she was not alone. Harland and Samael rounded the line and mounted the steps at long last, escorted to the far end of the table. She knew they were behind her in the line but hadn't expected for them to be invited onto the platform. The tension in Harland's shoulders and taut, forced neutrality of his face told her he was far from happy. Samael's expression was something else entirely, though she couldn't quite discern what emotion he was displaying. What an odd man he was. Maybe someday she'd care. More likely, she never would.

The food looked delicious, but nerves made her too queasy to eat. Piles of aromatic rices, spiced meats, brightly colored fruits, and dense, honey-coated pastries dotted the table. Pitches and goblets of waters, wines, and juices lined the table. Over the sound of the crowd and the music of the string instrument, she could make out the sounds of Lord Berinth's loud, inelegant sobbing, punctured by rough, disgusting pulls of sloppy congestion. It was fitting that the bastard was unwilling to die with dignity.

Ophir's hand flew to her ears as she realized something. She could understand nothing. Tyr still had her device. She could make a new one now if she worked quickly, but she was on display in a rather public way. The table had no cloth to cover their legs or make the banquet any more discreet if she held her hands in her lap. She fidgeted uncomfortably, debating whether she should risk exposure to create a new translation cuff for her ear.

An elbow gently prodded her bicep.

"Are you okay?" Dwyn whispered.

Ophir nodded. Yes, her nerves should have been about the execution, not about her translator.

Zita looked at her and offered the controlled smile of nobility. "Are you ready, Princess Ophir?"

Ophir dipped her chin again. She wasn't sure if she'd ever truly feel ready, but it was no more nerve-wracking than giving a public speech or being brought before the queen in the dead of night in a new country where she knew neither the language nor the customs.

All things were scary the first time.

The seat beside Zita remained empty, and Ophir's mind briefly returned to her conversation with Harland and Samael. They'd asked who else she'd met in the royal family. Was this seat left intentionally empty for that person? Someone she hadn't met, and would probably never meet? Something egged on the distrustful edge of her consciousness, but there was no point in questioning things now.

Zita stood and walked to the middle of the platform. The crowd quieted respectfully as she made herself known. Once more, Ophir encountered an itching sense of familiarity when examining the queen. Her gown was vibrantly orange on top, nearly as bright as the fruit that was so prevalent in the pastries Ophir had nibbled and set to the side throughout her week in Tarkhany. The dip-dyed nature of her gown gave way to a beautiful gradient of gray, ending in black, as if her dress were the sunset itself. Had the queen dressed like the garden's bird on purpose? Or, maybe that's what she was seeing—an enchanting déjà vu of the sun over the desert as it gave way to the blackness of night.

Zita turned to the table, offering Ophir a quick smile before she picked up her goblet.

"Citizens of Tarkhany!" she called out to the crowd. Any remaining conversation silenced entirely as everyone regarded their queen. "For centuries, our relationship to Farehold has been a tenuous one. I'm pleased to announce with peace and unity in my heart that when Princess Ophir came to our doorstep seeking aid and shelter, Midnah answered her call!"

The crowd cheered heartily, raising their waterskins, fruits, and breakfast foods. Ophir's heart skipped up as nerves coursed through her. She reminded herself to breathe, as if it were no longer an involuntary action. Each breath was an intentional inhale and exhale, lest she faint. She became too aware of her tongue, suddenly conscious that there was no comfortable resetting place for it in her mouth. She fidgeted uncomfortably in her chair. The air hurt. Her dress itched. The light was strange. She was no longer certain she wanted to do this. She wanted to leave. She wanted to go.

"Firi?" Dwyn whispered again, voice low.

Ophir grabbed for her hand again under the table, and Dwyn gave it a comforting squeeze. Her face creased as her worry deepened.

"Firi, what do you need? What can I do?"

Ophir swallowed, shaking her hand free to reach for a napkin. She began to dab at her forehead, her sweat evidence of her panic more than any indication of the early morning temperature.

"Her enemy crossed the desert to escape her wrath!" Zita continued.

The crowd booed the man in shackles, not needing to hear his crime to believe their queen.

"And now we'll offer Aubade the justice it deserves. Here! To the royal family of Farehold!" Zita raised her goblet high, smiling proudly as everyone in the audience and at the table lifted their cups in solidarity. "To justice!" she toasted.

"To justice!" they repeated.

Ophir reached for her glass, bringing it to her lips just as Dwyn made a face beside her. Her companion barely concealed a gag. "It's rather bitter. I'm surprised royal wine would be so low quality."

Ophir's ears rang as a powerful, familiar scent of roses filled her nose.

Roses.

Bile rose in her throat. The world began to swim.

She understood exactly what she was smelling. It had haunted her like a demon's possession. It had permeated her memories, soaking her clothes, invading her very fibers for days and weeks and months following that night. The thick, gagging perfume of too-sweet flowers that had wafted through her nightmares engulfed her senses. The rose-drenched smell from Berinth's party.

The champagne. The blood. The drug. *Caris.*

Her goblet tumbled from her hand as her face shot up, panicked.

"No!" Ophir cried out over the platform. She clawed toward Harland, who was making a sour, disgusted face similar to Dwyn's. It was too late; Ophir couldn't breathe. Zita spun on her, an unfamiliar rage burning through the woman's face. "No! Don't drink it!" Ophir stood, jumping back from the platform. She shouted at Zita, at Dwyn, at everyone.

Murmurs, gasps, and horror rippled through the audience.

Dwyn grabbed for her, fingernails dragging bloodied lines across her pale forearm as the fae's lids fluttered, eyes rolling back.

Ophir struggled to stand. Her vision flashed to a sensual masquerade. She saw flesh and bodies and sex. She saw flutes of champagne and masks and blood. Her sister's guard looked at her with fishlike eyes. Entrails twisted and pooled on the ground.

Roses. Roses. Roses.

Someone at the table hit the ground, tumbling from the platform into the fountain below. Chaos exploded in all directions as people began to scream, hitting food and water out of one another's hands. The crowd struggled against the information before them. The man called Berinth began to laugh, his voice a strained, cracked thing. It wasn't the low, murderous laugh of the wicked but the high, broken cackle of the helpless. Ophir's hand flailed wildly for Dwyn as pandemonium erupted. The drug hadn't taken her, but it may as well have. Her head swam, eyes watering, vision failing as she was dragged talon and tooth into hell.

Ophir began to cry as she fought to pull Dwyn to her feet. Hot, horrible tears choked her, gagged her, smothered her as she yanked and struggled to get Dwyn to safety, but her friend had gone limp. Caris was there, dragging her to hell. No, Caris would never do that. Perhaps Ceneth was sending her to where she belonged, desperate for her to join her sister. Maybe her parents had grabbed her and were gripping her by the bicep to thrust her into the life they desired, desperate for her to die in her daughter's place.

She screamed in panic and fury all at once, hands ablaze with hot, orange rage as she struck her assailant. Hands grabbed with rough, bruising strength as he tried to jerk her away from the table.

"Leave her!" She recognized the rough, masculine voice. A moment later a large, black-clad shape stepped into view from the place between things.

Ophir buckled against her sorrow. The sight of him shattered her. She was at Lord Berinth's party all over again, Tyr in his proper, dark suit and slick mask saving her instead of her sister. The command came from somewhere primal as Ophir bared her teeth and pointed to Dwyn. "No, Tyr! Help her!"

"Ophir—"

"Help her!"

With a frustrated growl, Tyr turned to the siren. She turned away from the pair, trusting Tyr to take care of it. He remained behind her, yelling at Dwyn, screaming at her to do something, to use her final borrowed power, to help, to heal herself so that she could call the fountain's water, to do *anything*, but she did not. She blinked uselessly, head lolling from side to side, breath coming with labored, rattling pulls. Dwyn's mouth parted as if to speak, but she was utterly helpless.

Ophir scrambled to find Harland as Samael struggled to haul the man to his feet. Samael appeared to be okay, to have been spared, but it was too late for Harland. The fast-acting paralytic was in his system.

A scream cut above the crowd. A single, high loud sound cut from the palace as someone sprinted from the ornate palace grounds. Ophir whipped her head to the side, tendrils of hair cracking against her skin as she turned to see who ran for them, only to see a lone woman in a deeply violet gown running on bare feet as fast as she could from the palace to the platform.

A vision of beauty and nightmare, of terror and misery stood before her. The cropped hair, the flowing dress, and the dark brown skin of the rarest calla lilies were unmistakable. Whatever was left of Ophir's sanity crumbled as her eyes shot wildly from one queen to the other, horror gripping her as she knelt in the presence of a second Queen Zita.

FIFTY-TWO

* * * *

6:45AM
00:00

F IRI." DWYN SLURRED THE WORD. SHE SPUTTERED, SPEAKING as if drowning in mud.

"Heal yourself," Ophir begged, not seeing Dwyn at all. She wasn't in Tarkhany. She was holding Caris's lifeless body all over again, pleading with her to be okay. She knew this could be fixed. She knew Dwyn was powerful. The ending could change this time. Dwyn didn't have to meet Caris's fate.

Tyr called from whatever distant part of herself was still capable of comprehension. He claimed Dwyn had one borrowed power left. He insisted it. Demanded it. He screamed at her, shaking her. "Heal yourself!"

Dwyn's sludge-like sputter came again, eyes in the back of her skull. "Firi—"

"Hang on!" Ophir forced down her sob. This time would be different. Dwyn would not die. Ophir gritted her teeth and spun on the woman before her wearing Zita's face. "Who are you?!"

The far-off queen—the one clad in lavender, the second queen who had screamed her outrage from a distance—had continued running and was now almost to the platform. She'd reach them in a moment.

The woman in orange, gray, and black disregarded Ophir entirely, turning to the queen in purple. "Stand down, Zita! If you won't bloody your hands to seek justice for your people, I'll do it for you."

The new Zita panted as she neared the platform. Hate burned behind her eyes as she outstretched a threatening palm. "Tempus, stop!"

The one in orange turned for Ophir, scrambling to grab the princess from over the table. Zita threw up her hands, and the woman in orange who wore Zita's face seemed to hit an invisible wall. The false queen began to scream, banging against an unseen container. She began to seek an exit, clawing as the box of Zita's shield appeared to shrink around her. Ophir had seen shields used in defense, but never as an offensive maneuver. Her breath caught in her throat as she turned to where she knew Tyr would be.

"Go and help Harland!"

"Dwyn or Harland, Firi?" Tyr barked back over the yelling crowd and the confusion around him. "Choose now, because I can only help one!"

Roses. Caris. Death.

She was paralyzed with panic. The crowd's frenzied screams and drowning hysteria acted like hands, outward panic gripping her and shaking her with indecision. She couldn't choose one and forsake the other. Neither could die. Neither would—

The world came to a glass-shattering halt.

Terror greeted her with open arms as the face of chaos screamed back.

Tyr had barely spit out the final word before everyone in the audience flinched, bending in half as they clutched their hands to their knees. Zita's shield wavered and dropped as both the queen and the imposter clutched at their skulls, protecting their eardrums from a sound so deafening, it may as well have been a jagged needle shoved into Ophir's ear canal. The sound was like bloodied glass, like rusted metal, like carpenter's nails dragged across porcelain, like the wailing of banshees all at once.

It was the sound of hate, death, and defeat.

Ophir yanked her palms from her head. She tore her eyes from Dwyn to the sky to see a black cloud encroaching. No, it was a bird. A storm?

The bloodcurdling cry tore through peace and sanity once more.

It was the sound of a dragon.

The gargantuan, winged demon was upon them before they'd even looked up. An enormous, quadrupedal black serpent with a wormlike neck and razor-sharp talons descended. Membranous wings like bats, nightmares, and cobwebs rolled into two enormous expanses flapped as the creature aimed to land in the middle of the crowd.

"Firi…" The sound was less than a whisper. Dwyn spoke her name, scarcely clinging to consciousness. She was trying to say something, to communicate, to help, to plead. Ophir didn't know.

Another gruff, desperate sound came at her side. Tyr was speaking to her.

"Command it!" he demanded, horrified. "It's yours, Ophir! Command it!"

He'd said it already, hadn't he? Tyr began yelling. No, begging. Goddess, when would it stop? When would this be a memory? She struggled to see the wings and fangs and claws. The sulphuric smell may as well have been roses. The screams of the audience may as well have been Caris's guard— the noble August—tragic, final, dying.

This wasn't Berinth's party. She wasn't holding Caris.

For fuck's sake, hold on, she begged herself. *Dwyn can't die because you're a coward. This is your fault.*

Ophir couldn't breathe. She was going to pass out. The smell of roses was too strong. She couldn't think. The scream-ing was too loud. The blood. The smell. Goddess. Mother. Fucking. Cursed. Shit. Roses. Fuck. Fuck. Fuck.

The dragon's mouth shot down into the crowd, plucking a terrified audience member. The wet, horrible crunch and slurp of the slain man was a music she hadn't expected. The dragon swiped, biting, crushing dozens of bystanders as it thundered to a landing. Their broken bodies were toppled by the weight of its legs, its tail, its knife-sharp talons. The too-long neck of the snake snatched a second unlucky, screaming civilian in its rows of hundreds of needle-like teeth, tossing the man into the air as he kicked, thrashed, and cried out in horror and pain. The snake caught the man in its mouth, crunching down with a wet, bloodied sound as bones shattered and his screaming stopped. The man went limp as the serpent lifted its wormlike head to the sky, allowing gravity to help it pull its victim down into its belly.

"Ophir, command it!" Tyr tried again, shaking her shoulders.

Ophir looked between the twin queens, her rapidly poisoned friend, the sprinting, crying civilians, and the enormous demon she'd created. It was then that she realized why it was there.

"I did," Ophir said, too stunned to explain.

Tyr said something unimportant. He didn't understand what she meant. Of course he didn't. He hadn't been there in the desert when she'd given the very instructions that had brought them here. She'd told them to destroy her sister's murderer.

She'd done this.

Smoke poured from the humanoid abomination's mouth as it flamed its wings, descending into the crowd toward the middle of the platform. Paralyzed with fear, the queens, their guards, Harland, Samael, Tyr, Ophir, and Dwyn were unable to move. It landed on the lip of the platform, near Berinth.

The winged, faelike monstrosity opened its mouth and spoke.

"Murdererrrrrr," the abomination hissed, waves of carrion and rotten eggs overpowering the scent of roses. "You wear the blood of Carissssss on your handsssss."

437

"Ophir!"

Tyr pulled at her. Tugged. Shook her. He'd crossed the bridge from desperation to madness.

"I did command it." She looked helplessly at the thing she'd made, knowing precisely why it had come. She'd stood on the sands outside of the city and told the demon to do exactly whatever it had to do in order to terrify the ones responsible for Caris's death. She'd first told it to stay out of the city and keep the serpent out of sight, but her second command was obviously the one it had followed. She never made anything right. Nothing ever turned out the way she wanted. Stupid, stupid, stupid. Her mouth was so dry. Her heart murmured arrhythmically. "That's why it's here. It's here because of me. It's here on my command."

The serpent beat its mighty wings, knocking a number of civilians to the ground as they attempted to run for their lives. Its black wings blotted out much of the early morning light, casting a deep and bottomless shadow over them.

"Call a door," came Dwyn's garbled, drug-addled words. She wasn't looking or seeing or hearing. This was the only sentence she'd managed. For all Ophir knew, it would be her last.

A request. A lifeline. Hope.

The dragon swatted at the audience, its nails biting into the flesh of all who ran, its foot crushing more. Its mouth still dripped with the blood from its first meal, but now it bit for sport, continuing to pick at things that drew its attention. Blood. So much blood. The cacophony of screams would never end.

"What?" Ophir couldn't think. She could smell sulfur, and spoiled eggs, and roses. This had to be a nightmare. None of this was real.

The two-legged demon with the body of a man took one step toward them, then another.

"Stop," Ophir tried weakly, but it did not.

"Killll…" it hissed, its head twitching from one side to the other like an insect as its horrible, black eyes looked between them.

"Firi!" Tyr demanded. She wasn't even sure what he was trying to ask of her anymore.

"Beast!" Zita screamed, throwing up her hands once more. She spread her shield to create a wall between the demon and those on the platform. The demon extended a sharply pointed hand to the wall to test it for weaknesses, thick, tar-like drool dripping from its mouth as it looked among them.

"A door..." Dwyn said again, unable to reopen her eyes.

Zita kept her hands aloft. She was confident in her shield until the demon called for the dragon. When its head struck out, it hit the shield, shaking its head violently against the impact. Zita cried out, absorbing the blow as if the shock flowed through her directly.

"Go!" she called to them. "Get to safety!"

"Zita!" The imposter turned to her, but she wasn't looking to the woman in orange.

"Where's Sedit?" Ophir looked around blankly. Screams filled her ears. The serpent's blackened, wormlike head struck the shield again. She looked into the bottomless trench of its maw, horrified at what she'd created. Chunks of flesh and cloth remained stuck throughout its rows of bloodied, needle-like teeth from the last man it consumed.

"Firi!"

The two-legged demon reached a hand toward Berinth, grabbing him around the throat. "Your massster will pay for your crimesss." Ophir heard the sickening crunch as Berinth's neck snapped in the demon's hands. It faced Ophir, taking one step, then another toward her. It extended its hand for her, running into the shield.

Tyr shook her too hard, too violently as he desperately tried to make her see the pandemonium. The lives of Midnah and everyone in it were in Ophir's hands, and she was frozen. His voice hitched with something near tears as he cried out for her to hear him. "For the love of the goddess, try something, Ophir! *Anything!*"

The dragon hit the queen's shield again. This time when Zita groaned, Ophir knew she wouldn't last much longer. The dragon satisfied itself with a distraction as it grabbed a wailing woman who'd dodged between buildings, nearly escaping the massacre on the palace grounds.

"Sedit?" Ophir cried, a little louder this time. She wasn't sure why she called for him, only that she knew he would help. He was her baby, her son, her beloved creature, her loyal companion. She needed him. "Sedit!"

Tyr released her and grabbed Dwyn by the scruff of her neck. "Don't you have a power left? Use a healer's power! Do something!"

"Door..." was the last thing Dwyn said before falling utterly limp. Her body doubled in weight as she went dead to the world.

Ophir saw it then. Like the serpent and the humanoid demon, her hound came bounding down the city streets for her. Seeing him filled her with a relief so tangible that it helped bring her back into her body. She took a deep breath, inhaling through her mouth for the first time since she'd smelled the sickening scent of roses. Sedit was nearly to the platform when a Midnah guard lifted his sword to protect his queen.

"No!" Ophir screamed, but it was too late.

The guard brought the sword down over Sedit's head, severing it from his body. Her bloodcurdling cries were as horrible as the dragon's. The creature joined her in her shrieks, a legion of ten thousand demons screaming from within its belly as it flapped its wings again to mirror her pain. This time when the dragon struck, Zita was thrown back against the force of her shield shattering.

"Tempus!" she cried out, and the imposter ran for her. Before the others could blink, Tempus had stepped from a woman in a gown into the shape of a horse. Zita grabbed on to its mane, and they took off away from the dragon as the city fell into chaos.

Tyr cursed as he released Ophir, pushing himself to his feet with a purely angry grunt. He sprinted past the two-legged demon without giving it the chance to reach for him and leapt from the platform and into the crowd. He pushed past the guard who'd killed Sedit and told the man to stand down, grabbing the dog's body and its head as thick, viscous blood began to stain his hands, his shirt, his very skin. He tossed the dog's torso onto the platform before swinging himself up.

The humanoid demon took several steps toward Ophir. She pulled Dwyn into her lap and raised her arm, smelling roses. She didn't see Dwyn; she saw Caris. She didn't see a demon, she saw men and their blades and the red, pooling blood of her sister. She heard the screams from the party. She felt the nausea, the fear, the need to drift into the ocean.

"Murderrrerrr…" the demon hissed. It would be standing over them in the next ten seconds unless Ophir did something.

Tyr rolled Sedit's head toward its body, and white, parasitic tendons began to stretch from one part of the beast to the other as it reconnected.

"Ophir! He's fine!" Tyr grabbed a sword from a guard who'd run and swung toward the two-legged demon. It hissed as it advanced toward Tyr. "Ophir!" Tyr cried out again.

Out of the corner of her eye, she saw Sedit stand.

Her heart began to beat once more.

That which had died could be brought back to life.

Time could rewind.

Things could be fixed.

This was not Caris.

"Stop!" Ophir cried to the demon. "Sedit, help!" She pointed at her creation, lucid for the first time. She focused on the scent of sulfur and blood, vastly preferring it to the scent of roses. A door. Dwyn had told her to call a door. To where? For what? She looked around to see piles of broken bodies. Her winged snake continued to strike, picking off

441

anyone who had broken their legs or been trampled by the crowd, unable to escape. They would not live to see another day.

Sedit leapt for the demon, but she didn't have the time to see what their battle entailed. She envisioned a door, focusing on how it would open to somewhere better, somewhere safer. She closed her eyes and lifted her hands, thrusting her intention toward the open space in the platform until a door appeared.

"Get Dwyn!" she cried to Tyr as she scrambled to her feet, tugging at the unconscious girl's arms. Power rippled through her voice as she rallied her strength.

Tyr growled his displeasure as he yanked Dwyn roughly upward, throwing her over his shoulder. "Go, Firi! Go!"

She ran for the door, twisting the handle as she called for Sedit. She sprinted through the door, out of the pastel morning lights of the desert and into the dark, cool, damp shadows of an overcast forest. Tyr pushed through behind her, Dwyn over his shoulder. Tyr dropped Dwyn to the sodden forest floor. With the anger and pent-up rage of someone who'd helplessly witnessed a massacre, he began kicking the door over and over and over again until it fell to the ground.

The wooden door banged. Its handle rattled as pressure pushed on it from the other side. Moans and cries and grunts poured from the crack as it opened. The Tarkhany crowd was quick to follow, and within a minute, they would not be alone.

FIFTY-THREE

✦　　✦　　✦　　✦

RAIN. MOSS. TREES. WOOD. MUD. RAIN. RAIN. RAIN. Cold. So fucking cold. How was it this cold?

"Where are we?!" Tyr gasped through the onslaught of ice-cold rain that greeted them.

"What?" Ophir blinked wildly around, trying through the torrential downpour to figure out where she'd taken them. It was as though she'd been tossed into the snow in her under-things. Her skin pinked against the frigid rain, showing early signs of pending hypothermia. She recognized nothing. The earth, the trees, even the smell was unfamiliar. She sputtered through the storm, wiping away at the water that threatened her eyes.

"Can you burn the door?" Tyr shouted through the rain.

"Not in the rain!" Her words came out in a frantic whine. She trembled against the cold, her thin, gossamer desert attire clinging uselessly to her in the frigid rainfall.

"Block it! Block it now!"

Yes, she could do that. She summoned a stone, allowing it to shoot up from the earth below it, blocking the door so that it could never open again. The creature on the other side succeeded in banging against the door, a single, razor-sharp claw scraping uselessly in a high-pitched ring that resonated through the rain. It cried out in horrified, bloodcurdling frustration as it found itself unable to pass.

The silence that pressed down on them was deafening. The forest was a dense, lush green unlike any she'd seen before. The tree trunks were enormous. The scent was vaguely pine, though she didn't recognize any of the vegetation around her. She looked to Sedit, who seemed to be happily chasing after a bird.

"Dwyn?" She knelt to where Tyr had roughly left the unconscious woman on the forest floor. She checked her pulse, and though faint, it was still there. Her black hair was plastered to her face, her neck, her shoulders as the rain drenched every inch of her. The flowing fabric of their gowns suctioned to their bodies with the rain, chilled gooseflesh running down their skin.

"It's a paralytic," Tyr said, rain dripping off his brow and chin as he reached out to her. "It won't kill her. Though it is useful to know she can't use her borrowed powers when it's in her system."

Ophir's eyes flashed a deep shade of ochre. "Are you making jokes? About this!" She pointed a shaking finger toward Dwyn. "This was the drug in my system—this was the drug…" Her voice broke off as a wave of tears hit her.

He softened, kneeling beside her. Even if he'd wanted to lower his voice, the deafening rain wouldn't have allowed it. He put a hand on her back. "I'm so sorry, Ophir. I know. I was there that night. The drinks…"

"Who was that woman? The woman who poisoned us?"

Rain doused him, pouring over his hair, his face, shrouding him in a thin veil of ice. "That was her husband. The man is a shapeshifter. They…disagree."

Ophir sank more fully into the mud, her gauzy lavender gown soaking up the chilly, wet earth and sticking to her.

"Ophir." He said her name gently. "Can you make a shelter? Blankets? You'll freeze to death in that."

He was right. They couldn't stay exposed in this storm.

"And Dwyn," she agreed. "She needs a roof over her head to rest and heal."

She coughed through the pummeling rain as she looked at the paper-thin material that had been so perfect for the desert only moments before. It clung to Dwyn's immobilized curves, revealing her chill, her shape, her deathly pallor. Ophir closed her eyes but not to concentrate. She didn't want to see anymore. She'd seen enough. She'd done enough. She kept her eyes closed as she waved a hand, certain that if she opened her eyes, she'd see that she had somehow managed to fuck up blankets. Maybe she'd made them out of barbed wire or knit them together with baby teeth instead of thread. She never made anything good. She never made anything right.

Ophir dropped her head into her hands as the tears flowed freely.

She'd done this. She'd done all of this.

She'd brought Caris to Berinth's party.

She'd created the serpent.

She'd told the demon familiar to pursue Berinth and to do whatever it took to terrify Caris's murderers once those responsible had stepped into the public eye. It had arrived to follow her command. And rather than fix it, she'd been utterly helpless. She'd been weak and worthless just as she'd been the night of the party. Only this time she didn't have the rose-scented drug in her system to blame.

She had no one to blame but herself.

The weight of a soft, warm blanket draped around her shoulder as Tyr wrapped her up. She sniffled, opening her eyes to see him cover Dwyn, however begrudgingly. He wasn't dressed particularly warmly either. She made a few more things, some that worked and others that didn't. A shelter in the forest kept them safe from the damp, misty rain. A fireplace quickly burned it down as if it were little more than a tinderbox, forcing them to escape the shelter until she made a new one. It was a struggle to find the patience necessary to try again, but once they were under a roof and within four walls once more, she found a safer, more controlled way to manage her flame within a manifested structure.

She'd expected Sedit to be bothered by the chilly forest due to his amphibious skin, but he showed no signs of discomfort. Tyr had enough discomfort for all of them.

She wasn't exactly sure what he was feeling. Was he angry with her for the monsters she'd created? Was he disappointed in her for her failure to save others, for her inability to command or control her demons? Was he angry that they were now in the middle of a cold, empty forest with no idea where they were or where they were meant to go?

"I'm sorry," she said quietly from where she sat on the small, oddly shaped cot she'd created.

He looked confused. Tyr left the fire, and rather than sit beside her, he took a knee in front of her. "You have nothing to be sorry for, Ophir."

She shook her head. "The monsters—"

He took her hand between his, looking up into her eyes from where he stayed on one knee. "This life you're living is something that has happened to you, not something you've done. You're doing the best with what you've been given, and it is not your fault that evil people have been put in your path." He shot a pointed glare at Dwyn with his final word.

"You blame her for my manifesting, don't you." It wasn't a question.

"I blame her for a lot of things," he said honestly. "But I don't blame you. Not because I think you're some innocent damsel incapable of being frustrating, or cruel, or shortsighted—"

"Is this a pep talk?"

"I'm not finished. Or selfish, or—"

"Okay, I think that's enough from you."

He smiled, and she returned it, even if it was neither warm, nor reached her eyes. "You're your own person, Ophir. You have agency. You make choices and those choices have consequences, and I see why you want to shoulder that guilt. I understand why you think this is your fault. But there were puppeteers behind this, Princess. Whether Berinth and his crew, or Dwyn and her contribution to your manifestation, you can't be blamed for things you were pushed into."

"Why are you being so nice to me?"

"Well, I was inside of you less than twelve hours ago."

She shook her hand free, and he grinned. That earned a real smile, even if it was accompanied by a disgusted eye roll. He got up from the floor and sat beside her.

"Will she be okay?" Ophir asked, staring at where the shadows from the fireplace moved over Dwyn's unconscious form. They'd kept her wrapped in the blanket and close enough to the fire to stay warm, but she hadn't moved once since the drug had taken her under.

He nodded. "Unfortunately, I'm pretty sure she'll be fine." He looked at Ophir's face, and seemed to understand that half of her fear had nothing to do with Dwyn, and everything to do with Caris, the drug, and the cycle of history and time as it collapsed in on itself. Once again she'd been defenseless as a man in power took away someone she cared about.

"I never want to smell another rose for as long as I live," she said quietly.

"I'll see what I can do about that. In the meantime, we need to be thinking of our next steps. We need to figure out where we are, what happened in Tarkhany, and whether or not there will be any retaliation. The king and queen of Farehold have been hunting you from the moment you slipped away from the castle. If your husband-to-be has any scouts out for you, we also need to have eyes on Raascot. Now that you're filling the southern continent with unkillable demons, I'd suggest we go to Sulgrave, but..."

"The Blood Pact."

"The Blood Pact." He nodded quietly.

"Berinth is dead, but her real killers are still out there," Ophir whispered. "I don't think I have any other purpose,

Tyr. I don't think I can sleep, I don't think I can breathe again until they're dead."

To Ophir, it looked as if his eyes had unfocused on a memory. It was lost on her that he was looking directly at Dwyn.

"I have an idea," she said, sighing. "My ideas never work out."

He touched her back again. "Yes they do! Look at this... house. Look at Sedit." He gestured to the creature that slept near Dwyn's unconscious shape, though he frowned unconvincingly at the demon. He'd always hated her hound.

She looked around at the ramshackle shelter that was better suited for centipedes and mold than humans or fae. She looked at her gray, amphibious hound as it slumbered. "You make an excellent point. Everything I create is perfect. And on that note." She sighed, getting down from the bed as she created a map of the continent. It turned out rather impressively, intricately detailed with names of kingdoms, cities, rivers, forests, and landmarks. "So far, so good." She sounded almost encouraged. She closed her hand into a fist, focused her intention, and then opened it.

She frowned at the object.

"Is it a top? Like a spinning top?"

She threw it on the map angrily. "It's not supposed to be!"

Ophir crossed her arms as she looked away, defeated. The top had begun to spin the moment it landed, swirling around the map as it wandered about the continent. It crept from the desert, spinning like a tornado as it wound its way through Farehold, shifting its direction north of the border. The top began to slow as it reached the northeastern edge, just beyond the mountains. It idled until it tipped, landing.

"Are we outside of Gwydir?" Tyr breathed, looking at where the top had landed just outside of Raascot's capital city.

She shook her head. "There's no way. I don't know how it's possible. I don't know how any of this"—she gestured around—"is possible. I've never heard of doors taking you to new places—not in mythology, not in religion, not even in wishful thinking. I've never heard of travel like this, not even in lore. How could Dwyn have known?"

Tyr looked at her where she rested, happy reddish-orange fire illuminating half of her face and body while the other was obscured in shadow. The comforting smell of smoke had filled the rough-hewn cabin.

She almost didn't look evil while she was asleep.

Almost.

"Well, Princess," he said quietly, "what would you like our next move to be?"

"I'm torn," she said, voice matching his. It held little emotion, so low that it was just above the crackle of the fire, or the gentle breathing of Sedit.

"Between what?"

"Aubade is up in arms, and between Caris's murder and my disappearance, they're falling apart. Tarkhany was besieged by a monster moments after Tempus tried to poison the only remaining heir to Farehold. Raascot has been suffering under the weight of the migrations. I feel like I'm standing in the woods looking down two very distinct paths. If I take one of them, I do what Caris would have done. Everything is so volatile, so precariously poised, that change is inevitable. I could heal the land. I could facilitate peace. I could unify the continent."

"And in the other?"

She paused, closing her eyes as she envisioned her fork in the woods. Voice muted with low conviction, she said, "I tear it all down."

EPILOGUE

To His Royal Majesty, King Eero,

I'm writing you to inform you that your daughter and her companions have sought sanctuary here in the Castle of Gwydir. They arrived in the night and were intercepted by my guards and are now comfortably sheltered on the castle grounds. I apologize for the unconventional nature of this conversation, and for harboring Princess Ophir, should that go against your wishes.

I suspect there is much to be learned about what transpired on her travels, and I will gladly share it with you, as Raascot continues to see Farehold as an ally and maintains an interest in our peaceable union. In that spirit, I will move forward with our intentions to wed to further unify the north and south. I will leave it in Ophir's hands to select the date for such an occasion, as well as give her the opportunity to return to her home in Aubade, should she wish, for the wedding.

My hope is that you have found this quill an acceptable gift for our correspondence and that you will use it when best you see fit. I will gladly resume more conventional methods of communication, should your preference be raven, though I do feel confidently that ravens can be intercepted, and a note that's written directly from one monarch to the other maintains a comforting air of privacy.

If there's anything I can do to help ease the burdens or assuage the worries of you or Queen Darya in the wake of these uncertain times, please let me know.

Cordially,
King Ceneth

To His Esteemed Highness King Ceneth,

It is with both relief and a heart heavy with misfortune that I receive your letter. I am indebted to you for locating and sheltering Ophir. I trust she is in safe hands and am infinitely grateful that she found her way to your doorstep.

As for her companions, it was my sincerest hope that you were referring to the men I dispatched to retrieve her from Tarkhany. As I have received separate letters from my men and from their queen just this morning, I now know this is not the case. If Ophir is traveling with a woman from Sulgrave, please exercise extreme caution and proceed delicately. It is my belief that she is responsible for much of the tragedy that has befallen the continent.

On to more serious matters, I do believe a problem greater than your marriage to Ophir has arisen. The word from my men was a message of warning that Tarkhany's king poisoned many at a banquet, including the successful drugging of Ophir's personal guard. They're safely outside of city limits but wrote of a winged serpent and demon as black as night devouring the city. They described a massacre. I do not know if Tarkhany is to blame for the siege, though the coordinated timing between King Tempus's subterfuge and the arrival of unspeakable monsters is both suspicious and problematic.

The second letter was written by Queen Zita of Tarkhany, calling for a meeting of the continent's monarchs. I suspect you will receive your raven soon, if you have not yet already. As we move forward with this diplomatic gathering of the kingdoms, I hope Farehold and Raascot will be able to continue to count on one another as allies.

With hope,
King Eero

ACKNOWLEDGMENTS

As a child, I knew firemen put out fires, doctors helped sick people, and authors wrote books. (I was also pretty good at my colors and shapes, but I digress.) On the rare occasion that I saw two names on the front of an illustrated book, I could piece together that one was the author, and the other was the artist. (My deductive reasoning skills were not too shabby, either.) It wasn't until my thirties that I understood just how many people went into bringing a novel into the world, and I'd love to use this opportunity to share just how many hands are on any given project.

Sure, I have an idea and I spend long days and sleepless nights putting it onto paper.

Then, if it weren't for my friends, my beta readers, my champions who tell me that it's a good story—one worth telling—I'd probably stop there. In a confetti cannon of no particular order: Allison, Haley, Kelley, Lindsey, Sara, and Bela, thank you so much for giving me self-esteem when I had none and for enjoying these adventures.

My agents, Alex D'Amico and Carolyn Forde, advocate for each project and match it with a publisher. (They also hold my hand when I have constant anxiety attacks and regularly scheduled mental health breakdowns, which, as it turns out, is the #1 reason having agents is the best thing that could happen to me.)

Then, before the book can be made, my publisher, Bloom Books, has to believe that my story is worth telling, which undoubtedly requires numerous signatures and nods and contracts from the Powers That Be, many whose names I may never know.

My primary editor, the fabulous Letty Mundt, helps take apart the story at the joints and rebuild it with developmental changes for emotional impact, pacing, messaging, and big-picture ideas. She then continues to put up with me in our line-by-line edits for word choice and clarity, to bring a book from first-draft drivel to its final, sparkly form.

My sensitivity editor, Jada, digs into the book from all angles to help ensure we're championing our diverse story conscientiously, particularly when playing the long game in a difficult message, so the pages are filled with both representation and love.

My marketer, Madison, advocates for spot gloss, checks on shipping, and helps orchestrate panels, campaigns, signed editions, and events.

My cover artist, Kyria of Wolf and Bear Co, has a vision and puts something new and spectacular on the shelves.

My character artist, Helena Elias, plucks the characters directly from my brain and brings them to life.

Lastly, I'd like to acknowledge the countless glasses of buttery chardonnay mixed with flavored sparking water that gave their lives and sacrificed their intended flavor profiles so that I might have a fun little hydrating drink while I tackle a new universe.

And of course, thank you to the villains everywhere. You're the best part of every story.

ABOUT THE AUTHOR

Piper C.J., author of the bisexual fantasy series The Night and Its Moon, Villains, and No Other Gods, is a photographer, hobby linguist, and French fry enthusiast. She has an M.A. in folklore and a B.A. in broadcasting, which she used in her former life as a morning-show weather girl, hockey podcaster, and in audio documentary work. Now when she isn't playing with her dogs, she's binging cartoons, studying fairy tales, or disappointing her parents.

Website: pipercj.com
Instagram: @piper_cj
TikTok: @pipercj